The Killer App

Would you die to be young again?

D1051848

By
JOHN WRITHER

FIRST PRINT 2014

ISBN 978-0-9928373-1-0
ASIN B00IP1ZUYW

www.killerapp-book.com

CONTENTS

Killer Application

http://www.thefreedictionary.com/Killer+application

(Electronics & Computer Science / Computer Science) a highly innovative, very powerful, or extremely useful application; especially one sufficiently important as to justify purchase of a new equipment, software or service.

Collins English Dictionary – Complete and Unabridged © HarperCollins Publishers 1991, 1994, 1998, 2000, 2003

Genetic Engineering

http://www.thefreedictionary.com/Genetic+Engeneering

1. the development and application of scientific procedures and technologies that permit direct manipulation of genetic material in order to alter the hereditary traits of a cell, organism, or population.
2. a technique producing unlimited amounts of otherwise unavailable or scarce biological products by introducing DNA from living organisms into bacteria and then harvesting the product, as human insulin produced in bacteria by the human insulin gene. Also c._biogenetics.

[1965–70] Random House Kernerman Webster's College Dictionary, © 2010 K Dictionaries Ltd. Copyright 2005, 1997, 1991 by Random House, Inc. All rights reserved.

There is no innovation and creativity without failure. Period.

Brene Brown

Part I

1.0 –January 15th, 2025

[…] The spiralling cost of pension, health and social care for the elderly and the disabled, means that Britain faces bankruptcy on tens of billions of pounds of debt.

The ageing population is forcing the public purse on an unsustainable path, unless we, as a society, accept severe budget changes. Simple spending cuts and increased tax pressure will not work – all those short-sighted measures have already been tried and tested on our loyal citizens, and they have failed.

This is why I come to power today, to bring about the reforms that our predecessors have shied away from, to stop kicking the can forward. I undertake to lead this Government with unprecedented determination, leaving no stone unturned, no futile privilege unchecked.

We will strip-search the finances of Britain, rallying every resource, saving what can be saved and exploiting what can be exploited. We will sow the seeds of a new land of success and prosperity, believing in innovation and funding research again. We will teach the basics of future technologies to our young generations so that they may find new ways to live and work.

This is what we owe to our children, this is what NewGo policies are all about.

Andrew yawned widely, closing the online newspaper. He had been reading his father's installation speech, given in front of Parliament. *How boring… whoever writes Dad's shit, lacks the gift of crafting stories,* he thought. Andrew Hand was the son of the newly-appointed Prime Minister, currently travelling on the 10.30 a.m. service from Cambridge to London.

He was looking out of the window. There was a black lake between Royston and Baldock that could be seen from the train. It was more than just toxic; it looked still, but minacious, unanimated yet ready to kill. Andrew was fond of the perverse aesthetic beauty of such latently destructive man-made collections of waste. It was an artistic attraction, an eager muse requesting his attention. Tranquil and serene, it reminded him of abstract painting; a bowl of soup, a chemical minestrone, behind which Andrew imagined a magnified old farmer with a wooden spoon.

The southbound train ran along the lake's east banks, flanking the view of its dark waters before a long left bend shielded it from sight. The magnetic image remained imprinted on Andrew's mind for much longer.

He was wondering whether things would float or sink in the black lake. Older boys on campus said you could throw a car in it and it would dissolve, leaving only a dense cloud of acrid smoke – he resolved to check that out sometime. Or maybe his imagination was tricked by the feeling he had about the warm, stinking, perennially-overcrowded train.

That day, the carriage was so hot that Andrew suspected the heat had been turned up in a last-ditch attempt to discourage passengers from train travel. He did not understand why progress had left such pockets of discomfort in people's lives. *Will Dad fix all this? Nah…* Twenty years old, he was a Cambridge undergraduate studying literature, film and creative writing, much against his father's advice of engineering. At parties, he described his writing as, "hungry-for-camera novels that would make Ian Fleming turn in his grave." Complex plots would spread through his mind like summer wildfires. He chased his storylines night after night, alone, leaning over his laptop.

To be fair, his father could see his talent for writing, but refused to support it because he argued that cinemas would soon be deserted. He said "subversion would be the new entertainment – who would want to watch a movie when they could start a revolution themselves?"

Andrew didn't listen to his father, Robert, anyway. He was confident of his writing skills and didn't worry about the future or an income. Sooner rather than later, he was going to plunge his aunt's old Volvo into the toxic lake, filming it going up in smoke; a short stop-motion sequel to *Battleship Potemkin*, tossing acid on the last few frames to convey the toxicity of the pond. *Look Dad, how I've learnt your science's shit!*

His head was foggy, still wrapped around the text he had received from his father. The dissolution of Scotland and Northern Ireland from the United Kingdom left his dad newly-appointed as Head of His Majesty's Government of Britain. No more greatness about it. The message read: *Hey, come to London, dealing with accident, can introduce you to King…*

Andrew didn't know what to make of it. He suspected his Dad wanted to use the accident, once again, to make him reconsider science over literature. Heck, his father was so determined he had probably persuaded the King to lecture him over the matter!

It meant bunking off lectures, but Andrew was intrigued to visit his father at work. Besides, the crisis management involved in the previous day's accident was excellent material for a scene that was tormenting him: *the young truthful politician turning into an insincere and pretentious statesman.* He returned to flicking through his phone's browser: *"Fracking earthquake in Greater Manchester kills at least 10,000, fires still raging…"*

*****

Half an hour late, the Cambridge train pulled into King's Cross station. The undercover security guard who accompanied him said to let everyone get off the train first, then they slipped silently into a black sedan, which was waiting for them just outside a side access to the station. This subterfuge gave Andrew mixed feelings about the new jet-set life that came with being the son of the Prime Minister. *A necessary evil*, he thought. He was happy for his father to get the top job in politics he so craved, because Andrew knew that since the death of his mother, Robert had never stopped working for one minute. He had plunged himself into politics, divorcing himself from his own private life, with the exception of time for his son; their relationship remained strong, despite their differences.

The car proceeded swiftly through Cavendish Place on its way to Whitehall, the Edwardian buildings looking anything-but-affected by the consequences of shale-gas fracking. The powers-that-be were escaping the miseries that were likely to stop at Watford; their role remaining to sit still and radiate strength and wealth to the outside world.

Once inside the government compound, Andrew was passed into the hands of a uniformed policeman, who walked and talked briskly, explaining that the Prime Minister was holding an emergency meeting about the Manchester situation. Confidently sailing through the complex, he led Andrew through secret doors, swiping badges, scanning fingerprints and twice producing a card that identified the Prime Minister's son to bored security personnel.

Their winding journey ended as they entered a smallish windowless room, leaving Andrew puzzled and unsure what floor they were on. Immediately, he was asked to remove his coat and leave all electronic equipment in a tray on the table. Then, he was briefed on how to conduct himself in the COBRA meeting room – basically, only breathing was allowed. The policemen were whispering even before opening the door, "Sit on the first chair on the left-hand side of the room and watch the show, courtesy of His Majesty's government."

Going through a double-door system with red and green lights was like being in a film, but once the second set of doors opened, Andrew panicked. The room he entered was pitch black and he had to follow the wall with one hand while seeking the chair he was meant to occupy. Once seated, he took in the images in front of him. On one wall there were nine boxes; the top six screens projected several characters in *grey* suits, while the lower three showed aerial views of the Manchester disaster, complete with large fires, smoke, destruction and hordes of firemen dealing with the hellish aftermath.

In the middle of the room stood a twelve-seat oval table. Andrew's father was hosting the meeting from the far end of the table, the youngest and yet the most senior politician. He sat slightly back from the desk, his left hand held his right ankle, which was nonchalantly resting on his left knee, and his right arm was down by his side, the hand torturing a grip exerciser. Behind the inner ring of seated people stood six younger members of staff, each next to a lectern, their eyes quickly scanning the screens as their fingers swiped over invisible keyboards. No one acknowledged Andrew's presence, and he tried to tune his senses into the staggering conversation and information flying around.

"... Casualties at 03:50 a.m. were 10,566; civilians 10,101, service personnel 465, most fatalities are still unidentifiable because of burn injuries."

Robert asked the next question: "Can anyone expand on that earlier report about the servicemen involved with plugging the fracking?"

Silence stretched out for ten seconds; in Andrew's naivety, it was due to the delay in satellite link.

A doctor in white overalls answered from the top left screen, looking awkward and like he needed a double gin and tonic.

"We've just identified higher-than-recommended quantities of radiation in some of the casualties, sir; others carry unexpected signs of injuries caused by caustic agents."

"Should you have expected that? I mean, you know, from fracking… should this happen?"

This time the answer came from a man at the oval table. Andrew took in the grey hair, round glasses, dark green jumper and light green shirt and presumed he was another scientist.

"No sir, which is why we are drawing up a map of the areas we believe are contaminated, and by which pollutant or chemical compound."

"I am concerned," said Robert. "I am very concerned actually, about this radioactivity. Why is it there?"

The scientist answered again, uneasy with what he was going to say. "When you push up the shale gas sir, you also bring up the natural radioactivity contained in the ground and..."

Robert interrupted him. "You say 'natural', then why is it killing our service men?" He was looking around the table for consensus.

"The concentration of Radium 226 around the area of the accident seems higher than anything that was forecast by the Environment Agency."

Robert grimaced. "So all you scientists and consultants, employed by previous governments, have landed us with a fracking accident and the contamination of a large and densely populated area with radioactivity and chemicals, and are now saying, 'Sorry, we were wrong?'" He paused, but no one intervened before he resumed.

"People are going to demand we stop this fracking practice; is this clear to everyone in here? I want the Department of Energy on the case, they have to come up with alternative energy mixes, fast. From the Treasury, I want a projection of life without fracking, finances, penalties on contracts, imports…"

The standing attendants were typing furiously.

"Sir, we will need to liaise with the owners of the drilling permits on this," someone in the room said. Robert turned to the Business Secretary, "We'll meet them in due course. Let's talk about how to relieve the pain of the people affected first."

The same voice spoke again, "The topics are connected, sir; according to the kind of response we give to the fracking licensees, we may get more or no help at all from our partners…like the U.S., sir."

Someone else added, "Also, affected businesses may want to help more once they are reassured that they'll be treated fairly when it comes to compensation, sir."

Andrew didn't understand these concerns. Robert did.

He paused for a moment. "Is there anyone in here not working for a corporation? We need to give them the impression that we will be soft," *even though we won't,* he added silently to himself.

Someone around the table pushed an earpiece in his right ear to hear more clearly. "Sir, we have a request for a videoconference from His Majesty, though this audience may be too extended for it…"

Robert swiftly wrapped up the session, "Ok then, let's adjourn the meeting for half an hour, thank you all for your good work."

Everyone winced as the lights went on and they adjusted to the brightness of the room. The disappearing video-links made the meeting room look smaller, and everyone left except Robert and two technicians rearranging equipment. At the edge of the room, Andrew started to leave when Robert caught sight of him. "Andrew my boy, you made it! Have you been here long?"

Andrew turned on his heels. "Hi Dad, no, just five minutes really. What a mess…"

"Yeah, self-inflicted too. I'd like to skin the people who said that fracking was safe and cheap energy."

"What are you going to do?"

"Survive it? That's about the best I can do. Listen, I know I said I was going to introduce you to the King, but I was only kidding. I actually had no idea he would call in as he's on holiday, but I can ask him if you can stay."

"Video-link's ready, sir," the technicians said as they left the room. As the lights faded once more, Andrew instinctively withdrew back to the wall.

"Rob?" the face of the young King appeared on the wall of monitors, occupying the whole surface that had previously been displaying six people. He was tanned, regally charming, with thin golden hair.

"Your Majesty, good evening, how are you finding it down under?"

"Warm Robert, bloody warm!"

"Your Majesty, this is my son Andrew," he gestured, signalling his prodigy to come closer, "a rare appearance in the household these days - would you mind if he stays?"

"Of course not, nice to meet you Andrew."

The King didn't wait for a response, which was fortunate given that Andrew's mouth had turned inexplicably dry.

"I'm boarding a plane home shortly, but I wanted to ask you something."

"Of course your Majesty. The number of casualties has stabilised slightly north of 10,000. Servicemen less than 500, the rest civilians. We have encouraging reports on regaining access and control of the area."

"I have the figures, they're unreal… when are you due to appear in public?"

"1.30 p.m. today."

"Good luck with that Robert; I believe our offices have already liaised with regard to your speech."

"Yes, and I'm hopeful that we will have the country with us, your Majesty. We haven't been here long enough to be deemed responsible."

"Good, we will speak again once I'm back."

"Thanks for your support, your Majesty, I look forward to seeing you. Give my regards to the Queen and the children; have a safe journey."

"Goodbye Robert, Andrew…"

The screen went black and a soft light diffused the room.

"Well, that was our King!" beamed Robert.

"Your boss," Andrew noted.

"My boss? No, the people are my boss. You're just a presumptuous Cambridge fresher, you'll learn. Let's go and find some lunch, are you hungry?"

*****

Andrew trailed behind his father in a daze. He found Dad's coolness in the face of current events disconcerting. He dealt with stress like water off a duck's back. Andrew felt like he was in the middle of an anthill; people with all manner of uniforms and ranks moved mindlessly around the doors and corridors, as if under the control of some higher order, all designed to serve the PM. He was the only one lacking any sense of countenance or direction.

A man much older than his father stepped forward to salute Robert. He had a blue uniform adorned with numerous badges, boards, flags and titles, and was clearly very high up the food chain – even Andrew couldn't ignore MRAF emblazoned under the name R. LLOYD over a light blue flag with three red horizontal stripes.

"Prime Minister, good afternoon."

"Marshall…" Robert was reluctant to stop and lightly touched his son's elbow in an attempt to keep moving along.

"Sir, we haven't previously met, I'm part of the Secretary of State for Defence's procurement team. May I have a quick word with you?"

"Marshall, I'm heading for a hurried break with my son, before I resume the COBRA meeting, can we talk later?"

The Marshall smiled briefly to Andrew, whilst continuing to address Robert. "It will be just a two minute affair, sir, please a very brief word indeed."

Robert sighed his annoyance, "OK, where?"

"Just in here sir, thank you, it won't be more than a couple of minutes."

"Andrew, follow this corridor round to the dining room, I'll join you *in a couple of minutes,*" Robert commanded, mimicking the Marshall.

As Andrew walked on unsteadily, Robert entered a nearby room and the Marshall closed the door behind them.

"What's up Marshall, what's the urgency?"

"Sir, thank you for seeing me without previous arrangement. As I said, I head the procurement for our Air Force and this, as you can imagine, gives me some privileged relationships with the various industries in our country."

"You can't possibly be talking about weapons at such a tragic time?"

"No sir, it's the impact of what is happening in Manchester... in the interests of the oil and gas industries."

"I'd say that the families of those who have died are more affected than your oil and gas friends."

"Yes of course, sir, and we all want to help alleviate their suffering, but the oil and gas interests are more complex affairs than they may first appear, and I want to offer you my support in any immediate decision making."

"Are you worried that your force will run out of fuel, Marshall?" Robert snapped provocatively, obliging the Marshall to expand on his previous statement.

"The industry offers you its insight and knowledge in dealing with these matters."

Robert remained silent long enough to appreciate that he was in the midst of his first encounter with the dishonest and corrupt elements of government. He looked at his watch: just 27 days, nineteen hours and 33 minutes since he had taken on the job. He was oddly relieved to know that the worst lobbying of the State could not run without his involvement for a longer time.

"Marshall, are you aware of the Bribery Act of 2010?"

"I am an expert, sir."

"I am concerned it's not working properly. I think perhaps that's more your domain, your knowledge could really help. You see, I was thinking of pushing forward a flagship policy called "anti-depraved officers"; something that would address those seriously debased officials, who are so obsessed with corporate interests, that they lose sight of the common good. You know, the ones who represent the most decadent and putrid form of power manipulation. Do you think you could help?"

The Marshall's complexion turned puce and he began grinding his teeth. His confounded face was a perfect landscape for Robert to press on.

"Go on, Marshall; I think you should leave the service and find employment with your friends. Dishonest and disloyal as you have turned out to be, we have no use of you in the government of this country."

"You are treating me with disrespect sir, abusing your powers too. Now, if I may—"

"No, you may not," interrupted Robert. "I give you 24 hours to pack up your office and leave the force with the honour of an early retirement. If you don't resign yourself, I'll tell everyone you have tried to taint me. Thank you for insisting on talking to me today, you have done your country a last great service." Robert nodded, turning towards the door, leaving the bewildered airman behind, kicking his heels, looking older suddenly, trampled. In a last attempt to fight back, he warned, "You don't stand a chance in hell of succeeding with your idealism."

Robert stopped, holding the door knob in his right hand, he didn't turn, but said, "I'm prepared to see things get worse before they get better." He left and tried to shake off the unpleasant conversation as he headed to the dining room. Close to the window, at a table for two, Andrew was staring outside, marvelling at the Thames and south London sprawling out in front of him.

"Sweet spot."

"Everything all right Dad?"

"Sure, I'm starving."

"God, he had a lot of decorations that Marshall…"

Robert looked at the menu and muttered, "Well, he just got the last recognition of his career. What are you eating? The fish looks terrific."

1.1 – January 31st

It was snowing as usual for winter in Davos. The World Economic Forum attendees were nursing their hangovers under the fluffy duvets of their luxury accommodation. The delegates had excelled at the après-ski "networking", which consisted of drinking at the various alpine bars and corporate parties into the wee hours.

On top of the hotel, the small heliport hosted a waiting room large enough to contain a baggage x-ray, five leather armchairs and an espresso machine. The only guest there at 8.00 a.m. was Janet Icks – a tall and attractive woman with broad shoulders and an angular appearance. She had a beautifully-shaped mouth, and intriguing pale blue eyes. Her naturally-blonde hair was seldom allowed to brush her shoulders, instead being permanently scooped back in a ponytail. She looked beautiful clad in a pearl-white jumper and striking red trousers, wistfully sipping hot chocolate and admiring the majesty of the mountains.

A man's voice interrupted her reverie. Without turning, she instantly recognised the unmistakable American accent of Bill Haugan, his deep, composed and embracing tone increasing as he slowly entered the waiting room. Having noticed her, he was delaying his approach, hovering at the entrance. Bill was tall and slender with a round face hinting at well-blended mixed origins; he had smooth skin, thick dark hair and black eyes that could not be immediately penetrated.

Janet had heard him address a small conference regarding stem-cell burgers the evening before. The gathering was hosted in the underground ski depot of a luxury hotel, the kind of underbelly Davos gatherings that gave venture capitalists an orgasm. But she already knew his voice from a short speech he had given at the inauguration ceremony of her laboratories in Oxford, two years earlier. He was there in his capacity as main donor to the University research programs, including hers, and she had desperately wanted to be introduced to him to thank him for his financial support, but his reserved style meant she remained an anonymous admirer. Now, she felt the rush of adrenaline at the exclusive and odd chance of contact. Her British restraint and the confines of the small room didn't help, leaving her unable to turn to face him while he was on the phone.

"No, we won't exercise the option," he said as he paced the doorway. "Let's make them scream first, all right? Gotta run, just leave it with Anne, she'll spoon-feed me in a couple of hours. It's past 1.00 a.m. there, get some sleep."

As he hung up the phone, silence stifled the room. Unease hung like the clouds outside, descending over the room like a veil. Looking in opposite directions across the panorama, they remained awkwardly aware of each other, every passing second making it more difficult to strike up dialogue. His cool control versus her shy reticence.

They were saved by the ping of the lift doors opening, revealing Robert Hand.

He walked confidently towards them, escorted by a member of his staff and the director of the hotel. Still a young man, he was trim, but youthfulness had left his face since the death of his wife and his blond hair was prematurely greying. His sharp, slightly feline features hosted two captivating blue eyes beneath a wide forehead.

It was Bill who had organised the morning's skiing trip – Janet had found an invitation in her room on her arrival, while Robert had received it through his PA. Neither were aware of the other attendees.

"Good morning," beamed Robert, addressing Janet and Bill at the same time as only seasoned politicians can. "Talented ski team this morning!"

Bill confidently moved to shake the Prime Minister's hand, allowing Janet time to rearrange her thoughts and to acknowledge them both with a charming smile.

Robert and Bill fell into an easy conversation and Janet soon joined in as she found they were all similarly switched on. From differing, interesting backgrounds, each 40-something was driven to be a leading character in his or her respective domain. Sinking comfortably into the low brown leather armchairs, they chatted effortlessly until they touched the raw nerve that was the financial crisis which had crippled the economy.

Here Robert backed away from the conversation a little as the enormity of the problems afflicting society exerted its pressure on him, the captain of the ship. Being a boss had its drawbacks. Instead he observed his off-piste players: Bill had huge assets and skills;

Janet depended on government grants and donations, like those from Bill, to continue research and retain the international recognition of her genetic laboratories. Both could guarantee confidentiality, after all it would not be appropriate to broadcast the Prime Minister gallivanting in the snow on the seven o'clock news, just fifteen days after the fracking accident, with smoke still rising into the North West's skies. The country was naturally weary of politics following the electoral campaign and recent installation of his government. The people at home did not need to be tested on their belief in his *NewGo* policies by some clumsy skiing pictures splashed all over the *Daily Mail*. However, he had chosen hedonism over cautiousness, creating the opportunity to outline an active alliance of big business, science and government.

Soon they heard the noise of a helicopter's rotor blades approaching. Two large mechanical birds hovered and landed on the helipad outside, the first was reserved for the three skiers, while the other took the security personnel.

The ten-minute journey was wordless as the passengers took in the beauty of the world beneath them. Fingers pointed excitedly at a famous peak, a deep blue lake, a cloud shaped like an animal. At their destination, the hypnotic mountains mesmerised the VIPs as the morning sun spread over the Swiss Alps. A gentle breeze whistled around them, replacing the deafening drone of the helicopters. Nature had captured their spirits, making them feel like the sole inhabitants of a secret world crushed between the infinite blue sky, the mountains and the layer of grey clouds beneath them.

"Lass uns gehen!" said the local security officers who knew the slopes like the back of their hands, and Robert, Janet and Bill launched themselves on a thrilling downhill ride. The energising rush of off-piste blew away the negativity of the conference.

After five minutes, Robert was the first to stop, positioning himself a few meters away from the security personnel. He was closely followed by Bill and Janet - they had ceased to be a leading elite and just felt like kids in a playground instead.

"It's amazing!" exclaimed Bill.

"Beats a day in your lab, Janet?" asked Robert.

"The panorama, the snow, it's stunning! Why would anyone work?" she marvelled, adjusting her hair under her fluffy hat.

"I want to ask you about your research, next pit stop maybe?"

"Sure, there'll be cows grazing here by the time I'm finished talking about it."

"World innovation can wait then." Robert said.

"World? What world?" teased Janet with a grin, before turning her skis downhill once more.

The boys just had time to nod at security, before following her into the valley, a good 20 minutes of skiing away.

Janet's disinterest had piqued the curiosity of both Robert and Bill; the latter speculated over the dollar value of Janet's discoveries, whilst the former wondered at the mix of clever scientist, attractive woman and superb skier as she raced away.

Passing through the carpet of low grey clouds as they descended, the sense of isolation started to wane.

Bill's thoughts returned to the company dashboard and the unprecedented slowdown of demand across all markets, while Robert was wondering how he could generate some positive headlines in the aftermath of the Manchester crisis.

When they stopped again, gasping the cold air, Bill's security guard addressed him in a thick Russian accent.

"Sir, shall we acquaint your guests with the bacon and mushroom pancakes?"

"Good idea!" Bill replied. "It's a small chalet before the village, do you feel like it?"

"Sure," chimed Janet and Robert in unison.

Ten minutes later, they were approaching the outskirts of the village, skiing through exclusive chalets with lights on and smoking chimneys. Half-hidden by months of snow, lay Frustuck-Platz, a mountain hut emanating the irresistible smell of bacon. Although it was still shut, the security guard arranged for the VIPs to have a seat in a secluded room.

*****

Left alone in their private den, the trio allowed their conversation to turn to business.

"I wanted to thank you for the trust you place in our labs Bill," Janet started. "I know you want to know more about how we're doing, and I apologise for not co-operating with your guys when they came nosing around. We just weren't quite ready to talk then."

"Not to worry, we picked up on the anticipation buzzing around the university and understood you would be keeping it close to your chest. But you understand that we had to read the report?"

Janet recently had an immense breakthrough in her research program, but had tried to be discreet – she had only just complied with the internal requirement to make a report to the Dean of the University, but now it was clear that Bill, a major sponsor, had managed to read the report.

"I was told that it was confidential, considering that everything could still be ruined if leaked outside."

Robert then admitted that he too had vaguely known about the report. "I wouldn't worry about confidentiality Janet," he jumped in, "the majority of what you do is beyond the understanding of us mere mortals! What exactly do you do at the OGL?"

Robert looked at Bill for agreement, but instead saw an expression, which suggested that he didn't need explaining.

Janet hesitated, modest as ever. "Sure. Where should I start? Well, basically, we have come up with a procedure that can program the human gene to act after life." She stopped, suddenly feeling the impact of her statement. *Maybe he'll understand, most likely not.* Speaking those words for the first time outside the lab, made her sound like Princess Leia talking to Luke Skywalker.

"How would you use that, if the human body is dead then?" Robert asked politely, again turning to Bill for confirmation.

A blond waitress came in wearing a traditional Swiss outfit and carrying a tray of fresh pastry, warm coffee and orange juice. They all smiled as she laid the food down, only resuming their conversation once they were alone again.

Bill spoke, revealing he understood more than perhaps he had let on, "I guess you're thinking of people who could envisage part of their DNA being transferred into someone else after death?"

"Yes, the DNA could be inserted into a vehicle and carried into a new body that, if young enough, could let new instructions prevail over its original genetic programming."

Robert's bright, but logical mind, failed to grasp the benefit of the technology. *See son? You need a scientific background for modern life.*

Janet paused to let the Prime Minister process their conversation, then added, "we targeted a way to program the human gene to take over someone else's body and carry out certain instructions, and... we have succeeded."

Robert was still bewildered by the concept, so he asked Janet to explain further.

"Imagine, for the sake of vanity, you wanted to inhabit a younger body of the same sex. Well, we could pick-up all your current genetic information, pack it into a carrying solution, and transfer it into that new body."

"And what would happen to the person already living in that body?" asked Robert.

Janet shifted uncomfortably and explained that the first few experiments carried out on chimpanzees had been at the expense of the young specimen's life. "So we discovered that it works only with newborns, though...technically, the personality of the carrier would still die."

Here Bill entered the conversation, giving it a commercial twist. "Imagine you want all future generations to vote for you – Janet could create a concentrated juice of consensus from your best supporter and implant it into all the newborn babies of the country. With a compulsory 'vaccination procedure' by the NHS, you could serve for longer than Mugabe… How about that?!"

Visibly shocked, Robert laughed, "Well, that would definitely win me the title of craziest dictator of all times! He mimicked a documentary narrator, "Hand resolved the imperfections of democracy…"

Janet was uneasy with the direction the conversation was taking. "I am glad Bill already has a killer application for the technology, but for now, we're still happy testing on animals. Though on paper we're ready…"

"For what? Human testing?" Bill's rushed question hung over them as the waitress brought in their hot bacon and mushroom pancakes.

"Careful, dzei are very hott," she warned.

While Janet and Robert focussed on their food, Bill was distracted. He fiddled with his fork while he gave the matter some more thought.

"Would you be interested in testing the technology on human beings?"

Janet nearly choked on her pancake. She had in fact started drafting procedures for human tests already, and had been thinking of setting up a secret laboratory. She knew such practices would be frowned upon by the university, so for a while she had been trying to work out how to continue that part of the research independently, but it required immense funding. It also risked compromising newborns' lives during the trial stages and she was sure no donor would allow that to happen. Now, sitting with two very powerful, influential leaders, she wondered how much to disclose. Bill had just asked a very direct question...

Robert observed her – as a politician, he knew the value of an internal debate before answering an important question. He could see Janet was weighing up how much to say and decided to support her. "Janet, I guarantee you absolute confidentiality for whatever you tell us here. We all know how hard it is to trust someone when you reach our positions."

Janet felt the pressure throbbing in her temples. It dawned on her that she had been summoned to the skiing trip specifically to answer questions on her findings. Looking directly at Bill, she asked, "Did you set up this excursion in order to question me?"

Still chewing, he frowned then shrugged. "I just wanted to get to know you and Robert better. It seemed a valuable opportunity to speak in a relaxed environment, that's all."

"Ok," hesitated Janet, unconvinced. Turning the tables, she tentatively probed Robert instead, "So, how's work for the Prime Minister going these days?"

Bill got the message; *tit for tat.*

"Not so good, to be honest. I've inherited a country without a penny in the coffins and— coffers, I mean coffers," he corrected as he saw Janet and Bill smirk. "And I've presented the citizens with the most ambitious program of reform since the Middle Ages. Other than that, it's business as usual, I guess."

Whether Robert's Freudian slip was intentional or not, the tension was broken and they all smiled with complicity. Janet switched the focus onto Bill, spinning round to him pretending to be a hard-hitting reporter: "And now, in other business news, I ask Mr. Haugan, 'how is the country's business faring?'"

Bill went along with the role-play. "If you want to talk about economy, ma'am, you may as well order the gin first – we'll need gallons of it to drown the disappointment that such topic may cause to our audience."

Robert wasn't quite as amused by Bill's flippancy as Janet. "We may as well, since we built an empire over booze as Orwell liked to write, but really, that said, corporations are making wealth creation even harder..."

"Creation. That's the keyword Robert, spot on. That's what we do, us the *evil* corporations, whereas the government's redistributions have always failed."

"I know that much, Bill. The problem is, creation takes time in a crisis... And the Chancellor may be broke by dusk."

"The people too if things don't change," said Bill. "I see spending plummeting in all sectors of our economy…"

Silence. The plates were empty and the subject was just as barren.

"I once asked an RAF commander, with whom I was flying, how he could manage to keep hundreds of instruments under control while flying a thousand miles an hour. His cool reply was full of bravado, but made me think: 'Oh, you know where each device should be, and all you have to do is try to spot if anything is moving away from its target faster than usual.'" Robert paused for a moment, "It's the speed of the movement that signals an impending emergency."

Silence again.

Janet had followed the exchange with interest, but the economy wasn't her forte. Utterly absorbed in her bubble of DNA research with money pouring in since the publication of her paper on cross-sectional analysis between genetics and computer sciences, she was somewhat divorced from the struggles of the man on the street. Still, she strived to make a contribution to the conversation, shifting it to how molecular systems dealt with crisis and how they developed accordingly. She brought a scientific angle to the discussion that enriched the exchange of opinions.

They continued to discuss the current situation well beyond breakfast, drawing parallels with the end of Ancient Egypt, the Roman Empire and the Middle Ages. They touched on the depleting resources, the role of energy and the challenge of introducing structural reforms. It was nearly 11.00 a.m. when they acknowledged that they just had the most stimulating time of the whole conference. They felt connected, motivated and energised, keen to work together to fend off the threat of decadence threatening their country.

"I know this makes me sound like a dumb public servant," offered Robert, "but I'd like to propose you two to setup a *working table* on these subjects."

"Don't worry Robert," laughed Janet, "I also have a stupid term for this type of brainstorming – it's the Delphi method."

"I can offer you a whole year of stupid definitions about how to do things – it's called an MBA!" Bill's joke prompted an amiable laugh from his co-conspirators and the meeting came to an end. They decided to meet up again, reasonably soon, in a convenient location with the aim of identifying new ideas and remedies.

When they finally emerged back onto the slopes, the security guards were waiting, wondering what on earth could have taken so long as they had finished their own breakfasts in a few quick mouthfuls.

1.2 – February 1st

It was like a long-distance love-affair for Janet and Gaia, the time they spent apart reinforced the sisterly bond and it meant they appreciated seeing each other all the more, though Gaia would have preferred to have her big sis closer to counterbalance the demands of her young family.

Janet was a hard-working career-obsessed woman, while Gaia had developed more in other aspects of her personality – like friendship, family and love – things which Janet had avoided behind a thick wall of screens, books and ampoules. Their differences largely counted for the attraction, making their relationship work.

Gaia was the mother of a five-year-old girl and three-year-old twin boys, picking up 100 percent of the responsibility as her useless husband failed to support her in any way. Drowning in kiddie-duties and sleep deprivation, Gaia would forget to eat herself while feeding the kids. Janet, on the other hand, was far from even conceiving the idea of a family; in fact she was married to the job. She had become one of the country's leading genetic scientist, overseeing more than 100 people working at the Oxford Genetic Laboratories (OGL), eating, sleeping and breathing her work.

The two sisters desperately needed each other's time, but each was so bogged down in her own mess she could not help the other. Gaia was dealing with a bad marriage while taking care of children, while Janet was swamped under managerial work on top of demanding research activity.

Gaia's tablet tracked Janet's aeroplane as it started its descent after circling the skies of Kent for over an hour. Gaia had brought the children to the airport and they were blissfully asleep in the central row of the seven-seater, a pod travelling through the dark and damp wintry evening. Gaia was idly listening to Magic FM, or *Tragic FM* as her husband Marco teased, when Janet texted to say she was finally out and through customs. Suddenly she was on the pavement, waiting to see her sister in a brief parenthesis in the interminable Heathrow traffic.

"Hi sis, is that really all you took for three days of meetings and dinners with the world's leaders?" whispered Gaia, looking at the cabin size trolley and trying not to wake the children. Janet climbed in the people carrier, closed the car door and leaned forward to kiss her sister. "I had my other stuff sent home separately by the airline." She turned to look at the children, "Are the little ones asleep? How sweet."

"Travelling first class, sis? Wow! Tell me all about it, who did you see, what did you do?"

"Oh, you know, a lot of CEOs, dictators, prime ministers, including ours, and various other characters – good fun overall, but tell me, how are you, how are the children?"

"They're well, but I'm exhausted – we've had a long day, they got up at six o'clock this morning..."

"How's Marco?"

"He's fine thanks, he went to work. He promised to come home to look after the kids so we could catch up."

"Sounds good. Have you heard from mum and dad recently?"

Gaia was stop-start driving in the terminal exit traffic. "I was with them on Friday, well I only saw mum really; dad just dropped her off at ours. He blamed the parking and said he would just come back in a few hours to pick mum up, but I think he's really—"

"Mummy?" whispered Luca, one of the twins.

Gaia instinctively stopped talking, but was about to resume, hoping it was nothing.

"Mummy??" Luca tried again.

Gaia sighed, "Yes love, what is it?"

"I'm hungry," he said.

"Always the last to sleep and first to wake up! Baby, we'll be home in half an hour, sleep a bit more sweetie and we can have some food when we're back."

"Not tired, hungry," repeated Luca.

Janet remembered she had some chocolate from Switzerland in her handbag. Leaning towards Gaia, she whispered, "I have some chocolate, shall I give it to—?"

"Chocolate! Chocolate! I want chocolate!!" chanted Luca, waking Matthew and Sophia who, though drowsy, soon understood what was happening and promptly joined the "I want chocolate" chorus.

"Well, I guess we have to now… at least it'll give us a break," acquiesced Gaia wearily.

In fact, the kids monopolised the rest of the journey home and Gaia's opportunity to chat with her big sister vanished, she didn't even have the chance to hear anything exciting about the world leader's forum. Janet had steered the conversation to her niece and nephews and had fallen foul of a common mistake; people without children don't realise that mothers often *don't* want to talk about children, they would rather look for escape in news of anything else. Gaia, who didn't even have time to read *Grazia*, longed to hear about all the exciting things people without kids did with their lives. Not to mention Janet's global travels, hot-footing it with all the big wigs, she could only imagine all the things they got up to – far more interesting than, "has Matthew potty trained yet?"

But instead she drove home, having the same inane conversation she had every day and silently praying Marco would be home as promised to take over.

****

Coming back to a house in darkness confirmed her fears, Marco was not home yet.

"Something must have happened at work," she covered, "I'd better call him." She left Janet with the kids in the front room and called her errant husband from the downstairs cloakroom. He answered from what sounded like a busy bar; recently he had taken to installing himself in the White Horse after work, spending the rest of the day chatting and drinking, occasionally flirting, the same old story told over and over again to the casual new joiner or the well-established group of time wasters. He sounded pretty drunk: "Yeah?" Gaia tried to control her anger and give him the benefit of the doubt. "Marco, what's going on? We are home and you're not even in yet."

"Sweetheart, can't you spend some time alone with your beloved sister?" he slurred.

"And who's gonna put the kids to bed again, you idiot?" she snapped. "Me, as usual."

"Love, it takes five minutes…"

"You bastard! How would you know? You're never here."

"Gaia give me a break, will ya? You know I don't like being around your judgemental sister. Besides, there's a game on, so we're having dinner here."

"What an ass you are," she hissed. "I can't believe you're leaving me alone with the kids again, when you know I want to see my sister – fuck you!" Gaia hung up and caught sight of her red face in the mirror, her blood-shot eyes filling up with tears. Composing herself, she fake-flushed the toilet, switched off the light, closed the door and dragged her heels on the walk of shame back to her sister. Fortunately Janet was absorbed by the attention-seeking children. "Is Marco coming?" she asked without looking up. Gaia felt obliged to make up an excuse for her AWOL husband; "He's caught in traffic around the office and doesn't think he's going make it for dinner."

"Are you ok, hon?" Janet asked, now studying her sibling's face. She doubted her little sister would admit what was going on, but she had to ask and wanted to help, not that she knew anything about relationships.

Gaia stubbornly shifted focus away from her messy marriage. "Hey! You've just got back from the Mecca of the movers and shakers, and you're fussing about my silly husband – are you kidding? I want to know *everything* about your trip!"

Janet softened and finally saw it: *she really wants to escape the shit.* So she started describing the gathering of the super-wealthy and mega-powerful, but seconds later Luca started crying, having been hit in the head with a toy by Matthew. Gaia rushed over to console one screaming son, while simultaneously scolding the other. Gaia was clearly embarrassed about the usual déjà-vu situation whenever she met Janet: no Marco, looking after three screaming kids, dinner, bedtime and so on. Janet wanted to help, but was clumsy with anything other than test tubes or computers and certainly didn't know what to do with children. "I'll fix a macaroni cheese if you want to put them to bed," she offered. Overwhelmed by such a simple offer of support, Gaia wasn't able to stem the tears this time. She smeared mascara across her cheek as she wiped the escapee drops with the back of her free hand. "Don't worry, they had tea earlier, I'm just going to give them a banana in bed and read them a story. I'll be down soon."

"Shall I order a curry for us in the meantime?"

"Thanks, the number's on the fridge door." Halfway up the stairs with one twin under each arm and her daughter in tow, Gaia added, "And pour me a large one please!"

Janet negotiated the order with the heavily-accented Bangladeshi restaurateur and agreed the delivery time of *I'll-do-my-very-early-best-for-you-madam.* Then she laid the table, lit a few candles, turned on music and poured two large glasses of Pinot Grigio. She had just taken her first sip when Gaia came back into the room, looking as if she had been run over by a bus. Looking tired and pale, Gaia sat at the small table opposite Janet, absolutely shattered. They stared at each other in the low light for a minute, both pondering what was in the other's eyes that hadn't been seen before in a lifetime as sisters.

Janet spoke first. "You are doing a great job with the kids, Gaia, you're such a good mother."

"And father… Thank you sis, I don't hear that very often, it's an invisible job I have between these walls. Tell me about the glamorous forum finally, I'm begging you."

Janet paused for an instant as she flash-backed to the two of them at the dinner table listening to their father telling a story. "It was weird," she said, snapping back to reality. "It's an odd setup – too much security to move from one place to the other, so you end up just hanging out in one part. The place is small though, so you still bump into a lot of people.

"The day starts with breakfast meetings, for instance I was mostly booked in by pharmaceutical CEOs, then I attended conferences, all day, passing from one theatre to another, sometimes as panellist, other times as a guest. I spoke twice and sat in five panels, actually old Piers Morgan was moderating one of them!" She knew Gaia would love that detail and on cue her face lit up.

"Is he tall, is he still cute?"

Janet smiled, she hadn't recorded any of that information. "Sorry, I wasn't really paying attention to his looks. You have to listen to every word, these are *clever* people talking, though I reckon they live in another world! Then, the afternoons are about schmoozing and evenings are for parties, business-card-swapping and grandstanding." Conscious she might sound like she was showing off, she quickly added, "It's all a bit cheesy, lots of awkward people huddling around each other, laughing loudly at their own jokes; I'd say I prefer my labs at the cost of sounding nerdy..."

"Who was the cutest person you saw?"

"I don't know..." Gaia was so desperate to live in this fantasy world of her sister's that she forgot Janet didn't look at men like that. In fact, as a successful woman in a man's world, Janet was used to being stared at and so built a shield around her. "The highlight of the trip was a skiing trip with the PM and Bill Haugan..." Although she had tried to say it casually, the statement blew her little sister away. "No way! How did that happen? Are you supposed to all go skiing out there?"

"No, no... not everybody goes skiing, but... well you know how much I like it and there was a group going on the last morning, but the only other people there where Robert Hand and Bill Haugan," she bluffed, concealing the actual invitation.

"No way, what did you do?"

"We took a helicopter up the slopes at 8.00 a.m., skied for a while and then had breakfast," downplayed Janet. Gaia was suitably impressed and kept asking *how, when, why and what* had brought her big sister to such intimacy with the Prime Minister and Bill Haugan.

"British attendees usually hang out together at such events and I guess as a female scientist I was interesting to politicians and business leaders."

"So you could have hung out with an engineer from Dyson, but instead ended up skiing with the PM...?" probed Gaia inquisitively.

"They are clueless Gaia... I mean these politicians and leaders. They are drifting, drowning even, like they've lost their course and they look up to scientists like guiding stars. You know, the financial crisis, dwindling energy resources, the accident up north... they're seeking answers."

"Ah, that's what you talk about while skiing," said Gaia wisely. "Were they nice to you?"

"Robert Hand is really nice," smiled Janet. "Bill Haugan is too, but he's more reserved and I found him a bit awkward. But they are both really switched on, so we talked about a wide range of philosophical stuff, as you do in Davos: energy, genetic research, money..."

"Do they understand Genetics?"

"Yeah, with all the issues on the table, they see it as a possible solution to some of them."

"How? I mean you're talking about genetic food, right? In what way? Did you tell them what you're doing?"

"Gaia, believe it or not, they know everything I'm doing pretty well already."

"Really? How?"

"For the reasons I just told you; plus Bill is one of the main sponsors of the Uni's research program – he even funded the scholarship I had in Computer Sciences years ago, do you remember?"

"Wow! And did the Prime Minister know who you are too?"

"Apparently so. They go to such meetings really well prepared. Like you, I previously thought Davos was just a place where important people went to show off their power and influence, but I was surprised to discover that they mainly go there seeking for help from one another. It's a big bunch of disarrayed companies without future, crumbling institutions, fading politicians…" Janet joked, "I mean, some panels looked like AA meetings: people sitting around chairs, passing a microphone from one to another, sharing dreadful experiences, begging for help!

"They crave insight from science, that's why interest in genetics is pretty high." She paused for a moment, "That's why the PM knew what I was doing, I think."

Gaia took a moment to let it all sink in. "Well, I'm very proud of you big sister, you've really kicked some asses to get where you are… But what is it really that you are doing with this latest project at the labs, because…" Gaia wanted to make sure she got her words right to get the truth without irritating her sister.

"I may as well ask you now," she continued, "Mum and dad think that you… well, you're not experimenting with genetic manipulation on live animals, are you?"

Janet smiled. She knew the concern wasn't that of her parents. It was a stand-off between flower-power and science; she believed Gaia had no idea of the challenges faced by the human race, that she was just a nouveau-hippy, a meliorist crusader, ignoring the logistics of life for seven billion individuals crammed on the overspent planet. She did not understand how diseases spread, the endogenous life within them – she abhorred the use of any chemical compounds and would happily spend weekends making her own soap and vegetable stock.

Despite thinking that she knew better, Janet had never enjoyed lecturing her little sister. In fact, she could see the common genesis between them and how their different life experiences converged to the same outcomes: they were each helpless in the other's domain, they were both overworked, lacking a partner to support them. So she refrained from sharing the true nature of her discoveries and hid behind a white lie, "We experiment only on animals that are already condemned to die."

That didn't pacify Gaia who was baffled that her sister seemed to represent everything she stood against: genetic manipulation, chemistry and computers. In her world, scientifically-organised destruction of the natural environment. "I don't think GM has a future in mankind," she sneered. "Do you know anyone who would try genetic manipulation knowingly?"

Janet knew. "Someone who's not happy with what nature has bestowed on them and wants to change it, for instance, or someone who's ill. Imagine your doctor told you that Matthew had a degenerative condition that condemned him to suffering and an early death – wouldn't you consider a genetic cure for him if it was his last and only chance?"

"Gosh, no!" exclaimed Gaia quickly. "Why would I save him from a disease that gave him and humanity a thousand other issues?"

Janet was used to such illogical arguments and had given up on Gaia's views of the world a long time ago; she was family, a flesh and blood relative whose life could not be separated from hers, they were held together by an undying love.

Janet chose to sidestep the quarrel. "Maybe you are right Gaia," she said softly. "We have taken a strong fancy towards these molecules, that can cure diseases and lengthen people's lives, but for what reason and to what end?

"Anyway sis, what's the plan, shall I wait here for Marco with you?"

It took Gaia a moment to move on from the conversation. "Yes, no, no, no, you don't have to stay sis, Marco will be here any minute. I will just pass out in bed; I am a wreck after a weekend alone with the kids."

"Alone? Wasn't Marco around at all to help?"

Gaia looked uneasy, instantly regretting her slip. "No, I mean without a babysitter, or nursery for Sophia…"

Again, Janet felt that words would have hurt Gaia more than silence, so she restrained herself from inquiring further. Gaia quietly sipped her wine. The doorbell rang, their take-away had arrived.

1.3 –April 11th

It was a sunny weekend at Chequers, and Robert was inside studying the figures he had received from the Chancellor. It was his exclusive preview of the cash crisis his government was facing and, overwhelmed by the gravity of the matter, his throat tightened. He felt the urge to get some fresh air before his guest arrived. He walked to the window, rolling his shoulders as he walked, trying to relieve the tension in his neck and back muscles. He had invited the security guards to bring their kids over to play football in the grounds. They were too beautiful to enjoy alone. He wished Andrew was there too, but apparently he was too busy "studying" in Cambridge.

A gentle knock at the door disturbed his abstraction. The head butler had moved stealth-like to just one foot away. "What's up, Jeeves?" Robert asked his favourite member of staff. He liked to banter with this giant, an institution at the house, in his early sixties, he was donning a grand uniform. "A reincarnation of Mr. Steve Jobs has come to see you, sir," he smiled at his own joke. "He's downstairs, sir."

"Great, I'll be down in a moment or two."

Robert recomposed himself as he walked back to the imposing period desk, closing the Treasury binders and instead refocusing on the meeting ahead with Bill. He felt light-headed; a powerful cocktail of two parts exhaustion and one part desperation, mixed with bending over to access a secret compartment in the old desk.

He collapsed in his chair with a single sheet of paper in his right hand. He peered at the well-crafted informal letter from Bill requesting a personal meeting, and his aching eyes automatically shut in protest. The handwritten note in an age of digitalisation, imbued a certain sense of gravity. Robert read it over again, causing his teeth to grind involuntarily.

He vividly remembered the first time he had met Bill – it was at a charity event years before and the guy had just donated ten million pounds to a hospice treating terminally ill children. What had impressed Robert back then was the ease with which Bill had handled an unplanned Q&A session started up by a tabloid "reporter". When asked whether he preferred taking or giving money, Bill answered, broadcasting serendipity, "oh, it's true, I'd never seen things from your angle…" Years later, his name popped up in one of Robert's first government meetings, flagged as a source of concern for the Office of Fair Competition unhappy about his dealings. He had also upset the Treasury, producing a confidential file for the Chancellor and the PM entitled *BIG Tax Avoidance Schemes* where *BIG* stood for the size as well as the stock market mnemonic for the Bill Investment Group.

An involuntary connection in his brain, a broken synapse, sent Robert's train of thoughts towards Janet. He told himself it happened just because she was at his last meeting with Bill, but in reality he couldn't stop thinking he rather liked her; she was interesting, pretty, mysterious. Under other circumstances, he wouldn't have minded a date, but his private life had to come after everything else at the moment. Besides, he guessed she would rather prefer Bill, who was richer, younger and more academic, not to mention more able to date away from the media... *And they both understand science better than I can drink beer*, he thought.

Shaking off the array of conflicting thoughts, Robert stretched and headed off to the private meeting. He saw Bill sitting on a small wrought-iron garden chair, listening to one of the children – he was nodding with interest at what the boy was saying and managed to smile as Robert approached, without taking attention away from the child. Robert nodded and laughed, "Young man, are you confessing your sins to the God of e-commerce?" The boy looked deadly serious, as if he was about to spill the beans over some secret affairs. Then instead, he grinned and said, "I was telling Mr. Haugan about some funny videos about him on YouTube." Robert chuckled. "Good lad, did you know that in this country we treasure Mr. Haugan more than Santa? Now run along back to your game of footie with your dad and let me speak with our national champion for a moment – you never know, we may decide to bring Christmas forward this year!"

Bill and Robert watched the boy run back to the game. Robert was amused by the genuine attention shown by Bill and suggested, "Why don't you hire him as your YouTube security agent?"

"Because if I started to worry about those videos, I would probably have to ask the Prime Minister to shut down the entire Web!"

"I reckon you'd be jobless pretty soon if I closed the whole Internet..." quipped Robert back. Bill was glad the PM was in good spirits and hoped it bode well for a pleasant meeting.

Although Robert had meant his answer as a light joke, it reminded him of the general public's discontent: a recent poll showed youth unemployment above 25 percent and it was broadly accepted that shops around the country had definitely boarded up their windows as they were impotent to compete against internet giants such as Bill Haugan's BIG. Robert's face fell after his light remark, as he realised the gravity of the situation. "And if I shut the whole Internet venting machine down, there would be so much malcontent around, Bill..."

Fortunately the businessman caught the curveball and realised it was time to shift gear in the meeting. "Well, let's face it, we're swimming in an ocean of crap without any safe harbour around us." Bill felt his answer might be slightly harsh, but it was hard to hide how he felt about the economic and social situation. He had spent the entire previous day in an emergency meeting with his top security guys planning how to protect their inner city assets from the next round of social unrest. "My guys are concerned," he continued, "they see it coming thick and fast, and I myself spend the days jumping from melting businesses to security conclaves. That electronics depot, Robert, it seriously scared the shit out of us." He was referring to the news of a large electronics distribution centre which, attacked by thugs intending to rob it, had gone up in flames courtesy of a rival gang. The untrained security guards didn't know how to handle the situation and it ended up with the loss of millions of pounds of goods.

Robert was prepared for this topic and fell back on his spin doctor's well-rehearsed stance in the face of big businesses. "I know Bill, it was awful. We have caught some of them already and are in the process of sentencing them, and we will not rest till they're all in prison, believe me." He continued, "We've moved over several thousand policemen from the north to be deployed watching sensitive business targets in the city." Delivering his well-rehearsed lines, Robert appreciated how hard it was for people like Bill to feel safe. Those who stuck their heads above the parapet with assets and wealth were painfully exposed.

The conversation lulled for a moment while they watched the kids playing football. Bill nodded in thought. He had recruited the best analysts to study the security threat on behalf of BIG and wasn't ready to swallow the empty promise of more bobbies deployed on the streets – he knew from his own reports that the police required more powers, intelligence, forensic resources, vehicles, security rooms and surveillance equipment, but he didn't want to press the point just yet. The weather was fair, though getting chillier, and the wind started to swirl around them. "Robert, I meant to ask you – how are things, really... I mean financially?"

Robert's thoughts were preoccupied with the spin prepared to fend off concerns of an immediate danger of default, but then he considered the depth of relationship he was intending to build up with Bill. Gazing into the distance, Robert could see the kids running to kick the ball through the defence line of proud fathers, and further away the countryside foliage swaying in the westerly wind. For an instant, he felt unable to carry on running the whole show by himself, the burden of his failing country weighing him down already. He had the feeling that Bill would make a great partner to government, and remembered his offer of support during the meeting in the Alps. He decided to open up a bit: "Bill the finances are anaemic to say the least. Lower income and business tax receipts, higher social security and health costs, security, policing – it's unsustainable. We're looking at fixes with treasury and budget offices, but it's not easy. Bricks and mortar businesses are going bankrupt and retreating from the high street as if there was no tomorrow, while others, like you, expand through cheap labour which does not help improve salaries or taxes. But that's not the main point," Robert quickly amended the tone, trying not to be too confrontational, "the issue here is that our social model is broken. The government has too many people to take care of and too few resources: the old, the poor, the sick and the unemployed. One low level employee per four pensioners doesn't go very far."

He paused, wondering in which direction to steer the conversation, when Bill asked him directly, "How long do we have left before it all goes belly up?" Robert, who didn't like confrontation stiffened. "We have some time, not much admittedly, but we are—"

"How many days or months?" interjected Bill. "Is it as long as a year? Do you even know?"

Robert's face tensed: his brows furrowed, expanding his forehead, and his mouth pursed. He shifted his gaze beyond Bill, looking as though he was trying to find an escape route. *What a shit-bag, is he here to fight?* He was reminded of a note left by the previous Prime Minister: *So many options come with power, shame the problems are so big that choosing becomes silly.*

He composed himself with a deep sigh. He refocused on Bill's face. "Bill, everyone has his cash flow issues from time to time. You're a businessman, you know that I won't be dragged into disclosing such information."

"I've come to the conclusion that we need to do something quite radical," proposed Bill in one last assault, unimpressed with Robert's avoidance. "Economy and demographics come in as a pair as you know… we can't fix one without adjusting the other." Now Bill paused to check he had the Prime Minister's attention. He then continued, "Robert, lately I've been thinking that what is most needed in this country is demographic reform. Previous governments dabbled with it through immigration, remember? Back then, politicians and businessmen alike thought that the positive influx of young people could drag them out of the mess, but they learnt the hard way… it all fell apart. And now, we're stuck with overcrowding and an insane density of population."

While Bill talked, Robert replayed in his head the meetings and political negotiations of that era, which coincided with the early stages of his career. *What have we learnt?* He felt like asking Bill the question, but he knew he hadn't become PM by asking embarrassing questions. Instead, he turned it into a statement which he delivered in a thoughtful tone. "We've learnt a significant amount from those policies."

Bill shifted in his chair, leaning forward and resting his elbows on his knees. He could feel his palms getting warmer. "Time to experiment Rob…" he said, looking straight into Robert's eyes.

The PM felt uneasy. He tried to regain the distance Bill was eroding. "What do you have in mind?" he asked, pushing back and wrinkling his forehead.

"Well, I've been thinking about Janet's work at the labs."

"Oh great, mass genetic manipulation!" exclaimed Robert. "Come on Bill, be serious…"

"I am serious Robert. I have a case to discuss if you want; I think we really have something."

"Go on."

"OK. Government and business both need more productive people in their headcount. On the other hand, a lot of people in this country don't want to hang around in a life of misery for a long time." He paused, staring intently at Robert for any acknowledgement. "We could propose a deal where people voluntarily terminate their lives in exchange for a new start."

Robert looked incredulous and sneered, "Good God Bill, where did you get that harebrained idea, in a Sci-Fi magazine?"

"No, I'm serious. We'll do it discreetly, starting with people who want to relive their youth, and if it works all right we expand the scope of the demographic swap."

"You've got to be joking if you think you can get away with that."

"Trying is better than being swallowed by an ageing overpopulation that will eventually drag the whole place down into terminal depression…"

"Your idea just sounds like a creative cost-cutting strategy where you try to keep the workforce young and cheap! Imagine what our international partners would think of us." He doubted his idea of working with Bill.

""Yes. Young people, in good shape, who work and pay their taxes to cover up your pension black-hole, who shop and spend again and again, keeping companies in business and employing more young people…. Am I a dreamer? No. Janet's discovery allows for exactly that Robert. I think it's worth a punt – I mean, do you see any alternatives out there? We all want the same thing: a chance to live, work and enjoy ourselves."

"But you're a marketing man for Christ's sake, Bill. Have you given any thought to how unsellable this whole thing is? The day you say a word about it will be like walking in a t-shirt saying shoot me down."

"Do you really think so?" Bill questioned, oozing confidence. He referred to the growing trend of plastic surgery and how it had developed to become a dominant force in society in just under 30 years. People picked up on the trend to avoid aging. Bill had it all clear in his head: a fair share of society was ripe for a scheme which offered the chance of living a second life in youthful vigour. There would be individuals, probably those who did not want to have kids anyway, who would happily trade a decaying lifestyle for the promise of a new rise.

Bill was capable of portraying an entire universe in concise sentences when he spoke. He possessed the gift of acting, performing with care and precision. Robert was a visualiser and could actually picture the people Bill was describing in his head; he could see them queuing in abundance, their hopeful faces waiting to apply for the end of their dreary lives in exchange for a fresh exciting start. The not-so-good-looking, the shallow narcissists, the decadents, the socially inept who'd rather change everything except themselves and their ideas.

Questions started to fill Robert's mind: Would anyone accept the consequences of death? At the hand of who, their government? A corporation? Would it work? And how much would it cost?

Bill could see the bait being taken and reinforced his argument. "I've thought a lot about the details Rob and I'm ready to present you with a blueprint when you're ready."

Robert was shocked to realise quite how far things had gone – for him, the country and mankind. Just sitting there to consider letting this man and his crazy ideas contribute to government was a testament to the prevailing disorder of things; *entropy full on.*

"After lunch maybe, spare me from genetic manipulation before my only quiet meal of the week. I tell you what, let's have a drink now, then we'll resume our talks this afternoon." With that he ordered the trolley bar, pushing his finger onto a small wireless device he had in his pocket.

Bill, satisfied with his initial bid, agreed to sit quietly watching the game of football.

The heavens opened and everyone ran in to take cover from the surprise downpour just as a member of the staff appeared with a tray of aperitifs.

1.4 –April 12th

Bill's office was a geek den. Programming books lay close to product prototypes, A2-sized charts covered almost all available wall space. His post of command contained everything he needed: knowledge, privacy, inspiration and control. In front of his crammed desk stood an empty round table for meetings, and the side wall housed a console with a mini-fridge filled with healthy snacks and drinks.

Sundays were manned by a skeleton staff, with a PA facilitating a few top executive meetings for new product development. On a working weekend he alternated office hours with long outdoor walks – this was Bill's favourite method of meeting as he focussed entirely on the other party to fully understand the roots of an issue. Indoors, he would listen to a weekend soundtrack broadcast throughout the offices. When the pressure rose, he would get out of his office and take a stroll through the empty floors of temporarily uninhabited offices, listening to Pink Floyd. It soothed him, he liked it this way.

This Sunday was no exception: key staff wanting to see the boss came in a succession from 11.00 a.m. to 4.00 p.m., but his first meeting was someone he had squeezed into the agenda, confidently thinking that it would be a quick affair.

"Alex, I called you here to give you a new role," he began.

"Of course Bill, what do you have in mind?" Alex was very English; tall, stiff, balding, with small blue eyes, he had an understated image of himself.

"I'm putting together a team of scientists, up north, and I need a coordinator, someone in charge who can help them achieve what I want."

Even after many years working together, Alex was flattered by Bill's demonstration of trust. "What do you want them to achieve?"

"It's the next big thing in genetics, it will be huge. Have you realised that the government has fucked it up big time? They have no money left and the country's demographics are all wrong. I want you to head up a team to come up with a lifeboat, before anyone else and before their heads slip under the water."

Alex was used to taking some time to understand Bill's ideas, but he was struggling more than normal with this request. "Why did you pick me for this, are you sure I'm the right person to help you with it? I'm a marketing guy."

"Oh, don't get your knickers in a twist, you're far more than that to me. I need someone trustworthy to act with limited information, who can work with his head down, undercover –under the sand, like a beetle, hidden, nonexistent. I know you can do that, remember online groceries? What was your cover name then?"

"Mark Vickery."

"Exactly! That was a magic job you did then, really. That's why I think you are the man for this one, Alex. I want you to become… erm, Mark Twain if you like. Help me set up an undercover lab. You'll be my eyes and my ears. We'll spec it up in due course, but for now, just get yourself ready, wrap up your stuff here and pack a few more jumpers for a trip up north." Bill was smiling. He was thrilled to be taking the first steps into his ambitious new project.

"But I rather like what I'm doing here, Bill…"

Bill didn't like the sound of Alex's objection. "I bet you fucking love it! There's nothing left to do here, you've rolled out 500 stores in over 25 countries. That's it. No, Alex, time you got your feet out from under the table, get your juices flowing again. Pull this last rabbit out of the bag for me and you won't have to lift a finger for the rest of your life."

The PA buzzed the intercom. "Bill, your next meeting has arrived."

"Thanks. I'll be five minutes," Bill answered without taking his eyes off Alex.

"So… Mr. Twain, are we in agreement?"

Alex didn't react fast enough. "For Christ's sake Alex, what have you turned into? A fucking vegetable? I still have that note you left for me at reception after our first meeting, when you worked for those Muppets, remember? *I'm your trusted soldier, call upon me as you wish.* I refused to let you rot away on my watch – if anything, I should have made you sharper. That's why you're here Alex, to grow, with me. Otherwise, find yourself another circus."

Alex focussed on the grooves in the parquet floor without speaking.

Bill sighed his frustration. "Oh boy, I guess there is no substitute for hunger…"

"It's not that, Bill. I need the money."

"*I need the money? The options, the plane* – listen to yourself Alex, it's embarrassing. What do you want, another swimming pool? Did you ever think there would be more zeros in one month's pay now than the total of your previous employer's salary?" Bill banged his right fist on the solid oak desk. "Listen to me Alex, you owe me this one. You've got to go up north and lead those valuable minds to develop what I need. Do the setup at least, 8-10 months, then you'll be free if that's what you want. You can keep your package here and get an extra top-up from our friends in the Alps, alright?" Alex raised his face to receive Bill's stare again.

"We'll talk again next week, Alex. I've got some government entertainer waiting now on the other side of that door…"

Alex left, feeling confused and uneasy. He didn't want to spend a year in the north of England. Nor did he want to work on an isolated genetic research project. If anything, he wanted to quit, but he was left broken in spirit by Bill. It was out of character for him to be so aggressive. He wondered about Bill's latest infatuation with genetics.

Bill, on the other hand, angrily punched the keys on his laptop: Alex – bonus +350k Swiss francs, private jets membership. He knew the task would be a hard one. Less than a minute later, Bill's PA announced the entrance of his second appointment of the day. Bill had anticipated this visit for a long time, though he was unsure what form the secret envoy appointed by Robert would take.

1.5 – April 30th

Janet arrived later than usual at the lab. She parked the car in her allocated space and started the five minute walk to reach "the aquarium" – her glass-walled office at the centre of the single-story building.

Janet was used to recognising most people at work, partly because they had only recently exceeded more than 100 employees and partly because she had usually been involved in the recruitment process or knew the people previously, through publication or academic achievements. Today, more so than the last few days, she couldn't help noticing new faces, people she could not fit in her mental organisational chart. There were awkward looks, stolen glances and sudden bursts of activity as if people were intent on hiding away from her. The previous day she was stared at by an attractive young man with the appearance of a model or bodybuilder, certainly not someone who fitted into the common genetic laboratory landscape. Almost unconsciously, she took a detour from her regular route to her office, observing the staff a little more closely. Without engaging anyone in conversation, she conceded a smile here and a nod there in order to examine her staff better. *Yes, I recruited that one, and I know him… but who is she, and the other one next to her?*

It was tall order, trying to recognise and mentally tick people off without getting noticed or interrupting their work, not least when they were all dressed in white overalls. The more she looked around, the more confused she became, and concerned.

Suddenly a memory from her childhood flooded over her. She was being pushed in her pram by her mother when an unexpected rain shower occurred. A plastic cover was thrown over her and the protective sheet distorted faces and objects on the other side. Janet had hated it and screamed. Startled by the flashback and suspicious of the unknown faces, she jumped to the conclusion that explained it all: *could they be spies?* The idea that someone may have infiltrated her research facilities made her feel physically ill, it was as though she could smell an acrid plastic sheet draped over her laboratory.

Quickly closing the door to the aquarium behind her, she walked over to sit in the black leather chair, immediately flicking her computer to life. She was thinking fast, trying to work out how long it could have gone on for. She remembered the famous *Cambridge Five*; the ring of English spies recruited by Russia, who passed information to the Soviet Union during the Second World War. She was just about to insert her access password when it occurred to her someone may also be infiltrating her computer, collecting information on her sensitive research. She completed her login and started browsing the apps on her desktop, looking for the one called CloudMarshall. She clicked on it, inserted her credentials and started browsing the internet traffic monitor. There was nothing on the surface, but after applying her networking skills, she discovered three machines seeding documents outside the labs, the app showing the sheets of paper flying from the labs computer to a picture of planet earth.

The nightmare was real. Someone was spying on the labs, and in turn on Janet. A pain developed in her chest, she closed her eyes and sat back, trying to work out what to do next, kicking herself that she had been caught up in her work, without focusing more on security.

She decided to confront her Chief of Staff immediately, hoping to catch her by surprise for an explanation about the new faces around the labs. She summoned Lily via text. A 43-year-old scholar, Lily was the most senior manager at the labs, known for her skills at scouting and moulding young researchers. She seemed anxious as she walked in and was uncomfortable accounting for the replacements. "James caught a stomach bug during his last holiday… Sally? Unfortunately we had to let her go over security concerns, nothing major…a previous boyfriend. Security… um, they served voluntarily, about a month ago…"

"Where is Al?" Janet asked the whereabouts of another senior manager. "I want to talk to him," She was unconvinced and wanted to cross-check Lily's answers with the HR department of the University.

"Al's on jury service. He's caught up on a long case, he'll be back in four weeks."

Janet had always been disposed to accept a lie from someone smarter than her, and that rule had been part of the belief set that allowed her to climb to the top of the tree. In this instance, however, anger took over. Adrenaline rushed around her body and was urging her to fight. *The old cow should have known better!* Janet stepped closer to Lily, grabbing the hem of her tunic and pulled her down onto the side of the desk. Speaking through gritted teeth she asked, "Why are you giving me this garbage about staff departing in all directions?"

Janet had forgotten to obscure the glass walls of her office, potentially allowing anyone to see the physical confrontation. She released Lily's dress. "If you can't justify this turnover of staff to me, you should go too."

Lily felt threatened. Her face reddened and her breathing was unnaturally short. Janet was about to launch into round two when her phone started vibrating on the desk. "You're released."

Lily stared in disbelief. She wasn't sure if Janet meant that she should get out of the room, or leave the facility or the whole world of genetics research. "Get out of my sight!" shouted Janet. Lily nodded and fled the office.

Janet walked back to her chair and sat with her legs under the huge desk. She seldom did this, as she hated the *aquarium*; she thought she looked embarrassing in it. She finally pushed the button that frosted the glass walls, she needed to think. Lilly had provided no real answers – *what was happening with the staff, who was taking over her lab*? It was all a mystery. She reflected on whether her head had been turned by the glamour of Davos, meaning that she had her eyes taken off the risks of her research.

She was determined to remain logical, to work out who could have possibly interfered with her work. First of all, she assumed it was the work of one of the big pharmaceutical companies – they were the usual suspects, but somehow she didn't fall for such an easy explanation. The motivation could have been money, or ideology. Her work was extremely sensitive, and Lily had mentioned at least five staff substitutions. Plus Lily herself was clearly involved... that was a fairly comprehensive spy ring.

The image of Bill Haugan crossed her mind twice during the thought process. *Bill?* She realised of course that there had been quite a heavy exchange of opinions with him, and Robert for that matter, but why would he spy on her? *No, it was too farfetched.* Now that she thought about it, the best course of action she could consider was to run her concerns past Robert to see what he made of it all. He seemed a good guy and with his connections, maybe he would be able to find out who could be behind the operation. Having excluded Bill from her suspect list, she thought about asking him too, but then changed her mind. As in *The Godfather*, she thought, the one who comes offering the negotiation is the traitor.

She found the number Robert had given her in Davos – a semi-direct line with a slightly nicer gatekeeper managing his personal communications, making the PM's ring fence a bit easier to leap.

She wrote the number on the back of her left hand before starting to rearrange her desk. The small microphone sticking out of her telephone gave her an idea: she could broadcast instructions throughout the whole lab over the public-address system. She cleared her throat and pushed the green button. "Hi everyone, this is Janet Icks. I would like you all to take the rest of the day off. You have half an hour to wrap up any process that cannot be terminated quicker. Thank you for your terrific work so far, an afternoon of relaxation will not spoil it, so take it easy and enjoy!"

The reaction was exactly what she wanted – a growing buzz of confusion and excitement, spurred on by the unexpected release. People were frowning, asking each other what was going on, but the gorgeous weather meant most people did not need to be told twice. The majority of staff happily started to rearrange test tubes, close laptops and file paperwork. Janet figured that whoever had ordered the infiltration of spies would be receiving a phone call soon, and she felt pleased with her stroke of genius, actually Mario Puzo's.

She grabbed her mobile and prepared to leave the building herself, thinking of Lily, and whether or not she had been too hard on her Chief of Staff after three years of working closely together. She cleared the aquarium walls to reveal staff acting like students deserting the campus at the end of term. She called security and asked to speak to Ecto, her favourite caretaker. He had long hair and was covered in tattoos, he was rough, but reliable, which was exactly what she needed. She asked him to check that everyone was out of the building in 30 minutes.

"No worries ma'am," he replied, "I'll play some metal so loud that every single one of them will be out screaming on the road in no time!"

"Great," she laughed, in need of some light relief. "I'll go shortly myself." She sighed, there was no reason to remain there and somehow she needed to find out what was going on.

She invested the last 15 minutes changing as many passwords as she could remember, knowing that it was fairly pointless, but it would at least force them to overwrite all of her logins again.

She made her way back to the small management parking area and found her cabriolet basking under the sun of the warmest day of the year so far. She was about to take the roof off, but remembered she needed to make an important phone call. She cursed whoever the intruder was as she climbed into the new-smelling coupé, plugging her phone into the hands-free kit and waking up the 200 brake horsepower. Leaving the labs and warehouse, passing the saluting security at the barrier, she turned left onto the gorgeous Oxfordshire country lane. During the few moments of bliss that followed, Janet rehearsed what she was going to say to the Prime Minister's secretary: *I'd like to talk to the PM about some security issues at the Oxford Genetic Laboratories. I reckon beyond doubt, it could be of immediate interest to him.*

As expected, the lady on the other end of the phone sounded very experienced and sympathetic. A premium, well-trained 999 operator, used to sorting luxury emergencies on behalf of the busiest man in the country. She gently identified the caller, qualified the nature of the call and left Janet on hold, feeling that a meeting with the PM would take place imminently. In the end, she promised to call back shortly and Janet played Stevie Wonder while she waited, the soundtrack to her imagination. Driving along the meandering lanes, passing only a few villages, Janet was not accustomed to having spare time, so she used it to draft a plan to uncover her spy.

Meanwhile, Robert's secretary walked to the PM's office and handed him a note with an expectant look, urging him to call Miss Icks back straight away.

Janet's phone rang and her eyes flicked to the screen in anticipation. She was surprised to see Bill Haugan's face on display rather than Robert's. Her synapses travelled faster than the car: she had been wrong earlier, the infiltration was Bill's work after all. She almost felt relieved. She had almost spotted it, she now knew who was behind the operation, she was even a little flattered that he had taken such an interest in her work. *See little sis? They need me more than you know.*

She touched the button on the steering wheel to answer while the music faded automatically. "Bill, surprise, surprise… *not.*"

"Hi Janet, how are you doing, are you driving?"

"Surely you know where I'm going better than my navigator?"

"Let me guess, you're in your car driving around in circles, thinking what a scumbag that Bill Haugan is?"

"Yep, you got it. And if it wasn't for the soothing countryside, I would have shouted at you already. Bill, what is it that you want from me? What's the invasion of my labs all about?"

Silence. Finally Bill said, "You're a scientist Janet, you know that a tracking system requires triangulation among three points to accurately predict one's position…"

"So you have a buddy who's supposed to help you following me?"

"I suggest that the three of us meet again, as soon as possible."

"Oh, sure, why not?" She used sarcasm to hide her shock. "Are you two in a gang now?" Janet pulled over in a quiet lay-by.

"It's more like the Alpine triad – you're in it, remember?"

"But then why follow me, why do stuff behind my back?" Janet was thrown by the insinuation that Robert was also involved and wanted to confront him about it as it didn't seem right. "So where do you propose we meet next – on top of Mont Blanc?"

"Well, I was going to suggest a slightly more convenient location in Oxfordshire. Have you heard of RAF Benson? It's thirteen miles south-east of Oxford."

"Benson… I guess so, what time?"

"Robert and I could be there in an hour and a half. If you get there earlier, there is a good pub next to an antiques shop, in nearby Wallingford."

"Sure Bill, maybe I'll find a pendant light that looks like your balls."

Bill ignored her anger. "Your name will be at the gate of the Air Force base. If you want to familiarise yourself with the base, I'm sure the boys will be delighted to give you a...." *What an arrogant pig*, thought Janet as she hung up on him. She wasn't in the mood for banter, things had moved much too fast that day: discovering spies in her laboratory, identifying the principal and his henchman, all before lunch, and now she was about to meet... She had to think fast, work out how to defend her secrets until she could at least get a sense of what deal there was on the table for her, if any. This acceleration of events gave her motion sickness, but she tried to stay calm, inhaling deeply and loosening her grip on the steering wheel. She reassured herself that her research would not go anywhere without her; this was her life insurance policy, for now.

*****

There were no houses in sight where she sat in the lay-by, it looked as if Janet was the last survivor responsible for rebuilding society. She gathered her hair in a clip and sighed deeply before starting to program RAF Benson into the navigator. She decided on a quick detour first, driving by a restaurant she knew in the area; her idea of a *last lunch*!

An hour later, she was finishing a small glass of white wine to give her Dutch Courage and polishing off her favourite cake, lime tart with warm raspberry compote. The sun filtered through the two large Edwardian windows, giving Janet access to the magnificent views rolling away from the back of the property. The decor inside of men hunting deer and other game made her think: *how long would there be meat for everybody on the planet? Or will Gaia and the hippies have it their own way with everyone eating quinoa?* She imagined what it must have been like living back when you had to hunt for food, *it must have been a struggle without hygiene and scientific research, death at every corner.* That lifestyle was definitely not for her; she was a city girl and grateful to live in modern times with technology and scientific progress. She didn't understand how nostalgic people could romanticise the *bucolic* past, forgetting the grief and the ruthlessness that came with it. Gaia was like that, forever celebrating past times, the balance when man and nature lived in harmony… *Yeah, whatever, balance my arse when all your offspring die of the plague or starve to death.*

That was her fundamental reason for pursuing genetic manipulation: she wanted to earn her place in medical history, improving life for all human beings, collectively.

Janet left the restaurant, both sated and nervous. She leant against her car, drinking in the sun's rays for a moment to restore calm, but her mind filled with thoughts of Robert and Bill. *Hard to divide the two now*, she thought, *when you call one, the other calls you back…*

She wondered if that had been her doing, whether or not they had united over her more than they would otherwise have. It was the power embedded in her research that acted as a magnet, attracting the two most influential men in the country. They had already proved how determined they were, by putting the labs through deep undercover espionage, polluting the sanctity of the research centre in order to gain information, or control, or both… *bloody bastards!* And it dawned on her how tough the challenges ahead would be: meeting with them without being squashed, without being hurt or cornered into a position where her control of the technology would be lost.

She looked at her watch, half an hour. The moment she would have to disclose the whole truth about the potential of her work was approaching fast; time to drive into the arms of the enemy.

1.6 - April 30th

The blue eyes of the young airman scanned her deeper than the searching device which was digitally reading every millimetre of her car. His handsome face was looking down at her through the open window, and Janet noted his immaculate combat uniform over what looked like a healthy amount of muscles.

He can only be 25, she thought, distracting herself from the reason for her visit. After a short consultation on the radio, conducted slightly away from Janet's car, the soldier said she was expected and she should follow the jeep that was coming to pick her up. He politely wished her a good time at the base. Janet followed the jeep around the airfield, noting the rusting buildings near a long runway and the maintenance hangars. Parking her car as indicated, she was suddenly surrounded by four airmen, the older opening her door with one hand, saluting with the other. "Follow me, ma'am," he said. Inside, a sparsely furnished reception area hosted a further level of security. This time she had to leave behind her bag, phone and tablet, and walk through a body scanner, before being escorted to a tiny, crammed meeting room, with nothing more than a small round table, four chairs, a whiteboard, some pens and a phone. The equipment looked a good 20 years old. She glanced out of the window onto the empty runaway and wondered what function the base had – was it completely abandoned or used as an occasional site for aeroplane maintenance? The eerie, run-down feeling intuitively made her think of a secret service outpost. Despite the brilliant sunshine, the gloom of the place frightened her, she had been drawn into the lair of her tormentors.

Five minutes later, she heard airborne traffic, one or more helicopter's rotors noisily announcing the arrival of her VIP hosts. She just had enough time left to prepare herself for the meeting: *I must understand their relationship,* she repeated in a mantra. She had learnt from the pharmaceutical company recruiting rounds that it was key to identify who in the team was the real engine behind a discovery; often referred to as the *splitting technique* by head-hunters, Janet figured she needed to separate Bill and Robert as much as possible.

To the background noise of the helicopters, a soldier opened the door to the little room and ushered in Robert and Bill, remaining outside himself. Janet, waiting to meet her fate, unconsciously adopted an inquisitive yet obstinate look. Robert and Bill, on the other hand, were smiling cheerfully, looking like comrades coming back from a hunting trip. They greeted her merrily, their charm tentacles reaching out, which only served to annoy her further. She sat on the windowsill staring alternately between the two men, until her stillness suppressed their talk.

Robert attempted to break the ice with small talk, enquiring about her arrival at the base. Janet conceded a few short answers, delivering replies in a sharp curt tone; her mind staying ready for any event. Then Robert got down to business. "I know you've noticed that we have some people in your facilities and the reason we're here is to explain our recent initiatives. You see, we want to support you in your work, because we're interested in what you're doing." Janet sneered at the word "support".

"The good news is that, with the information we've gathered, we're in a position to offer you a significant upgrade in your research program, to the top level, with maximum priority of funds and support."

Janet remained quiet, capitalising on the power of silence. Robert, who had finished what he thought was a whole sentence, didn't quite know what to add, but in the absence of a response from Janet, he could not refrain from continuing. "Hopefully, together we will take your technology to the next stage."

He felt he had made an enticing opener to Janet, yet she failed to return any feedback to him, remaining still in her stony expression.

Bill decided to try. "Janet, everything that has happened has been because we see great potential in what you're doing. Since our first conversation in the Alps, I haven't been able to stop thinking about an idea that I have consequently outlined to Robert. It's about… well, marketing an application of your technology."

Instead of being flattered, Janet only felt more provoked by Bill's platitudes, her heart pounding faster; it was with great effort that she managed to speak at all, her whole body tensed in her attempt to look calm.

"So, when you like a technology you send in your spies. And then when you are caught red-handed, you simply show up offering 'support'... no flowers, no card? You have no idea what the findings of my research mean for me; all the years of blood, sweat and tears. How dare you bully me like this?"

Robert blushed and felt the need to explain their behaviour further. "All we ever wanted was to see if we were right to believe in what you had. We needed a due diligence, a quick and discreet one, that's all."

Janet bit back. "Too much fuss asking the actual owner?"

Bill answered that question. "Janet, you may be right on that, but leave it aside for a moment; we're here to ask if you want to work together. Both government and business are proposing to use your research for something practical in the very near future."

"I'm amazed you bothered asking at all, or was it only because I caught you?" She didn't want to let them off the hook just yet. "So now I believe the 'proposal I can't refuse' will be introduced – well come on, where is the gun?"

Robert jumped in. "Janet, we have a practical use in mind for your technology. I think we should talk to you about entering an—"

She interrupted him. "Come on, what's this use you have in mind Bill?" She was using the splitting technique, to divide and conquer, purposefully interrupting and redirecting the conversation, and it seemed to be working. Bill looked at Robert, unsure as to who should answer first, but the truth was that neither of them was comfortable in releasing any information yet. Janet scanned the body language in the room: Bill was a bit more relaxed and looked like he was in charge, while Robert looked stiff and sheepish at getting caught. Bill started to speak. "From a business point of view, people will do anything to combat ageing these days, undergoing various treatments and procedures in an attempt to look and feel younger. This market has grown immensely, I'm not going to mention figures, but it's significant. Still, they've failed to find a durable fix, something like a quantum leap." He paused for effect, "That's what we'd like to achieve, offering the chance of a voluntarily interruption of what they themselves define as a miserable existence, an opportunity of a second life, where they'll be younger, better and stronger."

Still no inkling of a response from Janet, Bill felt obliged to continue. "Of course, marketing would be easier if the candidates could keep some sort of knowledge or awareness of their previous life – it would make it an even more appealing proposition to a larger group of people. I estimate fifteen percent of the global population would use our service within three years, based on the growing trend of cosmetic surgery and its correlation with suicides."

Janet stared at Robert while Bill was making his case, he looked fascinated, like he had just heard the stuff for the first time too. As far as she was concerned, having worked on genetic transfer technology for half of her life, she wasn't impressed. She had spent years improving the process of inserting human DNA into newborns, allowing life to relocate between bodies and throughout her field work, she had seen just how difficult it would be to present these findings outside a small circle of scientists. It was now her time to comment: "Gentlemen, if you didn't occupy leading positions in our country, I would think you were mad, that somehow you had suddenly turned into a pair of silly..." She checked herself, they both looked quite startled by her opening. "I have worked on this technology my entire career, believing in its potential to become a life-saving treatment for critically ill patients, the hideous diseases that remain uncured. And you waltz into my lab with spies, proposing a revolution in plastic surgery?"

Shocked by her attack, they hardened their body language. She continued, "Have you asked yourself anything at all about Janet Icks? It appears to me you haven't – nosing into my job, extrapolating my ideas and coming up with indecently inappropriate proposals."

"That's not really—"

"Wait Robert, I'm not finished."

"Apologies, go on."

"Remember, I've managed the migration of life from one body to another. I've proved that it works, but I'm not finished yet and I don't want to jeopardise my findings. So, whatever haste you have in cashing in on people's desire to stay young, please don't mess with my work. If I ever think of launching a hair colouring spray, I'll give you a ring."

*****

Silence pervaded the little room at RAF Benson. Bill awkwardly attempted to pacify Janet. "What we want to do goes beyond the pharmaceutical use. More serious social and economic issues are incorporated into our plans," he looked to Robert for support, since Janet offered none.

Robert picked up the plea. "Imagine we asked you to reframe your outstanding discoveries, looking at the broader picture? For instance, you say you want to save lives because you believe that's an absolute priority – well, that's understandable in the context of the information you have available, your career objectives and your aim in life, but if you could, for one moment, look at the situation with my eyes, through the evidence I have at hand, you'd realise that things are just a little more complicated than simply saving lives."

"I'm all ears…"

"Do you really want to know?"

"Of course I want to know, Robert."

"The fact is that we have reached a point where most basic social dynamics have gone awry. I may lead 'government', but practically I can't control anything anymore, the whole affair has run past the founding rules of society, the entire thing has entered into deep crisis…"

Janet grew impatient. "What are you trying to say, Robert? Are we here today to change the social contract?"

"I wish we weren't, but your technology could help control demographics, for instance. If we could voluntarily swap some of the older population for a younger generation, well that would be a more sustainable rebalance; our economy and the country as a whole would improve."

Janet remained silent before mumbling, "Un-be-lie-va-ble."

Bill, well used to difficult conversations, tried to get into the detail to help Janet see sense. "From what I recall in Davos, you said that you have found a means to transfer DNA from a grown-up to a totally unrelated person, is that true?"

"Yes, I was broadly portraying the nature of my research."

"Not only that, but you also hinted that your process could allow retention of the entire memory background of the, let's say, donor?"

Janet sighed, "Yes, I said that was one possibility."

"Lastly, I remember us saying that it could one day be tested on human beings because you…even deemed it safe for a wider—"

"One day…What are you going on about anyway?" interrupted Janet. "Why do you keep quoting me? I think we can all remember what I said, though it was over three months ago. I'm not here to answer your questions, rather the opposite I reckon, and, please leave my research out of your abstractions – it's not fit for shaping demographics, anyway."

"Janet, it's very straightforward," snapped Bill, keen to wrap things up, "there is a lot to be gained from rebalancing the demographics of society. Because of the nature of such endeavour, it's more suitable to start with the people who would express their consent to being… transformed." He stole a glance at Robert as if to ask, "Can I say that?"

"Janet this is the future. It's improvement of society, genetic evolution." Robert took over. "The preliminary idea is that government will approve and sponsor an exclusive provider offering an application of your technology, which will enable people to voluntarily commit to being born again."

"Social churn?" Janet asked provocatively.

"A killer application. For you and your technology, backed, funded and implemented."

*****

"Oh dear me, you make it sound like a bloody party!" exclaimed Janet, staring hard at the table, thinking *these two are crazy…*

Fuelled by the belief in *his* plan, Bill continued with what he defined as massaging: "You and the OGL will request funding from the government and they would agree to help, partially buying you out in exchange for an exclusive right to sell the technology via an established British company. A prime example of science, government and business working together for the good of the country; that's what it's all about, Janet. What do you say to that?"

Thirteen-seconds later: "That you've gone insane!" After a second, shorter pause, Janet elaborated, "Half of what you just said is material that will secure you a life's membership to any psychiatric hospital, restraint bars and straight-jackets all-inclusive."

"Of course we can pursue this without you if you feel that strongly," Bill suggested in a Machiavellian tone. "If you decide to miss this opportunity, then effectively we would be left with the burden of finding ways to make the application work without you, by either stealing your ideas, copying your designs, recruiting your people and so on. We would probably have to make sure that you won't interfere with the project, considering that a very restricted number of people will know anything at all about it."

Janet was stunned by his open threat. She looked out but found no evidence of the beautiful Oxfordshire countryside outside the small window. Everything sane and normal seemed thousands of miles away, suppressed and paved over by the concrete runway and rundown buildings. *It's all going to look this same depressing grey one day*, she thought, *tarmac, buildings in need of repair, a dim man-made sheet covering what had once been nature. How can I even start to fight it?* She alone wasn't going to be able to stop the run towards annihilation. She looked at Bill, then Robert, addressing the latter in one last attempt to confuse. "So, I either work for you or you'll have to shut me in a room while you steal it anyway? What's the deal for me if I'm in?"

Robert and Bill caught each other's eyes and tried not to look too smug; they seemed to have passed the hurdle. Robert answered, "Our proposal is to make you the head of the project, and co-owner with Bill. We want you to lead the scientific function, with him running business and security." He paused for a moment, sipping water from a plastic cup. "I can't be directly involved, as you can probably imagine, but my office will be represented. I assure you will have as much autonomy as you need," he promised looking her straight in the eyes.

Bill continued to flesh out the detail. "There will be very few people involved, initially briefed on carrying out one single experiment, that's it. Only the three of us in here will know the reach of our work. We'll outline the rest to them in due course, should the experiment work."

Janet wasn't sure she had much choice, but she wanted more time to think. "When do you expect me start swapping monkeys for humans?" she asked of Robert, but Bill pushed on, reassuring her that they would work out dates to suit her once she confirmed that she was onboard.

While Bill talked, Robert was ready to move on; he gave one passing thought to Janet and briefly repeated to himself that working with her was a going to be good. He then assumed the closing-up tone of a seasoned politician: "Janet, you deserve a huge payoff for taking the time to discuss these matters with us today. I know it's not easy to see government like this, but the situation we've portrayed to you today is urgent and we wouldn't have bothered you otherwise."

"Partnership in crime, you mean," Janet replied. She turned back to Bill, with the aim of closing the meeting in the least damaging way. "Thank you for understanding my work, I'm flattered, even though this still looks to me like the craziest endeavour in the history of mankind. As you can imagine, I need some time before accepting. I'm not convinced we'll ever get away with it."

Not a word for Robert, Janet's eyes moved from Bill to the cheap vinyl flooring while chasing a thought. Robert guessed that he had to take the blame for the undercover ring at the OGL. It didn't really matter though, as long as she decided to come onboard the project and work with him.

She finally asked them the one question that had been nagging her throughout the entire meeting: "The people you seconded to my labs – who are they, what do they know?" This confirmed Roberts' intuition that Janet was yet to forgive them for the intrusion.

"They're from my team," offered Bill, "a small unit, a magic circle if you will, who are never inclined to discuss the details of any operation they undertake."

"They're not government agents?" asked Janet, looking at both of them this time.

"It's common to employ private contractors for certain security assignments and in this instance we are using Bill's."

"I ought to know what to do with them, how to carry on?"

"Their only assignment is to protect you," Bill said.

Janet shook her head, he had sent a chill down her spine. *Criminals protecting criminals?* "Ok, enough then, I'll meet you again soon," said Janet, now exhausted and wishing for the meeting to end.

"We'll meet in a couple of days. If it's a yes, we'll draft an agenda together; Robert will be with us again once we have completed the first key stages, right Rob?" Robert nodded and Janet nodded back at him in agreement. They both looked at Bill who gazed off into the distance for a moment, following his thoughts: *it was an exciting business he was getting into, finding people who wanted to die for the prospect of buying new life.*

1.7 –May 1st

The meeting at the airbase left Janet feeling drained, exhausted and weary. Driving back to the lab was not an option. She also excluded going home, for all she knew, the place was probably bugged. Being scouted as the most promising scientist in the country carried burdensome side effects; feeling pinned down, under surveillance, and deprived of the privacy she had previously enjoyed. She decided to drive to a small spa retreat she knew near the village of Woodstock, stopping on the way to buy a change of clothes.

Nestled in the hills and hidden from the world by trees was a former country house for nineteenth-century Londoners. Janet had spent a few weekends alone there working, sleeping and eating room-service meals in front of the TV, and now the remote setting appealed. She likened it to a monastery, a sanatorium in which she could take refuge.

Being alone in a hotel allowed her to sever all relationships with the outside world. She hid behind a shelter of impersonal furniture and toiletries, in a separate universe, run by professional people on behalf of those who had temporarily given up.

She arrived feeling emotionally distraught, but as she entered the room, it was like stepping into a soothing bath: the natural colours, the way the bed was made, the order of new interiors and the gentle hiss of the air-con.

Dropping onto the sumptuous duvet, she reviewed her day so far, and immediately regretted opening up the secrets of her work to Robert and Bill. *No one can be trusted, only genes, they behave better than the people they make.* It had always been the case for Janet that when she connected with people, it caused her to withdraw, to reject the bond that it created. This cycle of behaviour had proven necessary for her career: the more she worked alone, pushing her discoveries beyond everybody's boundary, the less she felt inclined to share the results of her solitary ransack through science. It was a vicious circle that fed her confidence and the confidentiality of her work, but withdrew her further from interest in other people.

She had been inspired by Ovid, the ancient roman poet: "Bene vixit qui bene latuit" – *he who has kept himself well hidden, has lived well.* She had always managed to keep a fair amount of distance between herself and the world. At 38, she only had to report to the university dean, not least as this represented the majority of her waking hours. Her private life was left extremely lean; she didn't see her parents much and, though she was emotionally connected with Gaia, they seldom talked more than once every couple of weeks. Outside the family circle, she didn't yearn for relationships and only cultivated a faint connection with the worlds of love and lust through Claire, the anaesthetist she was intermittently dating.

Not so much to offer to the altar of life, she thought; will that potentially make me the best positioned person to start testing genetic technology on people?

She left her thoughts hanging over the bed and moved to the bathroom, taking one of her usual searingly-hot showers. She emerged wrapped in a thick white bathrobe, the only exposed part of her body being her thin pale ankles, designed, like the rest of her body, by mother nature on one of her good days.

She started to unwind, with the last 24 hours occasionally reappearing in her brain, unable to classify the key events of the day – even managing to assign them a clear bearing was unachievable. Had she advanced in her career, could she call it a day of achievement? Or rather, had she just been raped of privacy and independence? A minacious air was moving around her, like a suspended knife threatening to fall over her head. Working with government, shoulder-to-shoulder with the most powerful CEO in the country, tasted bitter. She sighed and reached for the minibar, studying the various bottles through the glass door before deciding on a vodka. She unscrewed the lid and drank it in one move, throwing it on the floor and falling back onto the bed. She felt the familiar burn in her throat move down to her empty stomach. *What the fuck have they got in mind? They're the sick ones.*

She was not inclined to have any association with them, their objectives, means and timing felt wrong. She wasn't ready, no one was ready. *What was that strange noise?* There was no way she could see the scientific community accepting it. *That was definitely the sound of furniture moving.* Every single stakeholder in society would be at their necks pretty soon. *That was a smothered moan from next door.* Her thoughts were distracted by what she discerned as the sounds of sex on the other side of the partition wall. The clear grunts of a man were joined by increasingly vocal moans of a woman. Janet's upper-body stiffened with curiosity and she held her breath in order to catch every sound. *This called for another drink*, she thought, reaching for the minibar again. She grabbed the first miniature at hand, a Gordon's gin, and felt its poisonous taste quickly travelling to between her legs.

During the extensive travelling on her own, she had developed a strong interest in hotel sex, in all its forms: couples, call girls, colleagues, she could tell them all apart, her brain highly tuned to every detail of off-the-wall intercourse. As a result, she was sure she would herself be inadequate to an eavesdropper if she should be overheard.

The seasoned couple next door began moaning in rhythm with the regular movements of the bed creaking, and Janet began to feel turned on. Soon she was at the point where she couldn't fight the idea of efficiently relieving herself with an orgasm; no men or women were needed, she would satisfy her own desire to come. She stood up quietly, reached to close the curtains and returned to the bed where she undid the belt of her bathrobe. A moment later, she was writhing on the bed, responding to the waves of pleasure unleashed by her actions, until the inevitable result – an intense release that took her away from the world for a while, shortcutting her body, mind and soul, freeing all the accumulated tension. The very strange day was coming to an end, and all she had left to do was lie in the comfortable bed while her pleasure turned into sleep.

*****

Janet was woken up hours later by her rumbling stomach. *Breakfast? Dinner? What time is it?* she wondered. She checked her watch. It was 6.00 a.m. on the first of May, 2025.

Janet turned on the TV to order. "TV, morning, breakfast," she said. The big screen in front of the bed lit up, casting a light blue tone on the whole room and displaying a choice of breakfast menus. Janet wanted it all, but settled on a Danish pastry, apple tart, black coffee, orange juice. Once breakfast was ordered, she used voice commands to switch the screen to TV and advance through the channels until she was shocked by a news report. The rolling banner underneath the scene read: *80 bodies have so far been extracted alive from the clinic, they all show evidence of plastic surgery.* Now she heard the on-site reporter. "Fire brigades are still inside," commented someone with a thick south-American accent, "a spokesmen confirmed that people, mainly in their thirties and forties, come here for all types of cosmetic surgery – breast augmentation, facelifts, – thankfully the weight-loss and dental clinics were located in another building. Back to you, Joanne."

"That was Kerry, reporting from the Santa Barbara Clinic, where following a fire in one of the main buildings, 80 people are now known to have died with many more severely wounded. On to other news—." Janet commanded the TV to pause for a second while she closed her eyes, she rubbed her face with the palms of her hands and sighed deeply as she massaged her temples and eyes in turn. *We are losing it,* she thought. She could not believe the misery people were prepared to go through in order to appear younger. The faces of her two new associates passed quickly through her thoughts. When presented with the folly of the world, their idea to dispense a shorter-better-faster life to people who, apparently, didn't want to grow old gracefully, didn't seem such a bad scheme after all. Those images made the reduction in overcrowding and exploitation of the planet look like an ancillary bonus. In the ghastly face of reality, the genetic adjustment of society made sense, a compelling argument that she could not argue against. Taking control of demographics by steering human life to youth suddenly didn't seem like such a desperate endeavour.

She opened her eyes and focussed on the contemporary desk on the other side of the room. Sitting in just her bathrobe in the black designer chair, she put on her reading glasses, fixed her hair in a quick ponytail around one of the hotel's pencils and opened her laptop. In the sterile environment of the hotel room, she turned her mind to the goals offered by Bill and Robert's idea. In her first act of solid commitment to the "Killer App," she began writing in haste; the blueprint of the human mass genetic manipulation.

Checklist 1
DNA Donor approaching 40 years of age
- Keywords: consenting, unhappy, not integrated, poor links to society
- Requirements: sound of mind (mental profile checks), look up genetic code at specific

location, get information about genealogy and ancestry

- Recruiting: samples of behaviour to assess psychological construct and environment
- Procedure:
  1. Record genetic map
  2. Insert genetically modified amino acid containing instructions
  3. Program knocking-out function at 40 years old
  4. Copy genetic material and clone molecules
  5. Scan database of newborn, max elapsing time 6 hours
  6. Insert DNA sequence in target carrier
  7. Check newborn extensively for malfunctions and behavioural disorders
- Critical Issues:
  8. Ensure that only healthy DNA sequence is carried in across to the recipient
  9. All materials biodegradable to clear eventual examination and/or dissection of donor body
  10. Cut cause-effect links of death/changes produced by procedure.

She stumbled over one of the key issues raised by Bill: the procedure undertaken by volunteers in order to die. *Will they endure suffering? Will it be an accidental death, peaceful euthanasia?* Janet spent some time assessing whether an exact shut down time could be programmed, or whether death had to be sub-ministered by staff at the very last moment. The delivery of a pleasant death was imperative, for the donor as well as the other stakeholders: a decent, well planned process that would pass the scrutiny of society was essential to the acceptance of this programme. *How can I help them sell it?* She was thinking of ways to conceive a procedure delivering natural death for all donors, resulting in *"fatality attributable to previous illness or internal malfunction not directly correlated to any external force". Better life, ending suffering without agony*, she was typing furiously on her laptop. Janet knew first-hand how much resistance genetic manipulation attracted from all layers of society; she typed in capital letters: *LEGAL*.

Her expression was reflected in the window as she gazed outside. Watching a bird passing over the tall tree tops, she nodded in confirmation of her thoughts; the key was in engineering a genetic material that once inserted would fully match naturally occurring biological products, leaving no evidence of artificially modified molecules.

A knock at the door startled her. "Room service," called a porter. "Thank you, just leave it outside," replied Janet, preferring to chase the trail of her thoughts than sate her hunger. She typed fast, her fingers flying over the keyboard as her mind raced through the options: *active agent to carry awareness of previous life into the newborn, requiring more encoding and hence more alkaline solution.*

Her confidence staggered slightly in front of the enormous task of delivering all that was expected of her. She paused in awe, thinking, then continued keying her notes once more. *Occasional memory flashes vs. behavioural traits?* She inserted an arrow, followed by the word "BILL".

She finally got up to retrieve her breakfast, dwelling on how Bill had stressed the awareness of the past life as being a unique selling point. He had mentioned research evidence of people who were willing to live a new life if they could benefit from their previously accumulated experiences. This was appealing to people who struggled to make the most of their own competitive advantage first time around. She collected the tray from the floor, closing the door with her heel while resting it on the bed. Grabbing the juice and Danish, she scurried back to the desk again and opened a new page, writing *Newborn, what can go wrong?*

She paused mid-chew, everything can go wrong! She swallowed and focussed, could the shuttle get corrupted during the transit? A sip of juice, what if only part of the instructions are delivered?

She got up for the coffee, still steaming by the bed. The hot vapours rising from the cup made her think, the intrusion in the newborn would create new toxins in the body that could end up killing its defences, as well as its resistance to medicines, making the host body vulnerable to new diseases that were harder to treat.

More notes followed, a reference to the secretions of the host body potentially becoming toxic to other humans and organisms. Each of the new components of the risk profile daunted her resolution to make this work. She took another bite of her pastry and cast her mind back to her university days: *an incorrectly folded form of an ordinary cellular protein, can, under certain circumstances, be replicated and give rise to infectious neurological diseases.*

The pastry tasted bitter as the experiment looked more and more like a lottery. She Googled Dr. Michael Antoniou, a name long-since abandoned in a dark alley of her academic knowledge. Up came references to the core of his research: *whole proteins will be transposed overnight into wholly new associations, with consequences no one can foretell, either for the host organism, or its neighbours.*

Shit, she felt herself being swallowed by a sea of negativity and the waves of problems associated with her research. Fortunately, the sugar-rush from her breakfast ignited her willpower again, sparking the belief that on the opposite end of the spectrum there would have to be success: a new breed of men and women programmed to live better-faster-stronger lives, spared from the preoccupation of old age, freed from the grip of medicines, removed from the detriment of the country's finances.

Had Robert and Bill really thought about all that? She was impressed with how quickly she switched from curing hereditary diseases to addressing old age problems by completely removing elderly citizens from the equation. She was pleased with the flexibility of her paradigms, though she was disappointed that she had taken so long to understand that quality of life was going to win over quantity. Still, she was satisfied to realise she had finally found an adequate payback for her expensive education.

Part II

2.0 – May 20th

Standing in a small rundown lift, he read the advert one more time: would you die to be young again? Relieve your youth – the years when you were stronger, healthier, and more prone to action and adventure!

The candidate was a tall man in his late thirties, other than an aquiline nose, his features were dominated by thick dark hair, bushy eyebrows and a salt-and-pepper beard that made him look at least ten years older. He was tall and lean – some would call him gangly, kinder folk would say he looked every bit of the misunderstood artist he was. Once on the small landing, he put his tablet in the pocket of his jacket and closed his eyes for the few moments before a buzz accompanied the green light on the right-hand side of the door and it automatically opened. On entering the large room, he saw sparse furniture, bare walls and two large windows behind the drawn roller-blinds. In the middle of the room stood a chair, in front of a white and stainless-steel Robot.

It was hovering above the floor and the candidate had to do a double take to check that the thing was actually moving around the room without wheels, tracks or wires from the ceiling. It looked like a piece of expensive medical equipment; it had a light-blue screen projecting a male avatar face and a set of camera lenses that looked like a cluster of scrutinising eyes above the screen.

The robot spoke in a soft, welcoming, digital voice, inviting the visitor to take a seat in the lone chair.

Pretty soon, it became clear to the candidate that the interview would be conducted solely by the robot. He felt commoditised, he was a man, not a number, and being dealt with by a robot swung open the doors to his disappointment. In protest, he decided to be economical with his answers, and gave the machine a mere nod before sitting down, appearing like a sulky teenager. He began doubting the interviewing company and wondered why he was there at all, but the robot interrupted his internal dialogue. The mechanical voice explained that it could imagine what the candidate was thinking, almost offering an apology and confirming that the use of computers was demonstrative of the sophistication of cutting-edge technology adopted by the firm. This partially reassured the candidate and glossed over the reality behind the use of a machine: it was employed to avoid having any humans meeting and interviewing the applicant, so that no one had to physically take responsibility for the process.

While the robot moved around, as if to gather a full picture of the candidate, the latter looked around the room and noted its temporary nature. Still performing a slow-motion dance, as if truly equipped with the power to read thoughts, the robot went on to say that the interview location was mobile, to be regularly moved across the country to accommodate the large numbers keen to take part in the project. The robot finally stopped about one metre in front of the candidate, calibrating the height of its screen to be exactly in line with the candidate's eyes. Suddenly it shifted to a colder, business-like tone, signalling the interview was about to begin.

"Central London, Wednesday the 20th of May 2025, you are Experiment Candidate 1456, do you confirm?"

"Yes."

"What's your date of birth?"

"15th of June 1986."

"Are you comfortable to talk about yourself?"

"To a certain extent, perhaps, no, definitely, yes."

"How did you hear about us?"

"I started to notice this ad – *would you die to be young again?* and all that – you know what I mean, it started to quietly creep into my daily routine, and it just kept coming up."

"Where did you see it?"

"Oh, once in the appointments section of my favourite broadsheet, then in a blog I read… I think I even noticed it on a billboard hidden in an alley and half-covered by a lamp post. I thought it had started to follow me actually."

"What did you make of it?"

"Nothing, to begin with, but a few times later, or even the third or fourth time that I noticed it, I started to feel moved, stirred rather. As I said, the first impression wasn't much, but then I realised the message…had a kind of deeper meaning? It was really talking to me. It was as though the universe really wanted me to see this message."

"Did it prompt you into any particular action?"

The candidate launched into conversation, like someone who doesn't have a wide circle of friends with whom to make idle chit-chat. "Yes. I remember one evening; I was travelling to some god-awful place with a colleague on business. He had a girlfriend in this town, so he went off and I was left, sitting on my own in a bar, at dusk, with people engaged in inane banter all around … These were not the kind of people I would mingle with, so I was eager to find some form of entertainment, something that I could do by myself to pass the time. I was browsing the internet, flipping through things to do – theatre pages, lists of concerts and the like – when all of a sudden, I see the bloody ad on my tablet again: *become younger etc...*

"It really stopped me thinking about anything else, and threw me into another dimension. It appeared just when I was dreaming of escaping – so I thought, instead of escaping for just one night, what if I escaped my whole life, my entire existence? You see, I'd been feeling so depressed and was fed up of seeing other people, morons, getting on with their lives, in all sorts of dreary occupations… And I couldn't bear my job and was frustrated at not being recognised as an artist.

"I was essentially already living two lives, if you see what I mean, so when I saw your enticing proposal out there, I thought how amazing it would be to drop off the grid altogether and start again. Whoa, to be given the chance to use this as a rehearsal, to have the opportunity to see it all and then get to perform it over again – well, it seemed ideal!"

The robot looked puzzled. Well, the metal didn't change, but the avatar appeared to struggle with the abundance of information, though the candidate had already convinced himself that it possessed superior intelligence, "I understand your emotions; just tell me what actions you took then."

"Listen, I was feeling unbearably lonely, so after a few minutes of wild thoughts, I decided to call a friend and put the question to him, hoping that he had not seen the ad himself. I wanted to kill the anxiety I felt, but I was also trying to get some advice on what to do next with your ad, because it was rather dry you know, a website with a contact form to fill..."

"Please continue," the robot interrupted, pressing the candidate to get to the point.

"Yes, yes. So I called my friend, who was always open for a transcendental chat about off-the-wall subjects. Making the question my own, I asked him if he would have liked to live for a number of years, die, and then live again, rather than having to roam through a longer meaningless life, without knowing how long it would be before it ended, or how you would die, and he said..."

"Candidate 1456, please keep this interview to the subject: yourself and your motivations for being here."

"But I am!" he said, increasingly frustrated by the robot. "So he thought exactly what I thought – that obviously, to live two lives would be nirvana, if you were still able to be yourself of course."

"Why did he, I'm sorry... why did *you* think so?"

"I think most people would want that, if you ask it the right way and explain what it means. People want to keep young, fashionable, slim, fit... just look at rates of people divorcing and remarrying; everyone wants a second chance. But my friend is much better off than I am, financially I mean, and listening to him list all the things he would do again if given the chance, when I hadn't even done them once, kind of depressed me further."

"What did you do then?"

"Well... I called someone else, another friend, she's a married woman I used to date; we had become friends on Facebook, but I hadn't called her for years. I thought I would sound interesting, intriguing, you know – an old flame resurfacing from the ashes, asking clever questions? I wanted to meet her again, impress her, make love. I had already spent hours looking at her pictures – the wedding, the nights out with girlfriends and so on – and I was as horny as hell for her, and cross that I let her slip through my fingers..."

"You must keep to the subject."

"Listen to me, I am keeping to the subject; so we chatted a bit, then I asked her the question from your ad, again pretending it was my material. But it was a disaster. She was the most opinionated woman, who just ranted, telling me how horrible it would be to go back and live another life. She said she had finally found some balance in life and that reaching 40 was the best thing. I asked her if she was happy being a wife and mother, hoping to pick some hole of uncertainty, but of course she was. She said, consistently happy, 'how else could it be?' I even suggested that she was obliged to say yes for the sake of her family, but no, she said it wouldn't be possible for her leave the loved ones for the fancy of being young again. Her smug content made me even more depressed.

"I had obviously not thought it through before phoning her up, but even then, how could I possibly have imagined it going so wrong? How could she not want to be young again? I felt so alone and worthless, and hated myself for having sounded so stupid, and probably desperate."

"Tell me what happened next."

"I'm telling you, aren't I? Be patient. So, there I was, feeling very lonely, and as though I had achieved nothing in life – no money, status or family. Not only did I feel I had wasted my life so far, but I had no prospects. I could only keep thinking about being born again, not dying, but reborn," he nodded at his own dialogue.

"Why did you come here?"

"That night, stuck on my own in an unfamiliar dead-end town while my colleague was off gallivanting with his girlfriend, was the moment I wanted to get involved in this project. First I Googled it to find out more, but couldn't find anything online, so I decided to be brave and complete your online form, giving out my personal data, even though I never do so and would have liked more information to read first."

"I'm glad you did anyway Candidate 1456. Can I now ask you a few personal questions?"

"I would prefer to hear what is it that you do here."

"Soon, as we finish section one of the interview; do you have problems at work?"

"Listen, who hasn't issues at work – robots?" he replied animatedly, laughing at his own joke. "I'm an unqualified architect, unrecognised artist, and mediocre insurance salesperson – my problems at work range from under-appreciation and lack of career prospects to the complete absence of a social life. I have no hope of changing anything, I will just continue doing more of what I'm doing already, day-in, day-out, till I'll drop dead and get replaced. By something like you, I guess, but I get paid at least, although the money is pitifully low and asking for a pay rise would equate to a resignation. "

"Are you in a relationship? Do you have a family?"

"You don't ask interesting questions, can I ask some questions?" he was getting heated.

The robot pushed back, "In due course Candidate 1456, we need to finish this section first, please respond to the question."

He stood up. "This is not how I expected it, at all. Why do you want to know? Ok, I was married for a few years, but I've no children, you should know that, and I have not really settled down since then – are you happy now? What I want to know—" the avatar's expression was changing regularly, and he was clearly outraged by the outburst.

The candidate sat down again, landing heavily under his own weight. "Listen, the marriage ended with a miscarriage. Hannah blamed me, she was..., well I would prefer not to talk about it, it's all too depressing anyway."

"Would you have liked to have children?"

"I sometimes think I would have liked to have had children, but they are less and less frequent. I think my interest in children faded after Hannah, after we separated; life is..., but, listen, you're a robot."

The avatar smiled sympathetically, "Briefly describe your parents."

"They are dead. They were always old to me, or at least my mother was old, my father was just sick.

They died a long time ago and I'm happy for them that they went before having to endure too much aging. I don't miss them."

"Are you scared of growing old?"

"God you robots are stupid; who isn't scared of ageing?" He sighed, looking up at the ceiling. He thought the interview was losing whatever significance and value. "Listen, you have no hair, no skin, nothing to age you – that's *why* they sent you here, you wouldn't be asking all these silly questions if your trademark beautiful locks were thinning or greying, or if you were sleeping badly, had a dodgy back, thought you looked like a ripened plum in the morning… Gosh, you don't even gain weight, you don't have to worry about bloating after a second serving… and I see you have no legs, while I've got sore knees from too much sitting at work and I've started to get those hard feet old people have." His voice was starting to crack and his tirade was broken by a few hiccoughs. "Young people call me *sir* now, I'm sure they do it just to provoke me. The lads in my office aren't kind, I am the oldest and you would think that they should respect their elders, but…" he shook his head as he tailed off. "God, I could do with looking ten or 20 years younger in the office."

"What's your ultimate dream?"

He spoke without listening to the last question, "I lack purpose in life, and lust for adventure and desire for women. I used to be interested in doing wild things, but now I feel incapable, deluded and inadequate." The robot let the candidate's monologue continue, seeking for more answers. "I've had a few opportunities thrown at me over the years, diluted in a sea of poor judgement. The women I have not kissed, the people I have not impressed, the things I have not said or done... it makes me sad," he sobbed.

"Do you fear humiliation?"

The candidate took a minute to recompose himself, adjusting his posture on the chair before clearing his throat. "At work, there are younger people who earn more than I do, and are promoted above me... I have no stories to tell my manager, no trips to Vegas, no dancers, no boozy nights out. And yes, it is humiliating sitting there listening, pretending to join in, while they share their mischief, the fun and frivolity in their lives; it hurts. I feel like a has-been. Listen, this is too depressing. I mean, this interview is so... You're just trying to humiliate me, making me tell my sad existence to a robot. I want to speak to a human, I want your boss."

"Candidate 1456, we're almost finished with the questions; if you don't complete this interview, your chances of proceeding further will be zero."

"This is not how I envisaged this would happen."

"If you had a new life, would you make the same mistakes?"

The candidate felt the urge to leave, but he also wanted to pursue the opportunity. "I don't think so," he continued, staring at the floor, his hands gripping the side of the chair. "I wouldn't make the same mistakes, I'm not stupid," he sneered.

"What would you change then?"

He replied without hesitation. "I'd make myself heard, you can be sure of that; I'd have a better job, I would succeed as an artist, I would manage to hold down a relationship, I would drive a flashy car, and people would *have* to take notice of me. No more talking to robots!"

"Candidate 1456, you are doing really well, thank you for all the information."

"I'm not happy about this meeting. To be honest, all these questions are getting in the way of me asking about the opportunity described in the ad. Can you tell me more now?"

"We will come to our offer in due course; remember, a lot of people want this treatment, and questions are asked to discern the fittest."

"Yes, but—"

"I'd like to ask my questions now. Please answer yes if you exhibit any of these behaviours, and remember, we cross check your answers."

The candidate nodded wearily.

"Do you abuse alcohol?"

"No, I mean I drink like most people, but I don't abuse it."

"What is your daily consumption?"

"Well, that depends on the day, but probably just a beer or two."

"How often do exceed that quantity?"

"Rarely, very rarely and only if I'm having a bad spell."

"Do you make use of drugs?"

"No, God no! Only sleeping pills. They help me—"

"Do you find the male body sexually attractive?"

"What? No!"

"Have you had cosmetic surgery?"

"Isn't that normal? Yes, I've had some work."

"Please detail."

"Gosh, well, I had a few lines filled in around my eyes."

"Anything else?"

"I had my ears pinned back when I was much younger."

"Are you obsessed with young people?"

"What do you mean, sexually? No!" The robot detected the candidate's lie, before he could elaborate on his answer, instructed to do so remotely, it terminated the interview abruptly.

"Candidate 1456, thanks for all the important information you have provided so far; we will revert to you once we have analysed your profile against other applicants. You are free to go now."

"What? Are you crazy?" He stood up in disbelief. "I came all the way here to find out more, and you've not told me anything?"

The robot moved around the large bare room, trying to put some distance between them. "Listen, this is not acceptable," the candidate shouted. "I need to know more about all this; I applied because I wanted to learn more!"

The robot continued to move backwards, readjusting its lens accordingly and changing its avatar to an authoritative mode. "You are entitled to a short overview," it increased the speed of its speech, "this is a unique opportunity reserved for selected people. We endeavour to provide you with a pleasant termination of your life on your 40th birthday. You will be guaranteed a new life of matching duration, commencing within hours of your natural death. You will be born healthy and grow as any other normal child. By the time you reach puberty, you will become aware of your previous life. From then on, the freedom to express yourself will be subject to strict conditions; you will not be able to alter or exit the experiment and you will be terminated if you disclose anything about the procedure."

The candidate was in awe watching the robot talk through the process. "You will be supplied with certain products and services, and we will direct your vote in any democratic ballot. This is the end of the overview; you can leave now."

The candidate jerked his head back as though he'd been slapped in the face. *That was a lot of information in 30 seconds!* A smile slowly staggered across his face, he was impressed. "Wow! What a plan, this is fascinating. But tell me more about the way it works, I mean medically, please can you explain—"

"We are not able to disclose more information at this stage. We trust that you will be progressing to the stage of the selection where you qualify for further information on the procedure."

"Can you at least please tell me when can I meet your supervisor… a human, someone responsible for all this?"

"We will contact with you via the secure server. In the meantime, you must not disclose any information about this meeting to anyone. As per the terms and conditions you signed, your obligation to refrain from disclosing any information is already binding."

"Are you threatening me?" the candidate asked, a little incredulously.

"We have our ways of guaranteeing our privacy. You will hear from us in 24 hours. Remember your ID is Candidate EA1456, your identification password is KillerApp. Goodbye," the robot said, moving towards the door.

"I remember my username, but—"

"You may leave now."

The candidate hated being ushered out when he still had so many questions. He looked at the room once more before turning to leave and saw the robot projecting a waving hand on his screen.

Back out in the real world, the candidate wondered what had just happened. He felt excited at the opportunity and couldn't wait to hear if he was successful, but as the interview was with a robot, he wasn't sure if it had gone well. The weather had turned and, the grey day combined with a brutal return to the drudgery of work, quickly brought his mood back down to its usual depressed level.

2.1 – May 21st

He would sit for hours at the windowsill of his first floor studio flat, looking down at the half-empty street, feeling a mixture of distress and unhappiness. Even before starting to feel stale following his divorce, the candidate had always been an ill-humoured, negative person. In fairness, during the good times of his marriage, he would suppress his bad mood and temper. But now he could only hide his true nature at the start of a new encounter if he deemed the person to be interesting enough. If the stranger scored highly in his peculiar rating system based on looks, wealth and status, he would lay on the charm; smooth-talking witty repartee accompanied by dashing smiles and intense glances. He was naturally talented at flirting and instantly connecting with someone. However, being in a long-term relationship would inevitably reveal his complicated personality and irreversible tendency towards the dark side.

Of course, if he didn't deem the person worthy of his attention, then they stood no chance of seeing his lighter side – he reserved that exclusively for the chosen few. Rank and class were an obsession for him. He only pursued people who were well-connected and actively despised anyone of a lower social standing and went to great lengths to avoid them. Despite his discerning attitude towards others, he was desperate for their approval, and seeing that most friends tended to desert him once his negativity showed through, he tended to cling to new acquaintances in the hope of garnering their friendship for a while.

He would often talk to strangers, smiling profusely to show off his good teeth while seductively twirling the ends of his thick black hair. These were his prized assets and he saw them as testament to his heritage, which once belonged to the elite of society, though maintaining his hair nowadays was an immensely time-consuming affair, consisting of foil wraps, conditioning masks and specialist clippers and brushes.

During the warm evenings in May, when everyone else kept their windows shut to block out the ravaging air and noise pollution, he would insist on sitting at his open window, dressed for going out in society, even though he hadn't spoken to anyone in days. With his bad temper interfering with every thought, he saw a young woman walking a dog down the otherwise-deserted street and his first reaction focused on the *disgusting* animal. He reflected that city laws, levying dog-owners with a £10,000 annual tax, were very finely crafted. Then, something rare happened – his negative spiral faltered, allowing his mind to drift to a positive consideration: *if the woman is able to maintain a dog, she might as well take care of a fine young man in his late thirties, someone looking to marry into high society for example.*

This thought spurred him into action; he briefly checked his appearance in the mirror before dashing downstairs to street level. He reinforced his resolve as he strode across to meet her, *a woman can't seriously find a filthy dog more likeable than a man like myself!* He rearranged his hair and started walking along the pavement, endeavouring to casually bump into the girl and her dog. He didn't like to think of himself as a stalker, chasing a woman he had seen for 20 seconds from a window; instead he imagined her, like him, as a lonely character, perhaps mourning for the loss of a man, someone who had left her a sizeable inheritance. He fantasised that she was going to be totally entranced by him, captured by his spell, and that they would be engaged before the end of summer.

Snapping out of his dream world, he sought a good opening line, a touching, well-composed ice-breaker, like in the movies. He would be like a charming actor, softly speaking something magical that would supersede anyone's expectation for a successful conversation starter. He thought of *Casablanca*, his favourite movie, but she was moving too fast for him to become Victor Laszlo. In fact, she was already walking in his direction, leaving him grasping for determination. He couldn't figure out why she was already coming towards him, it was almost as though she had no definite destination, that she was merely zigzagging the pavements around his flat, but he dismissed that possibility, *who would venture out without a destination these days?*

He was close enough to bump into her that very second, and so it was with irritation that he abruptly paused his internal dialogue. He looked stern, uncompromising, and hesitated a fraction too long to sound natural, "That's a rather lucky beast... blessed I'd call it, belonging to a fine young woman like yourself."

She stopped in her tracks, literally speechless, utterly unsure what to do with such an awkward opening line. She took one quick glance at him and he was saddened to see her reaction. Only the fading souvenir of his original purpose, pushed him to a second endeavour, addressing her once more to make up for her lack of response. "I fancy that I would rather like to be this dog to be looked after by you... I am quite put off by the smell of such beasts, otherwise I would be entirely capable of paying the city tax."

His mention of heavy-duty tax made the girl clear her throat loudly, which he interpreted as her discomfort at his blunt approach, but she responded to his nonsense, "Yes sir, spot on."

"Aha, you're a very funny girl," he exaggerated a laugh as he interrupted her. "Calling me sir, when I am no more than a few years older than you! This age of cosmetic surgery means you can never really tell anyone's age anymore, have you not noticed? I'm always so distressed at guessing people's age – how old are you my dear?"

She wasn't taken aback by his rudeness. "I'm … I'm 30, sir."

He suppressed an urge to show his annoyance as he still had an interest in her. "Listen, you may think I was your age sometime before the turn of the century," he chuckled, "but I'm actually very much within your age group, and would appreciate being addressed as John, as in John Keats … *My heart aches, and a drowsy numbness pains …* "

The woman was really not sure what to make of him or the conversation, yet she seemed to want to continue talking to this stranger. Out of nowhere, she asked whether he liked the neighbourhood. He was pleased to see his charms working on the pretty young woman and in a few seconds he realised how fruitful the new subject was – he could launch into a stimulating debate about the deficiencies of the area compared to more secure compounds in north London. "Areas like these can only be trusted for trouble – dead poor when you need society, but wealthy enough to attract all sort of wicked attentions," his thoughtful expression nodding, before boasting about how he had developed a necessary "sixth sense for spotting ill-intentioned people," in order to be able to "live safely in this government-forgotten pocket of hell."

Having established his views and self-perceived position in society, he turned the table and started asking her questions: where she lived, if she was married and why had she decided to take such an expensive companion onboard, all done in an increasingly posh accent.

He was distracted by someone rattling a gate in the background, but the delightful dog-walker grabbed his attention as she pulled out a tabloid newspaper with an alarmist headline: *Family deprived of food stamps kill to sell organs abroad.*

She spoke soberly, "Look here, I know what you're talking about!" In that brief moment of communication, he believed she was the real deal, that she knew and was accustomed to the daily tragedies of life. After the disaster of the interview with the robot, he grinned, eager to connect with a new human. "Me and you, we understand each other perfectly! These are rotten times, not a chance of happiness, it's a terrible sign of... Are you alright dear

– you look very hot, do you feel unwell?" He stepped back, "Could it be the city bug?

"It could be heat pollution from global warming, it's a disgrace. I myself have not been able to sleep well since that terrifying accident in Manchester, no matter what they say, I think we are all gonna be contaminated this side of the Chilterns too. Listen, I don't like the way the world is going and I think all we can do is to choose the company that we want to be with while navigating our way through this awful society… hence my earlier question asking you whether or not you were married?"

"Yes, I mean, no, well I was, but I have not been able to..." she stumbled, unsure of her answer.

"I understand," he said conspiratorially, "It must have been difficult for you to bear marriage. As a matter of fact, I too have suffered my share of hell for being married once. Listen, such restrictive schemes are hard, they're not fashionable any longer, just confinements from an archaic society. Actually, I am what I am and that alone makes me special…"

"I'm sorry," she interrupted his preaching, "but you're right, I'm not feeling well." She took her leave in haste, giving him a half-smirk half-sneer which he didn't immediately understand. *Is she dumping me before I've even asked her out?* He concluded that the inconceivable was happening: she was cutting him short, there and then.

He attempted to retain her company, but she sang a well-known refrain, "We'll meet again – don't know where, don't know when..."

Her rejection was a slap in the face, turning him into stone. With an air of contempt, he started talking to himself in a low voice, "Go to hell, pathetic dog-walking bitch." She couldn't hear, she was long-since gone with the dog struggling to keep pace with her.

Left alone in an empty street, the candidate nursed his disappointment and found himself in one of his terrible moods; despair was a familiar feeling which he had inhabited most his life. He shook his head and ground his teeth in frustration. He ran his hand through his black hair, a gesture he often did subconsciously when experiencing discontent or disgust. He headed home with his head down in a sulk, chewing the bitter bullet of being dumped again. Once at the front gate, it took him a moment to register the light that was creeping from the inside – a most peculiar occurrence since all doors and gates had to be closed at all times according to strict building rules. No one would have left a door open and risked a fine, not even his idiotic neighbours with money to burn. Pushing the gate open without the use of a key confirmed that it was unlatched, but once through he realised it also would not close properly behind him. Unsure of what to do, he tentatively climbed the stairs to his flat. At the top of the stairs, the gravity of the situation hit him in its entirety, like a ton of bricks: the door to his flat was wide open, his privacy exposed for the world to see. His jaw dropped as he quickly pieced things together: the pretty girl wandering aimlessly on the street, her agitated conversation and sweaty appearance, the noise of a gate rattling as she distracted him with a newspaper cover. He had been robbed. At that moment, everything became crystal clear. He hated society more than ever.

He let out a loud scream of aggression and his legs buckled under the weight of his naivety. He remained rooted to the floor at the entrance of his flat for several minutes before he could make it inside to survey what was missing. His heart pounded and his stomach churned as he took a mental note: his tablet was missing from the desk, his wallet and phone from the bedside table… everything valuable was gone. He was so angry, he didn't know whether to shout or cry. He had lost everything that was valuable to him. He couldn't possibly afford to replace them. More than ever, he wanted it to end. Then despair wrapped an icy grip around him as he realised he needed his technology in order to receive the instructions from the research company. Without them, he could not be born again; he felt like killing himself.

2.2 – May 22nd

Early in the morning, the day after the robbery, the candidate was visited by the building manager, an unemotional, business like, short, white-haired man in his sixties. He didn't deal with complaints as methodically as he did rent collection, often disappearing at length just when he was needed. Still, he was here now and he had gently knocked on the side panel of the broken door, patiently waiting for an answer. He was aware of how difficult this particular tenant could be, so he knocked again and waited some more. Without receiving a welcome, he took a few long strides into the flat and started surveying the place, taking pictures and notes. He then sat down at the small table and began calling, texting and emailing the office, contractors and suppliers to get the mess sorted.

Unable to emerge from under his duvet, a mere ten meters away, the tenant listened to his crisp voice. Conscious that hiding wasn't sustainable long-term, he eventually got up to face the consequences of the previous day. He threw on a jumper and trousers, and did his trademark move running his hand through his hair as he walked towards the other side of the room. The view around the house wasn't pretty. Last night he had taken in the event of the burglary, but now he was confronted by depressing daylight: drawers were pulled out, clothes strewn on the floor, pictures were askew, cupboard doors were left open and worthless belongings were scattered where they were discarded, signalling the route the burglar had taken around the flat.

In the middle of it all, the building manager was still on the phone, barely acknowledging his presence, talking tactlessly about a number of complications for the tenant. The latter headed for the coffee machine to get some perspective in a mug, but he couldn't find it; had that really been stolen too? The tenant slumped at the table opposite the building manager and held his head in his hands. When the visitor came off the phone, he continued speaking without a pause: "Don't worry about coffee, I've just had one." He pressed on, without any consideration for the tenant, asking what had happened the night before, and whether he had been home during the crime. The tenant gave brief responses and started shaking his head in the negative when asked awkward questions – had the alarm been set, were the police informed, had they written a report, did he have insurance? All the sticky points came out in a quick succession, none of which the tenant seemed to be able to answer satisfactorily. "There's nothing I could have done differently," he offered meekly. "I had no phone or computer. I knew you'd arrive quickly once you heard about the door and gate."

He just about refrained from provoking the accusation of "endangering behaviour," a charge which could be brought when a tenant exhibited conduct attracting or facilitating a crime, or letting undesirables in the building. And a successful prosecution would mean automatic eviction.

The manager's main concern though, remained the repair of the main gate, which had to be carried out by the authorised security company the same day. "You don't have sufficient money on your account, can you top it up now?" The tenant tried to reassure him that he would have the money to pay for repair by the end of the month, but the promise did not cut any slack with the manager who only left when the tenant committed to be back by 6.00 p.m. with the money. The manager also made it clear that it was the tenant's duty to look after his property and presented a number of incomprehensible forms for signature which the tenant didn't read. Instead of wading through the small print, he pushed for the manager to leave as quickly as possible. Finally alone, he tried to gather his thoughts. He had no idea how he was going to get the money to pay for the repairs, but he was more concerned about the interview he had had and how to check his emails to find out if he had been accepted into the experiment.

The paranoid side of him began to form a fatalist notion, that the robbery was a premonition, a guiding event pushing him definitively towards the chance of a new life. This was his one opportunity; otherwise, he would be condemned to a wretched life of misery, bankruptcy and loneliness.

Without a tablet or phone, the project organisers couldn't contact him, and without money he couldn't work out how he was going to find out his fate. On top of that, he was getting hungry since he'd skipped the previous night's meal following the robbery. He couldn't think where else to get a free meal, other than joining the homeless queues at a soup kitchen, but he had no idea where the nearest one was. Then he remembered the Jediist temple, and he thought he was likely to find a meal there, even though it meant walking at least two hours. He used the walking time, to think about his plight. He remembered how he had first seen the adverts for the chance of a new life in his favoured broadsheets, so he began scouring the streets for discarded newspapers. As soon as he found one, he would scan it quickly then fold it neatly before storing it in the pocket of his dark brown trench coat, like any good lunatic would do.

He arrived at the corner where the Jediist temple was located around lunchtime and was dismayed to discover it wasn't a pretty line of people he was joining. Queuing behind an array of down-and-outs, beggars, weirdos, tramps, addicts and drifters; he was mortified, but starving all the same. The line stretched endlessly and over an hour later he finally reached the door of the temple.

To enter, he had to pass a short interview with an activist and commit to attend mass after the meal. Inside the wide corridor, two more volunteers were sorting people out, checking for lice and separating those who needed washing before queuing for the canteen. He was allowed straight into the large refectory, *I should think so too, I'm not homeless!* He was handed a tray on which lay a spoon, a bread roll, a paper napkin and a religious pamphlet. He proceeded further down the line where a bowl of thin vegetable soup and a slice of cake were placed on his tray. Hungry and tired, he sat down and dipped the bread roll in the soup and started cramming it into his mouth.

Still chewing the last mouthful of cake, he reached in his pockets for the newspapers. He examined them, line-by-line, without lingering over the meaning of anything, simply scouring for that advert. Page after page, he scanned indiscernible articles and stories, and left other adverts undeciphered in his brain. He could visualise the ad he needed and, like a child looking for a shape to put through a hole, he focused solely on that unique sentence… *would you die to be young again?*

He checked each paper, again and again, but found nothing. Fatigued by the effort, he allowed himself to be corralled by the staff to join the mass. He moved passively with the rest of the desperate guests through the corridor into a larger room used for the brainwashing rituals. He didn't mind, he let it wash over him, his mind racing around a myriad of thoughts, from what would become of him if he couldn't pay for the door repair, to what had happened to the experiment and the ad.

His attention was drawn back to the mass by the arrival of an elegant, refined and sophisticated tall man on stage, with long black hair combed back into a ponytail and a very pale complexion. He appeared to be the leader of the religious movement, a spiritual motivator, speaking before his flock with a commanding posture and captivating voice. He opened with a typical salesman gambit, "He who is hurting, comes to the Jediist temple to heal; he who is lost, comes to the Jediist family to be found; he who is hungry comes to the Jediist bosom to be fed. If you think the government does nothing to help you, raise your hand and say, 'Hi'," he raised his right arm theatrically and was copied by a large part of the congregation. "What is your government doing for you? Your government is killing you. That's what it's doing!"

The spiel didn't catch his attention for long and soon his mind turned once again to the daily papers. He wondered why they weren't carrying the ad anymore. He couldn't give up, it wasn't an option, a new life was waiting for him on the other side of that ad; he had to take control of the situation and prove that he was motivated. That's when he got the idea of going to a public library to search for an old paper.

Buzzing with excitement, he could hardly wait until the mass was over to put his plan into action. By the time he left the temple, after zigzagging his way through the various activists trying to recruit him for spiritual exercises, he realised it was too late; the library would be closed.

He trudged home, grateful to have had at least had some food and devised a way out of his misery. He didn't arrive home until early evening, and was thankful to have avoided meeting the building manager again. His entry code to the compound gate didn't work, but fortunately one of his neighbours was coming home from work and he slipped in behind her.

Walking upstairs to his door, he was greeted by all his possessions stacked in a few boxes in front of the repaired, repainted and sealed door. A message was attached to the top box, framed by red-and-white-striped tape, he took it off and read: *This is an eviction note on grounds of Endangering Behaviour. A moving fee of £300 has been escrowed from your account together with £350 for repairs. We wish you all the best with your future endeavours, The Management.*

He squatted in front of the door holding his head between the palms of his hands. He felt tears approaching his cheeks, followed by an overwhelming urge to kill "The Management." He was sure his neighbours were enjoying the scene from behind the peepholes of their doors – he knew all too well that the eviction procedure comprised all residents being informed, and he could imagine them all cheering for the burglary and his eviction. *Rats, they were all despising, hateful rats.* He was sure no one had stood up for him, putting in a good word to help him.

He got up and kicked the new door blocking him from his old apartment, but was too exhausted for any further physical retaliation. Instead he sorted through the meagre contents of his life, assembling a small bundle containing only few days' worth of clothes and cosmetics. He left the building without a destination in mind and wandered the streets for a couple of hours, bitterly regretting not coming home earlier to try and save his haven.

Tired of walking the deserted streets cursing his landlord, he felt the evening air cool and snuck into the unmanned gate of a nearby tube station. Inside, he cursed the temperature which was still stifling, but welcomed the prospect of being able to spend the night somewhere sheltered – well, at least until 4.30 a.m. when the trains resumed service. He ventured to a hidden corner on one of the platform concourses where he nestled up for the night. Physically tired and emotionally distraught, he fell asleep quickly, but was rudely woken less than an hour later by a cleaner who threatened him with his mop: "Leave now tramp or I'll have you arrested."

Back on street level, he wandered aimlessly again, until he passed the front of a closed convenience store with a wooden bench outside serving as a fruit stall. Exhausted as he was, he carved a space for himself among the stockpile of empty fruit boxes and snuggled underneath the structure, hiding from the cruel world. When he finished covering as much of his body as he could with newspaper, he realised the cleaner was right – he was a tramp. He could barely suppress his tears and an intense storm of negative emotions raged through him, from anger and anxiety, to guilt and depression. He finally gave in to sleep in the early hours of the morning.

*****

Suspended between the realms or dream and reality, the ex-tenant heard people talking a foreign language, and smelt curry spices as someone kicked his left foot. He woke abruptly and immediately became aware of an intimidating situation: he was lying on the ground, surrounded by a group of tall young foreigners, who were gesturing wildly and talking over him in an incomprehensible language. He scrambled to stand up and grab his stuff, then fled, much to the amusement of the men.

Running wasn't his strength; unaccustomed to physical exercise, he stopped when he was completely breathless. His throat burnt and his ribs ached from breathing deeply, his legs were leaden from the effort and he felt lightheaded. As he calmed down and caught his breath, he saw the dawn breaking and noticed a page of newspaper still hanging from his body. Any pride he might have felt for surviving the night without shelter, was soon replaced with terror about the day ahead of him. He had no money, no means of contacting anyone, no friends to whom he could turn, and he was presumably fired since he hadn't turned up to work the previous day. Then he remembered his plan – go to the local library and find the advert in an old paper.

It was still early, but he picked up his luggage and slowly headed towards the only public library left locally, which was a good hour away by foot. As rush hour started, he noticed that no passer-by would make eye contact with him; unwashed, uncombed, in wrinkled smelly clothes, he projected an air of despair and desperation. While walking, he couldn't help worrying about what a second night on the streets would be like, and a third, or fourth… He accelerated his pace and steeled his determination to find that advert.

A sense of relief washed over him when he saw the old gothic building housing the public library. He was frustrated by the line of people queuing outside, but knew it would be worth the wait. He lined up and moved slowly towards the gate, where he filled out a registration form (bluffing with his old address as contact details), had his picture taken and went through airport-style security. He reluctantly parted with his luggage, which had to be left in a locker, and asked for directions to the newspaper room.

He rushed up the flight of stairs, two steps at a time, and found the archive room consisted of an already overcrowded table covered in papers, in the middle of rows and rows of shelves. With no empty chairs to sit on, he scanned the volumes of papers standing up, which was tiresome. Nonetheless, he went through each page of every paper, scanning them like a machine. Two gruelling hours later, he found it: *Opportunity knocks once in a lifetime – would you like to die to live the first 40 years of your life again? Contact us at www.eandiamo.com.* His heart almost skipped a beat, he stopped breathing for a second, and he felt dizzy, emotional. Suddenly self-conscious, he suspiciously surveyed his fellow researchers to preserve his secret. Next, he had to locate the computers with internet access, and of course there was another queue. His stomach started to make deep, long growls, reminding him he hadn't eaten since yesterday's lunch. Weakness replaced the tension in his body, and he was increasingly aware of the fragility of his situation. Time passed slowly in the queue, and when a keyboard and screen finally freed up for him, he almost lacked the physical strength or willpower to type the website in the address bar of the browser. An almost blank page was loaded, with just the words, *Already interviewed?* appearing on the screen with a *Click here* button in the bottom right corner.

His hand was shaking as he clicked it, and a new page appeared in front of him with two blank boxes requesting information: *Candidate number* and *Date of Birth.* He remembered the first from the interview, he was Candidate 1456, and he entered his birthdate, 15th June, 1986. He clicked go and the screen refreshed to a single line asking for his password. He cast his mind back to the interview and had to work hard to retrieve it from the back of his brain. The effort exhausted him and brought on a debilitating headache, but he finally settled on something that sounded like it... He nervously keyed it in and held his breath as he watched a video load. With great anticipation, he pressed play and the screen showed a close-up of a young doctor in white overalls, directly addressing the camera, giving the impression she was talking straight at him, live.

"Message for Experiment Candidate 1456: please get in contact with us as soon as possible on the phone number written below. Alternatively, kindly report to the Oxford Genetic Laboratories, Superseding Life Unit, Oxfordshire. The Labs are located fifteen minutes outside of Oxford town centre and can be reached by bus route 35."

The video ended with a bird's-eye view of the labs next to a text-box with the phone number, address and directions. Candidate 1456 had not realised how much this meant to him, but he found he had tears streaming down his cheeks, there in the middle of the library. He was flooded with emotion; he was moved that they hadn't forgotten him, they knew he was their man, they had remembered him, all the way to making contact, expressing their wish of seeing him again. He finally felt whole again; wanted, needed, useful. He had no time to waste; the team at the Oxford Genetic Laboratories were waiting for him.

2.3 – May 23rd

Janet arrived early at the lab, donning her white lab coat straight away, leaving her hair swept back in a ponytail; within minutes, her face was lit up by multiple screens displaying information on the candidate who had been chosen as the experiment adept. She connected to the network, eager to see the results of the work carried out overnight on the adept – she would use these findings to arrange a complex schedule of tests to be carried out on EA1456 later that day.

She had been so relieved that the candidate had made contact, as they feared he had gone AWOL. She had received an email alert when EA1456's contact request was made from the public library, which included a surveillance picture showing him as pale, tired and scruffy. Somehow, he had managed to arrive at the premises later that night, starving, smelly and unrecognisable. She had already gone home when he arrived, but she had put staff in place with strict instructions on checking him in: a room with a bed, a shower, fresh in-patient clothes, and food and water.

Janet was excited about her maiden visit with the adept, the first one-to-one encounter. She flicked through his personal profile once more, even though she knew it inside-out: *NPD, Narcissistic Personality Disorder, refuses to deal with criticism and rejection, quick to anger, self-centred, egocentric, lacking empathy, selfish, emotionally unstable.* She made a mental note to be careful not to be manipulated by his dark character. She also remembered how the systems had picked him up as the only suitable person to use because of his DNA structure.

Her tablet buzzed, the adept was ready for her in one of the lab's rooms. She walked towards him, full of anticipation. The selection process had been the result of complex algorithms and careful negotiation with Bill and Robert, and now the product of her hard work was here. Somehow EA1456 had made it through, even though he appeared a bit of a nut case, a whimsical oddball, an eccentric character – these were all attributes that intrigued her, although some of the traits could expose the experiment, and she worried about the responsibility she held should things go wrong.

She walked confidently, rehearsing her strategy based on the team psychologist's advice: don't disclose you are the leader of the experiment, just hang around casually and let EA1456 approach you; gain his confidence by defending him against the people he will certainly attack. This should give her more freedom of approach at a later stage, by gaining a handle on his narcissistic nature.

She appeared in the room from behind the sliding door and, without greeting her colleagues, edged closer to the bed where he was lying propped up on pillows. He looked different from how she'd expected –relaxed, at complete peace with himself. As well as his freshly-washed hair and beard, she noticed his thick eyelashes and foxy eyes. His slightly ruddy complexion was testament to the last two days. With his thin arms folded across his chest, she saw he held a religious amulet. Janet looked at it while he assessed her angular features; it resembled the intersection of a cross and a hook. "That's a fine piece of art you have with you, is it a good luck charm?"

"Oh, just a souvenir of the last restaurant I ate at… the Jediist Temple in London."

She was wondering how he could balance religion with the experiment, no liturgy could possibly have accommodated what she was going to do to him.

"What was your name before coming here?"

"I waived it, I'm Experiment Candidate 1456, but you can call me EA1456."

He made her smile. "Sorry, I forget these things, I've not been here long myself." She paused to phrase her next question carefully. "Hey, do you want to know what we're going to do with you now?"

He nodded, again seeming at ease. "Before the procedure," she continued, "we make sure that certain health parameters are checked, so we can take good care of you while you're here." Against her expectation, there was good chemistry between them and she found herself giving him a cheeky look, "So, will you cooperate, yeah?"

He nodded.

"Do you have any questions?" she asked raising her eyebrows.

"A million," he replied quickly, "though it seems to me that one of the house rules is not to explain how things work."

She was a bit taken aback by his bluntness, as she thought they were forging a good relationship. She revised her expectations slightly and reassured him,

"All in good time, we'll try and give you a million answers after these tests."

"You talk less than that bloody robot... but at least you're prettier," he said grinning. His mood swings disarmed her, but she smiled back at him and prepared herself for the challenge ahead.

EA1456 didn't push his luck further, he was happy to be taken care of and this latest one looked like a goddess; he wasn't going to complain. He considered the recent turn of events enough, even, to think about forgiving the robot. Janet spoke to him in a soft voice, "I think we'll put you to sleep for a while."

He felt like a beaten dog since the burglary and was happy to give in to the accumulated fatigue. Anticipating the drugs crawling through his bloodstream, reaching his brain to switch it off, he shut his eyes and dreamt about waking up in the body of a young boy, proud and strong, playing rugby in the gardens of Eton College. He pictured himself as a handsome teenager, when he was in fact pale, weak, and middle-aged, but at least he fell asleep with a dumb smile on his face.

*****

Janet spent the rest of the morning directing her team, taking samples of just about every single part of his body, through a variety of needles and other apparatuses. The adept's body was connected to a range of machines checking his entire status every four seconds. His blood was filtered through continuous flow centrifugation, he was injected with all manner of solutions, measured, marked and mapped from head to toe.

Eight hours later, the team were holding a comprehensive debrief of the day, detailing everything about his genetic, medical and psychiatric state, while EA1456 was still asleep. Like a Rubik's cube, they were trying to manipulate all the data and DNA to find an exact match, but the information was not being compliant. One hour into the meeting, the result was still slipping through their hands like an eel. A few hours later and nerves were frayed after an intense day; they were very animated, without structure or solution in sight.

Janet was annoyed with the lack of progress. She waved her arms dramatically above her head to shut everyone up. "Wait! What's going on in here? What has happened to us?" she ranted. "Why can't we analyse a simple tramp and produce an accurate diagnostic map? Let's go back to basics and recap for a moment.

"That man," she pointed to the adjacent room, "will cease life three weeks from now, by our hand. We've promised a bunch of businessmen in suits that the day of his clinical death, that vagabond will reappear in the body of a newborn, together with features from his current meaningless life. ARE WE ALL ON THE SAME PAGE HERE?" She paused for effect, the room deathly quiet after her tirade. "Now, if you will stop behaving like a bunch of amateurs, I want you to speak in an orderly fashion and please tell me what the situation is here – is he compliant or not? Who wants to tell me? Dan, is this your time to shine, maybe?"

Dan was one of three colleagues in the trusted circle, allowed to stay in the research program with the agreement of Robert and Bill. A short, stout man from Essex, in his early thirties, he was accustomed to dealing with Janet's outbursts through years of research together. He had learnt how to break his answers down into easily-digestible pills, so that she wouldn't spit them back at him straight away. He took on the mission of saving the meeting. "Ladies, gentlemen," he started, making eye-contact around the room. "Janet's right, we we have no fucking clue here, even though everyone has rehearsed a lifetime for this. Let's hear from each one of us at a time and see what we've got, ok?" his strong Essex accent got everyone's attention. "Clinical lab?" he addressed a bald guy in the far left corner of the room: "65 percent positive."

Dan continued, targeting the other side of the room, "Pathology?"

A tall man of Indian origins answered, "Not compliant."

The next question was aimed at a blonde woman in her early forties, "Radiology?"

"All good."

"Nuclear?"

A curly-haired British woman replied, "Not compliant."

Dan pointed at an elderly short man at the end of table, "Neurophysiology?"

He fired back, "90 percent positive."

Finally, addressing Janet, "Genetic frame?" He held his breath for her answer; she was carrying the final relay baton and although she would have liked to avoid it, the guys in the room were far too clever for a lie. "Close to matching the required *mask*, but with all your reserves, I don't know if I can give the green light," she admitted, followed by a long sigh.

It sounded like a death sentence. They collectively realised they were trying to transport the wrong specimen into their futuristic experiment. They fell silent, all waiting for Janet's direction. She spoke, staring blankly at the far wall, "Go back to your machines and find out how in hell we could get this so wrong after all our preparation. Walk back through the chain of events that brought him here, carry out the tests again, double check every piece of information, find the slack. If we really can't resolve the issue, I'll handle it, but not before you are 200 percent sure that this is a failure."

They shuffled out of the room in silence; she stayed a minute longer before going back to theatre.

*****

EA1456 woke up with Janet looking down at him. He felt rested, although most of his body ached. He sensed immediately that something wasn't right with the pretty doctor, which annoyed him as he expected to wake up to a cluster of hand-clapping doctors looking satisfied, congratulating him. In reality, the room was grey and empty, except for this one doctor looking at him with a face like thunder, plunging him into a gloomy sorrow.

He broke the silence. "I hope I behaved well, you look..." *Disappointed*, she thought. "Well, anyway, what have you done to me? I'm aching all over," he continued, trying to move through the stiffness in his body.

"You've been a wonderful specimen of a patient," she said gently, "it's just, well, some of the information we gathered contrasts with our previous tests, and so we need to repeat part of the process."

"I am easy, as long as you are," he replied, "see, you'll soon be convinced that I'm your man for the experiment." He nodded.

Fit for the experiment or hasty selection? Is he going to give us a run for our money? she wondered. Janet sat on the edge of the bed and tackled a sensitive subject. "EA1456, during the analysis, we thought you may have some psychological... how can I say this? We found some genetically pre-determined features that influenced your behaviour. We initially thought this was happening in an otherwise compliant body, but then, not everyone was happy with this interpretation," she said. The adept was giving her his full attention. "It felt like an approximation," she continued. "Me too, I was perplexed by your case and started reassessing the data... and I ended up asking myself whether you are too different from what we expected."

He raised his eyebrows inquisitively; he didn't follow her any longer. But she wasn't finished, she offered more explanations and sounded like she was talking through the outcome of her day with herself as much as informing him. "The fact is that we find you healthy, but completely out of balance – your mind is in such a chaotic state, that it confuses the neurological and biological processes of your body. You're... a complicated case."

He remained silent, letting the information percolate for a moment, before addressing her in a solemn tone. "Janet, I inhabited a very dark cave for close to 40 years, which is kind of sad if you think about it. But, it taught me how to walk in a blackout, finding my own way. I can recognise a source of light when I see one, even if it's well-hidden I can spot it straight away, and you look like one to me, Janet."

Rather than flattering her, his charming offensive annoyed Janet. "Perhaps this is how you swayed the people who selected you into believing that you're sane and healthy. In reality, you are neither."

This confirmed his impression that, like all the others, she would behave like a bitch, just as his whole body was hurting like hell because he had trusted her. Apparently, she too had decided to dump him in a tip. With immense effort, he tried to control his emotions, building up for an unusually moderated reaction – no cheap scores, no unyielding fits, but cogitated words that would help him out of the corner. "I assume you have weighed all the pros and cons, and I respect your opinions..." that was how far his disappointment allowed him to go with his good intentions, he felt the urge to sting her, "but I think the problem is more with you than me, Janet. You look like a pretty unhappy camper; have you perhaps tasted the bitter pill too? Maybe many times, like me?"

Her heart started pounding, her instinct told her to leave the room, to get rid of him, but she was waiting for the second round of tests. If they were negative too, she would certainly dispose of him, but thinking of the shame of going back to Bill and Robert with a failed experiment, motivated and fuelled her determination. "Do you really think, I would be creating genetically manipulated human beings if I was interested in the opinion a piece of dirt like you holds of me? No! All I want is to see this experiment happen, and you don't seem to be facilitating it. On the contrary, you're carrying over 400 DNA defects, and your head isn't really vibrating like a bell. I'm starting to think that you are a phoney, an unsuitable poser who targeted this experiment knowingly."

"There's no getting rid of me, Janet," he hissed back at her. "I am part of the family now, I'm the selected one. I passed the most difficult selections to be here today, your supervisors will understand."

She was stunned, the situation was paradoxical – he had no idea that she was the leader of the experiment nor that he had been groomed all the way into it. She couldn't entertain the conversation further without breaking boundaries, so she decided to leave him alone. She simply confirmed that he was correct, that the decision was in the hands of her bosses. She took the role-playing further and had a laugh at his expense, "Perhaps you're right, I'm the one who's not ready for all this, a more experienced doctor will take over soon, goodbye." She went to leave him alone in the semi-dark theatre room, but he didn't relent.

"All my life I felt like a pushover, Janet. If anything, I have proven the heliotropism misconception, never knowing where the sun shines… You owe me this, you owe it to us all, to all the people you have outdone in—"

She recoiled and left him there, lying in the darkness of the room, head on one side, half buried in his long thick hair. She sat in her office, but her heart felt as if she had never left his room. She pictured him lying flat on his bed, hands gripping the metal frame, inhaling, exhaling, unable to make any other movement because of all the pain she had inflicted on him. Recalling his retaliation made her see him as a weak and wounded animal, propelling himself by fierce determination to rescue whatever was left of him; a thorny creature, trying to raise his head above the underbrush hoping to reach the sunlight. Like her, he was strenuously pushing forward, kicking in all directions to make things happen despite whatever hurdles he encountered. They both summed up the struggle faced by the entire human race.

She sighed, appreciating that they had common ground – she had been doing the same all her life, engaging in every battle, turning a geeky shy girl into an internationally acclaimed scientist, they shared the same gut instinct to fight. She took a deep breath to shake off the confrontation, she was re-emerging, different, better disposed. She decided to reassure him, feeling it wasn't fair to leave him there all night feeling miserable. Watching him on the CCTV, she activated the intercom and spoke in a reconciliatory tone:

"EA1456, it's Janet, I'm sorry for earlier." Hearing her voice, he registered that she was in charge. "I respect you. You're putting your life in my hands as I am putting mine into yours, and I'm inclined to think that this experiment could possibly hurt you more than anything you can say to me." She watched as tears started rolling gently down his cheeks.

"I could turn my head away and let life keep trampling all over you; but instead, I'll give you a chance to crawl into the new order, where you'll get a fresh 40 years of life, as promised, even with all your deficiencies and disabilities…" She too began weeping slightly. "Nature doesn't know perfect DNA anyway

– there will always be inadequacy in the future. It may as well be yours."

She released the intercom. She had said too much, but felt better for it. She pulled the *Patient Results Due Diligence* assessment form in front of her. She studied it briefly and inserted a short line of text, before ticking the "Yes" box twice, confirming the dialog window appearing at the centre of her screen.

A second later, a message flashed on all the screens used by the project team: *EA1456 deemed compliant, good job everyone, J.I.*

Puzzled looks flew around the laboratory where most of the staff were still working. No one spoke, or understood what was going on. A few smiles and sighs of relief eventually marked the achievement; their feelings were overtaken by gratitude. The weight of an impossible decision had been taken off their shoulders.

2.4 – May 31st

Stillness filled the air, even if the sea would not stop moving; it rocked a persistent dance threatening to gain more territory. The Lungomare di Monterosso was a desolate place, so far from life that it was hard to imagine how civilisation could have endorsed it for over 800 years. Since the last great flood, the town had been abandoned and the coastal railway line closed. The land had joined forces with the rising sea, assaulting the old borgo with salty waters and wild vegetation. The still-accessible buildings were originally used as squats, then became dilapidated and abandoned, until not a single soul was believed to live in them any longer.

The bleak location had been chosen by Bill for the informal Sunday meeting. It was where he had met his Country Manager for the Italian enterprise one year earlier – a proud local, who had persuaded Bill to pledge to preserve what remained of the seaside village. He had found Bill's soft spot, in his fond memories of walking the *Cinque Terre* with his father as an eight-year-old boy. Bill had quickly agreed to sponsor the work to reopen the famous walk, under one strict condition: access to the path would not be granted to the public, until he said so, and as he had not yet consented, he had secured that wonderful walk, piercing the wilderness between mountain and sea, for himself alone.

It was Janet's turn to be slightly late for the meeting. Bill was waiting in what had once been the car park behind the sandy beach, now reclaimed by the sea and covered by shallow water. Bill's staff had picked Janet up at the decommissioned Genoa airport, where she had landed in one of Bill's private aeroplanes, arriving in Monterosso in an armoured vehicle through the old railway tunnel.

Genuinely looking forward to meeting her, he dismissed his assistants as soon as she came into sight. The warm temperature was mitigated by a gentle sea breeze. The sun was slightly shadowed by a thin veil of high clouds. Everything was just the way Bill liked it. He anticipated it would be a great day to share the majesty of the place with Janet. He wanted to be briefed on the progress of their endeavour, but he also wanted Janet to realise how much he held her in high regard. Behind his black sunglasses, his eyes followed Janet walking insecurely along the shore. He was smiling.

She approached with her head down, studying where she was putting her feet, and once she raised her head, she saw that Bill was happy to see her. *He'd better be ecstatic!* she thought, *having managed to drag me to such a remote location for a walking meeting.* She had previously heard about his fixation with holding his most important meetings while taking long walks and thought it was a quirky habit which only someone so successful and powerful could impose. *Rich men's jokes are always funny...*

Bill offered her his hand, then kissed her cheek awkwardly. "Hi Janet, welcome to Gaia, isn't she beautiful?" he said looking at the promontory.

She smiled back. "What an amazing place – how did you discover it?" She made a mental note to call her sister that night.

"My main man in Italy comes from this area. I funded the restoration works of the beautiful path that crosses the *Cinque Terre*, up there, can you see?" he asked, pointing at the headland rising up to the horizon. "I fell for the place straight away. I was here many, many years ago, well before the flooding."

"I wonder what it must have looked like back then."

"Oh, very different indeed. You could smell the fish restaurant from here. It was built on stilts, right there in the middle of the beach." He pointed to the centre of the bay, "I'll show you, shall we start the trek?"

"Ready, I am, sir" she replied, affecting an army-style salute.

"Ok, we're carrying a small backpack each with some provisions. We should be on the other side in three hours or so. Security will walk behind us, as usual."

"As usual…" she said, indicating she had learnt security had become an essential part of her life. He smiled, "Let's go."

Janet put on the small backpack and moved to Bill's side, striving to walk on the narrow limb of land remaining, between the mountain on her left and the sea on her right. They eventually managed to pick up a brisker pace, having negotiated a compromise speed between the two very different walkers. They marched without talking for a while, both concentrating on where they put their feet. The path was climbing up into the landscape, it looked like the back of a white snake slyly moving uphill.

"How's work these days?" Bill asked, looking at the track ahead.

"Very busy managing the adept, he's quite a handful."

"Not behaving according to plan?"

"Well, as you know, we lost contact for over two days, which was an initial concern; apparently he was living on the streets for that period, so when he arrived he was a real mess. Actually, I meant to tell you – I think security needs patching up." She was relieved to be able to focus on the poor security, rather than the incompatibility of the adept.

"Yes, I'm aware of that. It was a disgrace, but you know, we couldn't look after things until the contracts were signed and all references removed. But we should be all right now, with the adept and the other stuff... Tell me, what do you think of him, how is he in real life?"

"Rather a specimen I'd say. Pretty fickle, with a variety of personalities on offer. The switches are quite interesting, you can even almost see the eye colour adjusting to the new identity. Beyond that, we've got a good grip on him, and given the trouble recruiting him, I don't plan to change him."

"Why, would you have had any reason for it?"

"Just that he wasn't all that compliant, but I sorted that out by changing the receiving side. We have selected a different newborn for him."

"I see. It sounds like he's making you miss working with the chimpanzees..."

She smiled, "Yeah."

Their breathing was becoming laboured as the path gradient increased. Janet looked for a moment over her right foot, all she could see below was grey rocks, green shrubs and spiky cactuses, beyond which was a steep descent to the deep blue sea, with its white floating outline. She knew she wouldn't survive one minimal slip and took extra care of her footing. Abrupt gusts of wind were building, sometimes pushing her slightly off balance, just enough to make her very aware of the dangers of the walk. For a moment, she fantasised he would push her down to get rid of her and take control of her project.

"Janet, I wanted to tell you that I think what you're doing is great. You're pulling off one of the most amazing projects ever, with barely any help. I really respect your work."

Bill's words caught her by surprise, *I think I'm falling off the cliff and he's pulling me up into the clouds!* but she had never liked pedestals. Janet was unable to articulate an answer – he had sounded sincere, but she was sceptical. There was so much at stake with this project, that having no hidden agenda didn't seem a natural option. Even she, the weakest link in the chain, had a side plan, a sort of insurance to retain some control over future stages of the experiment, so long as her Claire would help. The guilt of her own mission grew in her chest, preventing her from formulating a straight answer. "I'm not on my own, you've always been at my side, clearing the path to success. Like this track here, I'm sponsored by Bill's Investment Group."

He was taken aback by her response and couldn't quite discern whether she was still bitching about being forced into it. This snarky attitude was just at the time he was reaching out to her. *Damn people!* he thought, *thinking with their stupid minds.* "Janet, I mean what I've just said, you're working on my most interesting program and I'm very excited about it," he reiterated, sounding as sincere as he could. "I'm not trying to flatter you or anything, I've nothing to ask, all I want is to hear a little bit more about how you're doing... because you're shaping what I've envisioned for the good of our planet."

Janet was wary, but she hadn't flown for three hours just to pick a fight. "Bill, you've had a good deal of informers in and out of my labs lately. Are you sure there's anything I can tell you that you don't know already?" This was delivered with half a smile.

In a typical alpha male move, he stopped walking to look at her; he couldn't manage to walk, talk and look all at once. She fascinated him, he couldn't help it. He decided to proceed further, offering his hand to help her navigate the slippery rocks covered in moss ahead. She was cool about holding his hand – she knew he didn't fancy her and was just naturally awkward. She could see that he was a genius, and as such, he couldn't always be understood; she knew that of herself too, anything could come out of him at any given time. Besides, he was distant; he needed a wide comfort space in which to move.

*****

As they approached the tip of the peninsula, the sea was visible over 180 degrees around them. The sun was shining less shyly and they were both perspiring and short of breath. The walk had been tough, but it looked like the route ahead joined a dirt road coming down from the peak of the mountain, before turning sharply left to go south. They stopped to catch their breath for a moment, and drank in the incredible views that demanded their full attention.

In the most prominent point of the headland, they found an old wooden table and bench under an old lamp post, corroborating the idea that civilisation had once touched this beautiful, isolated spot. Janet took off her backpack and reached straight for the aluminium water bottle. Bill, still lost in his thoughts, kept staring at the sea while addressing her, "Imagine how many things we could do together, Janet."

"Don't you think we are already doing quite enough?" she replied casually, while raiding the pockets of the backpack for a chocolate bar.

"I feel we're just beginning. Let's face it, if this thing works we'll have a blueprint to tackle the overwhelming wider mess of the planet." Janet was looking at him now, listening. To her, he looked and talked like a tramp – one of those unhinged characters who's never had anything or had lost it all. She could picture him as a clochard in Paris, smoking the butt of a self-rolled cigarette. "I mean, you also see the people in disarray," he continued, "the complete loss of direction of this—"

"I am confident about the experiment Bill," she interjected. "I think it's great that you have come up with the Killer App for my technology, but I still believe that the social consequences will slaughter it." She sighed, "They will not allow widespread use, because—"

"They? Who's they? There's me. And we've got government with us, remember?"

"Yes, Robert is with us, but society, where power is... sorry, I'm just being sceptical."

"But why?"

"I doubt that you will find as many willing candidates as you need to effectively dent the demographic map with this process."

"You don't put much confidence in my work. You know that research uncovered quite the contrary of what you're saying."

"Maybe I'm wrong," she shrugged, "but I struggle to imagine that you'll attain a new order, with the Killer App becoming mainstream. It would take you years…"

"Same thing I was told when I started BIG."

"You can't compare your Internet empire with genetics!"

"But you're right, the reach of our work together is bound to create a new way of living. Robert and I honestly believe in it."

Janet remained silent at first, absorbing the weight of what he was saying. He sounded like a motivational coach talking about marketing a headache remedies. "Let's see. I have the impression you have shifted your offering from a service to people who were prepared to pay for it, to a more, how can I say this, compulsory model affecting everyone?"

"What do you mean?"

"I remember drowning in your PowerPoint presentations, each one filled with projections on how many enthusiastic people would eventually like to swap their old life for a new one. Now you sound different. It's like you're a car manufacturer recalling vehicles: 'hey everybody, come back for genetic upgrade, now!'" She paused, "Perhaps you're changing the business model or you have a new strategy that I don't know about?"

He was supporting his chin with one hand, the other tapping on the boards of the picnic table, and getting frustrated. "Janet, do you see what's going on around you? Perhaps you spend too much time in your labs? Remember what state society is in for a moment. Here, for instance. Look here, just look around you: a few years ago this was a worldwide renowned walk, people would fly here from all over the world to walk this very same track. Up here, on the back of the mountain, locals used to grow wine grapes and down there others went fishing. And this was only a few years ago Janet, only a few years ago...

"Look at it now, it's all abandoned! It's going to waste, it's unsafe, like the rest of this country. Here is where I really see a society unable to adapt to change. Before them the Greeks, the Egyptians... you name them, great civilisations lost because they couldn't keep up. It will be our time to be erased soon, if we don't change our game Janet, before the people lose their patience and faith, before they revolt, and we all end up defeated."

"You make quite a pessimistic futurologist."

"Maybe you bite into their same hypocrisy? I don't. Most people want lives they can't afford."

"You're right on that point, but they won't allow you to change their ways."

"Well, lots of them are prepared to die for their greed, trust me, I know the way to their hearts."

She watched him venting his sermon. *He's mad,* she thought, *elated.* "Who do you really want to get rid of?"

"I think the people who can't take care of themselves, should be let go. Those who require society to work for them, they're dragging the rest down."

She hated listening to him preaching like this. "So you want to use the offspring of the people you reckon are a liability to society and get them implanted with the DNA of the successful ones? Can't say you lack imagination Bill, perhaps restraint…"

He gave her a nervous look. "I want to break the chain reaction that would otherwise kill everyone, no distinctions made! We need to allocate what's left efficiently, don't you see it? We need everyone to row in the same direction. And if your procedure delivers, we'll make it, people will flock."

"And you think pharmaceutical companies will let you do that?"

"Fuck the pharmaceutical companies, the bane of society!" he cried. "All they want is to turn people into zombies, lying in hospital beds pumping their fake therapies through a cannula, at the expense of the rest of society. Janet, we need to crush them, we ought to take the lymph out of their business. Robert agrees… I will spend my last penny seeing them cleansed from our system."

Whereas she found the conversation had swayed into surreal, she remained committed to it. "As soon as they work out we want to provide a shorter life to sick people, they will go for our jugular."

"Maybe. Or maybe I won't allow them to. I'll have the people behind me, remember?"

"Not all…"

"A great deal depends on you and what you will be able to offer them, with your research, in the future. A DNA that protects from the risk of cancer – who'll be needing pharmaceuticals any longer?"

He's a derailing train, Janet thought, *turning into a mad dictator.* She smiled and turned to him, "You sound like The Joker, in *Batman*, do you realise that?"

His body language conveyed disappointment. *She doesn't get it*, he thought and decided to give up on her for the time being. "Janet, my dreams are always larger than life, I recognise that." He paused, "Let's talk again once we have the technology tested, it's more likely that our ideas will converge then."

He started to prepare for resuming the walk.

"Is Robert fully behind you on this?"

He sneered, "Hopefully the three of us together can have the vision and the firing power to make the Killer App work. That's all he cares about."

"But whose idea was it, originally?"

"Robert is an exceptionally good guy, but you couldn't possibly expect him to pull this one out of the hat alone. Politicians, in general, are just bags of shit, Janet."

"Hey, is this the same Robert we are talking about?" Janet was genuinely surprised by Bill's candour. She thought he might be threatening Robert too.

"Don't worry, I like him. Just remember he's a politician, an administrator – he is the person you put in charge to run your affairs for some time. These are times for revolutionaries, not administrators." Janet interrupted him, "Bill, wait a second, I'm not a revolutionary. My entire life I've studied to create cures for diseases, to alleviate life-threatening medical issues... endless nights spent in godforsaken labs, studying the mapping of DNA genomes—"

This time Bill interrupted her. "And it's paying off, Janet; did you ever doubt it would?"

She shook her head to indicate she wasn't conceding. "I never doubted myself. I often pitied fellow scientists."

"That's the same frustration I feel, Janet. I think we are blessed in our awareness, Janet."

Janet tried not to look too unsettled. She sure didn't want to hear any more preaching for the day. "Come on, the security guys are getting impatient, let's move on."

He nodded, she stood up too and prepared to walk again. Two contrite smiles were exchanged, they had agreed to disagree for now. Bill also nodded to the escorts.

Minutes after, they turned round the head of the cape. The wind abated and the sea, now less than 50 meters below them, seemed to calm too. Further along, an unexpected splash of colour appeared in sight: the remains of Vernazza, the old fishing village that lay in the middle of the Cinque Terre region. Also abandoned after the flood that half-covered it in mud, it still looked like a colour palette.

They started their descent towards Vernazza, which vanished from view and suddenly reappeared as the path zigzagged down the mountain.

Bill asked one more question. "Do you confirm that we will proceed with number one as scheduled?"

She nodded rather pointlessly as she was behind him. "Yes, unless I will get too bogged down by Robert's legal team, the 15th of June should be fine with me."

Bill nodded and looked out at the remains of a house that once stood tall and proud on the path. Not long after it, they came to an abrupt interruption of the walk where the mud from the mountain had hardened like lava, claiming the tail of the path leading into the old village. A small wooden boat was waiting for them nearby, two men inside waved before helping Janet and Bill onboard.

A short transit took them to the other side of the flooded village, where a jeep was waiting to pick them up at the bottom of a dirt track. As spectators sitting on the edge of a floating moon, they looked at the passage of that celestial body that was the skull of Vernazza. To Janet, it looked defeated; Bill instead saw it screaming out loud how unprepared mankind was to receive the consequence of its exploitation. In the stillness of the landscape, the sea was lapping off the mud that had covered the corpse up to its torso. On a last look, Vernazza looked like it had consciously given up its battle against the sea, resigning itself to the wrinkled mantel of cold water.

2.5 – June 15th

What a lovely day to die.

EA1456 woke up with this thought in his mind, even before remembering that it was also actually his 40th birthday. He roused from his slumbers happy. For once, he had made it all the way through something important, the experiment. He was the first, the chosen one, the pioneer. He felt very proud. *Soon*, he thought, *I will be on the other side of getting old – I will be born again.*

He looked forward to being able to re-enter the world through its main gate, through the womb of a loving mother, who would later today deliver him into his bright new future. EA1456 lay in bed, daydreaming of experiencing the beautiful stages of life again: ages ten, fifteen, eighteen, 20... He was confident that, with the promised awareness of his previous life, he would finally be in the position to blossom, to thrive, to leave a mark. He was determined to leave behind his melancholy and depression, the wickedness and wretchedness of his miserable experience first time around. Unwilling to drag himself into a sulk on the day of his new birth, he pledged with himself to be in a tempered state of mind, to remain in a positive disposition. He could almost feel his spirit filling with harmony – something he wasn't used to – a sign that he would soon be entering a new life, full of the joys of which so far he had been deprived.

He sat up, yawned copiously and walked over to the mirror. He pondered what his appearance would be like in the future. Holding his chin as he turned his face side to side, he hoped that they would make him look as handsome and interesting, but more so.

He went for a long hot shower, that was to be his birthday present, a cathartic, purging wash, consigning a better self to his new life. He dried himself on the not-so-bad towels provided by the lab, and put on the clothes that they arranged for him on the chair. His clothes had been the topic of much discussion among the staff: at first he only wanted warm pyjamas for *the day*, but he had changed his mind – he decided he wanted to wear a doctor's tunic, a wish which they had been happy to fulfil. Today, he was very pleased with his choice and made up his mind that he looked really good in it. He combed his thick hair back and made his way to call the people on duty.

A doctor came into the room and greeted him with a friendly smile and a warm handshake. He felt important at last. Walking towards the main breakfast room, they chatted idly about the exceptionally hot weather. When they entered the room, EA1456 could not believe his eyes: over 20 members of staff had gathered in the canteen, and they were all clapping and singing happy birthday. The tables had been rearranged to form a single, long white surface in the middle of the room, piled with breakfast food, juices and coffee. At the far end, blue and silver balloons in the shape of the digits four and zero bobbed gently in the aircon.

EA1456 was overwhelmed. He was so happy that he struggled to control his emotions, and eventually wept with joy. He couldn't remember the last time he had so many people to celebrate his birthday he wasn't used to so much attention. Then the exceptionality of the event dawned on him: it was his last birthday they were celebrating, the last day of his life. It was only through strenuous effort that he avoided collapsing under the weight of his emotions. One member of staff put his hand over his elbow to help him walk the last few meters to his seat at the head of the table. The rest of the staff had finished singing and were now cheering *EA-14-56, EA-14-56*, some of them were already reaching for chairs at the big table.

The only missing member of staff was Janet, who was still finalising details via videoconference with Robert and Bill. Their two faces filled the wall screen in the meeting room, Robert was speaking. "That's for the dean of the University Hospital, but in general that last final endorsement we received means that we may achieve a larger backing than I had previously anticipated."

"Great work, Robert."

"That's nothing, thanks to you guys for pulling this together."

"One concern we have still is security at the London hospital. Can we review it one more time? Like who's going to collect Janet?"

"Sure, I did ask the same question and I've been assured that the team we have deployed is first class, it's composed of three officers, a pilot, co-pilot and doctor from our Genetic Engineering Warfare Unit. They'll fly Janet and the biotic material to the Royal

London Hospital, where two more men will be waiting on stand-by."

"How can I be sure that I'll be free from any nuisance while operating there?" asked Janet.

Bill stepped in. "Here's the briefing from your guys, Robert: J.I. will have support from five undercover agents who have been active at the hospital for over a month [...] they are trained in the germination process and they know the various doctors, nurses and procedures at the hospital. So you'll find a number of stand-by personnel both visible and invisible, who will be alert, ready to intervene. Clearly, we all hope you won't need to engage with them, but in the unlikely event, they'll offer valuable support for you."

Janet asked another sticky question, "What about the family of the carrier, who's there and what procedures do we have in place to keep them at bay?"

Back to Robert for this answer: "This is exactly the kind of work that will be taken care of by our resident staff onsite."

She let him off the hook easily. "Right gentlemen, thank you for that, I've got to go and celebrate the last birthday of our man. I look forward to speaking with you both at the 5.00 p.m. debrief."

Robert jumped in quickly before the video-link could be closed. "Janet one last question, are you 100 percent sure that you are gonna fire it today? I mean, is there any remote possibility that we'll have to delay the procedure?"

Janet was slightly irritated by the question. "I've got the best team, you've both done a great job with the logistics and the patient is keen, so I'm confident. We'll have a positive result today."

"Excellent work Janet – good luck," concluded Robert, while Bill's salute was stunted by Janet ending the call too quickly. She was still uneasy with Bill's grand plans for world domination, and more than a little nervous about the day. She was eager to spend some time with EA1456 before the *slaughtery*, as it had been nicknamed by an inconsiderate member of the team – the process that in a few hours would see him cut into pieces, pressed into juice, distilled to essence and injected into a newborn baby.

She picked up a parcel the size of a binder, covered in red wrapping paper, and headed out of the meeting room. She stood for a moment at the doors of the breakfast room without entering, watching through the glass at the reception party given in his honour. EA1456 was sat at the far end of the long table with about ten members of staff on each side; they were all chattering away like old friends at a house party. The sight filled her with pride, she had put together the best team, around the most prodigious experiment ever attempted in genetics, while at the same time providing a loving family to him, the adept.

As soon as she entered, all eyes turned to her, the conversations ground to a halt. She beamed a broad smile to break the ice and walked over to the birthday boy. Putting her right hand on his shoulder, she looked at all the people assembled around the table, asking herself if they were celebrating life or death.

Instead of voicing her doubt, she spoke softly, addressing her colleagues. "Good job everyone, you've all been very kind to organise this party for EA1456. I'd like to thank you all for the good work you've put in so far, including you EA1456, all your patience and diligence. Today, history is in the making. With your contribution, the progress of the human race and its relationship with planet earth will take a giant step forward." She paused for a moment protocol prevented her from saying anything more.

Turning to the adept, she praised him further. "We all know this wouldn't have been possible without the bravest of us all here, EA1456. He's about to climb up the mountain ahead of us, to see what lies on the other side. He'll go first and sow the seeds of what we'll come to harvest in due course. This is the proudest moment of my career and I'm excited to share it with you, here today at the lab. You should all feel the same... but not before we go and finish our work; people expect great things from us today."

They all stood up, in silence, rearranging chairs, removing the party pieces they were wearing, and walking out of the room in a composed fashion, knowing they were on a mission. It was time to take their assigned posts, ready for battle. When alone with EA1456, Janet thought there was no point bullshitting someone due to die within the hour, so she took the chair on the right-hand side of EA1456 and sat in front of him. "How are you today?" she asked, with genuine compassion.

"I'm... all right actually, thank you." He could not find more words to describe how he was feeling. He didn't know whether to be happy or sad, whether to think about what he was going to lose or the rewards that lay ahead.

"I also have a gift for you, here, open it," she proffered. "This comes from just me, and it's a secret between us. I shouldn't have, but I thought it would make you happy."

He looked at the package, puzzled, he couldn't imagine what it could possibly be that he could take with him to his new life. He unwrapped the parcel to discover an A5 sized white photo album that had "EA1456 New Family" written on the cover page.

Just as he opened to look at the pictures, Janet started to speak softly. "I want you to meet your new family, Cleo and Samir." Janet was smiling in anticipation of his positive reaction. He turned the pages, staring at each photo in turn, with his mouth half-open and a sense of unease on his face. He hadn't understood the names Janet had pronounced. As he browsed the pictures, everything became clear to him: he had been setup, framed, completely defrauded and deceived, hoaxed by smart doctors in their white tunics. He couldn't believe it. He glanced at two more pictures before taking a long deep sigh and slamming the album closed. He looked straight into Janet's eyes, unable to articulate his thoughts.

Janet raised her eyebrows, gently requesting an explanation to his reaction.

He tried to stay as calm as he could manage. "Janet, I'm very disappointed. Who the hell are these... Lamirs? What is this, some kind of discount laboratory?"

She was both surprised and shocked. "What do you mean?"

"I mean that they look like third-class citizens. Not something you exactly want to die for... Ah, what a mistake I would have made!"

"Excuse me? Can you explain what's wrong, without sounding so arrogant?"

"Forget it, Janet. All this time we've spoken about being born into some first-class family, we had agreed on that. I made it clear that I had expectations that I'd be improving upon my condition."

"So what, you think I've had it easy to match your messy genome—"

"You've let me down Janet, completely. But that's not important anymore," he said, picturing himself orderly resigning and quietly leaving the laboratories.

Janet resented his cocky attitude and accusations. She wanted to tell him, "*you are no fucking better than them,*" but instead she kept her cool and explained how she had sweated buckets to find the right couple. She detailed her efforts to break the rules imposing an anonymous transplant, so that she could have properly introduced him to them before the procedure.

EA1456 wouldn't stop ranting about the mixed backgrounds; she felt like injecting him with potassium chloride there on the spot.

The only thing stopping her was knowing how close she was to the final stage of the experiment, she couldn't bear to lose it now. Her success depended on convincing the moron that he was going to have the good life he so desperately wanted, within his newly acquired family. Even though she really wanted to strangle him, she spoke softly and calmly. "They'll give you everything you never had, everything that you want and need for your future. They're a wonderful couple."

EA1456 continued to refuse on the grounds of race and class. But she would not have any of his narrow mindedness. "Consider the effort required to find a matching couple, with the right DNA sequencing, who are having a baby on the day of your birthday, within six hours of the procedure to be precise, and within a limited radius for a swift transition – it is a tall order by all accounts."

He was still shaking his head resolutely, and Janet realised she wouldn't convince him with the technicalities of the procedure, so she changed tack. "I can assure you, Cleo and Samir are top people. They've wanted this baby for a long time…"

"Have they gone to college?" he interjected. "Will I go to college? With what money, Janet? I want to have a better life than I had, otherwise, I am not going to do this, full stop!"

"But you will," she stressed, pleading with him to reconsider the opportunity. "These parents will walk on burning coals for you, what's more important than that?" When EA1456 refused to answer, she tried to play him at his own game. "Seeing as it's so important for you, I guarantee you the money for college. I'll create an endowment fund with our sponsors, ok? I promise you that, all right?" She wanted to sound sincere, though she did think it would be a good idea, or that the proposal would pass the legal advisors.

"You don't understand Janet you're not putting yourself in my shoes, probably because you don't have an appointment with a lethal syringe later this morning. My point goes beyond education – with parents like these, where would I live, what connections would I ever make and what opportunities?"

She couldn't take any more racist nonsense, he was being an arrogant snob who had conveniently forgotten where he came from and how much he had begged to be a part of the experiment. "EA1456, first of all, think of the immense competitive advantage you'll have because of your awareness of your previous life, how about that? Secondly, let me remind you that a few days ago you said you were willing to do this at any cost. I concede that you would have preferred to be born into wealth, who wouldn't? But your adoptive parents *do* have very good jobs, one in medicine the other in IT, so the conditions haven't changed, I'm delivering what we promised – now it's your turn to be cooperative."

He had stopped listening to Janet and hadn't followed her recent arguments. His head was preoccupied with a mishmash of images: a Far Eastern family; himself wearing Hindu clothes, with a huge third eye on his forehead; his father singing Bollywood songs whilst driving a taxi; his mother kneeling to pray in the corner of their small, messy living room; outside, a stretch of council flats reverberating with the bleakness of his life, against the cloudy grey sky. He spoke from his trance. "You've cheated me. I'm not going, the future you've prepared for me has no hope, I'd rather die now than bear this accursed new life you want to inflict on me."

Janet felt like slapping his pathetic, disappointed face. "Stop this nonsense, I have just qualified your new family to you, everything will be—"

He interrupted her, "I am not going—"

"Yes, you are!" she screamed over him.

"No," he snapped back.

"Oh - yes - you - are!" she hollered.

"No!" he yelled.

"Yes!" she shouted.

He jumped at her, going for her shoulders and trying to push her down to the floor. Shocked at the attack, she screamed for security, her mouth half-covered by his hand. They were wrestling on the floor when, less than 30 seconds later, security burst into the room. Two uniformed guards pulled EA1456 away from Janet, twisting his arms behind his back. He tried to resist, but found himself weaker than the pair and could only resort to screaming out his frustration, drool running from his open mouth.

Janet, still on the floor, ran the back of her right hand across her lower lip where he had inadvertently head-butted her as they fell. She had a fine streak of blood down her chin, but otherwise she was ok, if a little shaken.

He continued yelling, repeatedly shouting the word "cheated," until the guards turned him onto his stomach to handcuff him, at which point he started to cry. It was a sad scene, something she would have very much liked to avoid. Wanting to regain control over the situation, Janet tried to stand up, but felt light-headed and fell back down onto her bum. She beckoned to one of the assistants who had entered the room behind the security guards to come over. He asked how she felt as he came closer, but she signalled for him to bend over, so she could whisper in his ear. "Put him to sleep, we're going into assisted germination, now."

EA1456 either heard or guessed what was going to happen and started screaming again as he was dragged out of the room by security.

Janet got up with the help of her assistant, supported herself on a table with one hand and rearranged her messy hair with the other. She walked the short distance to her office, collapsed onto her chair and sighed deeply. *What a shitty start...* She revived her computer screen and started to compose a message.

To all - every great mission encounters its hurdles. Our complication seems to be that EA1456 has now changed his mind and is entering the procedure reluctantly, as was displayed by his tantrum. We expected this would happen, and we will go ahead with the experiment anyway. I ask once again for your full professionalism, to make sure that this mission is smoothly executed. You have done a great job, let's keep doing our best work for one final push! J.I.

She hoped this would help her people understand what had happened, she wanted to quickly resume a sense of normality, as she really needed everyone to be fully committed and focussed. She felt stupid for having risked the mission, attempting to treat EA1456 like a human being.

*****

EA1456 only relented when he entered a secure room. It contained a wall-hung bed, equipped with wrist and ankles straps, a reading light and an oxygen connection. He let the security guards strap him into the bed, where he was administered a large dose of sedative. Although he tried to fight the drug, unwilling to give in knowing that would be the end of it all, the medication gradually started to numb his body. He cursed everyone around him, including himself, for being too naive. Most of all, he condemned Janet for being a wicked palatine of the cruel world, hounding him to the grave.

The drug reached his brain. He pictured himself as a small guinea pig in a big pond, unable to swim, slowly sinking to the bottom, doctors looking on from the edge of the water, clapping their hands. His last hallucination was of a grave stone shaped as a coffin, marked with EA1456 in gold. There was a hole at chest level, which was being used by people to dip their fingers, in order to get fresh DNA. His life, his blood, his genome... exploited by ungrateful unknowns, with nothing left for his survival. He fell asleep, convinced that he was going to struggle even more in his new life; uglier, unrecognised, disadvantaged, and further away from the happiness he had been seeking all his life.

The seal on his existence came in the form of an oath: If I ever wake up again, I'll kill anyone who dares to mistreat me again.

He was gone. He was going to wake up a warrior.

2.6 – June 15h

The operating theatre was the wintriest of environments: lighting, walls, IT, medical equipment, laboratory machinery, all aseptic and white, as required for the intersection between life and death.

Most people had smelt the antiseptic cleanliness of surgeries at least once in their lives -- either at birth, death or both. EA1456 was going to be the first person to use one to both die and be born in within the same day.

His sedated body was ushered in by two porters, who placed it in the middle of the room for the harvesting to begin. Medical staff busied around his still body. There were machines to connect, tubes to lay, cables to make way for, sensors, cameras, readers, interfaces, ports, scanners; a paraphernalia of equipment impatiently waiting for EA1456 to become their hub. Janet was coordinating the team, monitoring progress on wall-mounted screens and ticking-off stages on a long checklist. There was no emotion in the process, just smooth, well-rehearsed action. Everyone had gone through the details of the day many times before as part of an obsessively practised program imposed by Janet since mid May. Team members moved as professional ballet dancers in a west-end show, their costumes comprising white caps, gloves and overalls, each knowing exactly where to be, their movements revolving around the unconscious body of EA1456.

He was going to be inhumanly dissected in the name of preservation of his species, humanity. The technique consisted of numerous surgeries to the main organs, with various sizes of scalpel, scoring and sinking into his skin. Each and every main part of his body was targeted, according to its consistency and texture. His body would sag until a change of posture was required to vivisect a different organ. The surgeons kept going, descending on it with their instruments, sinking deeper into EA1456's placid body. But there was a craft in it all: they wouldn't allow the body to decline or die, they always repaired and made good the parts they had pillaged, reconnecting all processes required for life.

This preservation policy was an integral constituent of the agreement strenuously negotiated by Janet with the government. Section 3.6 of the contract: *[…] undertakes not to provoke the death of the EA by means of extracting DNA encoding […] death will not happen until confirmation is received that the solution has been successfully implanted into new carrier...* Government had requested that the EA's body was to be maintained until they were sure the transplant had worked, they didn't want to end up in a situation where the donor died prior to his genes being germinated.

After four hours of surgical assault, when all the required materials were collected, EA1456 was stitched back together in his temporary wholeness. In the meantime in the adjoining room, his genetic information was distilled in a solution combined with proteins and other molecules to increase the shelf-life of the mixture and improve its ability to propagate into the carrying body.

Once the hardware contained in the DNA sequence was captured in the fluid, the so-called "shuttle" was poured into an ampoule and placed under the largest piece of equipment, which occupied the majority of the operating theatre. Under Janet's scrutiny, the DNA sequence, now a software program, was being manipulated, effacing some of its traits and enhancing others. The aim was to achieve a level of awareness of EA1456's previous life, in order to spark recollection after the age of ten. It was important to make sure that defined traits were retained, such as responsiveness to certain images – a positive reaction was coded for preset symbols, among which Janet had chosen the Jediist Church logo EA1456 had first brought with him to the lab.

Conversely, the DNA sequence was programmed to forget the circumstance of his previous death, which again was a stringent clause demanded by the government to avoid the new carrier being aware that he was a clone. Janet had resisted over this point, because she wasn't really able to provide the guarantee required. In the end though, realising the impossible add-on was non-negotiable, she decided to play along, knowing that there was no way to find out before the carrier's adolescence.

The software encoding stage of the procedure took the best part of an hour, after which the fluid was ready to be inserted into the newborn – in the meantime, the liquid was chilled and stored in a purpose-built carrier. All the while, EA1456's body was kept alive via a number of cutting-edge life-support machines. His blood, above all, was cleaned and transfused back into its original container, to cover all evidence of intrusion. He lay unconscious in the dark, in a clean set of garments, waiting for the signal to come for his complete shutdown.

EA1456, in his first incarnation, was out of the spotlight now, off the main stage, and the attention shifted to the next steps of the procedure: transportation of the DNA sequence to the germination site, the delivery of the newborn and the insertion of the DNA solution.

*****

It was a warm day outside the lab, the stillness of the air broken only by the heavy army helicopter arriving from the nearby Air Force base of Benson. Everything in the surrounding landscape seemed normal, just watching another day pass without anything exceptional. The Oxfordshire countryside gave no indication of the imminent experimentation of DNA recoding on newborns.

The landing set off a frenzy of activity, and a number of staff ran from the main building to the helipad, under the rhythmic spin of the rotor blades.

Janet and two escorting agents made their way into the rumbling machine and fastened their seatbelts; moments later, they were hovering high above the labs, the pilot turning the canopy 180 degrees to point towards the capital. Janet was feeling deeply agitated. She didn't even watch her beloved laboratories, kissed by the June sunlight, disappear into the distance because she knew she was going to scar the landscape forever with her experiment.

"Mum and child are all right?" the older of the two guards asked, referring to EA1456 and his DNA encoding in the slang of the Genetic Engineering Warfare Unit. Picking up on it straight away Janet replied, "Never an abortion that one, though it turned out to be quite a caesarean." Both soldiers smiled at her, appreciating the banter and effectively accepting her as "one of the boys." She, on the other hand, distrusted them.

Janet smiled. They nodded and Janet smiled back in silence, thinking they didn't stand a chance of grasping the complexity of the experiment, like the pain, commotion and drama that came with EA1456's tantrum. She went over the basics of what was about to happen once again: an otherwise-normal newborn child would be injected with the fluid of a *thoroughly compatible*, but detestable, human being, who had agreed to give up his life (although he technically changed his mind at the end), to enter a new order of society where people lived, worked and voted for an allotted period of time. *Huxley, you're a child...*

She spotted the hospital compound in the busy East London skyline. From above, it was just a sign proclaiming *The Royal London Hospital* on the roof of a massive set of connected buildings. Nerves were making her feel sick, or was it the helicopter, which had started to circle the helipad at a 45 degree angle.

They soft-landed on the top of the tallest tower, and two red-uniformed personnel came out, reaching for the handle of the sliding door. Janet climbed out of the helicopter and disappeared into the building, carrying the small stainless steel suitcase containing the DNA shuttle. She was glad to leave the noise of the helicopter outside, though immediately noticed the uncomfortable presence of the resident doctors staring at her in silence.

Following the doctors to a waiting room, she appreciated the parenthesis between life and death was coming to an end; these men were about to deliver into the world the baby boy she would inject.

"Morning... afternoon rather, how long before the birth?" asked Janet.

The bald guy, who looked more senior and loquacious, answered politely, "The mother has been in labour for three hours, we expect delivery within half an hour." While changing into the light green tunics of the hospital, Janet asked, "What's the latest medical picture of the baby?"

"Mum and child are faring well: position, heartbeat and blood pressure are all good for an easy delivery."

The other guy scuttled along behind Janet, clipping her heels as he negotiated the various doors, lifts and obstacles they met on the way. He explained that it was a fair walk to the maternity ward. "Upon delivery, you'll be behind an opaque glass. Once the baby is born, we'll bring him to you – take your time, you'll have up to ten minutes, after which by the rules of the house we'll have to claim complications with the hospital." He checked around for potential listeners and lowered his tone, "Once you're done and the baby is all right, we will switch rooms: the mum will be given the baby back and you'll move into theatre, from where you'll be able to monitor progress without her seeing you."

"Thank you," said Janet, her thoughts running away, imagining all the things that could still possibly go wrong, a reaction probably provoked by the simplistic description provided by the resident doctor.

Whoever designed the hospital really didn't make it easy to get from the helipad to the maternity ward. They went down another lift, then along another corridor, interrupted by further sets of doors, turning and twisting inside the belly of the huge hospital complex. Finally, they reached the designated area and Janet saw a young British Asian man walking nervously in circles in front of a room: *Samir, the baby's father.* She recognised him, she knew he was an anaesthetist at a Surrey hospital, you could see he was a doctor from a mile away, as well as a worried soon-to-be father.

Once inside the room, she took in the layout of the space and was grateful to have previously requested a floor plan of it, so that she could prepare for where she would be working. The air was stuffy and she wanted to take off the overalls, but they allowed her to blend in perfectly with the rest of the hospital staff. As agreed, they left her alone, looking through the window into the adjacent theatre; she could see Cleo lying on a large hospital bed in the middle of the room, looking like a bumblebee, surrounded by busy servants preparing her to yield new life.

Janet reached for her mobile to text Claire: *arrived at LRH coming down in 30 mins. Xxx.* She went back to the desk and opened the suitcase she had come with, checking the temperature of the ampoule it contained. She took out one of the two syringes that were encased in the top part of the case, carefully removing the plastic needle cover. Her phone vibrated in her pocket, *Claire answering,* she thought picking the phone up: *Not in the ward before an hour. Miss you Xx.* Janet was annoyed at the news, though a little relieved she may not compromise Claire as much. Still thinking through the best course of action for her secret plans, she jumped at the sound of a baby crying: a long call for help, a loud utterance proclaiming grief, sorrow and pain. It was emotional, the baby was announcing himself to the world, whilst his mother, in pain too, was weeping, appealing to the midwife and the nurses to remedy the child's cry. "Take care of him, he's my son, wrap him up so he'll feel warm again. Is all this light necessary? Oh, my baby boy…"

One of the two men assigned to the experiment had already entered the room; to the eyes of the naive mother he was just another good doctor sent by God to take care of her baby. The undercover agent went straight for the boy, pulling a puzzled face to the midwife: "Better take the little one to the other room." Then he addressed the mother who had winced at his words, and said reassuringly, "Congratulations, we will give the boy a good clean and a measure, then you'll get him back in no time." Both mother and midwife nodded at him.

The baby continued crying while the doctor carried him out. He was calling for his mother, instinctively knowing that separating from her wasn't going to bring any good. The doctor lay him down and adjusted the heat lamp to irradiate him, while Janet filled the large 25 centilitre syringe and expelled the air. She looked at the doctor, they both nodded.

An injection like no other, which looked no different from any other. She put a little piece of cotton with disinfectant on the baby's chest and with a firm hand inserted the needle just above the heart, turning the cries of sorrow into ones of excruciating pain. The little boy was releasing impossibly loud exclamations of fear, anger and despair. Janet withdrew the needle and covered the hole with the cotton pad. The mother was calling, "Don't cry baby boy, the nice doctor's only washing you. Oh, sweetheart, don't cry." On the other side of the wall Janet and the doctor stood completely still, watching the baby's reactions like hawks.

His complexion turned dark red and he was unable to catch his breath from the convulsive crying. The doctor started massaging his little chest to ease the breathing, in a moment that seemed to last an eternity. Half a minute later, the baby started shaking in a spasmodic, insane set of convulsions, his entire body contracting and stretching in twitches. It was painful to watch the little boy jerking uncontrollably on the table, unable to determine what was causing the reaction, or what was going to happen next. During the interminable fit, the baby discharged a reflux of fluids smeared with blood out of his contorted mouth. The mother, preoccupied by the terrifying noises was becoming restless herself, begging to be given her son back, she even tried to stand up while still being sewn up, the nurse struggled to keep her in bed.

The situation was critical, Janet was running through her mind all the possible scenarios: *the baby's death, paralysis, sedation of the mother...* nothing seemed to make sense anymore. She didn't know what to do. All she could do was repeat the mantra: *It's just an experiment, none of it is my fault, it's just an experiment.*

A moment later, the baby fixed his wide-open eyes on Janet's face. He suddenly stopped crying and convulsing. He gave her the most intense stare that no newborn could have possibly given. That reminded her that the baby personality had to be killed for the experiment to succeed. *Must be EA1456!*

The mother quietened too with the baby, listening carefully to catch more signs of life from him. The baby eventually started to blink, vexed by the sharp light in the room, before closing his eyes altogether.

A cry came from the other room: "What have you done to my baby… why has he gone all quiet?" One nurse was trying to calm the mother, while another filled a syringe with morphine.

Janet took what seemed to be her first breath in over a minute, relieved that the boy's condition was stabilising, though she knew that the real boy was gone, forever erased from the face of the planet. A small step for a giant leap… The resident doctor also exhaled audibly, raising his eyebrows at Janet as if to say, *that was close!* He connected some cables to the baby, tilted and adjusted a screen that was protruding from the wall on a telescopic arm, and, after swiping the touch screen, pronounced his diagnosis from underneath the mask covering his mouth: "Vital functions OK, breathing clear and blood circulation regular." And after a while he added, "I think the crying must have cleared his lungs, he'll be fine." Then in a higher tone of voice called, "Nurse, towel him dry, wrap him up and take him to his mother please."

The nurse nodded in response, placing her palms together on the side of her face, tilting her head signalling that the mother was asleep. The doctor understood and everyone in the room relaxed, apart from Janet.

2.7 – June 15th

EA1456 was lying unconscious on the hospital bed, covered in sweat, his body busy trying to restore itself with the help of a mass of tubes and wires protruding from everywhere. His connection with time and space had dissolved, his mind was broadcasting pictures of him sprawled out on a highway, being perpetually run over by cars and lorries, unable to get up and move away.

He slowly started regaining consciousness, which meant he could feel his entire body aching, helplessly tasting defeat in his mouth and smelling death through his nose. He spent some time discerning if he had in fact died, or if life was just playing one last cruel game with him. He had a hazy recollection of events: surgery, fighting with a young female doctor, immense nausea. Then, the perception of distance from the rest of the world, from which emptiness was emerging, carrying the weight of a promise he had made to himself, that he wasn't yet able to recall.

Unable to move one inch, he was drifting in and out of consciousness, awareness bouncing like a pinball between his various organs, which were making themselves known to him through pain. He was also worried about what more could happen to him, what to expect next. He was scared he would have to endure more surgery and pain, and feared they would be coming back for him. He had a suspicion he had been left waiting during a break, perhaps their lunch hour, but he couldn't think straight, the cocktail of medicines and anaesthetics had polluted his brain.

A sudden reflux of his own juices came out, filling the mask that was holding the tubes firm into his throat. He panicked, worried that he would drown in his own puke, until something distracted him, someone apparently. Like a shade, a pair of cold hands went over his face, inexperienced, unsteady hands pulled the mask away and wiped the vomit dripping down his neck.

He heard a familiar voice. *It's the pretty doctor I attacked – what the fuck is she doing? Move that tube an inch, bitch. No, not like that, stop the breathing machine from pumping puke back in my lungs! Ah, fucking hell, is she panicking or what? Is she drunk?* He tried to raise his head, at which point, something hit his skull: "Fuck! That hurt..." he said and fell unconscious again.

The voice was still there. "Is he in a coma? He's gutted, are you sure you want to take him?" A young man was fiddling with the wall-mounted screens and machines on the other side of the bed. "Uh-um," he conceded, removing a box connected to the blood pump from the side of EA1456. "I think I bumped it on his head, other than that I'm doing fine," he said proudly. "Now, I just need to work out how to arrest the flow before I disconnect it."

She was less sure about what was going on: "Is there anything I can do?"

"Jesus, he's in a real mess, I'm not sure we can put him in the car… perhaps we should look for the keys to that ambulance out there?"

She nodded, looking through the glass panels dividing the laboratory spaces; she could not believe her luck that the place was deserted.

Gaia left Andrew fiddling with the tubes and went exploring through the endless spaces, hoping to track back to the entrance they had used to come in. She thought the place was weird: part hospital, part chemical factory, part mutilation farm, all blended together by white walls without signs – not a place suitable for unaccompanied visitors.

She finally recognised the corridor in which they arrived, leading to the back entrance used for supplies, *or bodies*, she thought with a shiver. *I wonder how many people they planned to torture…* She was shaken by the state in which she had found EA1456; a mass of entrails stuffed in a sack before discarding. She couldn't believe that it was her *big sis* who masterminded this horror show. Through a window, Gaia noticed a room with a fake mirrored glass: a security post, temporarily unmanned.

She ran across to it and entered, determined to find her way out of the scary laboratory complex as soon as possible. Inside, a desk with a battery of screens displayed every corner of the lab in turn, including Andrew passing his hand over EA1456's eyes as if checking whether he could see him or not, then empty corridors, rooms, and the staff party in the canteen area. *Oh my God!* Gaia startled, her heart racing in her chest: the party was disbanding, a flood of people would soon be hitting every corridor, reoccupying the workspace. She shivered, rummaged around the room quickly, hoping to spot a set of ambulance keys, but no such luck. Another glance at the screens revealed that the once tight gathering of people in the refectory was dispersing. With a fright, she bumped into a torch, making it fall and smash, then she rushed out for Andrew, inevitably getting lost on the way through the indistinguishable corridors.

Seeing two doors opening ahead of her, she almost fainted, expecting a bunch of doctors coming out of there, but was overwhelmed with relief to see Andrew's bum appearing, followed by the rest of his body and the bed with EA1456 in it. *My angel!* "Andrew, they're all coming back! I couldn't find the ambulance keys, we have to hurry and slip out while we can!"

Andrew smiled proudly; he had managed to separate the remains of the man from the bundle of machines, leaving only one piece of hardware lying on the trolley bed between EA1456's legs. He nodded, "Yeah let's go."

They started running back through the maze of corridors with identical stainless steel doors, at one point hearing the voices of some people coming back from the canteen. Accelerating, pushing and pulling EA1456's trolley, they made it outside, stopping just inches from the back of the old white Volvo estate. Andrew opened the tailgate, looking to make space in the messy boot. Scratching his head working out how to move the dead weight into the car, he grabbed the thick blanket he had brought and, with Gaia's help, he managed to slide it under the body. They then manoeuvred the blanket with the body into the back of the car, covering it with a piece of blue rug, before closing the hatchback. They both ran round to their respective seats in the front.

The movement and sound of the boot closing woke up Lucas, the lighter sleeper of the twins, activating his cry, which in turn woke up the others. By the time Gaia and Andrew were ready to go, the three children were making some pretty loud noise. Andrew looked back to reverse the car and saw the three crying children: *Perfect!* he thought, grinning. He rapidly swung the wheel to head the long white Volvo towards the main gate, hitting the trolley bed they had left behind as they pulled off.

Andrew was more excited than scared. He found the action thrilling, challenging his father on his turf, over his pet project, and with a gorgeous MILF at his side. He loved it, he thought he must have looked pretty cool at the steering wheel when the security guard stopped the car on the way out of the compound.

The scene revealed to the crouching guard consisted of a stiff young woman in the passenger seat, three screaming children in the back seat and a wannabe-man looking silly in his aviator glasses. *Can he really be shagging her?* "So you guys found what you were looking for?"

"Yes sir, thanks for your cooperation… good job," answered Andrew authoritatively, having anticipated the question and figured that answering positively would bluff the guard who could never guess what they were removing. Determined to follow the protocol, the guard came closer to the driver, looking around one more time before releasing the car. The smell of children's farts and the stench of decaying flesh emanating from EA1456, mixed with the general stink of an old Volvo, assailed the guard's nostrils, making him withdraw his head fast enough to salute them and step back, indicating they were free to move on. Andrew took advantage of the beloved smooth automatic gear of the Volvo to swiftly leave the danger zone behind.

It appeared they had made it out safely, for now. Andrew was elated with the turn of events: they had entered the compound, withdrawn EA1456 from his death bed and were now driving through the English countryside in the old Volvo.

"I still hope we can save his life Andrew, he looks horrible… what if he dies in our hands?"

"Gaia, *they* would still be responsible for his death, not us, with everything they've done to him. Anyway, let's not think about it, my mate in Cambridge is real good, a medical trainee who can work miracles with a stethoscope."

The children were still crying. "Kids, be quiet – Sophia, stop screaming, sweetheart."

"Mama, I'm hungry."

"Uncle Andrew's gonna take you to Burger King, but only if you behave," he offered as a bribe.

"No, what? Burger King, are you mad?" Gaia told Andrew off. "Here Sophia, have some raisins for now. Relax."

"I don't want more raisins, I want Burger King…" wailed Sophia between sobs, refusing the small packet of raisins. The noise faded into quieter whimpering. Andrew passed his tablet to Gaia. "Here, invert the destinations on the map, so we can find the quickest way back."

Gaia took the device and fiddled with it for a while before asking Andrew, "How do you do that?"

He answered, keeping his eyes on the road: "Just flip the names on the screen, with your thumbs."

"Ah, yes got it."

Andrew found anything she did or said very sexy indeed. A millisecond glance at the outline of her breasts gave him an erection, which he hid by shifting position in the seat. One hour and 20 minutes, *let's hope the car doesn't die before we get there*, he said to himself whilst switching on the music. They drove in amiable silence; he mentally rewound all the amazing things they had done in the last half an hour, while she projected all the risks posed by their recent actions.

*****

In the back of the car, EA1456's operating system started to reboot, having been literally knocked out by Andrew hitting his head with a swinging piece of medical equipment. Before awareness came pain, in his head and chest first, then, a strange feeling of moving at speed. It took him a while to realise he was in the back of a car, lying in an awkward position. He felt weak and sick, he could barely open his eyes. He asked himself, *What kind of prank is destiny playing now. Who are they? Why Magic FM 105.4?*

He decided to try and make himself heard. He wanted, needed, to understand what the hell was going on. He tried to mumble something, but he could barely even hiss. He tried again, and again.

"Mama, man…"

After a short pause Sophia repeated, slightly louder this time, "Mama... man."

Gaia, dealing with her growing anxiety, responded distractedly, "Cows love, they're cows."

"No mama, man..."

"No Sophia love, those are cows, see? Black, white."

"Mama, man, talking, back..."

Gaia sat bolt upright in her seat, looking at Andrew who finally understood too. "Do you want to go and look? Can you—"

Gaia turned to Sophia, "Yes love, man talking at the back, it's all right. Mummy will come to have a look. Let me see…" and without looking at Andrew she commanded, "Slow down, please." With her right hand she unbuckled her seat belt and tried to climb over her seat to get to the boot. Although she was a relatively small girl, she barely found any space left to plant her foot on the back seat because of the chunky child seats. Irritated, she asked Andrew to stop the car, half knowing that he would refuse.

"Not a good idea, Gaia."

"But I can't do it while you drive, it's too dangerous."

"I can't stop the car, I don't want to attract attention; besides, time is of the essence."

"Ok then, slow down at least, Andrew," she said, trying again to complete the passage. Extending her left leg into the back of the car with the rest of her body following, she crouched slightly and caressed her children tenderly, there were raisins and sweet wrappers everywhere. She stretched up between the twins heads to look into the boot. She raised a corner of the blanket where she thought EA1456 would be, but he wasn't there. She recoiled and moved to her right behind Andrew's seat.

"Police car!" Andrew said with a shout, "Quick, under the seat!"

She did so, with her face up looking at her puzzled children, and smiled pretending nothing was happening. She remained crouched uncomfortably, long enough to hear the moan coming from the trunk. When Andrew gave the all clear, she stretched back up and reached behind the line of rear seats lifting the opposite side of the blanket, uncovering the emaciated face of EA1456 with his eyes half closed. Even though she felt her throat clogging, she found the strength to address him, mindful that the kids were listening in. "Hello, I'm Gaia and we're taking you to see Andrew's friends, they're good doctors. I know you are in pain and we will be there very soon." She wasn't sure if she saw him nod, but he had at least stopped moaning.

EA1456 was completely confused. Who the hell are they? She sounds like the doctor, but she isn't.

"Mama, where are we going?" Sophia asked Gaia as soon as she could see her mother's face.

Is it kids I'm hearing? What am I doing in a car with kids? Isn't this an ambulance, I'm sick! He thought perhaps these were the children implanted with his DNA, though he couldn't understand the role of the woman, the mother, who sounded like the doctor… His head pounded as he tried to unravel the situation, but his motion sickness was growing with every bend.

"No love, we will go home a little bit later -- we're driving the man to Cambridge first and then we go home."

"I'm hungry," replied the little girl.

"Ok, let me see if we can stop. Andrew, what do you think?"

"Where are we?" asked Andrew, lost in his own thoughts.

"Can you check the tablet? I'll stop if I see a drive-through, better not showing our pretty faces around too much…Looks like we're not far from Luton."

"Sophia? Baby, we'll stop soon, ok? Mummy will get you some food."

"And a milkshake," added Sophia.

"Milkshake, milkshake," cried the twins in unison.

Andrew's driving was slowed down by traffic lights turning onto the A505, but once they were on the road, it was wide and traffic-free, he could have sped if he wanted. After about ten miles, he found a gas station with a drive-through restaurant and pulled in. Andrew ordered food and drinks for everyone, including a Coke for EA1456. Within ten minutes, they were on the move again and Gaia crawled back to ask EA1456 if he wanted anything to eat or drink.

He was getting really nauseous by the car trip and tried to make this point across to Gaia, who misinterpreted his arching eyebrow and tried to force the straw in his mouth. He sipped some drink, pulling back immediately as the fizzy drink hurt his throat, cola spilling down his chin and neck.

Andrew made good progress with both the driving and the sandwich he was eating, while the kids chomped on chicken nuggets.

Soon they started to smell the foul odour emanating from the contaminated pond near the road. Andrew turned left as per the computer's instructions, slowing down on the dirt road, although EA1456 was still being tossed around the boot like a rag doll.

Andrew stopped the Volvo beside Gaia's SUV, which was parked on the road just before the pond. He sprang out, simultaneously slamming his door and opening the back door to start moving the children's seats across to their normal car. Gaia was impressed that Andrew moved each seat with the child still in it, and she herself went round to open the Volvo's trunk to check on EA1456. Andrew arrived and together they moved EA1456 into the other car boot, this time cluttered with baby equipment, but more comfortable and not smelling of petrol.

"Are you OK?" Gaia asked the patient, pushing some hair back from his forehead. He nodded, making an effort to see who she was – she was cute, he liked her, she was definitely related to the doctor, though her blond hair was longer and she was younger, with rounder lineaments on the same distinctive face. More importantly, she seemed to care about him. "We will save you," she said over the demands of the kids summoning her.

The kids and EA1456 had been transferred, so he reverted to his master plan for the day: sinking the Volvo in the toxic pond. He flashed a dazzling boyish grin at Gaia and ran around the seven-seater to climb in the Volvo. He switched the old banger on one last time and studied its auto-pilot lever on the right-hand side of the wheel once again to make sure he did not make any mistake when jumping out of the moving car.

Gaia, who knew nothing of his plan, was waiting in the driving seat of her car when she started screaming, frightening the children to near death. Through her windscreen she saw the Volvo tipping into the pond at quite a speed. She jumped out of the car and started running towards the cloud of smoke that was coming up from where the car had hit the water. Then she saw Andrew, lying on his side with his mobile phone held up in mid air filming the car tumbling into the dark, smelly water.

"What's happening?" she shouted, not registering that he had escaped the accident. He ignored her a little bit longer, getting up to his feet to walk towards the pond for a close-up of the bubbling surface, before holding his phone up for a 360 degree panorama to capture the landscape. He stopped the recording and walked back towards Gaia, grinning.

"What the hell were you doing?" Gaia shouted again. "Trying to kill yourself? You scared me!"

Andrew, busy fiddling with the phone, answered coolly, "It was something I have been longing to do for a long time."

"You scared the hell out of me, why didn't you tell me?"

"I dunno, I thought you might have tried to stop me."

Idiot, she thought, shaking her head in disapproval.

Andrew brushed some dirt off his shirt and trousers and, with Gaia, walked to the rear of the car to inspect EA1456: he was awake, but looking feeble, his face distorted in pain. Andrew tried to reassure him, "We Are Tak-ing You To A Hos-Pi-Tal," he said loud and clear. "We Will Be The-Re In A Dash." He covered him back up with a rag and closed the boot.

Who's that idiot now? EA1456, hating to be treated like a child, didn't have the time or energy for the arrogant boy. A streak of pain crossed his body, as if his nerves were being stretched and squeezed, making his burning eyes close again.

As soon as Andrew was in the passenger seat, Gaia started the car and left she was driving the last stretch. In the meantime, he took off his dirty shirt, wearing only the white T-shirt he had underneath.

Reaching the intersection with the main road, Andrew watched Gaia scrutinise the traffic to enter the main road safely: he wished he could pull her over to him and kiss her all over. She felt his stare and looked straight back into his eyes. She felt the same emotion, her mind riddling *kissing or driving, kissing or driving?* She was close to stretching out to him, inviting his mouth to join hers, when the corner of her eye caught sight of her three little children neatly arranged on the back seat, staring.

She winked and raised her right eyebrow at him, reminding him of their presence as they had completely gone off his radar too. They faced one another, looking into each other's eyes for a long moment. He awkwardly took her hand and clenched it – that was it, contact had been made.

She had liked him since they had met at Robert's reception at Chequers. For the first time in years, she craved for a body that didn't belong to her husband. Sighing, he remained with his head slightly tilted, giving her a passionate look. Gaia eventually regained her self control, looking again in both directions of the road they were joining, before pushing her right foot on the accelerator and leaving a cloud of white dirt behind them. The car picked up speed while they remained still in their seats, not talking, just looking at the road ahead, both interpreting the noise of their recent feelings. With the unbestowed kiss still hanging in the air of the car, they unwarily passed the *Welcome to Cambridge* sign.

2.8 – June 15th

Janet was relieved to see the doctor's thumbs up, signalling everything was going well, and her back briefly sought the support of the wall. As nerve wracking an experience as it had been to implant the first DNA Killer App into a newborn baby, without the knowledge of the mother, she wasn't finished yet. Now, she would go on to secretly inject another unaware pregnant woman.

Janet was studying the officers moving swiftly behind the glass wall dividing the theatre from the room she was in; she needed to temporarily get rid of them to make the second part of the program happen. She pushed away from the wall and headed for the sinks, where she washed up, waiting for her opportunity. She exchanged a few words with the resident doctor, who was getting out of his overalls – he noticed she was tense and reassured her that he was only going home for a few hours, and that he would be back later that afternoon to check that the baby was fine. "In the meantime," he said, "Dr. Patel will be guarding the patient. He is informed of—"

But Janet wasn't listening, instead thinking it would be less noticeable if she left the room with him. She suddenly became interested in the doctor, chatting him up, asking questions, selectively listening to whatever he had to say while subtly spying on her escorts. They were waiting on the other side of the doors she would need to use to get out of the theatre, one was busy flirting with a young nurse.

With a little attention, the doctor had turned into a chatterbox – Janet had picked up on his comment about the revolutionary intracytoplasmic sperm injection he was working on at the Reproductive Technology Centre a few floors below, and he was now telling her all about his assisted procreations.

She asked him if she could visit the centre and the doctor was suitably flattered, *beautiful, clever girl*, he thought, "Let's go." He faintly touched her elbow and Janet played the game, staying close to him, carrying the small briefcase under her other arm. Quickly through the doors, she took the waiting officers by surprise. They waived at her when she didn't stop, but she casually called back, "I'm popping downstairs to check one of the doctor's famous sperm injections, I'll be back in half an hour, max."

The young guy saw it as an opportunity to spend more time with the pretty nurse, but as Janet turned to face the lift entrance, she could see that the older agent looked uneasy. He was thinking of protocol, but thankfully the lift arrived and the doors closed between them before he could take any action. The doctor kept on talking, she half pretended to be listening. She needed to find room AC3034 as soon as possible, where she would inject the pregnant mother with the spare DNA shuttle she had prepared.

Janet was convinced she was doing the right thing: she was assuring an independent continuation of the experiment, away from Bill and Robert in case they decided to take over her work. An insurance cover for her career, a side job only she knew of.

She had planned it in typically minute detail: through Clare, the girl she had been quietly dating for the last six months, Janet got access to the database of pregnant women at the hospital. Claire worked as an anaesthetist and knew the hospital inside-out. Date after date, Janet had made conversation about the Assisted Reproductive Clinic, finding out as many details as possible to store in the back of her brain, as this was the department of the hospital she had targeted for her private implantation of the Killer App. Claire was blissfully unaware of Janet's plans, thinking she was an amazing listener, really interested in her and modest about her own amazing career as a researcher.

This way, Janet had learnt about an interesting young couple where the want-to-be father, a real gutsy fighter, had managed to beat his battle against AIDS. Claire had portrayed the young man's recovery as being nothing short of a miracle, with scans corroborating evidence that the virus had remained undetectable in his blood for two straight quarters. He had found out, aged fifteen, that his mother had deliberately injected him as a newborn in order to contaminate him, to be her get-out-of-jail-free card and secure state support.

Having managed to counteract the consequences of his awful past, they were now struggling to conceive a baby; the large doses of highly toxic drugs he had taken had inhibited his ability to reproduce. Janet had suggested to Claire that she wanted to help – using her knowledge and status as a researcher, she could select the best DNA profile from the global sperm banks, thus increasing the couple's chances of having a healthy baby on the first attempt. But it would have to remain their secret, Claire couldn't tell a soul.

In reality, all Janet wanted, was to control their DNA mix to see if it matched with EA1456's spectrum. With a little manipulation at the encoding stage, she discovered it would. Janet really wanted her secret carrier to be a baby girl, and the study of the couple's DNA suggested a 76% chance of procreating a female offspring. So she decided they would be the conceiving couple for her own experimentation of the Killer App, the DNA to be inserted into the mother and then transferred through her body into the foetus.

Janet spent hours studying this procedure alone, at night, enjoying not having to share her work with Robert and Bill. She had carried out a private and confidential investigation of the couple's medical history, far beyond what was in Claire's possession, modelling it against the available donors. In the end though, to enhance compatibility, she had provided Claire with a sperm sample from EA1456, to swap it at the hospital with the one supplied by the national sperm database.

The moment she had finalised her side plans seemed years away now. The lift was carrying her closer to accomplishing her task. Success depended on her chance of remaining alone with the mother long enough to inject her with the shuttle. Then, all that was left was to wait. Wait for a positive delivery, or death, death of the mother, the child, or both.

The resident doctor woke her from her myriad of secret and scary thoughts: "Here we are." She decided it was time to get rid of him, putting up a good definitive excuse by checking her phone, "Sorry Doc. I actually don't have time for this, I'm needed back upstairs. I'll just pop to the ladies here, then go back up. Thanks for all your time and sorry to be a pain." The doctor lacked the strength of character to insist, "Shame, I thought I was going to—" he trailed off, looking at the back of Janet walking down the corridor.

All room numbers starting with digit three were on the third floor. Janet tried to orientate herself, looking for the department she was after, Embryo Transfer Unit, Fertility Medication Unit, Hormone Treatment Clinic, she was definitely close. The hospital gown made her look like one of the doctors, helping her to negotiate her way to the target room without being stopped. Eventually she found it: Assisted Reproductive Clinic. Inside, a door panel was marked AC3034, Bingo! Shit, there's four beds per room. None of the women looked like the small profile picture she had seen of her target, now she struggled to recognise the patient she was looking for, so she called "Sharon" from the door, looking around the room.

"Yes, that's me," the woman in the far left bed reacted to her name. She was shorter than Janet had imagined, with straight light brown hair and pale blue eyes, she spoke in a slow soft voice. Walking towards her, she shook her hand confidently, introducing herself as Alvina Lunday, the General Practitioner, a supervisor, *the guarantee that you will have a good overall experience at the hospital.* Janet stood briefly at the foot of her bed pretending to read the girl's medical record, when in reality there wasn't anything more she could know about the girl, or that would have made any difference at that stage. She asked the patient whether she still suffered from back pain as reported before, the girl replied she was better, that it was nothing to worry about.

"I'm glad you don't worry dear, because sometimes I do, believe me. Now, have you been administered the vaccine against the hospital superbug?"

The girl shook her head gently, naively. Janet taking immediate advantage of the girl's timidity and ordered, "Open your gown and lie on your side, while I prepare you for the injection." The girl cooperated. Janet shot the needle under the girl's armpit, close to her left breast, whilst holding her arm straight up. At the beginning the girl winced with pain, but took it well. Janet explained to her how the protection against these new viral defectors worked, immunising her from hospital-born bugs which harmed patients with weak immune systems. She pushed it so far as to quote made-up figures supporting the case for vaccination.

Then something happened. After around a minute, the girl started to sway, yelping three or four times before going completely stiff with her eyes wide open. Janet bent over to look into the girl's eyes with a penlight and noticed she was biting her own tongue. Aware of at least one other patient in the room watching, she smiled at her before slipping her right thumb into the girl's mouth to release the bite.

The patient started to breathe again, through exaggerated gulps accompanied by a slight jerking motion on the in-breath. Janet panicked that she would be discovered and found out. She wanted to run away, but had to stay to calm the girl. "Don't worry dear, everything is fine, you are doing absolutely great," she soothed, while caressing the hot forehead of the girl, whilst disentangling her tongue one more time. She was red faced, her eyes still wide open, lost in a trance. Janet was probably out of her focus, so she seized the moment to go, turning to close the syringes case, her phone vibrating in the pocket of her overalls. Excusing herself to the patient for the fleeting visit, she was ready to go. To her utmost surprise, one of the other patients in the room spoke in a frightened tone to her, "I don't want one." It was the same woman who had been looking at her from the opposite bed.

Janet startled, "Want what?"

"The vaccine, I don't want it."

Janet breathed a sigh of relief, her phone still vibrating in her pocket. "No dear, don't you worry, I know you don't need one," she said as she left the room, wanting to make as much progress as possible to remain unnoticed by the staff. On the way out of the ward the doors swung open in her face, revealing a nurse looking straight into her face. Janet nodded at her, and the other woman, snowed under with duties, passed without questioning Janet's presence in her ward.

Janet was out, tracing her steps back to the helicopter, her heart beating like a hammer. Another call attempt attracted her attention, she looked at her smartphone: *the lab,* two missed calls and a new one on its way. She had to take it, "Janet here."

"Janet, we have a problem, have you been informed?" It was the lab's security head.

Feeling guilty for disappearing and the consequences it may have caused, she excused herself for the blackout and asked what was going on.

The guy's voice trembled. "Janet, the adept has been abducted, two people, took him away in a car."

"What? What! Are you kidding? Where was everyone?"

She listened to explanations that didn't make sense, burying her face in her free hand. She couldn't believe what she was hearing. *Could this be Bill's sabotage?* So little did she trust him after the meeting in Cinque Terre. *How else could anyone have entered the premises and taken EA1456, half dead? And to what end?* The lift arrived, but she didn't want to lose connection, so she waited. "Who did you tell?" She was surprised to hear him answering *no one*, of course, she expected Bill to have been informed, *maybe even Robert and the rest of the fucking army!* She told the security chief that she was going straight back, that she would call him in five minutes and to keep his mouth shut in the meantime.

Janet got the lift up to the helipad. She nodded to the pilot and the two officers, "We've had a security breach, let's fly back as quickly as possible." Her phone was buzzing again, Bill's face came up on the display. "One second, I'm coming straight after this call," she said, turning slightly to seek some privacy for a difficult conversation. She waited a few seconds for encryption to kick-in, a metallic voice croaked through the phone, "What happened is fucking fiction…" Bill didn't hide his anger even at the cost of sounding unsympathetic. He was firing questions: why was she late, why had EA1456 not been unplugged according to schedule, more importantly, where the fuck was she? All Janet could do was lie to cover herself. "There were some complications with the baby, it wasn't as straight forward in the hospital, logistics have been shit."

"Not what I'm told Janet, not what I'm told…" Bill remained cold and inquisitive, possibly thinking that she may have been involved in the abduction. *Fair enough*, she thought, *here we stand suspecting each other.*

Confrontation was delayed, she wanted to fly back to the lab. Bill said he would take over coordination of the search, "I'm gonna get him back for dinner, Janet, I'm just waiting for the GPS activation from his body."

She had forgotten about the chip that security had requested to insert. "What do you want me to do?"

"Go to the labs, manage that bunch of Muppets of yours, I want everyone to stay put till the situation is clear. No one will leave the premises until we have recovered him."

"Don't you want me to find out how this happened?"

"No, I'll take care of the adept, you prepare to resume the schedule."

She moved back to the helicopter, its door sliding closed behind her. Her ears popped, the uplift acceleration surprisingly strong, dragging her stomach up. She was exhausted. Closing her eyes, she kept asking herself who could have kidnapped EA1456 and why. She was feeling drowsy, struggling to hold her neck up.

It had to be an insider, someone who knew what was going on with the experiment, someone associated with Bill or Robert. *Robert!* she startled. She had forgotten to ask Bill whether he had been informed at all. She messaged Bill: *How about R. Informed?* She closed her eyes again, haunted by the images of what would happen to her with EA1456 exposed to the public – jail, persecution – her brain again repeating the mantra: *just an experiment, none of it is my fault, just an experiment.*

She was brought back to reality by the pilot's voice. "Message from mission control," he said in a thick Glaswegian accent. A metallic voice from the radio took over: "14:58 GMT, stealth contact with offenders made. White VOLVO 240 GL station wagon, registration number OY08 LEU; nearer POI Foxton, Cambridgeshire, coordinates 52.1150 degrees N, 0.0586 E. Occupants, two adults identified as Andrew Hand, 20, and Gaia Ardelli, 32, three young children appearing to be Mrs. Ardelli's. UKSF despatched, regular services not informed yet. Mission labelled S.C.O. till further notice, over."

Janet's face contorted as she struggled to make sense of what she had just heard. *Gaia? The children?*

"Officer, please ask them to confirm, what are they talking about?"

The officer replied to a hyperventilating Janet that the communication was a broadcast, a one-way message like a weather bulletin. "I can't call the dispatcher." Janet was overwhelmed, unable to understand anything anymore. She looked at her phone to see if Bill had replied, but he hadn't. She tried to think what the hell was going on – *Gaia, the kids, Andrew, EA1456* – names floating in her head like pieces of a flawed jigsaw puzzle. *Robert's son was in it too?* She needed questions answered, insisting one more time, yelling, "Call them now, officer, call your damn control centre!"

He declined, "We're not part of that operation." His firmness provoked a tantrum from Janet, screaming, unfastening her seatbelt and trying to get to the front of the cabin to operate the radio herself. The agent blocked her and pushed her down to the floor, her screams filling the cabin above the noise of the rotor. The officer immobilised her and managed to yell over her, "Calm down! Don't move or I'll handcuff you, all right?"

Janet had to give up. She nodded, trying one last time to disentangle her arms from his grip, her eyes filling with tears. She sighed. Looking through the glass door, for the second time that day, the rolling countryside failed to soothe her spirits. The experiment had changed everything: Gaia, the kids, she didn't understand anything anymore. The officer led her back to her seat and soon she could feel the helicopter slowing, tilting at an angle to circle a couple of times around the labs in preparation for landing.

She composed herself, drying tears from her eyes and smoothing her hair up. Clearing her throat, she addressed the security guard, "Sorry for before, please let me get out in front of my people alone."

The helicopter descended vertically towards the helipad. She disembarked alone, but was very conscious of the officer keeping close, escorting her into the office building. She could leave the noise behind, not the embarrassment, the awkwardness of the large security failure, apparently induced by a member of her own family. She walked straight to her office without talking to the questioning faces she met on the way. Once inside, she opaqued the glass walls and dialled Gaia's number, no answer. She summoned the head of security, the guy who was in charge during the kidnap, and two senior members of the medical staff.

Three team members appeared within a minute, discomposed, disconcerted. Janet felt responsible for the abduction perpetrated by her sister, having herself delayed the termination of EA1456 in order to carry out her *private procedure*. Still, she couldn't refrain from putting pressure on them, questioning every step, retracing with them the smallest details to find out what had happened, making sure they too felt the pain.

Following her departure earlier that morning, the staff returned to the canteen to celebrate the success of procedure. Drinks had been served with a cold lunch, and people had hung out for about an hour or so, chilling out.

Hang out, chilling – what was this, a school summer camp? she thought, shaking her head in disapproval.

"During that time," the head of security continued, embarrassed, "a car with Ms. Ardelli approached the gates, telling the guards that she had come to pick up something you had left with an assistant. The guard, recognising her and the children, and seeing the innocuous look of the young boy driving, had agreed to let her enter."

"Andrew Hand?"

"As you may have been informed already," he said sheepishly. "What appears to have happened after that is that they disconnected EA1456 and put him in the back of a Volvo they were driving, leaving the premises in less than fifteen minutes."

Janet listened to the end of the story, holding her head between her hands. "Thanks for the briefing," she said without looking at the speaker. Clearly, the security breach had her sister at the core of it: Gaia had taken advantage of her known identity and the kids to enter and exit the compound. She rearranged her thoughts and sighed deeply. "Right, I'm sure we'll have numerous occasions to analyse these facts further. For now, no one can leave – all staff must remain inside the labs, until further notice."

The security guy looked like he knew already, the doctors seemed more puzzled.

"Everyone and everything is prohibited to leave. Also, no one is allowed in. There's an ongoing security operation to recover EA1456 and we have to wait for it prior to resuming schedule."

They all nodded, with various degrees of acceptance, the doctors leaving the room. The head of security stayed behind, awkwardly reporting to Janet that a reinforcement security team had already arrived onsite, sealing the premises off completely. She felt totally disempowered.

"Repeat that," she commanded in a threatening tone. He re-articulated, "Before you landed, I had a call from control centre, they told me that a UKSF unit was to seal the compound from the outside; they asked me to go on the intercom system to announce it wouldn't be safe for anyone to try and leave the site."

She wasn't the boss any longer, she was a hostage like all the others. She was embarrassed to be seen by members of the medical team, her credibility forever shattered at the hands of her own sister. She asked to be left alone and tried calling Gaia again, *the little bitch… what is she trying to do to me?* Her phone rang and rang without answer. She tried calling Bill instead, but no answer there either. She was extremely frustrated not to have answers, and furious to see her whole professional career going down the toilet in the space of a couple of hours. She even thought she should have secretly terminated EA1456 straight away after the operation, *no fucking lawyer would have been able to prove anything anyway*, and even if, she thought, the consequences would have been minimal in comparison to now. More than anything, he was the piece of the puzzle that had to be hidden from the world, at any cost. She felt a pain in her sternum, thinking of EA1456 being driven around in the boot of a car by her very own sister and a *juvenile* adolescent.

Outraged and hurt, she phoned the security chief again asking whether he could display the location of EA1456 on her screens. He sent her a link she could click on which opened a map application where she saw a green dot was moving through the outskirts of Cambridge. Even her powerful brain failed to make sense of that view. She grabbed her phone from the desk without moving her eyes from the screen. Her fingers flew across the keyboard entering text at the speed of light: *What the fuck are you doing? I hate you!*

2.9 – June 15th

Andrew repeated the navigator instructions, adding his manly interpretation to it. Gaia steered the large SUV around the old city buildings and the sparse traffic. They were guided to turn right into a smaller lane marked *Hospital Deliveries*, and they slowed down looking for signs of Andrew's friends. The grim hospital building was covered by bunches of useless pipes, most of its ground floor windows boarded up, except for one revealing a laundry room with two old women mending hospital gowns. At the end of the road, further ahead, they found access to a small square with a line of empty car parks and an overloaded skip. On the opposite side, a carport in great need of maintenance and, standing on top of a flight of stairs, Andrew's friend Giles. A 20-something with ginger hair, Giles had a round happy face and flushed red cheeks under his wide cheekbones. He was wearing doctor's overalls, voraciously smoking a cigarette with his gaze lost over the top line of the garages. Gaia found his appearance too youthful and unhealthy to inspire patients' trust; he reminded her of fried breakfasts and whisky.

Giles didn't acknowledge the approaching vehicle until the very end. He hadn't expected Andrew's face to appear behind the windows of a smart black SUV.

He realised it was them, only when Andrew stuck his upper body out of the passenger door waving wildly. He ran down the stairs to greet them at the vehicle, instinctively bending to look at the driver, his eyes lowering in line with the descending tinted window glass disclosing Gaia's pretty face. His expression revealed most of his surprise and appreciation, *where the fuck did Andrew get hold of this bird?*

"Welcome to Cambridge Private A&E, we pride ourselves on a confidential and friendly service." She didn't know what to make of him, one young man was enough, two made her feel somehow inappropriate. Her incertitude was broken by Andrew, "The patient is in the back, he's not feeling great, I believe."

"We'll address that, and see him feeling well again," Giles was talking to and nodding at Gaia, "I can assure you of that."

Gaia thought perhaps she had overrated Andrew's circle of connections, expecting too much out of his network, and was increasingly uncomfortable with his choice of doctor for EA1456. Particularly since she had seen his dire condition.

Behind the shabby and unprofessional facade, Giles was a top class student who could have easily entered the junior ranks of the NHS a long time ago. The son of a Harley Street luminary, he had learnt the medical art by sitting in his father's practice, for hours, most afternoons, pretending to do homework.

"I've opened the boot for you, doctor," Gaia said.

He went to the back of the car where the automatically rising door revealed the man Andrew had been talking about; slightly more than a corpse now, lying in an awkward position, looking up at him through half-shut eyes. Giles' medical knowledge rated him straight away, *with a feeble chance of making it for supper*. In fact, EA1456 did look in a terrible state, worse than he had done at the labs after the car transfer and the rough ride. Giles could see he was covered in bruises and stitches on every exposed part of his body. One look into EA1456's pupils revealed that he was probably just attached to life to see what other curse it could throw at him.

Looking up from the patient's head brought into focus three little children sitting in the back of the car – two asleep and one girl staring back at him with questioning eyes. He straightened and turned to talk to Andrew, who was now standing on his side, with both hands on his hips. "A factory of surprises you are, mate. I wish I had time to ask you where you picked up all of this cargo... But customers first."

"Will you take care of him?" Andrew was showing off his caring side to Gaia.

Giles looked quickly back at the body in the trunk. "Sure, who wouldn't? I just don't have enough staff at hand to carry him inside. We'll take him in on the blanket," he gestured like holding a stretcher. "We can put him onto a bed in the corridor, just as you enter. I'll fake the papers during tonight's shift."

"Great, thanks. Gaia, can you hold the door?"

EA1456 was horrified, thinking, *fuck no, not another hand transfer... this is going to hurt!* He tried to hiss "no," but was unable to voice his opposition, producing red stringy phlegm instead, clogging his respiratory channel in a way that made him cough and splutter desperately. His gasping increased the haste in which Giles and Andrew moved him, both competing for

Gaia's attention, creating for EA1456 all the pain he had anticipated.

*****

The last she saw of EA1456 was him resting on the first available bed in the corridor. She couldn't follow him further, the kids needed her more than him, having been hauled around like parcels all day at the mercy of their *crazy mother*. She needed to attend to them properly, *I hope the boys take good care of you*, she whispered to herself and walked back to the car down the little flight of stairs. She opened the back door, a flurry of warm, smelly air came out of the car – there was at least one bad nappy that required immediate attention.

Lucas and Matthew were screaming over Sophia apparently taking their last toy, only to throw it on the floor for no apparent reason. Gaia knew the real problem was herself, constraining them in the car all day. She was flooded with love and guilt while she sorted them out, *so innocent, my little sweeties*. She found it funny how they all looked guilty when asked who should win the prize for the smelliest poo that day, or perhaps they were just exhausted and puzzled by their silly mother. She had an idea, "Kids shall we go for a walk in the old building and discover what's inside? Mummy can give you a clean nappy there too."

The little heads nodded, in rare unison, in that funny way little children require conscious effort and coordination. Gaia was constantly amazed with how utterly and helplessly they put their existences into her hands. She released them from their child seats, having to physically move their bodies to reach the security locks. In a familiar gesture, she took Sophia down first, giving her the small carry bag to hold, then reaching up for the twins, curling each on one of her shoulders. She locked the car and ventured up the stairs again into the long, dark and empty corridor. Walking through the next set of doors, she said, "It's a very old building children, maybe some kings and knights have come here recovering from battles."

"And princesses," swiftly added Sophia.

"Yeah, and princesses." In reality, the place looked just like a forsaken minor-league hospital, showing its deep wrinkles of time, crushed under the weight of age, slowly turning into a pile of rubble.

Gaia was looking for a toilet, undeterred by the expectation of finding it disgusting and lacking a changing mat. She negotiated with various sets of doors, letting the children go through corridor after corridor. At the next intersection, she got annoyed at the place, thinking that Lucas would get nappy rash if she couldn't change him soon. Seeing a set of windows overlooking an internal court, she decided to utilise the large windowsill. She sat Lucas on the cold surface and told his siblings to sit down on the floor, swiftly unpacking the changing stuff like a seasoned pro. Within minutes, both twins were done. She was cleaning her hands with wipes when she noticed across the courtyard what looked like a playroom: blue walls, pink French doors, children's decorations hanging around its windows. *Definitely worth a visit*, she thought, taking the little boys back up in her arms. The building was really quiet, being the back part of an old university hospital outside term time, and she didn't meet anyone all the way to the playroom. When she reached the other side of the building, the light was brighter, due to it being south-facing.

The glass door revealed the contents belonging to the children's world, to which they immediately emitted sounds of approval. Ignoring the sign, *This room is reserved for hospitalised children only,* Gaia pushed open the door to let the eager kids enter. Under a hand-coloured *Arts & Crafts* sign stood two low tables topped with crayons, paper and plastic scissors. Further away there was a red bike, a yellow trike and, in a corner, some boxes containing dolls, dressing-up clothes, accessories and books. Lucas and Matthew quickly wriggled down from Gaia's body, heading for the ride-on toys, while Sophia went for the drawing station.

Gaia sat on one of the small chairs sighing in relief, although she wasn't going to relax knowing she shouldn't be there. She realised that if someone did come in, she had absolutely no reason for being in the hospital at all, without the name of a patient, or doctor, to say. That image reminded her of the car, randomly parked outside the designated areas. The pressure in her chest mounted, the whole situation was uncomfortable; she grabbed the phone from her pocket and commanded it to call Andrew.

"Hey."

"Hi, where are you?"

"Inside the hospital, I had to change two terrible nappies…What's going on there?"

"Giles is in a room, on the second floor, visiting him. What are your plans, don't you have to go?"

"I know, but the kids are having a good time now, for the first time today, as we found a playroom. I guess I'll go as soon as they are bored."

"Has anyone seen you?"

"No, I don't think so, we are all alone. We miss you—"

"Me too. I could come, no actually, I can't leave Giles now, but if you stay longer, I'll see you to say goodbye."

"Ok, I guess I'll be here for a while. I'll text you before I leave."

"Great."

"Bye."

She watched the kids playing, thinking what an awkward situation it was, with Andrew, the kids, the experiment guy. She was still holding the phone when she felt it buzz. The display showed her sister's face; one of her heartbeats went missing. Janet had probably found it all out already. Gaia grew more anxious with every ring of her phone. A small accident between the boys made her jump off the chair. Breathing fast, she scurried over to the boys telling them off just because they had crashed the trikes: "Boys stop, or you're gonna get us kicked out!"

The phone had stopped ringing, she messaged Andrew: *Got called & texted by Janet, not picked up. She knows.*

Andrew called her back straight away. "Hey, I saw your text. Listen, he's got a chip on his back, which can only be a GPS location system. Giles is seeing if he can quickly take it out."

"Why... is he going to be ok? I mean is that necessary?" Concerned that EA1456 could die any minute, Gaia was doubtful about Giles' ability to focus on the right priorities.

"I know what you mean, but if they take him back he'll be fucked anyway, and us with him, so…"

Gaia thought Andrew made sense. "Ok, ok, sorry, as long as it's not too dangerous."

"Gaia, I have seen him properly now – the guy has been opened up like a parcel, he's stitched from head to toe, like a rag doll. Even Giles keeps repeating he's never seen anything like it."

"And Janet's call? Do you think she knows where we are?"

"If they don't already, they will soon. As soon as we get it out, I'll take my bike and throw the chip as far away from the hospital as possible."

"Then, why don't I take it with me in the car and chuck it out somewhere on the motorway? I've got to go at some point anyway…"

"That's a good idea! I'll see you at the car in about five minutes. Oh, wait, Giles is saying something... oh, hold on, yeah, we'll call you if there are complications," he concluded.

Gaia went to gather the children, but they were having too much fun. She insisted through their moaning because she realised they weren't safe with that GPS transmitter around. Gaia, mother of three and expert negotiator, threw an ice-cream in the deal. It had been a day of strong bribery already; reluctantly, they let go of the toys. She scooped up the twins and adopted their usual formation with Sophia picking up the bag.

Gaia looked forward to getting out of the depressing building as soon as possible and immensely enjoyed the outside air hitting her face behind the back door to the parking lot. She secured the children back in their car seats, filled a plastic bag with some of the rubbish that had accumulated throughout the day and started a new movie on the headrest screens.

Walking around the car to reach the driver's seat, she rearranged her hair in a ponytail. Once inside, looking at her face in the vanity mirror revealed that she was looking shattered. What a hard day it had been, she prayed it would be worth it in the end, that EA1456 could be saved. She ignited the car's engine and started to peer out to reverse in the little court. As usual, any place was too small for Gaia when reversing her big car, but this space seemed particularly narrow.

She got distracted by her phone buzzing between her thighs, as she didn't want to miss Andrew's call. She stopped reversing to look at the display, but saw the picture of her sister instead. It kept buzzing and buzzing incessantly. Panicked, she threw it on the passenger seat and turned again to the manoeuvre. *I got to call her back*, she vowed, *perhaps once I'm on the highway...* At that moment, she reversed into one of the garage doors. "Mama, boom!" was the unhelpful comment from a smiley Lucas.

Fuck it, Gaia was thinking of an explanation that would convince Janet about the necessity of abducting the adept. The reasons for her actions, and her own beliefs, were beginning to look frail under the stress of the day.

She could feel a growing despair when Andrew appeared at the door above the stairs. In a typically teenage move, he jumped the ten steps in one go and reached for the driver's side window. He was carrying a transparent container, not bigger than a tube of vitamins and showed it to Gaia. "Hey, here it is."

"Yuk, disgusting."

"I know. The chip transmits its position, the silver bit looks like the battery."

Not bigger than two centimetres, the electronic piece of kit was stained with blood; she took the tube without inspecting it further and rested it on the coffee-cup holder under the armrest.

"Where are you going?" Andrew asked melancholically.

"I don't know, I'm confused… Janet must know everything by now, so I think I'll go to my parents, in the country."

"No, don't go there. They will come and take you, stay here, with me," he pleaded, putting his hand over her forearm. His offer was sweet, but she reckoned it was a bad idea. She wanted to hand the children to her parents, before leaving for London, to face Janet. "It's for their own safety, I can't waste anymore time." She looked into his beautiful young eyes, "Thank you for today, you've made it easy… and enjoyable." He leaned in to kiss her. Hoping that the kids wouldn't take their eyes off the TV screens, she didn't resist him. Their lips touched for a long moment, during which nothing else mattered. They became one thing, the rest – their families, the experiment – turning into stupid noise. They had been dancing around each other, sniffing the scent of attraction since their first meeting at Robert's party, back in April.

It was Gaia's job to cut the kiss short. Feeling ashamed for having kissed another man in front of the children, she looked meaningfully into Andrew's eyes. He had remained a second too long hanging around her lips, until understanding he had dared and conquered already. He retracted. "Get there safely, and throw that thing out as soon as you are outside town."

Gaia nodded, the kiss had left her dazed, she had felt nothing like that with Marco for a long time. She thought how many relationships were potentially coming to an end that day, first Janet, then Marco… Feeling uneasy, she focussed on protecting the children; she couldn't afford to lose them too.

She gave Andrew a clumsy smile and released her right foot from the brake, the big black car started to slowly pull away over the concrete slabs.

Andrew remained behind, immobilised, amazed at the events of the day. *Fifteenth of June 2025… definitely worth a note in my calendar!* Like a spring, he jumped up the stairs again, through the back door and into the hospital, running back to the room where Giles was dealing with EA1456. He stood opposite Giles, who was sweating, struggling to clean wounds on EA1456's chest. One look at Andrew's flushed face was enough for him to understand what his friend had been up to while he was working his ass off to save the patient. "Fuck you mate, that's not fair!"

Gaia wasn't feeling better. Whereas she liked kissing Andrew, the kiss had reminded her of the bitterness of her relationship with Marco. It was him, more than the kids, who stood in the way of the things she enjoyed: life, love, nature, everything buried under the wreckage of her marriage. The internal turmoil made her speed out of town, turning left at the junction for Queen's Road, making it just in time before the traffic lights turned red. She nearly took a second orange light and she quickly moved beyond the relatively small town-centre, southbound.

While waiting at the lights, she activated the satellite navigator, choosing her parents' address. The machine calculated her route … "At the roundabout take the second exit," it commanded. "Ooh, perhaps we'll find an ice-cream truck there," she offered the kids, remembering her bribe. "Mmm, ice-cream." The kids giggled at her Homer Simpson impression. Her heart filled with love for them, *they* made her feel better. She thought that whatever happened, no one would ever separate her from her children. *Not even in prison, they take away your kids…* She made a note to call Marco once she reached a straight stretch.

Just after the underpass of the M11, she glanced at the chip in the container. She was going to get it ready for it to be flung out of the window. She checked the rear view mirror to ensure there was enough distance from the cars behind, as she really didn't want to hurt anyone. Then she got a real shock: she was being followed fairly closely by at least three matching black sedan cars. Panicking, she attended the rear mirror a fraction too long, and when she flicked her eyes forward again, she had already invaded the opposite lane of the single carriageway. An oncoming truck was flashing its headlights. Gaia impulsively steered away from it, but her snatch at the wheel was too fast for the car to maintain its grip on the asphalt. She lost control of the vehicle: it swung sideways, doing a full circle and knocking down a lamp post, before overturning twice off the road, ending about 50 metres beyond the safety barrier.

The car had been hit on every side. Windows had exploded and part of the roof was ripped off. Gaia's last thought was for her children. The last noise she heard was her phone announcing a text from Janet.

The last image in her mind was Marco shaking his head at her. And then the drapes were pulled.

In her dying slumber, she dreamt she had avoided the collision and managed to save her innocent children; her three virtuous little angels, unaccustomed to the mean ways of the world. She saw herself giving birth again, three small fish swimming out of her body with tiny fins. She saw them breastfeeding like puppies, lying across her breasts, sleeping, cuddled on the masculine chest of their father. She never saw them crushing in the rubble of the spinning car. In the end, Gaia was killed by the pain of having inflicted harm on her cherubs. The broken wreck of her car was nothing compared with the thought of having to leave them in the world, alone, without her, so young, so unprotected, so beautiful.

Part III

3.0 – June 16th

After a quick meeting with the new chief of security installed by Bill, Janet spent some time talking with her key staff at the lab in small groups, casually formed around what had become an emergency camp. The people she had ferried from the general research program onto the development of the Killer App were now scattered around the canteen and the main meeting room, wearing wrinkled clothes, unwashed. They had been the chosen ones. Now they were the unwanted witnesses. Involved in a security breach for which they were being detained in the labs, dispossessed of their rights by order from central command.

The general mood was pretty low, with pockets of disappointment and anger. They were feeling irrelevant, subjugated by political forces outside the labs who considered them nothing, far removed from the time when they had been at the centre of decision-making for the greatest experiment of all times. Somehow they had fucked it up big time that afternoon, losing the adept to a couple of young campaigners. The staff were not cool about the loss of freedom, but as much as they bitched and moaned, they needed to be reminded that they had signed the red Employee Book, of which section 9.3 read: *Detention clause – allows the confinement and temporary stripping of rights to anyone who in part, or substantially, supported the leaking of confidential information about The Experiment, until the threat caused by such action is halted.*

Nevertheless, Janet had to deal with a procession of people pleading to be exempted from the policy on grounds of important personal engagements, sickness, inadequacy of the labs to accommodate people and so on. She repeated the same refrain to everyone: that she had criticised the clause at the time it was being imposed by the legal department, and that she had tried to negotiate it against money and benefits, because she "didn't expect them to fuck everything up with a party during working hours – a bloody unsound assumption that was."

So, they "had to stay put in the labs as long as it was necessary to clean up their shit," as she had rephrased it through various meetings that evening, then again, in a general assembly held at 22.00, and finally over the intercom just before midnight.

Another sticky issue had been the restriction of the staff's mobile phones, email and Internet accounts. Everyone complained about that, expressing perhaps more frustration about the loss of communication with the outside world than the prohibition on going home. Some had begged Janet to use her phone, which was still working, but she had denied it. When everyone finally gave up and started preparing for the night, Janet was exhausted. She was also expecting everyone to wake up in an even more hostile mood and didn't look forward to more conflict in the morning. *They'd better be able to leave tomorrow…*

With the labs quietening down, she asked the security chief for a last update on the process of recovering the adept. His answer was short: EA1456 was transmitting a good GPS signal and would be recaptured anytime soon... Nothing she could trust or believe, quite the contrary, Janet found him just another ass-licking lieutenant withholding information from her. *This was her damn project, she shouldn't be kept in the dark!*

After one more attempt to call both Gaia and Bill, she decided to call Robert's PA, pleading for her call to be returned. She knowingly breached the security protocol, soliciting the PA to make sure that everyone dealing with her sister and the children did so with extra care. She had done the same all evening with the new security chief, annoying him with endless requests to relay the need for care to the team in the field, with the result that security was now hiding from her. Annoyingly, she had had to wait in front of their temporary office to receive first hand news on the capture.

Since the afternoon, she had refrained from calling her parents, to avoid giving them unnecessary grief, repeating to herself that it would be kinder to wait for confirmation that Gaia and the kids were alright before phoning home. It had crossed her mind to call Marco, but she was warier about him, there was no sentiment of trust or friendship between the two. Above all, now that everything had to be kept TOP SECRET, she used it as a handy excuse to postpone talking with the *bastard*.

Deep down, she blamed Marco for Gaia's reckless behaviour, him and his arrogance, his lack of responsibility, his pothead ways and the complete lack of consideration for Gaia and the kids.

Feeling the weight of the day pressing on her temples, she dimmed the lights and frosted the glass walls around her office. Soon, the arms of Morpheus came to pet her. Fighting the need to sleep, she looked at her phone one more time: *23:59, no new messages.*

She fell into deep sleep, which was permeated by a terrifying and disturbing dream: she was running barefoot on hot concrete slabs, covered with debris, glass, screws and nails. She was being chased by a storm of black ravens flying low over her, closing down, blinding sunshine all around. On the edge of falling and getting caught by the terrifying birds, she sprinted until she finally ran out of air.

Her phone buzzed at 3.47 a.m., giving her a shock that made her jump out of her chair. Numb from the awkward position she had slept in, she looked at the message which popped-up on the screen of her handset, *There in 10, B.*

Partly relieved that Bill was finally making contact, she noticed that Bill did not even attempt to reassure her that everything was well. It was disquieting. The place was completely still, everyone seemed to have finally given in to sleep. She felt uneasy about seeing Bill, who suddenly appeared in her office without escort or introduction, restating, if necessary, his total grip of authority over the laboratories. He was wearing a black high neck jumper, under a long black coat, looking particularly bewitched, unhinged, and moving like a warrior. He nodded without greeting her, expecting her to start talking.

"Is your news so bad that you're holding back, where is he and how's my sister?"

"Your sister had an accident, the children are ok."

"What? An accident? What happened?" she walked closer to him in disbelief.

"A car accident. It happened after Gaia and Andrew had hidden EA1456 in a hospital and removed the locator chip from his neck. Your sister was driving the car, with the chip, when she had an accident, outside Cambridge. Totally unrelated to us. As I said, the kids are ok."

"You're gonna pay for this!" she screamed moving towards him. "What do you mean, they are ok, how's Gaia?"

She threatened to attack him so he held her forearms. "Hold on Janet, let's talk this through and I'll take you to the children."

Janet sensed that he hadn't answered her question completely. He was referring to the kids in the present tense, not Gaia.

"I need to see Gaia, take me to her!" she shouted, starting to feel a vacuum in her stomach, which matched the emptiness of his lack of an answer. Her knees buckled under Bill's reluctance to deliver the bad news.

He was uneasy himself, stuck on a line he didn't want to deliver. "Janet, Gaia is dead."

A long pause followed. Janet was struck by the atrociousness of the news. After a while, she spoke the words as they passed through her brain, unfiltered. "You have killed my sister, and you're getting us all killed." She was sobbing now, "I want to see the children."

He had anticipated she might lose her mind, though he resented her comment. "Janet, I had nothing to do with Gaia's death. Your sister got involved in this by her own volition, for God knows what reasons, and she was killed by her own driving. I take no responsibility in this."

"Take me to the children," she sounded like a record stuck on a wail.

"I will, shortly. Just remember the magnitude of what just happened to the experiment—"

"Fuck the experiment! Take me to the children," she screamed.

"First tell me one thing: do you have *any* idea why Gaia and Andrew did this? Kidnapping *our* patient from *your* laboratories? It's all too weird, those two of all people."

She wasn't engaging, "Bill this is over, we don't have to find any explanation," empty eyes staring in front of her, "my sister is dead, there's nothing to understand." She continued crying.

He waited a moment. "Janet, you know the experiment is covered by secrecy acts – the involvement of any person outside our circle puts a lot of other people under threat. We ought to—"

"Is this all you can think of?" She rebuffed him, screaming, "Is this all the sympathy you have to offer?" Holding her face in her hands she sobbed, "You've taken over my work and my family and destroyed it all…"

She had lost the endowment of reason, while Bill was thinking that if anyone had the right to feel pissed off about the events of the day, it would have to be him. He wasn't used to failure. He had put every effort into making the experiment work, despite all odds, only to see it compromised by his associates' family members.

"This is no time for phoney rhetoric, for regretting our decision to start, our intentions were good and *mine* still are. This tragic turn of events, your sister getting killed, is only because of her own foolishness, and Andrew's. The future is still firmly in our hands. We've recovered EA1456 and the newborn is still in our custody."

Janet couldn't believe it, the man was a cold-blooded, steel-coated monster. Images of the beginning of her partnership with Bill were flashing through her head, memories of past admiration, a faint recall struggling now to reconnect with the parts in her that had liked him – her previous appreciation offset by the misery he had brought to her life. "It's all about you and your project, I hear you, even after my sister has died. What have you done to the children? I want to see them now!" every sentence ending in a reverberating screech.

"Calm down Janet, they are in a clinic in London, being treated for minor injuries."

Janet reflected for a moment, turning to weeping again. "Who's with them now that their mother is dead? Take me there now, I beg you."

"I said I will." A harsh tone appeared on the surface of Bill's voice, betraying his annoyance at Janet's behaviour. He missed Janet the scientist, the logical computer programmer, the terrific manager; he really couldn't help feeling sorry for himself, hard done by.

He couldn't wait to get back to business as usual. The way he saw it, the situation was bad enough, with or without Gaia's death. The tipping point had been surpassed with the security breach, leading to the abduction of EA1456. *She's missing the fucking point,* he thought. They had lost contact with the testament of their wrongdoings, the living witness and physical evidence to an experiment that necessitated secrecy, before it could be shown in all its glory.

Bill himself had pushed Robert to keep security under his own control rather than involving many layers of government, *it would be best for confidentiality.* But now it had gone completely wrong, he had failed to account for errant family members infiltrating the labs withdrawing the adept. The problem with him was that he didn't know about family dynamics, those inner social interactions weren't his strength. His inability to understand love, this shady area of life, was striking back at him, hard.

Janet was too bitter and heartbroken to let any friction go. "What are you thinking? Can't you see that the experiment has caused one death already, and injured three innocent children? They've lost their mum, that can't be changed. Your reputation can't be saved either, not even if you spend your last penny trying, it's over."

"Shut up, Janet!"

"I'll shut up the moment you stop thinking how you can cover it all up. You have ruined people's lives. You have to make good. Shift your attention on getting the children and Andrew home safely."

The tension in the room was high. Like seasoned tennis players, they were sending the ball into the other's half, without accommodating for the other's position. The dam of Bill's patience broke first, stung by Janet losing whatever focus she had previously held.

He needed any possible clue. He was hot from recapturing EA1456, he had just avoided the adept appearing as guest of honour on the morning news. Still, he had plenty of things to straighten up, arms to twist, favours to ask. He wasn't interested in any children or family mourning, so long as they did not spill into the public domain. Steering the experiment into a positive direction again, that interested him tremendously and it required him to swear, contract, assure, warrant and plead. And a lot it, all before noon. His lawyers were already slicing and dicing any potential direct responsibility of the BIG. Police, security personnel, media, every potential source of information leakage was being silenced as grass leaves under deep snow.

Which is why he was so vexed at Janet: "Stop pointing your finger at me, this mess is the result of your actions, not mine! When did you tell Gaia about the experiment?"

She didn't answer, thinking about her mother and father, staring at the floor with a vacant expression.

"When the hell did you break the confidentiality of the experiment!" he demanded, raising his voice at her for the first time.

Janet perceived Bill's shift to threatening mode. In her head, she remembered playing with Gaia: Janet dressing her baby sister up like a doll, a thousand hair clips, suddenly it wasn't Gaia anymore, she was dressing up Sophia. *I need to save the children they're innocent...*

She looked at Bill, restraining the impulse to scratch his face off, feeling her head turning into a paper lantern, her breathing shortening. She withheld all the answers she could have given in accordance with his tone, feeling it wasn't the time to retaliate. She swallowed her desire for revenge, yielding a split second of strategic thinking: one, she was being kept captive in her own lab; two, Bill had taken the lead over her and Robert; three, it was a dangerous position in which to be; four, she had to tread carefully, abandoning her confrontational ways.

Remitting her deeds of vengeance to the future, she inhaled deeply before uttering a reassurance. "I'll cooperate." She was speaking in a low submissive tone. "Believe me when I say it – I have no idea how Gaia got involved in this and, least of all, why Andrew is also a part of it."

It seemed Bill wanted more. "I haven't spilled the beans. It must have leaked over those half conversations, the times we were all together."

"Damn Robert and his fixation for playing happy families," he sneered, "keeping up the relationships that count. Bullshit!" He was shaking his head in disapproval, "and I was the one being pointed at as being paranoid... See how those meetings of minds have repaid us?"

"He did it for Andrew. Imagine what it must have been like for that poor child to lose his mother to the bottom of the Atlantic Ocean in the plane accident." She sounded defeated, knowing he wouldn't understand.

He silenced her with one straight look. "Yet, they must have been given some pretty key information from either you or Robert, or both. Otherwise, no chance they would have managed to come here and succeed." He remained immune to the intricacy of family relationships, he was shielded from the entanglements procured by kinship. "Their success can't be explained in any other way. Somehow, either you or Robert must have leaked some information." Their success was his failure, "while I was preventing foreign secret services from accessing it; this was beyond my fucking imagination."

He really didn't care about anything other than the experiment, trying to seal a cocoon around it to protect his Killer App. All he wanted was to get out of the storm dry. Janet realised there wasn't much she could possibly do, other than reinstating the maximum safe distance between herself and what she deemed was a dangerous connection.

"I will ask for the last time, is there anything you told your sister and that fucking junior."

She conceded, unable to contain her tears. "I remember telling Gaia that you had found an application for my technology… and that there was a possibility, a way to be born again into a new person. Nothing else than that."

"Nothing else, huh? And she didn't take it very well, that Ayurvedic sister of yours, I'm sure? Even I know your sister better than you. Still, you come here bullshitting me about family."

"It was after we had just met in Davos, not a word thereafter. She was very interested in you," sobbing took over her, "she thought I should be flattered of your interest in my work. Somehow, she pushed me into your arms."

He was furious, "Bullshit! Did you also tell her about Robert? Fucking unbelievable, talking to that Hare Krishna rioter, as if she was a grown-up… what kind of reaction were you expecting from her? Not your finest hour Janet…"

Unable to hold her rage inside longer, she yelled louder than him. "What the hell do you know about talking to a sibling? Of connecting and sharing feelings? You and your pitiful life, packed with your carnivorous ego."

He waved his arm, "Leave it, Janet, you are—"

"No, you stop there! I tell you what you are: a ruthless asshole, a relentless, antagonistic bastard who thinks of himself as the centre of the universe." She was crying her heart out. "Just look at how you're treating me in the face of my sister's death."

He remained unshaken. He spoke as if he was addressing his annual shareholder meeting, insanely disconnected, distantly cold.

"Everything there is to know about family, I've tried before you. Anything you can possibly suffer, I've endured it already. Other than creating this technology, you've proven yourself to be an embarrassing little stain of a woman. You've got nothing to teach me about having and losing family. I've agonised in the most excruciating ways, through rejection and disdain. But I have resurrected to myself and I'm not going to listen to any shit coming out of your little sewer mouth. My mistake was paying attention to you in the first place."

That last sentence dealt her a fatal blow; Janet was overrun by shame. She felt as if she had let everyone down, foregoing her human feelings in the name of science. She was guilty of focusing on bio-genetics more than her own flesh and blood, and had failed to listen to Gaia, when she had pointed out that making people die to be reborn was the ultimate creationist lunacy. She despised herself for having caused the death of her sister, bringing grief into her own family. She felt broken at an inner level. Remorse descended upon her soul, regret stormed her mind, defeat permeated her posture. Bill had managed to break her, turning the tables in less than 100 words. She sat back in her chair, tears flooding her closed eyes. "You only ever liked your own reflection in me, Bill. And you're disappointed because you haven't been able to realise that it was just a shade, a fibre in a more complicated personality.

"But this isn't time to stab each other to death. I'll bear dealing with you a little longer and try to get to the other side of this incredible mess. I know what you want, you've made yourself clear. I will comply." She rubbed her face with the palms of her hands, drying her tears, trying to pull herself together.

He gave her a chilly look. "Let's go to the children now," he said as he started to walk out of the room. On the way to the clinic, Bill hinted that they were investigating Andrew's network of connections in Cambridge.

3.1 – June 17th

Andrew woke up in a security room. The air was stale, there were no windows, just a dirty sink with a dripping tap. Trying to clear his head, he cricked his neck and looked around, attempting to understand where he was. It felt as though he had laid forever on that thick beige blanket with three white stripes at each end, spread over a concrete raised-step that served as a bed.

When he tried to move, he felt nauseous. Struggling for some time, he eventually managed to sit up, his head hanging below his shoulders, his arms supporting the weight of his upper body. He remained in that position, striving to recollect what had happened to him.

The moments before losing consciousness were not clear memories. At first he could only remember the red laser lights appearing in the room, like a rave party. Then, there was Giles' puzzled face looking at him, questioning, *what the fuck is going on in here?* He also remembered seeing the life-sized copy of Jace Stratton, the warfare video-game character: black battle outfit, bullet-proof vest, assault rifle and so on.

He saw again the smoking-can, the black tub they threw on the floor, which exploded in a hiss of thick gas quickly filling the room, like a thousand chopped onions being rubbed into his eyes. Not a voice, not a sign of what was going on, except when he hit the floor, struggling to discern whether it was police irrupting the room, or terrorists hijacking the town. That bad taste was still in his mouth, confirming the sense of hallucination he felt in his head and throughout his body. His eyes, neck and legs still sore, heavy and stoned, dragging down his determination to stay awake. His psychophysical conditions threatened his attempts to make sense of what had happened, even before remembering about Gaia and the kidnap.

Finally, he had a flashback of himself running through the corridors of the Oxford Genetic Laboratories, pushing a hospital bed, with a corpse on, holding a bedside patient monitor. *What the fuck did I hope to achieve?* Fighting an inner feeling of complete helplessness, he stood up, trying to maintain his balance. He walked three steps to the thick stainless steel door, faintly knocking at it. No answer came through, just the clear sound of empty corridors. He knocked again, too hard for his nausea, which meant he had to step back, sitting on the edge of the stone pallet.

Nothing happened for five minutes or so, then the small window pane at the top of the door opened, revealing a girl in her twenties with a rugged face and short hair. She was wearing a dark green jersey.

"You're all right luvvie? Cup of tea?" she spoke with an Irish accent.

"I'm feeling sick, can you please help?"

"What's wrong, sweetie? Do you want me to call the doctors?" speaking cheekily, she sounded as if she was making fun of him.

Not feeling strong enough to stand the conversation, he cut it short. "I've just got nausea, I feel like throwing-up, may I have something?"

"It's just the gas darling," her vowels seeming infinite, "but I'll call you the doctor anyway, he'll see you're alright." She shut the door panel, leaving darkness and silence behind. Andrew laid his head down again, thinking about what kind of place he was being held in: *police, army, prison, perhaps he was back at those spooky labs?* Although he had tried, he couldn't identify the uniform of the girl. All he knew was that she looked bossy and cocky. *Where does the Prime Minister's son go when arrested?*

All that mattered to him was lying flat on his back again. He could only imagine his father's face at learning the news: his aide, interrupting his endless meetings whispering, *Sir, we have an issue… your son, something big. If you don't mind, MI5 would like a quick word with you?*

Picturing that scene unfolding induced the vomit. Suddenly, his right hand was blocking his mouth as he stepped to the sink to throw up. With his head hanging, he sneered at himself, *what a shock I must have given him.* He was not looking forward to meeting his dad anytime soon.

Unable to expel anything else, sticky spit hanging from his mouth, not feeling or making any effort to look any better, he groaned as he lay on his back again.

Off in a trance, Andrew was woken by the door lock turning three times. *Doctor or girl? Gotta make an effort to understand the uniform.* He lifted his head, slightly tilting to stare at the opening door. The single bulb on the ceiling lit up, disturbing his gaze towards the door

– but not as much as realising it was his father walking in and no service personnel.

Having the effect of immediately cleansing his grogginess, rushing awareness through his body, Andrew managed to mostly pull himself together. It was with fright and guilt in equal measures that he looked into his father's face. For his side, Robert appeared far more gloomy and preoccupied than angry, as Andrew had expected. One glance at his father's tall figure was enough to make him feel like a damned convict.

Robert was waiting for the door to be shut behind him. "Andrew," he said, kneeling on the side of the concrete slab. He hugged his hangdog-looking boy, squeezing him in his arms, willing to feel his son was in one piece.

Andrew's eyes quickly filled with tears, as the scent of the sole caregiver he had known all of his life filled his nostrils.

Robert sat himself right in front of his son. "How are you, mate?"

A nod was the best Andrew could manage.

"You're feeling ok?"

Andrew was still unable to find answers.

"Why did you do all that… What did you think you'd achieve?"

"That silly experiment of yours…"

Robert furtively looked around to see if anyone was listening. "Look what you've done to yourself and—"

"We've both proved pretty evil, lately."

"But why didn't you talk to me first?" Robert was whispering.

"I'm not a member of your cabinet, Dad, since when do you concede attention on political issues?"

Robert looked up to the ceiling for a moment. "I'm sorry, I didn't know you felt so strongly about this."

Andrew struggled to believe his father was acknowledging him.

"Andrew, this situation, it has created some serious problems for a lot of people…Lots of suffering, trust me."

This sparked an unidentified doubt in Andrew's head, shifting the attention away from himself at once. He perceived that something bigger had happened out there.

"How are Gaia and Giles?"

Although Robert had thoroughly prepared for this question, he felt all his preparation disappear. He was required to give a straight answer, there and then, it was inevitable – there was no obliterating or camouflaging, no place to hide, not for long.

"Giles is recovering, like you he is detained, somewhere else. He has suffered some minor injuries."

The description of Giles' situation confirmed to Andrew that Gaia was the real issue. That she was left unspoken meant her condition had to be worse than Giles'.

"What about Gaia, then?" he asked tentatively.

"Andrew, Gaia… went through a pretty bad car accident. The children are alive… but, she didn't make it."

A meteorite fell upon Andrew, crushing him under the weight of the unimaginable. He suddenly felt the utmost shock, disbelief and rage possessing him. Starting in his stomach, expanding to his head like a fireball. He stood up with a tortured face and screamed, louder than he had ever screamed before, wanting Gaia to hear that he was there for her, that they were together still. Though only a faint cry came out of his mouth, his blood pressure was close to non-existent and pushed him back to the flat concrete surface. He had fainted.

"Are you both all right, sir?" asked a voice through the door pane.

Robert was straightening Andrew's body. "He's fine, but perhaps you could help bring him round?"

The guard rushed in, going straight for Andrew's legs, raising his feet to increase blood circulation to his head. A few minutes later, Andrew was opening his eyes, turning his head slowly, looking for his dad's face, locking eyes with his father – a meaningful exchange of glances.

Robert felt he owed explanations – suddenly, he was the defendant in relation to what happened to Gaia, according to Andrew, it had to be someone associated with his father.

Sensing a difficult conversation ahead, Robert nodded to release the guard. Once alone, he told Andrew what had happened. "She was leaving Cambridge in her car, with the kids. I have been told that something probably distracted her, anyway, she swerved onto the opposite carriageway before losing control of the car. There was no contact with any other vehicles, though it was a fairly ugly accident."

Andrew didn't look convinced, tears fell copiously from the corners of his eyes, dispersing in his fair hair.

"Thank God you weren't in that car too." Robert didn't think of asking Andrew when they had separated, or anything else for that matter.

Aware of his father's scrutinising stare, Andrew curled up on his side, turning his back to Robert and facing the wall. Assuming such a foetal position reminded Robert how close Andrew had been to getting himself killed in the dangerous spiral of events spurred by his attempt to stop the experiment. He could have been in that wreckage with Gaia, or even worse, accidentally shot by one of the animals recovering EA1456; the same fate as had happened to Giles, *what a fucking nightmare.*

He spoke softly, asking Andrew how he hadn't better considered the consequences of his own actions. "Still, notwithstanding your young age, how did you fail to recognise that kidnapping EA1456 was bound to play havoc with your life, your family and friends?"

Receiving no reply, Robert ventured further. "What happened to you recently, what's the root of all this… I don't understand?"

At the beginning, he struggled with his own emotions, "Every woman I love, ends life with an accident, and leaves me mourning." He paused overcome by sobbing.

Robert understood – Andrew's mother and the aeroplane accident which had taken her over fifteen years earlier. Somehow Andrew connected it to Gaia. He was caressing his son's hair, "Did you love her? Is that what made you lose your head? You lemon… When did it all start?"

"April—"

Robert didn't need more details, "My reception party, right?" He remembered winking at him in relation to Gaia animatedly gesturing as a part of a conversation the two were having away from the main group.

"Yes," Andrew continued, filling in the silence left by Robert. "Since then, we've spoken every single day, she told me she had found out something weird about you and Janet. We started, phoning each other, meeting in cafés, parks and playgrounds, travelling miles not to be seen together... I was her friend, she needed it terribly. I didn't know she loved me, until...she left the hospital that day. We kissed, for the first and the last time." His voice trailed off and he was weeping again.

Robert felt like sobbing himself, moved, sharing his son's pain. He was witnessing just the kind of future he wanted to avoid for his son. The one that closely resembled his, losing his much-loved wife Linda in the Air France 447 flight crash of 2009, just three years after giving birth to Andrew.

"Andrew, my boy, it's ok, you loved her... but it was a cursed idea to get involved with my work. I'd never imagined in a million years that pulling you into my orbit could have such a devastating effect. I wanted you close, after all the day-care and boarding schools, I felt I was losing you for good at Cambridge."

Andrew replied in a faint cry. "I didn't like what I saw, Dad. I had you marked down as a different sort of politician. It was Gaia who opened my eyes. She worked out that you were planning to exploit people's worst fears from a conversation with Janet. We wanted to find more information, so I entered your study one night. You were asleep on the sofa. And that's when I saw it. You had fallen foul to the most wicked baseness."

Robert was petrified by the replay of his own behaviour.

Andrew concluded, "You should have known better."

"Andrew—"

"No wait, don't take it out on Gaia. She opened my eyes and I'll love her forever for it… She found out that we were the only two people who knew what you were working on with Janet. She suggested that we acted quickly to stop your evil experiment." He buried his face in his hands.

"Andrew, if you could consider the nature of power, and how it requires you to steer the vast majority of people through uncharted waters, then my decision would not seem so incompatible to you, but laid out for at the wellbeing of all."

It was hard for Robert to abandon his politics, saying, "No one ever immediately grasps the complexity of the choices of the political leader, his actions… If you knew how serious the crisis is… well, I myself found it challenging to appreciate what a disastrous office I was taking on." Robert was monologuing, trying to convince himself as well as Andrew, about his righteous doings, rambling and jumping around in his own thoughts. "So I responded with bold actions, Andrew. Gaia was a pretty girl, but I think she acted out of foolishness, because she didn't have a clue."

"You could have done a thousand different things with your power."

"And I have, you haven't seen them probably because you were blinded by the views of your friend. But I've undertaken a lot in my short time in government, Andrew. The Killer App is just one campaign… An experiment, to try and dig ourselves—"

"Campaigns?" sneered Andrew, "that's a ridiculous a name for mass genetic manipulation."

"Well, what would you call it, then?"

"Game Over."

"You know, Andrew, the game changes itself all the time, and we're only given a slim chance of adapting to it. I've sacrificed the smallest price in the name of survival for our country. A single oddball, who willingly signed to undergo genetic manipulation for his own gain."

"So he's the scumbag now?"

"Hold your tongue, Andrew; don't talk to me like that." Robert raised his voice slightly for the first time, while standing up, then he seemed to calm. "I've had my share of doubts about it, but I looked into the facts and I trusted two great minds. I never expected you to mess it all up."

He paused and took a long deep breath, he was walking back and forth the short length of the security room. Then he spoke again in a more conciliatory tone, "You ought to stay here while we normalise the situation. We need to patch things up out there."

"Am I going to be prosecuted?"

"God no, don't you worry about that – I can't afford it. Even if yes, you should be, big time, interfering with state affairs, I should have you electrocuted."

"When do you think that I'll be able to leave?"

"Not just yet. I need to trust you again before I can see you released. What you did was a proper disaster, really damaging for one."

"Worse than Gaia getting killed?"

Robert sighed. "I don't expect you to understand that, but you're pushing it."

"Will you please allow me to be at Gaia's funeral?"

"Not in a million years."

Andrew felt the urge to cry again, but was able to suppress it. They were both silent for a while, before he asked what had happened to the patient they had tried to save.

"He's back in the hands of the doctors," Robert lied, as he had not understood why Bill had insisted on keeping him alive in a hidden location for the time being.

"Doctors? Butchers you mean? Don't forget I've seen him. Have you?" said Andrew scornfully.

Andrew knew that Gaia would have fought that battle hard. He wanted to emulate her, to keep going for her, even though it was his father he was battling.

"Don't go there, Andrew." Robert ground his teeth. "The guy applied to take part in the experiment," Robert pointed at the door as if EA1456 was just outside. "We tested and retested his motivations: his desire to die was stronger than his ability to bear his miserable life..." Relaxing slightly remembering a late night chat he had had with Janet once, "Imagine that they wanted to replace him at one point, and he clung teeth and nails to the job."

"Perhaps he had nothing better to go back to."

"Exactly. He didn't want to go back to being a hopeless psychopath."

Andrew's strength to take on his father was diminished by a new bout of nausea. He forced out a last, feeble statement: "I suppose there's no room for the eccentrics in your new order?" He only sounded half convinced. Gaia wasn't there anymore after all. She was the one worth fighting for, no one else, *not EA1456 and all the other losers they'll recruit.*

Perhaps the whole nonsense didn't deserve more duelling with his father. Nothing actually did, now that the best person he had ever met in his life was gone. Wit, tenderness, beauty... wasted for good.

Robert didn't pick up on Andrew's last comment, he was happy that his son was behaving childishly – it made him feel like a father again. When he realised that Andrew was falling victim to his own ideals, he thought about leaving the room on good terms. He was hoping his son would be able to deal with his long detention – obviously, he was sad to see his son held in a prison, but at the same time, he genuinely thought that was the safest place to keep the boy for a while. He cherished being able to shield his only son, protecting him from the messy state of affairs connected with the death of Gaia, the traces of the chase carried out by Bill's security forces, and the disappearance of Giles.

"You will like it in here, Andrew. Think about it this way: you are here for your own protection. Yes, it's a punishment, but most of all, it's a way of preserving you. And when times are better, we shall be waiting for you at home."

"I don't live at home any more, Dad; I want to go back to Cambridge."

"You know what I mean, I'll make sure they look after you. I'll visit you again soon."

Andrew waited before talking again to Robert. Without turning, staring where the stained wall met the dirty mattress, he said, "Only a prisoner can understand another prisoner – you're being held hostage more than I am, by the same people you think you're ruling."

A hollow silence followed. After a while, Andrew turned to look at his father. Robert stood motionless, ruminating over the sharp, cruel words, still reeling from things he hadn't expected to hear from his son. For a split moment, he thought Andrew had caught him, *wishing to govern the power... he is damn right.*

Robert wished he could be the one nesting in that small room, in a forgotten air base, giving up the crushing responsibility, the people to save, the others to condemn, the fights. Decision upon decision, deal after deal, sinking in the uncertainty of being wrong. Like Andrew, he had acted for love of a woman. Widowed by the aeroplane accident that took away his beloved Linda, he had put his entire being into politics, trying to soothe and overcome the emptiness of her loss.

That last thought prompted him to making sure Andrew wouldn't follow his example, fall in the same trap. He walked the two steps back towards the door and, before leaving, reassured Andrew that he would come back soon.

Andrew wasn't listening any longer, he had departed for a flight of his imagination, bound for Gaia, wherever she might be. He was dreaming of driving her car together in the English countryside, never to stop again.

3.2 – June 17th

No words were exchanged between Bill and Janet during the entire flight. She studied the lights on the ground, trying to work out, without success, where they were heading. He was absent-minded, chasing some thoughts of his own and not in the least disposed to talking with Janet.

Upon landing, there was the usual fast march away from the rotor noise and its wind, entering a building Janet was unable to decipher. Inside, Bill started to talk once again about security.

"I'll be waiting outside while you visit them, we need to debrief still, remember?"

Janet looked at him without interest, not registering his suggestion of work ahead. Whatever he said, he did nothing to assuage the mounting grief at the thought of seeing her sister's orphaned children.

"I need your help before though."

She looked at him from the corner of one eye, whilst scrutinising the corridor stretching out before them. The sound of another request from him made her recoil. All she wanted was to be taken to the children's unit, *can't he fucking get that,* she thought, studying the interior of the building which was starting to look like a private clinic.

She nodded, without answering, walking, imposing silence as her temporary victory over his despotism. She was digging for distance from him, from the experiment, thinking of how much time she had spent walking hospital tunnels, like now, their regular neon lights, the web of exposed pipes. Altogether, they comprised the landscapes she had inhabited for a lifetime. All the steps taken over the linoleum flooring, the medical career, sacrificing family time, love, even when the twins were born or she knew the marriage had soured, she hadn't found the time to be at Gaia's side.

Hospitals and family, the antipodes of her life, were now tragically reuniting.

Undaunted, Bill continued chasing Janet's mind, whispering. "There are two spheres of potentially dangerous people: those who knew about the Killer App before the kidnap, and those who became involved in connection with the accident. I'll be producing both lists now, while I wait for you to come out. Any inputs from your side?"

She nodded again, without answering, struggling to be pragmatic, composed.

"I'm also wondering whether the consequences for being on either list should be different, somehow," he continued.

The gently spoken threat woke Janet up. Suddenly Bill was a priority again, above the concern for how the kids were, though the anticipation of their pain was growing in her as she penetrated the belly of the clinic.

Bill was staring ahead, walking, waiting for her to speak.

"Gaia was the only person I talked to… she was made well aware that it was highly classified material."

"How about the Italian connection?"

She explained that she didn't know much about him, that he was *also* an ass. "I would so much prefer if we resumed talking after I've seen the children," she concluded.

Bill carelessly pressed on, "Yes, but it's not possible to hold off the subject of Marco…"

Janet sighed, saying nothing as she kept walking, following her instinct, like a truffle dog, hoping to find the children without delay. She noticed him slowing down, he had to have his agenda fulfilled after all, before the children and any emotions.

"If you don't think he knows, we bring him here and feel him out. You'll meet him in private and won't say a word about the experiment. Your job will be to understand how much he knows. I reckon he does. I won't appear, but I would like you videotaped."

Janet suddenly stopped and turned to look at him with surprise.

He misread her face, "What's up, can't you handle it?"

In reality, she was utterly disgusted at the cheap trick he was playing to have her filmed during the meeting.

She sheepishly nodded, looking at the glass door that had finally appeared in front of them. It read *Children's Ward*, just what she wanted. Janet rang the bell.

A *beep*, followed by a woman's voice made Janet realise she had no idea of how to introduce herself. Bill intervened, "We have three children in your care," and the door buzzed open. Janet put her hand on the door to push it open, to signal her departure to Bill.

"Don't call anyone else other than me when you're out of here. I want to see you straight after. I'll send for Mr. Ardelli…."

She moved away from him quickly, desperate to see the children as well as to relieve the anger he was causing her. She really detested him now; his business-minded ways, his lack of humanity, his self-centred ruthlessness, and complete disregard for anyone but himself…She wondered how she could have possibly liked him.

She noiselessly closed the door behind her, a smiling nurse appeared from the second door on the corridor, dressed in light blue. "Are you the children's aunt?" The nurse's positive beam pervaded Janet's soul immediately, "Yes, I am, how are they doing?"

"Come with me." Her smile filled Janet with hope that they weren't too bad after all, causing her eyes to spontaneously fill with tears, which she wiped away with the back of her hand while following the nurse. A few steps further, she entered the room with two cot beds attached to one wall, a large window opposite the door with a long sofa underneath. It looked as any other hospital room, just with coloured bed covers and children's pictures on the walls.

She entered the peaceful room, the nurse leaning on the door frame with her arms crossed, watching the unfolding scene. Sophia was awake, propped up in bed, one hand behind her head, an open red gown that exposed three medication patches on her little white upper body. Her other arm was connected to a drip, while another cable attached her to a cardiogram machine, providing visual representation of her pulsing heart. She was staring at Janet in silence, holding on to her thoughts inside. Janet smiled at her, temporarily diverting the stream of tears that were falling from her eyes.

Lucas asked in a drowsy voice, "Mummy?" He was kept close to his twin brother Matthew.

Janet could barely hold herself together. The boys were dressed in light-blue gowns, looking in overall better condition than Sophia. At first glance, Lucas only had a bruise on his forehead and a small cut on his lower lip. Janet couldn't examine him or Matthew further, without feeling uneasy about Sophia's stare – a steady, but firm glare, indirectly inquisitive, which made Janet feel there was nothing else left in the world except questions: *what happened, where's mummy, how's this possible, can't we go home?*

Sophia's gaze drew Janet to her. When she reached the side of her bed, the nurse walked into the room describing the clinical picture: "They arrived unconscious, with minor bodily injuries. We have stabilised their conditions, cleaned them of debris and sutured Sophia's wounds. She has three cuts on her stomach and chest caused by a piece of the car."

Janet listened, immobilised, in a state suspended between horror and astonishment.

"We ran all customary examinations and the results are fine," then she lowered her voice and came closer to address her again, "I think the twins aren't aware of the situation, but this one," indicating Sophia with a slight movement of her chin, "I reckon she knows it all."

Janet bent a little over Sophia in order to get closer, but the girl edged back in the opposite direction, avoiding her aunt's attempt to come near.

Putting up an exaggerated angry face made her look like a mini photocopy of Gaia, the same mixture of stubbornness, beauty and charm.

"Sophia, sweetheart it's Auntie Janet."

"I want Mummy."

"Darling, Mummy is not with us now, but I'm here for you... I'm—"

"I want my mummy!" Sophia spoke as though her aunt was her greatest enemy.

Janet's tears only increased in size and speed, just when she wanted them to stop flowing, to be more commanding, to be able to stem what she hadn't anticipated: a confronting Sophia, straight in her face, complicating the building of bridges, increasing the urgency of breaking the news to the little girl.

The nurse interceded, "Love, I'm just going to speak to your aunt to see if she understands me better." With a touch of Janet's elbow, tilting her head slightly, she signalled to Janet to leave.

"Would a tea help?" she asked once in the corridor, walking into the little kitchenette to boil the kettle.

Janet followed, set to patiently observe the ritual, wiping her face of the tears that had been falling since she had entered the ward.

"Milk?"

Janet nodded, the nurse talked with her hands busy over the infusion. "It's a tough situation. Under normal circumstances, there would be a counsellor available for you here to talk to, but on this occasion, someone has requested that we keep the contact to a minimum."

Bill's face appeared in Janet's mind, she mentally cursed him.

"But I'll try to assist you."

Janet realised the nurse was an agent assigned to the clinic. Also, they were the only patients in the ward, no other people were in sight. She guessed the place was a mausoleum of discretion, where only must-remain-secret accidents were treated with circumspection.

The woman looked extremely fit, with short blond hair and somewhat plain features portraying a professional image of justice, security and integrity.

"I have experience with this from previous cases, the effects on the children can be profound. And, I know you don't have children yourself."

Janet spoke to her for the first time, "Do you?"

"I'm not prepared to talk about my personal circumstance."

The answer left Janet unable to pick a fight. "What do you want me to do?"

"I suggest you focus on avoiding the psychological trauma that, if instigated, can affect their future view of the world. If you talk the grief out with them and give them the right tools from the start, the impact will be lessened."

While talking, she realised Janet herself was in a state of deep grief; she looked totally frozen. Quite understandable for someone who had just lost her little sister.

"Do you feel all right?"

Janet nodded faintly.

"You'll be fine, let's concentrate on what you are going to say to comfort them. I suggest you stick to an open formula that allows them to fill in the gaps."

"Like their mum is sleeping?"

"I propose you remember that eventually you'll converge towards the word *died*. Perhaps avoid mentioning that it was a tragic accident. They should think it was a necessary thing in keeping with the order of life."

Even though she noticed Janet's tears flowing again, the agent went on explaining how Janet should allow the children to express their feelings, as bad as they could be, allowing them to ask any sort of question, to be answered simply and honestly. She also described how they may draw back into their own world for sometime, trying to make sense of what happened. "In which case, it's good practice to provide them with something to hold on to, an item they love like a toy or a teddy." Janet trembled as in a shiver of cold or anger, feeling those techniques would be no help at all.

"Finally, if they physically shut down completely, crossing arms or turning backs, then it's important that you hand them something, keeping the communication flowing."

Janet's head had stopped listening, her quick thinking had run beyond what she was being told, identifying for herself what to do, ordering it into manageable tasks. She knew the dynamics of her brain would never fail her, clinging to her basic knowledge of life was her way of coming out of testing situations, like being completely out of her waters in the grief-parenting experience.

She asked the nurse whether they would still recall the details of the crash and if they would be afraid.

"When death is caused by a violent crime or accident, it's vital to explain to them that they're safe now. Position yourself as the person who'll make sure they stay so." She turned to pick something up.

Janet was thinking, *how can I even try to keep them safe when I'm not safe myself?*

The nurse handed her a leaflet titled: How Do You Tell A Child That A Loved One Has Died? "Have a look at this."

Janet looked at it with scepticism; it didn't make sense. *And how do you tell her sister?* Gaia had died, she was suffering like never before, though she was being asked to pull herself together, pretending to be unaffected, unscarred by the loss of her beloved sister. She could picture the expectation everyone had of her, shifting herself further away from Gaia, closer to the children.

The nurse drank her tea. Janet, who never shared the national fondness for it, observed her thin lips reaching for the mug. Her mind all over the place, wondering whether tea-making was part of the nurse role-play taught in a class, or genuinely enjoyed. Her thoughts strayed, thinking why a girl like her would choose to have such a job, in the service, if like Janet herself, something had constantly pushed her closer to strangers and forever distant from love and family relationships. For a moment, she thought of the agent as an acquaintance in a bar, picked up and kissed, without ever knowing any of her secrets.

She refocused on the leaflet, reading the paragraph headers scattered across four pages Don't Know How to Talk To Your Child, Easy Conversation Starters, Words That Can Hurt, Children Express Grief Differently From Adults.

The nurse took her cup and stood up. "If you don't have any further questions?" she said, taking her leave and walking to the adjacent room.

Sipping the strong tea, Janet heard the dazed and weak voice of a child calling, "Mummy." It was coming from the children's room; she panicked spilling half of the tea on her blouse. She recognised Matthew's voice, which surprised her; she didn't think she would be able to tell the twins' voices apart. She ran to respond to the child's call. She entered, Sophia's gaze was still there, in all its strength and pervasiveness. *That stare could cut diamonds,* Janet said to herself, making it to the twins' cots, crossing the room under Sophia's firm glare.

As soon as Matthew saw Janet approaching, he turned his head away moaning, giving her the cold shoulder. Janet remained puzzled and unresolved, between the boys' and Sophia's beds. She had to make up her mind quickly, to avoid the risk of losing whatever authority she hoped to acquire. Her preference was to turn to Sophia, adjusting a chair though, in a way that was close enough to Matthew, eventually seeking both their hands.

Like a quiet transition of stage in a dramatic play, they sat for a few moments looking at each other in silence.

Janet, thinking about the construction of her sentences, her imagination struggling to come up with anything positive, was suddenly interrupted by Sophia.

"Mummy is dead."

For Janet it felt like Sophia had picked up the words leaking out of her own head. *Mummy is dead, my sister is dead…*

"I saw mummy flying in the sky." Sophia seemed calmer than Janet, more controlled.

She pulled herself through the accident and Gaia's death... I must really get a grip here! She recomposed herself fighting the many tears flowing from her eyes.

"Everything is going to be all right Sophia, I'll be here with you now, always." The commotion of discovering Sophia's maturity effaced any chance of Janet thinking straight.

"Will I ever see Mummy again?"

That was a tough one, nothing she could have prepared for, studied or analysed. Six words demolishing her choice of spending life between a microscope and a computer screen. She was left wondering what library could give her the knowledge to deal with it, where to draw the intensity of feelings from that the moment required. "Honey, perhaps Mummy will come and kiss us goodnight once, when we are asleep and dream of her."

She wanted to make the boys take part in the cathartic conversation. "Mummy's gone to a far away world, because she knew we four would be close together. She'll be among us if we still want to be her family, and you Sophia, can be like mummy for your brothers, taking care of them, it will be cosy..." Sobs prevented her from continuing. She felt totally inadequate, Sophia and the boys unexpectedly strong, *what a fucking good job Gaia had done with her kids*. She could only hope that she would be half as good. Matthew was sniffling, perhaps in preparation of crying too. Sophia, cleverly sensing the situation, let her hand go so that Janet could adjust her position towards the boys. Janet was at centre-stage of the unfolding life-changing drama, the collar of her shirt soaking with tears.

"Is Mummy in the sky?" asked Matthew.

Lucas' lower lip was trembling. Janet wished she knew the formula for stemming children's tears before they started. She feared the consequences of all of them crying, but inevitably, it happened. Moments later, all four were weeping at the loss of Gaia, missing the cornerstone of their existence, the person of whom they wanted more.

They were also crying for the condition of being left alone, quite unsure of how to move on from there. A loud utterance of emotion: fear, anger and despair comprised the notes of their joint tears, which eventually abated into weeping, and from weeping into snivelling, before starting to reveal its healing properties. A release of emotional tension, after an overwhelming experience, that left everyone feeling that they were in it together.

The children curiously looked at Janet, who reassuringly held their gaze, this time, allowing everyone to feel that the tragedy was possibly revealing a new family assembly. The spirits started to feel faintly refreshed, temporarily supported by each other. The children, subconsciously feeding into Janet's desire for a life change, after the disastrous experiment fall-out. For the little ones, Janet's unconditional commitment, the person most resembling their mother, empathic, kind, willing to lighten their difficult steps ahead.

The nurse peeked into the room, immediately sensing the change of air among the puffy eyes and breathing spasms. She recoiled in the corridor, filling with hope that they would eventually be happy again.

Janet stood up and went to kiss the boys' foreheads first, and then Sophia's. She was aware that although they seemed to have touched the bottom and found a tentative balance, more lows than highs would definitely come their way, testing their bond, forging their new familiar love.

In Janet's mind, Gaia's position had shifted from missing sister to guiding angel, inspiring figure, providing strength and determination to give the children more than had been taken away from them. Feeling somewhat childish, she started picturing Gaia like a cherub, the small angel with a chubby rosy face she had been in her childhood, whom she had protected and whose children she would now continue to protect.

"I'll look after you, always" she said, caressing Lucas' high round forehead.

Lucas said in a quiet voice, "I want Daddy too," unfolding the next challenge for Janet, revolving around making sure that Marco wouldn't take the children away from her. Gaia wouldn't have wanted that, she was sure.

"Daddy's rushing here Lucas, I'm sure he's close to arriving any moment." She knew she would have to work hard on her relationship with Marco, to shield the children from any pain potentially arriving from that direction.

3.3 – June 17th

A doctor came in to introduce himself. Tall with prematurely grey hair, mainly on the sides, he had energetic eyes under thick eyebrows. Janet thought that everyone involved with the mission seemed to look like an Olympian somehow. He was followed by the nurse.

He spoke gently, often addressing the kids directly, *I'm Max*, asking how they were feeling, taking the time to explain their respective medical picture. Janet became an observer, feeling that it was inappropriate to mention that she was a doctor herself. She had lost her interest in affirming who she was, *if he's in the service, he knows already*, she thought, *otherwise who cares.*

He asked her whether she wanted to stay while he visited them. She nodded and moved to the sofa seat under the large window, further away. From there, she admired the doctor's gift with children, his talent for entertaining kids. She wished they had a father like him. She wondered what percentage of the man was doctor and what portion was agent, soldier or spy. *Tinker, tailor, soldier, spy...*

She pictured his superior scribbling notes over the CV: *good with children, despatch to unit dealing with innocent kids involved in crimes against the government.* Pending the doctor's lengthy examination, her thoughts reviewed the haunting events of the last three days, the messy situation in which she found herself. Unaware, the sweet doctor had become a mirror, reflecting it all to Janet, though he was just doing a trick with a drip tube, which made the kids laugh profusely.

But it failed to lift her spirits, as she had also studied medicine, but without enjoying the prescriptive, non-inquisitive part of the curriculum. She had always chased the development of solutions to human problems, but in the abstract. Everything else would have felt like just dispensing medicines. Sometimes, in her obsessive conspiracy nightmares, she was selected by an evil dictator, resembling Colonel Walter E. Kurtz. *The girl has a gift for genetics... Plunge her into an environment, without escape, and watch her grow obsessed with it...*

Perhaps, Bill himself had sniffed the business back in the days of her PhD in Computer Sciences. They had met during Janet's graduation ceremony, he had attended it in his capacity of sponsoring trustee of the academic association. She always thought herself smarter, but now she felt more like a puppet than anything else; framed into a killer application she couldn't control. Definitely a different career path from the doctor's.

He looked like the real winner, lifting real kid's spirits from despair, giving them health and hope. Nothing like her, slaughtering weirdoes, injecting their guts into innocent foetuses, newborns and mothers, potentially seeding destruction for the human race. *What a career progression? Leading to Sophia, Matthew and Lucas losing Gaia...*

She didn't feel forgiving with herself, thinking she should have amused herself better at Uni, putting aside her dreams of improving humanity, which now made her look too similar to Bill.

Like the doctor, she asked herself what it would have been like serving society, even government, as a surgeon, helping people, radiating tranquillity. The weight of her old ambitions made her sink into the sofa – *eradicating old age for everyone… What lunacy!*

All that was left now was to quickly reinvent herself as the replacement mother for the children, avoiding at any rate, them falling to the mercy of their selfish and immature father.

Speaking of the devil, there was his voice in the corridor. Janet heard Marco talking above the doctor's voice, he was arguing with a nurse, in stark contrast to the innocent giggling of the kids. She could discern him saying that it was outrageous to ask him to wait for the end of the doctor's visit. He sounded loud and challenging, ranting about having her fired, if not arrested, *good start* she thought, *if only he knew who he is really talking to…*

He made an entrance worth of Tybalt rescuing Lady Capulet.

"Sophia, Matthew, Lucas! Amori di Papà come state! Piccoli!!!"

The doctor turned his face to the nurse, offering a glance of reassurance. Then, without sounding surprised or annoyed he spoke gently.

"Children look, your dad is here," and to Marco, "Buongiorno signor padre." His thick English accent reminiscent of a Rosetta Stone beginner course.

Marco ignored him, feeling the children with his own hands as if independently assessing the state of their health. The doctor, amused by Marco's behaviour, offered him a second chance. "They're strong children, they're absolutely fine, apart from the bruising, we're monitoring that nothing is damaged inside."

Marco finally acknowledged him. "Thanks doctor, I was very worried for them, for everything that happened."

Janet had a privileged view of the room, from a sort of backstage, in the far corner.

She remained concealed, camouflaged within the sofa, watching Marco's fatherly performance, *will she have a scar here? Have the grand-parents been informed?*

When the doctor glanced at her, Marco instinctively followed his eyes and her presence in the room was revealed. He wasn't pleased to see Janet and he didn't attempt to hide it, his attention quickly recaptured by Sophia.

"Daddy the doctors are good here, but they haven't saved Mummy."

Marco, struck by his daughter's bluntness, as if he was discovering her true nature for the first time, answered: "sweetheart, Mummy is asleep, you will—"

"No daddy," Sophia interrupted him, "Auntie Janet told me she is dead in the sky and is only coming in my dreams, sometimes."

Marco looked at Janet with wide cursing eyes.

Then Lucas spoke, "Daddy, your car not broken?"

"No sweetie, Daddy's car is all right" he replied, still staring at Janet.

"Mommy's car broken, boom!" Matthew said, gesturing with his hands, simulating his take on crashing cars.

The doctor noticed the kids looked happy to have their surviving parent around, and receded towards Janet, knowing that Marco would not insist on him continuing the visit. He preferred watching Marco's clumsy attempt to steer the children's conversation to how they felt at the hospital, if they were hungry, promising pasta with meatballs as soon as they got home. The boys cheered to the news, not Sophia, "It's not fair, because Lili got crisps when she went to hospital." Marco promised crisps and more, profusely, he was lavishly describing what they would all do once they got home, *trust me...*

Janet realised he was planning to take them home, alone. Although foreseeable, it was still a shock for her. It reminded her of Bill's instructions to find out what Marco knew about the experiment.

She stood up, to walk closer to the others, smiling. The children and the doctor smiling back. Marco's first line wasn't friendly, "When are they coming?" evidently referring to Janet's parents.

She sensed Marco was worried about something, he either didn't like to have her around or it was something to do with the imminent arrival of the grandparents. Either way, he would have to endure them as a necessary evil, for the help they could provide now that he was a single parent.

Janet felt very uneasy at the thought of Marco parenting. He was irresponsible and in her opinion, he was a broadcaster of negative energy, even if the children didn't seem to mind, they would eventually be affected by it, sucked into the vortex of his inadequacy. But first of all, she needed to ascertain whether he knew anything about the experiment;

whether he deemed her responsible for the death of his wife, or was just being his usual unpleasant self.

The doctor asked the children if they wanted to finish the visit. Janet immediately took the opportunity to push through a gentle invitation for Marco to leave the room with her. Marco, not getting the message at all, felt that he had just arrived and wanted everyone to acknowledge he was in charge, hence he patronised the room, until the doctor, in perfect tandem with Janet, asked him directly, "If you want to stay while I finish checking them, do you mind moving to the sofa too?"

Janet could see that Marco was avoiding going outside with her, but refrained from a confrontation as she was fishing for his knowledge of the facts.

She addressed the issue indirectly, "Doctor, isn't it better if we go out and leave you in peace?" Before the doctor could answer, annoying Marco further, she added, "it would let the kids relax from the excitement of having us here, and you could finish much quicker."

The doctor confirmed her theory, it worked. Marco finally got the message. Looking at Janet he took his leave from stage. "Bambini, papà torna tra cinque minuti."

Once outside, his cross expression made Janet struggle to find the right angle to start the conversation. As it happened, he wasn't going to keep his tongue checked for long. "Jesus Christ Janet, your sister has really fucked it up big time."

"Is that how much you mourn her?"

"Ah, don't even start Janet, you know what I mean."

They were walking along the corridor leading outside.

His comment unsettled her, *how much does he know?*

She tried to push him to say more. "She just died in the most tragic circumstances, this isn't the time to feel sorry for yourself."

Marco recoiled, looking both offended and irritated. "You can't possibly be impartial, can you?"

"I mean, you ought to be more sympathetic and consider that everyone has been hit hard. Try to be more understanding and grown-up, Marco."

He immediately reacted to her rebuke. "No, Janet, *you* grow up and stop being a fucking lesbian. And don't ever lecture me again!" He was poking his index finger at her, getting angrier by the minute, but not mentioning the experiment, which for Janet was the thing that counted.

She looked uneasy when the nurse carrying a bunch of drip bags passed them. She raised her eyebrows to Marco signalling they should continue the conversation outside the ward.

Once out in the foyer, Janet tried to calm things down. "It was a dreadful accident, the only thing we can take from it is that the kids are still alive"

"I wouldn't exactly call that an accident, Janet."

Janet's heart missed a beat. "What do you mean?"

"Gaia went out looking for trouble, you know what that means."

Janet's body reacted with a sudden, but barely perceivable leap. "What on earth are you saying Marco? You must be in shock to say something like that?"

"I told you once already. Stop bullshitting me or you'll regret it! Your sister went around the country with her pubescent toy-boy. He couldn't win a fight against a paper bag, that scumbag."

He knew about Andrew, yet was probably oblivious of his full identity. "Are you jealous? You're awful Marco, daring to throw mud over Gaia's reputation, in a moment like—"

"Listen to you, the way you talk… Was it me driving young dates around the Home Counties? Was I the one speeding the children straight into a truck, almost killing them in the process? Tell me who's the fucking mud slinger here?"

"You lame bastard, all that stuff you sniff and drink has cooked your brain up," Janet snarled, through gritted teeth.

"So, this *is* about me and the bottle? Was that what killed your sister, huh? Was it me having a line on your kitchen table donkeys ago that brought the kids to hospital? Or was it that *she* was the mental case of our household, huh? Only a bitch like you can't see that it's her who in the fucking end killed herself and almost took the children to hell with her!"

Marco shouted, Janet could not think of an answer as fast as he was talking. "And who are you anyway to tell me off? Fucking behaving like the marriage inquisition? You, who would let a goldfish drown in its fishbowl…Have you ever heard of couples falling apart, huh? After one child perhaps? Well, miss I-fucking-know-it-all, we had three! Bloody twins too, for that matter! And your beloved sister? Screwed up, going bingo in her fucking pot head, long before… You could have noticed, if you weren't a self-obsessed workaholic bitch. Fucking nutcase you are…"

Janet fought back. "Could have been you in that car, had you ever bothered to take care of the children!" She was getting loud.

"But it wasn't, you stupid cow!" He was blasting out. "She, alone, landed me in this pile of shit, with three children and a fucking dumb sister-in-law!"

The nurse appeared, from behind the slamming door of the ward, flushed, looking outraged. "You two are acting disgracefully, what sort of behaviour is this!" They had missed the door buzzing, so loudly they were shouting. "Get a grip will ya? And deal with your anger, this is a children's ward after all, right?"

Her temper had an effect on Janet who felt truly ashamed that she'd been so uncivilised around the kids she aspired to educate.

"One more scream and I get you two kicked out!" the nurse concluded.

Janet nodded and looked sincerely ashamed. Marco, wanting no more lecturing, looked in the other direction, pretending she didn't exist.

As soon as the nurse was behind the large door again, Janet resumed the conversation, lowering her voice to a more civilised level. "Let's try not be an embarrassment for the children, ok?"

Marco still looked around, avoiding eye contact.

"What do you plan to do now? Those poor kids have had enough taste of hell," Janet said. "Do you agree that you can't cope with them alone?"

He looked at her briefly, his tensed body according her the slightest attention, without talking.

"You yourself have been flirting with the grave recently… Are you sure you need sole responsibility of three children on your shoulders now?"

"I am their father, they need me."

"Yes, they need you, but not *just* you. How do you think you're going to raise them without any help?"

Marco's anger seemed to fade a bit; he looked like he was actually considering what Janet was saying. She seized the opportunity, cornering him further. "I know what a struggle it was for the two of you to cope with the twins. I don't think you'll find it easier on your own; above all now that they need extra-care, after losing their mother…"

"What's your agenda, Janet?"

"Helping, like family do…"

He thought for one second, before replying, "Your parents may be a help, but you Janet, you would not know how to take care of a teddy bear."

"Let's not start that nonsense again Marco. I accept that I haven't had my priorities straight for a long time, you're right on that, but for the surv—, I mean, for the wellbeing of your children, I am ready to change that."

Conciliatory talking to Marco was taking its toll. Whereas she found him a moron who had messed up her sister's life since day one, she was going after the bigger prize on offer: the welfare of her sister's children.

Marco on the other hand, remained silent, thinking *cold, depressed lesbian bitch, wanting to foster children, call after five…. not buying that shit.* Though, he decided to control his instinct to sting her with more poisonous comments.

"I love the children and I would do anything for them."

Janet also resisted the urge to uncover the hollowness of his statement and focused on the fact that he was opening up to negotiations. "What are your plans, what would you like us to do?"

Marco was fixing his gaze on the floor, his attention divided between a part of the grouting and the sizable task of single parenting.

"I don't know, this is big, Janet, and it's just happened. I need help, I admit that much. I think I'd draw a plan with your parents... and you perhaps, since you suddenly sound like Mother Teresa."

"What do you mean since—" she was close to lose it again, "ah, never mind." She sighed, "Let's leave it." She paused before resuming, "Of course I want to help you and the children, I think I can do more than my parents, if you think long-term... They're old and not so flexible, they'll have to deal with the shock of Gaia's death and at the same time of becoming involved with the little children, I can't see that happening."

"What do you propose then, this ain't writing software Janet, I'm not sure you're a child expert." His aggressiveness was relenting.

Janet paused. "I think what Gaia would have liked... is for the kids to remain together, to support each other, before everything else. Then, I think she would have wanted a replacement mother, someone to love them, ready to live for them the way she did; better of course, if she was known by the children."

"What about me, you— "

"Of course Marco, it's not the father that they're gonna change, you will always be there for them, anytime you like, do stuff with them, no one will take your place, as long as you live." She had to refrain from making it sound like she was wishing for him not to live long. "It's the mother figure that we're talking about."

Yet, he resented her for not including him in the main picture, "I'm still the closest relation they have. Get over it."

He obviously wanted to hear it from her. "Yes, Marco. You are their very next of kin. Just not the *only* relation to spend every minute of their life with until they're grown up."

He desisted from commenting further. Janet hadn't seeded this last sentence with enough material to stir him up again.

She could indeed feel she had struck a favourable chord with him, and moved on pulling that lever further, framing future relations with Marco around the impossibility of his being with them 24 hours a day.

"And who should this mother be..."

"Me."

He sneered, "Bollocks! You wouldn't be able love them more than your career."

She ignored his renewed spite, *he has no clue about the experiment.* Clearly his relationship with Gaia had not run deep enough for her to share her thoughts on what was going on at the labs, notwithstanding that Gaia had proven to feel very strongly about it, considering all the steps she had taken with Andrew... *Yes with Andrew, you Muppet.*

He seemed unaware that Gaia had died in murky circumstances. Janet felt liberated, the security spill started and ended with Gaia. She had just found the dam that would stop the flood of problems submerging her. Though she knew inside that the real battle from now on would be with Bill and no one else; he certainly wasn't going to approve of her decision to pull out of the experiment to become the children's guardian.

She spoke as if it was him she had in front of her instead of Marco. "I don't need my career any longer. I want to get off that train, it's the end of the line for me. I've lost enough over that cause. I'll be of better use taking care of the little ones, alleviating their pain, supporting their growth. I feel, I owe it to them, more than anything I can do in any laboratories." She was nodding at her own words, looking Marco firmly in the eyes. "I suggest we make a deal: I undertake the daily management of the kids whilst you can see them as much as you like. We see how it goes. Maybe one day, you'll want to be more involved, or perhaps it will be me begging to go back to work... But I'm firm in my commitment now, it would be good for everyone if we could share their custody."

Marco was silenced by Janet's determination for some time before expressing his part acceptance to Janet's proposal. He voiced it in his usual colourful way, "Jesus Christ you Icks girls, always running for fucking sainthood... So madly idealistic. You just sounded so much like Gaia," he smirked. "Maybe this could be good for the kids now... I mean, if you could take her place without turning them against me."

Janet was relieved to hear that he recognised their priorities were the same.

He continued: "I'll give it some thought, but I won't be rushed into anything. We'll see how it goes and if me or the kids aren't 100 percent happy, they will come back to me straight away."

Bingo.

"Because I don't really want to give them away. I may soon be in the position to take them back." He was sketching out the possibility of remarrying. *Thoroughly disgusting*, she thought.

He was doing all the talking now. "Gaia was a good mother to the children, even if in the end she screwed it all up. What about your parents then?"

Janet could not call them without Bill's authorisation and she would have to make sure he wouldn't call them first. "They're on their way…" she lied. "They were away… but don't worry about them, we'll talk all this through together. Go back to the children now, I'll join you in a moment."

"All right then."

"Ah Marco… may I ask you a favour, can I borrow your phone? Mine's flat."

"Sure, here it is."

"Thanks, I need to arrange somewhere to stay around here… If you want, we can tell the children together what we have—"

"Wait Janet. Let's tell them in a bit, I've just arrived and we haven't sorted out the logistics of it yet. Don't jump the gun. Too keen you Icks ladies, always."

He had a point. "Sure, you're right, let's wait. We can talk logistics in a while."

"Sure thing," he said turning to ring the buzzer.

Once he was behind the glass door, Janet sighed in relief before looking around to spot if any CCTV cameras were filming her. She wanted to use Marco's phone for a private call. She wasn't sure she could make it without being taped or logged, but she decided to give it a try.

3.4 – June 18th

It had to be done. Janet's guts opposed the thought of going to yet another hospital, working again on the genes of unwitting patients, but she knew she couldn't leave Cleo and her baby behind. Out of sympathy and shame, she was travelling through London to see NB001, the newborn, for what she thought would be once and for all.

Shattered by tension and lack of sleep, when Bill's face appeared on her phone, Janet reluctantly opened her eyes and swiped her thumb across his face.

"Hi," she said, forgetting to wait for encryption to kick in. "Hi" she repeated a few seconds later as no answer was forthcoming. They were totally unsynchronised, in life and in communications.

"How's the family?" Bill sounded crisp, possessed, not one bit as tired as Janet.

"What's left of it... fine," her eyes closing again.

"What a blessing that the children are well, thinking about it."

Janet didn't reply, too tired to react to his cheap self-help quotes.

"Don't forget that other baby of yours…"

"Going there now."

"I've just come out of central command; we've been thinking about something."

"Go on," said Janet, fighting thick drowsiness.

"Just a briefing with the head of the forces there… Robert's also informed…" he paused awkwardly. "We disband all staff left at the labs and reassign them all to different locations."

"Why such haste now… who's going to deal with the baby? I told you I need a break…"

"There are resources who can pick that up in the service, with a bit of training perhaps."

"This sounds so rushed. Also, how about EA1456? Because if he's still alive…"

"Him? We just need to enforce the contract, today, no further delays."

Janet realised with surprise that he was still alive, which forced her brain to momentarily regain focus on the experiment, for the first time in two days.

Straightening he posture on the seat and lowering her voice to avoid the driver picking up her conversation. "What do you mean, is he still alive? And are you going to have him—?"

"You know the agreement Janet. More than ever, it's a way to protect you, your staff and everyone else involved."

"But you spared him so far. It's not necessary anymore…"

"Leave it Janet, we've had our time to be sentimental, and it hasn't really helped us, has it? The guy goes and your staff are dispersed; different jobs, all over the country. Time to concentrate on our little wonder now."

"Jesus, Bill, if the guy is still alive…. After all he went through, he is a miracle! Let him be, also we could study what's happening now that—"

"Which part of *he's going* don't you get? There's an experiment that's ongoing Janet, remember? One comes, one goes… does it ring any bells? Hell, you only designed the programme!"

"I know…" the image of the pregnant woman she had injected flipping through her brain, "I know. But I didn't expect him to still be alive, I thought—" Janet was unable to find the strength to fight Bill.

"No ifs and no buts, it's not convenient to have two people with the same DNA around. I believe you said that to me once."

"That was the paper from—" she was thinking of herself allowing for her personal experiment with Sharon. He was feeling incongruous.

"You don't need to think about it any longer, we're forming a new unit to monitor the newborn, people from the service, professionals, you'll be relieved from the daily management of it."

"What about my close staff?"

"Gone. Mine too. The plans for a skeleton team were drafted before the security breach. We should all have been more careful."

She paused, thinking before replying. "If you leave me alone, without staff, I'm out completely."

"So you're leaving your little creature alone?"

Her leverage was weak. "You know that's not going to happen, but I want to have my say when we decide these things."

"I understood you wanted a quieter time?"

"Easier said than done… I'm going there now, as we speak," she was displeased. "Listen, can you stall the disposal of EA1456 till tomorrow? I'd like to see you first."

Bill waited for a moment, "I'm going to do it, tonight."

"You? You're kidding me?"

"The decision is to push ahead. I told you all about the meeting. The sooner, the better."

"Yes, but you? What do you mean *you* will take care of it?"

"I re-peat, we are cut-ting sta-ff, un-der-stand? Someone needs to do it, I don't mind getting hands-on, plus, no one wanted to take responsibility. There was no protection offered since he should have been gone long ago."

She was struggling to find an argument that would buy her some time, let alone save EA1456's life. The surprise of Bill carrying the murder out himself, was beyond her imagination. *How the hell will he do it, he's so nerdy?*

"Bill, hold on a minute, the guy is terminally ill, we didn't look to preserve him, we were told to dispose of him quickly, that same day... Then he's been taken out of care for two days, driven around in a car boot... He's a wreck of a man waiting to die, why tarnish your name with such an awful act when—"

"Janet, you don't seem to understand," he kept interrupting her at every sentence. "We're cleaning up after ourselves. There's been so much shoddiness already, it has cost lives... I want things to get back to where they belong – like the fact that he signed up for it, he's got to be finished off."

Janet was taken aback by his insistence. "I was just suggesting you think about it before doing it... you may save yourself some horrible pain."

Janet started to silently weep. Her understanding faltering as to why she had decided to associate herself with this heartless, vicious character.

"Do you really think we will ever get back to business as usual?"

"Concerning the experiment, we are, as of tonight, I think so. Janet, I'm aware that we have had our diversions, but we need to keep focused – remember: it's not about how you start it, but how you finish."

Janet kept weeping silently. Bill wrapped up the conversation, while question marks spread around Janet's mind.

"Go on, take care of our little wonder, he's everything we've been fighting for. I'll clean up after the messy start, then you and I will meet again and plan the next move together. No more surprises from now on, ok?"

Janet was wiping tears from her face with the back of her free hand, preferring her emotions not to be detected by Bill. She was feeling guilty, of having bought Bill a ticket into genetic engineering, of facilitating the unstoppable diabolical machinations associated with his devious character. Her attempt to persuade him to call off the termination of EA1456 had failed. It was all a sign of the turning fortunes in her career.

Bill had concluded the call saying he had the procedure explained. He was going to head to EA1456 and carry it out solo. Janet had raised her eyes to the sky, silently cursing Bill for his determination to kill. She hung up on him.

*****

Bill was satisfied that he didn't need any help from her; he understood how to do it, and was looking forward to having a chat with EA1456 before he departed from this world.

He walked out of his headquarters to climb into the black limousine, his chosen means of transport for this stealth mission; there was no leaving flight tracks with both Air Traffic Control and the Civil Aviation Authority.

"Good to see you, sir," his long-serving driver greeted him with enthusiasm.

Bill greeted him back, asking if he knew the address.

"Yes sir, it's programmed in already, it should take around 90 minutes."

Bill relaxed on the back seat, enjoying the drive in the pleasant summer night. He was thinking of EA1456. *He's the only person who really shared the spirit of the experiment with me*, he thought. *The guy has put his life on the line for it, he is sheer determination… not a spoilt pussy like—*. He shook his head at his own thought, stroking gently the few short, soft hair on his chin, He'll be glad I've remembered to deliver. My word is my bond, he's getting his new life. His left hand rested on the small case containing the lethal dose of dimethylmercury, encased in what could have looked like a posh bike tyre repair kit.

Bill enjoyed having no feeling of doubt or uncertainty. He was confidently reassured of being right, his belief tracing back to all the prep work put into the experiment. Plus, he believed in sticking to the good old original plans, basically delivering what everyone wanted; it filled him with a sense of moral justice. He had provided a clean experiment for a technology that allowed DNA transfer between two living humans. Poisoning EA1456 was a necessary evil, as much as protecting him in his new form, NB001.

He believed it was a good thing, everything was going great, if it wasn't for the disappointment Janet had proven to be. Nothing compared to envisioning the day, three months from now, when little NB001 would show the expected marks, signalling he had inherited the DNA of EA1456. A mini, new-improved EA1456 coming out the other end of the Killer App…

The desperation of millions would be over. Government granting himself alone the exclusive licence to operate the scheme for 25 years. All coherent with his life's values, eclipsing every other interest in his businesses empire. Now that he could reorder mankind, reshape society, commanding its levers like the pilot of a ship making it to harbour after the storm, he wasn't going to push boxes around for long.

Bill fell asleep in the back of the car. Dreaming of his youth, of the times when, only eight years old, he would fear his father returning home from his endless business trips. Little Bill, hiding behind the gown of his English nanny, escaping his abusive father.

His mother, slumped on the white sofa, perpetually sedated by her diet of Gin and Prosecco, talking nonsense; she had always needed him more than he needed her.

Years later, barely eighteen, his dad's birthday present to him was flying back at his father across the kitchen. Forty millimetres of solid stainless steel watch, cutting a gash under the old man's eye, the person no one dared to upset or contradict, ever. These were the mixed feelings that brought about the end of his life in the family home, and saw him travel to England, seeking shelter with his retired nanny in Bibury, Gloucestershire.

The car pulled up in front of the navy base camp. Bill was awoken by a soldier flooding the car with a flashlight, pointing it at his yawning face. A smile and wave, followed by some checks and some reciprocal despise. In his body of principles, young soldiers were the dumbest thing, members of all armies, armies of dullness.

Once inside the compound, a jeep escorted them, driving through countless constructions in the shipyard, circumnavigating chunks of ships and piles of waste materials. Eventually, they reached the back entrance of one of the buildings. It looked like a meat-packing loading dock, with no lights but a small green bulb on top of one of the doors on the raised platform.

The sight of the place sent a shiver down Bill's spine, he didn't like it. How different from the OGL for EA1456 to end up there; not for long though. The service had chosen such a location for the availability of ships to dispose of the body at sea. Upon opening the car's door, the place revealed its utter desperation, so severe that Bill felt the urge to ask his driver to wait for him there. A superfluous request, feeding into his need for reassurance, as he planned to be out in no time.

Reluctantly, he got out of the car, carrying a small hard leather case. He walked up the coarsely asphalted steps, leading to the suspended platform, where a soldier was waiting, a dumb smiley type, half his age.

The first door wasn't secured, the soldier just pushed it open. Once inside, a faint red light revealed a building requiring heavy maintenance, if not knocking down altogether. They walked the dirty floor up to a stainless steel door, from where the red light was emanating. They stood waiting without speaking for the intercom to return the call, looking into an infrared camera and at each other.

"Engine room…"

"Code GBRF, sir. You have a *VIP-sitor*," the soldier looked at Bill grinning, he thought the army at night was fun.

"Passcode?"

"Warm pizza, cold lager."

"Clear then."

As the door buzzed open, the soldier raised his arm slightly, signalling Bill to wait there. An older soldier, in his forties, with slightly longer hair and a grumpier face appeared from inside. His unbuttoned, wrinkled overall gave him a scruffy look, as if he had just woken-up from a snooze on the sofa. The two soldiers exchanged salutes, with efforts proportionally tuned to their appearance – the young guy believing in it, quick, sharp and clean, the older one, just keeping up appearances.

Bill was signalled to enter, to follow them into the dark corridor while they closed the door behind them. They entered a lift and went down a few floors. When the doors opened, the older soldier spoke.

"Your host is in that room there." Bill, who was following him in the semi-dark, barely saw him pointing at the last door on a corridor of four.

"How is he today… Doctor?" Bill had noticed a name tag on the overall indicating Doctor P. WALKER.

"Spaced out… absent, not quite dwelling with us any more… Enjoying the morphine I guess." He had stopped in front of the door, a dim light was coming from inside the room, though brighter than the one in the corridor. Bill could finally appreciate the full figure of the doctor who was covering the night shifts, in an underground and forgotten corner of an army base, looking after death sentenced patients.

Bill smiled arrogantly, entering the room without waiting for the doctor to show the way. The latter frowned, shaking his head while closing the door, *pissy civilians…*

Inside the sparsely decorated room, EA1456 lay on a white metal bed with a slightly open mouth as if seeking air. An emaciated figure of what once upon a time had been a man. His thick beard and hair whiter than ever, with a lost glance to an undefined point on the wall. His hands outside the bed linen, lying over his stomach, showing signs of numerous needle insertions, a drip still pending off his right wrist. He was clinging to some sort of amulet, shaped like an encased Christian cross with a hook of oriental appearances. *Must have got on marvellously with Gaia.*

Bill studied EA1456 for some time, during which the latter didn't acknowledge the visitor's presence in the room.

"Hi there, you must be the famous EA1456?" He knew his real name, and was tempted to use it in order to catch his attention, but refrained.

EA1456 ignored him.

"Don't worry, I appreciate that you are not very talkative… you've been whirling around quite a bit recently."

Feeling the stuffy air of the room, Bill made himself comfortable, unzipping his black jacket and laying the leather case on the end of the bed.

"First of all, I want to apologise for the complications you experienced, and I want to tell you how much I respect you for undertaking the procedure in the first place." His words were falling through the silence broadcasted by the adept.

"I'm fine doing all the talking… I always wanted someone to hear my story. One reason I kept you alive all these days after your city break in Cambridge." Bill put his hands in the pockets of his coat and started pacing up and down the room.

"Once upon a time, there was an unhappy man… A cursed creature who didn't like his life at all. Despised by the masses, he muddled on unhappily. The one thing he dreamed of was to have a second chance at life; something big and great, superseding his incredible social ineptitude. He promised himself, he would use everything he had learnt the hard way, yielding it all into a new round at life."

The opening made no apparent impression on EA1456.

"You know who am I talking about, don't you?" Bill's tone slipped into lecturing mode, scowling slightly at EA1456's apathy, telling himself EA1456 was only pretending not to listen.

"Yet the man, remained a vermin pushover. Until one day, a black knight, a hero arrived in his life. Someone with a great idea, coming to the rescue. A man with a procedure in mind, which allowed unhappy men to cease their distressed lives and be born again, new, young, powerful."

Bill paused to think before speaking again. "You should think the man knew that the gift he was given was immense, and that he appreciated it, because he really wanted what lay beyond the hills. Remember, how he had had enough of his empty, shallow life?"

A pause allowed him to change the subject.

"We're so much alike you and me, nothing ordinary in our mould. We have no part in that second-hand circus boring people live. We don't like doing what we're told. We have a million dreams. We have fighting tendencies, and we look beyond circumstances. Original, pristine, clear in our will, I like you for that. You came, you delivered, you went." Bill paused.

"Yes, you went. Because it's time to say goodbye, you know?"

Bill reached again for the little leather case that had been lying on the bed, before talking once more.

"I don't expect you to thank me." He was unpacking it.

"They told me you had some silly second thoughts about departing... But I credit those to that silly hippy that took you from my labs... ha, or perhaps it was that softie of a doctor treating you there. She must have inculcated you with some pretty big doubts. Trust me, she's a failure, you're cleverer."

He had unzipped on the side of the leather case.

"I'm sure you've read the terms and conditions. I've seen the mini-you breathing already, he's beautiful. Now it's time to kiss & fly."

He had screwed the needle onto the stainless-steel syringe carrying the poison. He looked in the backlight for any air inside, pushing the piston slightly to remove it. Through this ritual, EA1456 lay motionless, flat, his stare still lost on an indefinite point.

Bill was ready to inject, when he realised he needed to expose a more suitable vein on the opposite forearm. Whereas EA1456's right wrist lay closer, the vein was attached to a cannula already, with tape, plus various other scars denoted similar insertions. Bill decided to go for the left arm instead, resting the syringe on the night table close to the lamp. He leaned across EA1456's chest, just below the talisman, bending forward to roll up EA1456's sleeve.

Without any indication heralding that he was going to abandon his lethargic state, EA1456 quickly withdrew his right arm from under Bill's body, recoiling his right elbow between the pedestal and the bed. While Bill was rolling up the hospital gown over EA1456's left arm, the latter took a firm grip of the syringe in his right hand, briskly thrusting it with a seamless movement into Bill's left buttock, forcing its fatal contents into his body. Bill, who couldn't be described as the best bearer of pain, caught the gist of EA1456's action when the unexpected needle caused the painful shock to spread from his left gluteal muscle.

A few seconds elapsed, allowing Bill to discern the pain of disappointment for what he had just let happen. Both perceptions were soon overtaken by the realisation that he had just been injected with a deadly amount of poison.

As a consequence, his body stiffened first, arching above EA1456's torso, then, slowly giving in to the poison he started to relax, falling, crouching rather, over EA1456's upper body, his face looming closer and closer to his murderer's face.

Unable to scream, he wished for more sound to come out of his throat, his larynx had become too swollen and dry already, preventing Bill from expressing his utter dismay and fright.

All that was left, was to look at EA1456's inexpressive face, until, brushed by approaching death, he experienced a sudden and complete loss of control of his body. Ushered into a dream, he strolled along a beach with the boy he had loved as a teenager.

"Blimey, did you realise those two were so close? Bloody hell, he's fucking hugging him, check it out! Oi, easy batty boy… Told ya he looked like a backdoor bandit…" The younger soldier was watching the CCTV screens for the first time in five minutes. Amused to see Bill embracing the patient's body, he had missed the gravity of what was happening. The older doctor, reluctantly peeling an eye away from his magazine, looked at the screen too, but noticed immediately that the body of the visitor was shaking. Above all the right foot was quavering strangely with only the tip of the shoe touching the ground.

"You stupid moron! He's in trouble – go in, armed, now! Separate them, isolate the patient, he's fucking armed!"

The younger soldier looked at the screen for a fraction of a second, before getting the essence of the unfolding drama occurring under his nose.

The senior doctor was already shouting into the radio: "WALKER HERE, EMERGENCY CODE

RED, URGENT SUPPORT NEEDED, LOWER LEVEL B…"

Springing from his wheeled chair, the young soldier ran the few steps that separated his room from EA1456's, kicking the door open and pointing his gun right at the bed. Since his shouts of abuse did not yield any movement from the two intertwined bodies, he walked in slowly, finally noticing the stainless steel syringe sticking from the visitor's buttocks.

Two more steps, circling the left part of the room, still pointing the gun at the patient, he saw EA1456 clenching a mobile phone to his ear. Holding the gun with his right hand, his sight fixed on the patient, he got closer to him, bending his knees slightly to extract the medical instrument from the visitor, before looking for further signs of any other weapons.

Less than a minute later, a bunch of soldiers flooded the room pulling the two bodies apart.

Some immediately tried reviving Bill, while others roughly handcuffed EA1456. All were nervously shouting at each other and over the radio, but nothing seemed capable of preventing Bill from getting a taste of the afterlife he had meant to deliver to the adept.

3.5 – June 18th

Talking with Bill had plunged her into a foul mood. He had turned into a monster. Any good in him was twisted if not gone; he had turned into a destructive killing machine.

Janet was sure the decision to disband her research team was his. She sensed he was taking her people under his watch, before striking them off completely, in what seemed a death sentence for anyone involved in the labs.

But there wasn't going to be a Janet 'fierce-defender-of-the–labs' this time. She could not even imagine opening that front, when at home Janet faced the worst of situations. Gaia was dead, three orphans all below five years of age were left behind, with a useless father too. Her parents, both in their late seventies, were about to be absolutely devastated by the loss of their *preferred* daughter.

And yet, she felt for them, for EA1456, baby NB001, his family, AND Sharon, the pregnant mother…holy shit!

She held her face in her hands in the loneliness of the black cab that was driving her towards resuming her despised work; away from those who needed her the most, her newly acquired children.

She blamed her choices, recounting the story of her life, perched half-way between hospitals and laboratories. She felt as if she had turned into a sour cocktail, one part distant sibling, one part heartless scientist, everything looking hazy, evidence of tiredness all around, and now signs of car sickness, *great...*

Trying to think about something else, chasing some needed respite, she sought shelter from the sad events flooding her recent hours. The attempt to escape her sadness led her back to focusing on the essence of the problem, Bill: a vicious conspirator, a spoilt, super-rich brat, who had proven unable to connect with anyone else but himself. Someone so utterly determined to crush everything and everyone standing between himself and his ridiculous objectives, was to become, through her work, the father of mass DNA redistribution. He had embarked on it to sort out the imbalances in society, *the fucker*, and he was succeeding, against her will. She had let him do so. It wasn't so much that she criticised the experiment or its aim. Yes, she recognised it *was a bit of bloody mad*, but what really redefined her priorities now were the kids.

In an attempt to pull herself together, she tried to visualise what to do next. First, she thought, she needed to anticipate Bill's moves, as the evidence was that he would kill again if he deemed it necessary; just as he had done with Gaia, and was about to do with EA1456. *I need to stop this runaway train, but how?* Janet's head kept trying to work out the question until, with her energy fading, the question sent her to sleep.

The neon light of the hospital gates was so bright that it penetrated the blackened windows of the car. Janet was resuscitated back into reality. She rubbed her eyes in front of the orange-lit cathedral, realising it was time to get to work again, feeling she owed her patients her best shot, even if the whole experiment affair made her feel sick.

The ill-natured driver negotiated the right of access with the guard at the front gate, before releasing the feet from the brake of his automatic car, advancing beyond the entrance of the huge main hospital. Once beyond the concourse, the stout, Essex accented driver turned his head and massive shoulders, addressing Janet without a hint of a smile.

"Miss, here's your pass, you're Doctor O'Neal, visiting the patient on behalf of the council, all right? I'll wait for you one hour only. Then, if you're not back on time and I've been told to leave, don't you go moaning about the fucking driver, all right?"

Another damn bully employee of Bill's, when is this going to end?

Janet nodded. She got out of the car, trying to blend with the sparse flow of hospital staff, mainly cleaners by the look of it, moving in and out of the building.

Walking the long corridor lined with closed shops, all of Janet's mental energy was taken up with fighting the desire to quit and run away. She passed a WH Smith and a temporarily unmanned minicab desk, getting to the battery of lifts, where she resolved once again to stop thinking of Gaia and the kids altogether for at least half an hour. That was the time she estimated was needed to visit the boy and her second implant, Sharon, the unwitting mother she had secretly caught in the folds of the experiment.

She regretted her past selfishness, pushing number three on the lift button panel. Once upstairs, she headed for the post-natal care department, which was the closest. As the main desk was unmanned, she checked-in at the nurses' room, introducing herself as Dr. O'Neal, from the Hospital Trust, carrying out random visits to check the baby's post-natal recovery.

The nurses' faces confirmed her doubts straight away: this visit would not be popular with them, or the patients. They gave her a faint indication of where room DE04 was, but no one accompanied her. "Curious time for a visit this is..." said one of the nurses scornfully when Janet was too far away to hear.

She entered the room, mother and child were asleep, the short glimpse of them filled her heart. NB001 was laying horizontally over her breasts, in a seamless bundle, enough for Janet's resolution to crack: she thought of the twins, the first time she saw them, sleeping on Gaia's chest.

Immediately her eyes started to fill with tears, her eyelids struggling to contain the fluid, threatening to make her face wet again. Janet temporarily hid her face behind the clipboard with the medical papers she found at the bottom of Cleo's bed. *Healthy mother and baby... no signs of complications... weight, blood pressure, latching well, passing fluids...*

Neither carried evidence of the experiment. *Neat job*, she thought, praising her work for the first time in 72 hours. She moved to take a closer look at the baby: he had dark hair and skin with a slightly red complexion, he slept exhausted across his mother's bosom, having just finished his meal. The papers reported that he was a hungry little boy. No apparent concerns could be spotted on either mother or child. But the procedure she had herself designed months before required her to check the spot of the injection to look for any bruising or signs of rejection.

She had to be quick, the driver was counting her minutes, and she still had to move on to her secret patient too. Getting on with the play, she acted according to the part of the bitchy controller from the Trust, deciding to call the nurses in for a check of the baby, even if that meant waking both patients up.

That really clashed with her newly acquired motherly conscience. *Business… Business… Business,* she kept repeating to herself, *in the best interest of mother and child…* She walked back to the nurses asking a few petty questions, before requesting one of them to help her wake the mother and child for a quick check-up.

The nurse frowned, "Really? That's the first sleep that pet is gettin' since birth, are you really sure?"

Faced with a malicious nod from Janet, the nurse was compelled to comply with the superior authority emanating from Janet's badge and uniform.

The mother took the unexpected wake-up call better than the nurse. Her good nature meant she was able to deal with the hectic hospital routines and frequent nurse's calls. She classified them as necessary traits of the great British universal care system, and was almost reassured by it. Only when fully awake though, the mother became wary, somehow mistrustful of Janet, looking at her intensely for some time before muttering something.

"You? She's the doctor who made my son scream during the birth."

Janet had to think quickly, picturing it turning ugly. "Huh? No madam, I just need to check the health of the baby for everyone's benefit, yours and the wider community."

The nurse looked puzzled at the woman's suggestion, her confusion growing as the doctor and the patient continued the dialogue.

Cleo, trying to raise herself onto her elbows, whilst holding the baby in a tight protective embrace, looked suspicious. Her nervous movements eventually woke up the baby, who emitted soft croaking moans whilst turning his head around.

The nurse stepped in to avail Janet's request, but she found this harder than envisaged. It was some time before the mother unwillingly hinted at releasing the baby to her. "Calm down sweetheart. She ain't no midwife don't ya bother with that. Just'a doctor from the Trust, that's all."

Cleo eventually gave the baby up, though retaining her most distrustful look for Janet. The newborn was laid down at the bottom of the bed. He kept turning his head looking for his mother, while the latter scrutinised Janet guardedly.

To Cleo and the nurse, Janet appeared an inept handler of babies, leaving clothes unbuttoned, his head perilously hanging, and turning his fragile body far too many times for the baby not to start crying. Janet responded by swaying him to and fro, making things worse. He had only breathed for three days, but was very capable of a deep commanding cry.

Janet feared that they would soon find out she was no council doctor. In a bid to regain the situation, she stiffened her countenance and tone, embarking on a short lecture about the functioning of the baby's organs during the first stages of life; stuff she remembered from her recent readings. Cleo seemed to appreciate the display of her knowledge, but the nurse was alienated and chose to ignore Janet altogether.

Finally, Janet managed to spot the mark left by the needle she had used on the baby. It was now almost imperceptible, and she was satisfied the baby was all right as far as she could see.

She needed to move on quickly. She nodded reassuringly to Cleo, asserting the sound health of the baby, handing her the crying infant hastily, *because he needed his mother...*

"It's a wonderful gift to have a perfectly healthy baby, you ought to enjoy him now, because you never know what could happen." Janet immediately regretted being perceived as a messenger of misfortune. "Well, time to go now. Maybe I shall visit you two again soon."

"Oh yeah, that's gonna be a big help to this lot, *innit*," the nurse said to herself.

"We're going home tomorrow morning," Cleo said with a faint smile, trying to hide her defiance. Janet remembered the procedure she had set in place months before: the appointment of a visiting nurse from the service at the family surgery. She would look after the baby's progress, reporting to the medical team back at the labs. Janet looked at these arrangements from a completely different point of view now. All she could see was the invasion and violation of mother and child's right to a normal life.

Just a few months ago, she had been sitting in a meeting room, with specialists, drafting protocols and procedures designed to cope with a large flow of data coming out of the changes induced by her technology into what would be left of the unaware, innocent boy.

Unbelievable, she thought now. *The things I have imagined would work, that seemed worth pursuing…*

What she was asking herself now was, *how could I've forgotten that the subject of my study was an innocent unaware baby?*

Janet composed herself, outlining a smile to Cleo before beginning the walk of shame out of the room, escorted to the reception desk by the nurse in silence. A straightforward, committed nurse, together with a phoney public servant and scientist of the absurd.

A quick thought of Bill flashed through her mind, what he might be doing at that time, the question of whether that was the exact moment he administered the lethal dose of dimethylmercury into EA1456's malfunctioning body.

She needed to immediately dispel that painful image out of her brain and refocus on the mission instead. She stated a declaration of satisfaction to the nurse, shaking hands in a cold goodbye. Once outside the ward, she sighed with relief, at least the baby was well, though the mother had most certainly recognised her, and the whole situation had become uncomfortably awkward and dangerous.

Janet felt the strain of having to quickly change her role. She had to become someone else now. Disguising herself once again created inconsistencies and incongruences in her mind that were hard to conceal. The thought of facing up to an even more difficult role-play made her startle. First, she had to find the pregnant woman she had injected with the genetic shuttle, then, conceive a way to examine her, leaving unnoticed. *Ah, damn me, what a fiction this is!*

Taking long strides to make progress, Janet despised herself, feeling uneasy about the position she had put herself into. It was like she had been another Janet, when her brain had conceived and assembled all the layers of that conspiratorial plot.

Now, the structural frame supporting those wicked decisions was collapsing. Her personality was changing skin, revealing the new Janet. This thought accompanied her to her secret patient.

Testing whatever strength she had left in her, she struggled to accomplish the objectives designed in another life. Her new commitment she decided, would be to escort the unwitting people she had plunged into the experiment, towards the exit of the embroiled schemes. This meant turning into Dr. Alvina Lundy again, quickly and convincingly, at a time when the simple task of finding Sharon's hospital bed seemed impossible to achieve.

She felt severely strained, her sleep-deprived body shattering to pieces under the pressure involved in staying focused and getting the hell out of there, to tend to her kids again. She vaguely remembered the way up to the antenatal care unit. Starting to move insecurely through the belly of the hospital, feeling unsafe, feeling neither of the two characters she was required to impersonate, none of the two reflecting her real self.

She shrugged off the thought while dropping her fake Dr. O'Neal ID into a yellow hazardous waste container. Everyone she met looked inquisitive and distrustful, but she kept negotiating her way through the bowels of the large hospital complex, still she couldn't find the ward. She was lost in how much she hated hospitals and their neon lights, incapable of believing she had passed her entire working life soaked in that depressing environment.

The few nurses around seemed old, unhappy and unfriendly. She didn't dare ask them for directions. She appeared to be lost in the palace of a shabby ruler, with his army of underpaid and overworked soldiers. Her eyes forced to look down most of the time, walking apace, fearing the prospect of any conversation was bound to reveal that she had no business in there, that *she* was a cheat.

Her thoughts ferried back to Bill's sheer determination and calmness throughout the crisis. *But he hasn't lost a sister, has he?* She couldn't restrain from cursing his blessed inner strength, his serenely self-possessed nature in all events from murder to marketing, perhaps out of abundant insecurity, weakness, emotional numbness and unresponsive indifference.

Like a thunder of hope striking at the endless corridor, the set of lifts Janet had used three days before appeared in front of her. She pushed the button to call it, marvelling at how convinced she was of experimenting with genetics on infants the last time she used them. Now, all that she wanted was to wrap her arms around her adopted children, to give them a feeling of normality again. No more picking random children, no plunging people into abnormality, forever compromising their opportunity to have a life within the boundaries of ordinariness.

She boarded the empty lift, arriving in front of the ward where she had left Mrs. Sharon Besley 72 hours before. Upon arrival on the floor, Janet was questioned straight away by a sturdy Irish woman in her mid-fifties, one of the nurses on shift.

"Hello there, it's not visiting time, would you mind coming back in the morning?"

"Ehm, I kind of mind yes," gagged Janet hiding her felony. "I'm a doctor, but I'm not with this hospital. I was paying Mrs. Besley a visit, out of courtesy, before going back on duty."

"You're a doctor, you know how the house works."

"Sure, you're right, I know. It's just that I sincerely hoped I could drop in and say hello… I won't be a minute, really."

"Won't be awake, will she." She came closer to Janet. "That patient hasn't been well at all, she needs to rest. Come back another time for her sake."

"Why, what's happened to her?"

"Oh, she's a rather curious case that one. First, she developed a bad rash all over her left breast, then started feeling all itchy and warm. She has been fairly miserable for the best part of three days, but she's resting now since we gave her a ten ml intramuscular of Ziprasidone."

"Well that's not so strong though, perhaps I can—"

"But we can't load her up too much either, she is pregnant, you see."

Janet felt a weakness rising from her legs all the way up to the chest. All her organs converged over the task of keeping her upright.

"You don't look well either, love," the nurse continued, she was holding a bundle of sheets in her arms. "If you ask me, she's had a nervous breakdown, over her husband and all, I think. She's constantly speaking of someone trying to kill her baby. I suggested Haldol… but the doctors you see, decided it could worsen the rash." She was shaking her head, "Very difficult pregnancy indeed."

The picture of Claire popped into Janet's mind, cluttering further the trashy trail of demise she had scattered around. She became fully aware of having wrecked Sharon's life.

"Well… what can I say? Ok, I understand, it's not a good time for me to say hello. I'll be in touch, once she's better I mean."

"Jolly good idea then. You too need rest dear; you look rather distraught yourself, if I might say."

Janet minded being reminded of what a state she looked.

"Do you know when she's going to be released?"

The nurse shook her head, arching the corners of her lips down, meaning she had no idea.

"Thanks anyway, give her my love," Janet said unwittingly, turning her body to depart.

"And who shall I say was here?"

"What?" Janet's motion was stopped half-way through tracing her steps back.

"Who should I say?" repeated the nurse.

Janet was stung by the demand. All that she knew was she had to protect Claire, so there was no chance of using any name at all. "Just a doctor who worked with her husband, she'll know."

The nurse didn't pick up on the need for confidentiality, "All right miss secret service, I'll pass the cable on."

Janet nodded warily, putting up a contrived smile over her eggshell face. Aiming again to escape, she could hear the chatty Irish nurse talking again. "It'd be lovely if you came to visit that poor soul again, wouldn't it."

Janet's frozen brain could not vocalise that she meant to be back for sure. *Shit! What the hell is going on? All this is happening at once* ... A growing fear arose in her chest: she was dead scared of being uncovered, worried she would be found out to be responsible for Sharon's condition. She walked fast, fear turning into panic. She became a hunted animal, lost in the middle of a maze. She needed to get the hell out of there. Quickly; looking cool though, casual.

A wall mounted camera following her, made her jump. She thought of Bill again, *if he could just get a taste of all this...* Overwhelmed by fright, feeling lost behind enemy lines, she craved to talk to someone, and the only person she could call was Bill, unfortunately. Even Robert, who admittedly had been involved from the start, wasn't the right person to help, as he had no direct involvement and had specifically requested not be encumbered with operations.

Bill was the last man standing on duty, the sole living human she could refer to in her situation. She needed his strength, to even be able to walk out of that confusing network of passages. She found herself curious to know how he was getting on with the dreadful mission he had imposed on himself. Walking as hastily and casually as possible, she swiped her right thumb over the screen of her mobile and let Bill's phone ring a long time, almost to the point of giving up. *Bastard, busy killing...* The call was finally answered by no voice, but a faint hissing coming through the line.

To begin with, Janet thought nothing of it, she attributed it to the usual encryption delay, lasting slightly longer than usual. In the course of the ten seconds required by her brain to discern the tones constructing the texture of the long muted delay and its unusual patterns, all the constituent noises she could hear came together. She pressed her mobile to her ear, still walking briskly, and realised she was listening to a man breathing heavily, sickly wheezing in the microphone.

"Hello, Bill?" She was starting to feel uncomfortable about what was coming through, she was thinking of tentatively ask for an explanation when she discerned the croaking voice of EA1456: "He's dying, he is dying..."

Three words erased everything around her; she stood staring blankly into the corridor. It had all gone wrong. She put one hand on the wall seeking support from her heartbeat coming to a halt. The hand with the phone inadvertently covering her mouth in an expression of incredulousness, *what has he done to him?*

When she dared to move the phone back to her ear, she picked up mounting background noise taking over; voices of men, soldiers, shouting orders. The last thing she heard was the sound of the phone being snatched up and the call ending.

The worst has happened, she thought.

In front of her, a poster advertising a church service for patients read: Therefore hell hath enlarged herself, and opened her mouth without measure: and their glory, and multitude, and their pomp, and he that rejoiceth, shall descend into it. Isaiah 5:14

3.6 – June 19th

Janet's sense of security was forever blacked out, her eternal, intrinsic confidence ceased to radiate from her. For a long while, she remained dazed, standing insecurely as if marking the place where she had acknowledged the unexpected endurance of EA1456. She was fixating on an irregular printing spot on the poster that at a closer look revealed the mess of dots underneath the white printed surface.

She had called for support, seeking a much-needed lifeline. Instead, she experienced quite the opposite, witnessing more death, the murder of her associate at the hand of her patient. Her fears of being isolated and hounded increased, bewilderment overwhelming her ability to process information. Notwithstanding her recent hatred for Bill, his being killed made her even more defeated, adding further weight to her already heavy burden.

Unexpectedly, a lady in her early seventies approached her from behind. She was wearing a long white skirt and shirt, with a light blue cardigan, proudly showing her gold and purple "Hospital Volunteer Service" badge. She seemed happier to comfort what looked like a deeply agitated young doctor than push a book trolley around. "Are you all right, dear?"

Janet reacted as if, encircled by a monstrous creature, she was about to be attacked. The lady didn't miss her overreaction; she was repeating, "It's ok, luvvie, calm down now."

Still, Janet's body was trembling, she pushed her back to the wall until she turned to run. The unsolicited encounter embodied her fear of getting arrested, if not killed, as the next casualty in the pile of experiment-related deaths. Now she was running, on her way out, retracing her steps through that intricate system of passages. She recognised a set of stairs, ran down them, slowing only before forcing the mezzanine door open, pretending to be cool, slightly striding, neither fast nor slow, taking notice of anything, just pushing out of the cheap shopping arcade. It was the early hours, few shift workers on an unlucky roster, caught between work duties and sleep.

No one was taking any notice of Janet's worries. Shying away from the many CCTV cameras, she descended the last escalator, proceeding towards the main concourse, between the short term car park and the kiss-goodbye area, the agreed meeting point with the driver.

It was a pointless score, as no driver was there waiting. Disappointed, she looked around for a moment, shivering in the chilly air, wishing for her car to appear, looking at the chronograph on her phone, counting the three minutes remaining before the assigned hour elapsed.

It was an easy guess: she had been dropped, there never was going to be any pick up. She tasted defeat. She whispered, "Support team" at the phone, activating the video call. Ten seconds later, the answer came in the shape of a young boy in his early twenties, with a clean navy haircut and clear blue eyes. "Central operations, good morning."

"Janet Icks."

"Ms. Icks good morning, we have a message for you."

"I'd rather have a car than a message," Janet said, her free hand rearranging her blonde hair at the back of her head.

"I appreciate your comment. It reads here: Unforeseen circumstances mean that we are unable to undertake the agreed pick-up service. We suggest you make your way home by alternative means."

"Well, sure I could get that, but there's something else I'd like to talk about with mission command." Janet was pissed off, but kept it quiet, realising that she hadn't picked the shortest straw that night. Her main preoccupation was finding out who was in charge of the experiment now.

"We will have someone from OC contact you as soon as she's available. We appreciate your understanding, madam."

"Did they teach you any verb other than 'appreciate'?"

"Could you be so kind as to rephrase your question, madam?"

Fucking idiot. "Whatever, I'm on my way—"

"Bear with us, we will contact you shortly," said the boy smiling through the small screen.

She felt like smashing the phone on the pavement, if that could have somehow wiped that stupid beaming smile off his face.

"Good night," said Janet absentmindedly, already mulling over her next move. She thought that the security chief despatched to the labs by Bill in the aftermath of the intrusion may have more information for her. *Better get into a cab first, though.*

Starting to walk briskly towards the only black cab left in the taxi bay, she touched the left pocket of her jacket.

"Villiers Road, Clapham," she said opening the passenger door.

The aged driver was busy listening to a football talk show, barely acknowledging her before starting the car.

Janet sat in the back and started fiddling with her phone to retrieve the number of the guy she wanted to talk to. He picked up on the second ring.

"Hello?"

"This is Janet Icks."

"Good morning," he didn't sound anywhere near as cool as she remembered. "Are you aware this isn't a protected line?"

"Yes, sure. How are things after the last events?"

The guy sounded troubled, "I am not sure what you are referring to, most likely something I'm not inclined to discuss."

He sounded damned informed to her; *he knows*, she thought. She paused to think what information she could get out of him without him hanging up on her.

"I'd like to meet up sometime. Are you busy in an hour or so?"

"That's not possible, I am off duty. But I may be able to fix you a consultation with someone in operations, if that suits."

"No… I don't think so, I'd much rather see you, if I—"

"I was thinking of someone equally endowed…"

"Well, in that case, ok," Janet was equally hesitant. "I will be at my sister's place in an hour, you can pass my details onto your colleague."

She was puzzled that he didn't check the address before reassuring her she wouldn't regret her choice. He wished her a good morning.

Hanging up, she found her situation truly absurd. In the end, it was entirely her fault that EA1456 had not quietly disappeared, without any living trace of his existence. Now she felt the entire responsibility firmly on her shoulders, inconveniently crushing her, just at a time when her new children were hospitalised at a secret location. She doubted whether she would need to ask security clearance from mission control in order to visit them. *Who the fuck are they anyway, fucking fictional phonies.*

She was fuming, at OC, Bill and ultimately herself, while driving to Gaia's house for the first time since her death. She had been given her sister's personal effects: purse, house keys, phone, a packet of carefree absorbents, receipts, children's toys and other bits and pieces.

Less than a minute later, the cab driver opened the intercom, speaking from behind the protective glass: "Wasting your money you are…"

His thick cockney accent, as well as Janet's low disposition to talk, hindered her ability to understand. "I beg your pardon?"

"You didn't need to pay a fare to go all the way to Clapham. You should have asked for a lift from your friends behind," he had raised his voice, articulating each word.

Still, it didn't make sense. Janet didn't like the sound of it, her nerves already strained, she tried to decipher the enigma. "What friends, what do you mean?"

"See that Vauxhall behind us? I reckon it's been following us right from the 'ospital. D'ya you know them?"

After turning to look through the back window, Janet sunk further into her large leather seat, hiding her head behind the headrest. She needed to quickly process and reorder the numerous possibilities: *service, Bill's security, police...* "I think I know who they are."

"Scumbags, if you ask me. Are ya famous?" he was studying her through the rear mirror.

"Sort of, footballer's wife..." Janet was not happy to become the centre of his attention, it wasn't embarrassment, she was worried he might recognise her if questioned.

"Nah, you're far too fine for those animals... ya don't look like no gold-digger neither. Bet you're a doctor, a shrink perhaps?" he was getting far too close.

"Doctors don't get famous I guess," replied Janet.

"'Course, I know – you aren't famous, and those aren't paparazzi neither. Wanna see the pigs? There's a station just there?"

Janet was determined to keep cool, even if the driver had just exposed her clumsy attempt to disguise her being followed. "Police? No, need thanks, I don't think I'm in danger. Let's just continue to the address."

"If you're happy with that..." the driver closed the intercom. He thought perhaps she was just another silly woman, who didn't need to be helped after all.

Janet was happy that the conversation had ceased, but was still worried of the loose ends it may leave, picturing the driver reporting the conversation to the police if asked, *she was very dodgy indeed.* She was also uneasy about her followers. She sighed deeply, looking at the clock on the display of her phone: 6.00 a.m. Biting her lower lip, pondering whether to call Robert's PA or whether it was too early, she said to herself, *I don't care, I'm not in this of my own free will...* and started dialling.

The phone on the other end rang for a long time. Just when Janet was about to give up, the calm, reassuring voice of a woman answered "Prime Minister's Office, how may I help?" *Must've been hired because of her angelic voice...* Introducing herself apologetically, in light of the early hour, Janet explained the urgency of the matter requiring to be referred to the P.M.

"I'd be so, so immensely grateful if you could have him call back on the confidential link."

Robert's secretary seemed to take the matter to heart, replying she would attempt to pass the message on as soon as he came out of his breakfast briefing.

Janet's cab had hit the clogged south of London roads now, proceeding much slower in the morning queues starting to coagulate around traffic lights. Scars from the glorious industrial past of London had never healed. The landscape, prone to depress "*Norf-Londoner*" Janet, consisted of low buildings, different blocks united by bad taste, nothing quite fitting together, far from conveying any sense of beauty at all. Its cameos consisted of troops of defeated humans, their exhaustion matched only by their sadness, beset by toil, accumulated over layers of old preoccupation.

She was reminded of something she had seen as a teenager, when visiting a homeless charity. A milestone in Janet's life, contributing to her determination to leave her mark in genetics. She had undertaken already then to diminish the pain and frustration for the *less fortunate* people, relieving the most vulnerable parts of society of misery and pain.

It had seemed an unavoidable mission; the daughter of a wealthy architect and a fashion designer, who had equally divided their lives between working for rich people and spending their money. *High-time for the unfortunates now,* she liked to repeat to herself whilst studying.

A momentary sense of direction and bearing, penetrating the squalid view of the army of drudges. Her career, initiated to relieve others, had brought along much torture and pain, for which she now sought redemption through her mission of raising Sophia, Matthew and Lucas to be better people.

The car was stopping at a red light. A large black woman in her late sixties, with a dirty and swollen face, skin as tough as an elephant, straggly hair and disproportionate breasts, came begging at the driver's window wrapped in filthy rags. Suddenly angry beyond reason, she started to bang her fist on the car. The driver, with no sympathy whatsoever, yelled back, "Fuck you bitch, get the fuck away from my car!"

Janet startled. She was a nervous wreck resting on the black leather seat. Unable to cope with the threat embodied by that woman out of control, as if she had already slipped inside the vehicle, Janet went through a full-scale panic attack, more so than the time at the hospital. The driver didn't notice it because he was trying to avert his course in the tight traffic jam, getting away from shouting of the demented woman. After his skilful manoeuvre, he checked the back of the car to reassure his passenger.

"Don't ya get agitated over that boozer, I ain't seen her sober in years…"

Gosh he even knows her and I'm having heart attack over it.

She remained unable to outline the dry smile the driver would have expected in return. Instead, she stared blankly through the partition.

Her phone vibrated inside her tight hand. Janet answered it without waiting to return a sign of gratitude to the driver.

The screen read *Unknown Number.*

"Hello, Janet speaking?" No answer, just the familiar sequence of dial tones, unmistakably introducing the encrypted conversation.

"Janet?" a compressed digital noise followed before she could hear, "This is Robert here."

Checking the driver's intercom red light was off, she answered him, revelling in the solace of having someone who knew, to talk to.

"Robert thank you for calling back straight away," her heart pounding, under the ray of light opening in the torn sky of her day. She was finally talking to someone who would help her.

"Just checking you're not getting into trouble too, how are you?"

"Oh, truly miserable… I think I've just involuntarily witnessed the most unfortunate circumstances, affecting…"

She stopped before she said too much. She needed to test the water – how much did he know about Bill? Whether he felt like talking about it over the phone was another matter. She couldn't compromise him, or risk losing her vital communication channel with him. Timely, red flags had appeared in her brain.

"I have heard, dreadful... You there? Janet?"

"I'm here."

"I, I personally don't understand how all this can have happened so fast, I mean, this endeavour is proving very wicked. I'm not sure you ought to pursue it further."

"Neither do I, Robert."

"Listen, you can't afford more disasters like—, the events you just mentioned. I mean, three in two days... and the last one, a hard one to contain, do you agree?"

"Sure..." Janet was startled by him mentioning three casualties not two. She tried to figure out who the third victim was, clearly it was inappropriate to ask over the telephone.

He continued, "I want you to listen to me going forward... Replace everyone else in your contact list, and don't take any initiative, burn all bridges, ok?"

Janet was still trying to figure out who the third death might be.

"Janet, are you there? I need you on the same page 100 percent."

She was glad to hear he was taking charge; the opposite of hiding away and ignoring her, which could well have been in the cards, in light of his position.

"Sure, I'm with you."

"We ought to realise that circumstances are pushing us to think and act as one. It's our only hope of getting out of this in one piece."

"What do you want me to do?"

Robert answered from a practical point of view. "I want you to pack a bag and get ready to be picked up, for a secure location. You'll rest for a while, you need it before you think about anything—"

"What about the children?" She didn't let him finish his sentence.

"They have their father, the less we meddle with him the better."

"You must be joking?" all complicity vanishing from her voice. "He has agreed to give me custody, I'm basically their guardian," she lied.

Robert paused for a moment, thinking. "Fair enough, if you get him to pass them on with a clean cut to their relationships that's fine. Have you signed any papers yet?"

"Not yet Robert, it's all just happening so fast…"

"Sure, sure. I'll see if I can help with that, actually, someone will be in touch, but till then, please treat him carefully. Make sure he has no cause to complain about anything."

She liked his willingness to help and settle things for her, she needed it. "So back to your plan, where do you want us to go?"

"If you have his permission, bring them with you to this temporary address I'm providing. I think it's a suitable place for children, I'm sure you'll agree. Just trust me, it will be fine."

"Ok, but first I'm going to—"

He interrupted her, "I know where you're going. Just pack your stuff and get the hell out straight away. There's a chap driving behind you, his name is Mike."

"All right, but I've close to nothing with me. I need their toys—"

"Leave that all behind, we'll take care of everything later... we can speak properly face-to-face."

"Sure, thanks. Just one last thing, I was gonna meet the security guy who worked for—"

"Leave those impostors out..."

"Ok, got it, but—"

"Stay calm, take care, gotta jump."

Easier said than done, she said into the phone, but to herself alone, as he had already hung up.

3.7 – June 27th

Janet was sitting on an old white armchair, upholstered with a large yellow flower pattern. Her shoes were lying close-by, contributing to the rest of the mess spread around her. On the floor, an Ellesborough guide book, a newspaper and a binder. On the table, a pot and a cup of tea, while the side table on her left was crammed with a large lamp, a radio and more paper binders.

She was catching up with the last 24 hours of Killer App updates; laptop on her lap, brain catching up fast, skimming through the data.

The week had passed taking care of the children and liaising with her parents, finding a balance after Gaia's passing so suddenly. Just one corner of her mind had kept scanning the environment to see if anything had leaked, searching for clues on the identity of the third casualty. She was baffled to be unable to find any information over what had happened in the intervening days, all erased. The internal communication suite was running thin on details, as if a vacuum had descended over the live feeds and data rooms used by the staff at the labs.

Claire, on the other hand, had called and texted, but she had had to ignore her on the order of security. On the positive side, there was a newsworthy report regarding NB001. A resident paediatrician had been assigned to the local surgery and was carrying out the regular scheduled checks, all reporting that mother and child were OK. Janet felt it was her responsibility that they were having to spend so much time with medics, all because of the experiment. She felt guilty about not trying to shorten their anguish. In the end, she thought that was one piece of good news, even though the experiment wasn't exactly her priority right now, she cherished anything that seemed to be slowly moving back into place. Instead, only the grief from Gaia's death remained at an acute peak.

She took a pause from the screen and looked around the room, peeking out through the tall French doors. She enjoyed being at Chequers, the charming country home imbued with history and character, able to summon all her good parts. It provided the much-needed normality that helped her cope with her struggle of surviving the dead.

In the garden, her parents were entertaining the grandchildren with trikes and ride-ons, all courtesy of His Majesty's Government. A good hideout after all. She wasn't allowed to leave the estate because of security, but she had no reason to, everything she loved being contained within the gates of that beautiful house: the children, her parents, the memory of Gaia. And Robert, who was taking good care of her, like no man had ever done before.

A soft knock at the far door. As he was entering the room, upon seeing her he stopped immediately, remaining perfectly still, halfway, thinking, before saying with a kind air, "Remind me to show you that picture of Margaret Thatcher sitting in that very same chair."

It took all of her brain power to switch off the information she was processing, before Janet understood what Robert's comment was all about.

"I think I saw it actually, isn't it in the library upstairs?" Talking to him sent an unfamiliar shiver of warmth through her.

"It's impressive how much you remind me of her in that chair."

Putting on an overly serious face, mimicking a posh voice, expression and gestures from the Iron Lady, Janet said: "I am extraordinarily patient, provided I get my own way in the end."

"Did you know that she was originally a research chemist? Oh God, how much I wish this was 1983," said Robert, resuming walking towards her.

"In a way, this looks more like a bad version of 1984, more Orwellian than he himself could imagine."

"How are the kids," he asked, shifting the tone of the conversation. "I'm impressed by your parents, how physically strong they're proving with the children."

Janet liked him noticing whatever positive dynamics were left around her. She found his kindness attractive. "They've gathered the best of themselves, considering what horrendous circumstances they're under... Had the kids not been here, I don't know how they would have coped with Gaia's... I can't make out who's supporting who anymore..."

"You're right about the kids, they make all the difference, I think. Andrew did with me too."

Often during that week at Chequers, Janet had found herself admiring Robert for the way he had pulled himself together to living through the death of his wife and raising a child, while still climbing to the top of the country's political ladder. Three impressive achievements put together, culminating in the political leadership of the country, the nation bestowing on him the responsibility of dragging Britain out of its decline. She spoke softly, "Robbie, I appreciate being here a lot. It makes the whole difference for us all."

"Don't even mention it, after everything you have gone through," he was sitting on a chair in front of her, his casual posture making him look younger. His smiling seemed to be abating at the transition of a sad thought through his mind. Janet reflected over the emotion they shared: death, single parenting, experiment anxiety. More common ground than she had ever had with a man.

"Also, I couldn't offer you much alternative really, this is as safe and confidential as it gets... at least for a few more days."

"Did you speak with anyone recently?"

"Sort of, just a briefing."

Janet, naturally not inclined to scepticism, wasn't entirely convinced that someone as famous as Bill could vanish like that, leaving no trace behind, making Janet doubt Robert's frankness sometimes. "Any news on Bill?" She could see his reticence to answer. "How are you going to—?"

"They're all specialists now, best people in the country, dealing with it from every possible angle; I trust they'll do a good job."

"What I mean is – is there really a way to cover it up?" Still, she didn't understand.

Robert looked straight into her eyes, nodding slightly. Janet felt as if he was attempting to cast a spell over her, anything that would infuse a sense of trust in what was going on outside the high garden walls.

She hated his power of steering conversations away from the topic of Bill's death. He had done so all week in a way, with varying degrees of success, both on the phone and face-to-face. Sometimes she thought he had taken her home to brainwash her, and that he was waiting for her to forget everything, before being released from the grounds again. In reality, he was just cursing Bill inside his head, for having managed to be so convincing over pursuing the experiment.

The conversation was not progressing, they were both silent, thinking, when Sophia burst into the room, crying. It seemed an insurmountable problem. Her grandfather also ran in breathless.

Janet sprung out of the armchair to receive her, Sophia's earnest crying filling the entire room.

"What happened, baby, what's going on?"

Without stopping crying, she hugged her aunt, who had knelt on the floor for her. Janet's hair was caught in the draft from the large French door opening. Her dad attempted to explain what had happened, in between gasping for air.

"It's nothing, just Lucas has—"

"No!" screamed Sophia interrupting her granddad. "He pushed me!"

"Oh, sweetie, don't cry, everything is ok," interceded Janet, which only made Sophia angrier. She was looking threateningly into Janet's face. "He pushed me over and hurt my head, I hate him!"

Janet was growing embarrassed in front of Robert, every small occurrence making cracks appear in her scheme of normality. She hated that the pieces would sometimes separate before the glue could set. She was aware of the dangers of never recovering from the accident.

She carried Sophia back to the armchair, laying her little sobbing body over her shoulder. Robert and her father becoming the background of Janet's instinctive performance. The affection of a mother started to flow from a hidden source, together with her ability to calm Sophia.

The men exchanged a quick quizzical look, Robert recalling a recently read inscription: *This house of peace and ancient memories was given to England…*

Janet's father thanked God for rewarding him with a daughter who was being such a good mother to his orphaned grand children.

The twins also entered the room, stumbling over each other in a blast of noise. Followed again at some distance, by their breathless grandmother. Robert gestured to Janet that he would be back to see her later.

He didn't manage to leave the room without witnessing Lucas walking towards Janet, pointing his right finger, "You are not my mummy and you are not Sophia's mummy, you don't understand anything. I want my mummy!"

The sum of all the eyes in the room fell on Janet, apart from Sophia's, who was burying her face into Janet's shoulder. The former, discomforted, bit into her lower lip, hoping to sink Lucas's comment somewhere deep inside her before it would affect her too much.

Like a hurricane can take the roof off homes, Lucas was removing her belief that one day she would become their mother, wiping out the progress of the last 100 hours. The foundations of her parenting were shaking; she thought it silly that she had consulted the online dictionary to dig deeper into the meaning of the word: *Moth'er n. a female parent, holding the position of authority and responsibility...*

She felt a phoney. She had never been pregnant, let alone with any of those three children, her knowledge of eggs and sperms confined to academic experimentation with life. She felt incapable of conveying any particular wisdom that could command respect. Yet, unaccustomed with the origin of their lives, by means of a hurried adoption, Janet had undertaken to create a new matricentric system that would attract the children to her. She was convinced she could fill the vacuum left by the sudden death of their natural mother; she had no time to waste.

"Lucas, I'll be around only if you want me to be. Like the sun, I'll come up in the morning, peek through your windows, waking you up with my shining and warming light. I'll invite you to play with the rest of the family. You'll be able to see and feel me if you want to."

The boy didn't look convinced, but Sophia was holding her tighter, giving her strength.

"It's not fair, I want my mum," said Lucas more quietly.

Not much could be answered to that, thought Janet. Yet, letting her heart speak freely had helped lift her spirits.

"We all love your mummy, Lucas, but love isn't always fair. We have to accept the wickedness that happened to us. At least, we're all in this together and we can help each other. You can help Sophia feel less lonely, while Matthew can help you to play your sadness away. Then there's Grandma and Grandpa…"

She realised she was doing with Lucas what Robert had been doing with her all along: talking the loss down, focusing on the positive need of love we all have throughout life.

Again and again, she was finding great support in Robert, a really inspiring partner. That second, she realised how much she needed him close to her.

Like her, Lucas had a deep vein of stubbornness. Showing no signs of cracking his heart open, he remained sulky, apparently unmoved by Janet's words.

His brother Matthew, huddling between the legs of his grandparents, looked at the scene unfolding. None of them were too young to understand the criticality of the moment. They were at different stages of the formation of tears.

Sophia unearthed her face from Janet's sweater, looking up at her first, then turning to Lucas. Radiating calmness and composure, she beamed serenity. She addressed her brother, dispensing tranquillity all around.

"Lucas, you know how much Mummy liked Auntie Janet. Be kinder to her please."

Her words sounded conclusive, she provided a final and superior sentencing of Lucas' tantrums, above the children and the adults, crushing his nonsense under the meaningfulness of her words. Lucas turned his gaze to Matthew and his grandparents, seeking support, but was left unable to bear the unequivocal lack of anyone's sympathy for his statements. Cleverly, he decided to retreat, running fast towards the woody hedges of the garden.

Before worrying about him, the family came to embrace the armchair where Janet and Sophia were sitting, in a beautiful moment that lasted until Janet's phone buzzed under her thigh.

Though she ignored it for a while, she decided eventually to pick it up. The display read *Dr. McKinley;* it took her a moment to recollect that it was the name of the newly appointed doctor in charge of NB001. An RAF Chief Air Marshal seconded to MI6, a former specialist in dealing with children used in suicide bombings.

"Sorry, it's work," Janet said looking at her parents and the kids gathered around the armchair. She swiped her thumb across the screen, "Hi doctor, would you please excuse me one moment?"

"Sure." Dr. McKinley sounded kind.

The family dispersed: Janet's dad went looking for Lucas, while her mother asked Sophia to join Matthew and walked both back to the garden to get some lemonade. All under Janet's admiration for the strength demonstrated by her parents, followed by a bitter lapse of her spirits. *What would they think if they knew I was the reason for Gaia's death...* The thought depressed her.

She took the phone back and repositioned the laptop on her knees, putting on her most professional tone – trying to conceal her mood as much as possible, she spoke again to Dr. McKinley.

"Thank you for waiting."

"Not to worry Dr. Icks. I guess you have been informed of my appointment, I recently took service and—"

"Yes, Doctor," Janet cut him short, "I saw your profile in the data room," though she was actually reading it at that very moment for the first time: *34 years old, Lincolnshire-born, top grades at the Air Force Medical School, Afghanistan, Ukraine, Syria, PhD…*

"All right Dr. Icks. So, I've spent the last few days analysing what is expected from me here, going through enough information to get me started. I guess, I would now benefit from a meeting with you to—"

Janet interrupted him again, the same reaction of annoyance bursting out in connection to her responsibilities with the experiment.

"Dr. McKinley—"

"Jeff, you can call me Jeff, if you'd like."

"Dr. McKinley, I, I cannot guarantee that I'll be able to meet you anytime soon. I suggest you keep working on your own for now. I'll assist you as much as I can remotely. We can schedule a regular conference call?"

She did not want him to think that she was distancing herself from the project, but in fact she was.

"Sure, Dr. Icks; I understand you need some time off."

Shit, how much does he know? The whole UK intelligence service must be laughing its head off about this mess!

He continued, "I'll be as independent as I can and, to this extent, you may appreciate knowing that I've managed to squeeze in with the routine blood checks a Polymerase chain reaction…"

The boy knows his job, she thought. "Good work, doctor. When are you expecting results?" She spoke with an appreciative tone for the first time during the call.

"I already have Dr. Icks: the boy is on track to develop the DNA combinations carried by the shuttle. In particular, the synthesis rates of purine, pyrimidine oxyribonucleotides and deoxyribonucleotides are matching the benchmark."

Translated, it meant that the experiment had passed one of its hardest hurdles: the corrupted DNA belonging to EA1456 had been accepted by its new innocent body. She lied, thinking of the dead baby that had been overrun by EA1456's DNA. "You give me very good news, Dr. McKinley. I am happy that you are taking care of the monitoring activities. I shall be glad to see you as soon as I, as soon as it's convenient."

The experiment's breaking news almost got her scientist's juices going again. For a tiny fraction of a second, she considered exerting her powers once more.

"Let's keep in touch, and don't refrain from keeping me up-to-date via the shared platform."

"I certainly will, Dr. Icks. I'll look forward to meeting you soon."

"Goodbye, doctor."

Janet hung up, exhaling audibly in a long deep sigh, signalling that relief was taking the place of weariness. She reckoned that the life of the little patient wasn't at immediate risk. Nevertheless, there was still a risk of mortality for the mother she secretly injected, following all the issues she had developed post-shot... *I wish I had a Dr. McKinley there too.*

She was determined to avoid her dying at any cost and sometimes considered talking to Robert about her, coming clean, now that she felt him close enough to understand her. Still, Gaia, Bill, and whoever else the other casualty was, had to be the last victim.

Janet acknowledged that she was 100 percent responsible for Sharon's situation – opposite to Gaia and Bill, she could have looked after her life better.

As far as EA1456 was concerned, he was different from the other deaths. He had signed off his programmed departure, he had actively sought to die... at least until changing his mind at the very last minute. She tried to picture the scene of Gaia and Andrew withdrawing him from the labs, *had they talked? Had he spilled the beans on everything he had been going through, I wonder what Gaia might have said about me?*

But she felt sorrier for everyone else involved than him, shaking her head in the attempt to disperse her regrets. Until she thought that if there was one chance in a million that EA1456 was still alive, it was her duty to save him; to pull him out of a destiny he no longer wanted to pursue. She owed it to Gaia, her lovely sibling who used to copy and learn everything from *big sis*, until becoming a hippy teenager, with an acute alternative personality. Time had come for Janet to learn another lesson from her little sister, along with motherhood.

Janet wasn't sure who the *third* death that Robert had mentioned was. Because of the hospitality, care and attention he had given her family, she had not dared to push asking. But now, in light of the new relationship she had with Robert, she reckoned she could ask and he wouldn't hide it further.

She expected him to be on the other side of the spectrum from Bill, when it came to sparing an innocent life, but then again, she had sensed a dark side in Robert too. After all, the Prime Minister was entitled to easily ignore giving Janet any detail of what was happening with the security operation. He had her segregated in his golden palace, unable to ask questions.

His reticence to talk, had already translated into Janet breaching the agreement to cut all relationships with people previously involved with the experiment. She had tried, and failed, as no one answered any number she rang. She couldn't even make the labs' number work anymore. Switchboard, direct lines, mobiles, pagers... nothing seemed to be connected any longer.

As Robert had said, "there are specialists in intelligence who can do it, Janet..." His words resounding in her head in a way that made her ask herself whether she liked him beyond the appreciation for his help. *All men are murderers, that's probably why I've never loved one.*

She recognised the need to understand what was really happening out there in order to get clarity over the rest of her feelings.

She got up to go looking for him. She walked the empty corridors and the quiet stairwells, meeting a lonely security guard upstairs, roaming around the door that served the study where Robert was working. He nodded and opened the door for her. She found Robert sitting with his feet up on the big wooden desk, holding a cup of tea, looking outside through the large windows. He appeared thoughtful.

"Hey, good to see you. All sorted with the kids?" he asked, readjusting his posture.

Janet kept walking, passing his desk, coming closer to his leather chair than she had ever done during the week she had spent in his residence. He watched her approaching, thinking how attractive she was, pleased when she sat on his desk in front of him. His enchanted appreciation met her frosty charm: she hit him with a remark he didn't expect.

"You've disposed of EA1456, without telling me, am I right?"

Unwilling to lie, feeling he could not hide much from her anyway, he nodded, meaningfully tightening his lips.

Without waiting for him to excuse himself, she crossed her arms over her chest and lifted her buttocks from his desk, slowly walking some steps away from him. He couldn't bear to see her leaving, he stood up and chased her, rejoining her the middle of the room, where he took her shoulders.

"Janet, you knew all along he was going to die," he meant to sound apologetic but came out romantic instead, as he spoke softly, his heart feeling for her "it was agreed a long time ago."

Janet didn't concede any territory. "It was your duty to save him from the journey to some secret morgue... You knew he had changed his mind. Like me... You knew you would have made me happy."

At that moment, he realised their relationship had changed. She expected him to understand what made her happy, on a personal level, beyond any business of the experiment. She was revealing to him that there was a hidden door to her and that she was prepared to open it to him in due course.

Knowing she sowed the seeds of a possible future together, she resumed walking slowly to the door. They had talked without looking at each other, but they had communicated at the deepest level. Understanding the ritual perfectly, Robert contented himself with having held her shoulders and looked at the strip of neck exposed through her white summer top. For Janet, having allowed him so close as to touch her shoulders, after all those years thinking she was waiting for the right woman to cherish her, it came as a surprise to find herself ready to love a man.

3.8 –June 28th

Andrew was growing accustomed to the absence of rhythm of the detention centre. Fourteen days paving the way to forgetting what life outside tasted like, as if the real prison was getting built around him day after day, taller and thicker. Routine consisted of solitude. Alone in the room, without visits or calls, his only interactions were with a soldier bringing food every six hours and a nurse checking his temperature and blood pressure every 24 hours.

They both came in, avoiding conversation, going about their business quickly and then leaving. Between 10.00 a.m. and 11.00 a.m. every morning, he would be taken to an open-air high-walled ground for a walk. But it was a dull place: a thick stainless steel door as sole access, four metre high concrete slabs all-around, a black metal table with its four chairs and an ashtray. That was it, someone had worked out the bare minimum requirement for people not to go mad during their detention. A daily stroll in a 50-square-metre courtyard for one hour, breaking the monotony of the remaining 23 hours spent in an eight-square-metre cell. And that was the improved room assigned after the initial 48-hour transit, which he spent in the *clubhouse*: a shithole where detainees ate, shat and slept in the same room. Now he had a separate bathroom, with a shower positioned close enough to the toilet seat for him to sit on the WC under a hot stream of water; luxury. The TV was his biggest disappointment, most channels being blacked, he had found himself watching *Downtown Abbey* and *Teletubbies*. Other times, he lay watching the switched-off screen, scanning the air for noises, in the total absence of any, adding to the abstraction of the location, accentuating the impression of being the only detainee.

Robert had not called in as often as Andrew would have liked, only once, promising he would be out soon. Another visit coming in the form of a young analyst, so he said, possibly from the RAF or the Navy, wanting to see him for what he had branded an *informal chat*; he meant interrogation.

He had discussed the news, the fine line of his lips struggling with the training manual's wording for death: *it's with our greatest sadness and sorrow…* making the conversation sound like cheap police movie bullshit. For a moment he imagined the analyst leering at Gaia's photo with a colleague, *hot MILF mate, hot MILF*.

He couldn't show anger, nor voice frustration; whether he liked it or not, he was guilty of kidnapping. Pretty bad shit any day of the week. Worse perhaps, if you went about abducting the government's classified specimen. Behaviour that would possibly not help his father, *The Head of His Majesty's Government*, at the next general election.

Andrew chose to bury himself under the landslide of guilt springing from the recent loss of the woman he loved.

Within a week of the arrest, broadly acknowledging he had become a factory of problems for everyone surrounding him, he saw himself emanating evil, his reckless behaviour affecting his father, girlfriend and friends. God knows how much time he had for self-critique.

Since the interview, he had lost part of his conscience, settling into the lethargy of detention. Chewing his bullet, he stayed locked in his soul too, unable to think about what would be next for him, his only occupation was filling notepads with dark dialogues and horror scenes. Until one morning breakfast came without coffee or juice, "'Cause you're getting out of here later today – no fluids, no stops on the way."

Andrew didn't know what to make of it. He was reluctant to think it was good news. He spent the day in agitation and disquiet. The silence of the place hitting him even harder. Speculating over his next destination, he oscillated between ghastly cells infested with worryingly rough convicts, mostly up north, to more remote and isolated locations. A fact, he thought, was that being transported meant his detention had been extended, otherwise they wouldn't bother moving him. He still hoped, though, that his father's influence would spare him from the worst jail landscapes, like a multi-sharing cell. Because what really made him shit his underwear was the fear of other inmates.

Dad was his hope. Andrew wished his father would forgive him quickly, as he had already helped with the iPod. The 40 terabytes of British rock that had become the soundtrack to his confinement. Real oldies like The Beatles, David Bowie, Pink Floyd,

Queen, as well as more recent stuff. He would lie in bed for hours, dissecting lyric arrangements, changing his mood accordingly, mainly picturing with fear a nasty trial with the press involved, and the demise of his father's career. Other times, when the music was just too good, he would imagine his friends and booze, reminiscing about the afternoons spent downloading songs and drinking ale.

Now he feared they wouldn't let him keep the iPod during the transfer. *Dad will find another the way to let me listen to his music...*

*****

A strong June sun was beating on the little window high up on the wall, amplifying the drowsiness of the early afternoon spent listening to Coldplay... *and it was all yellow.*

The agents found him asleep, it was 2.00 p.m. They quickly gathered his minimal possessions, everything he owned on the small reading desk. He stood up, woken up by their noise, instinctively offering his wrists.

"No handcuffs lad, shame you have to go now that we had you trained so well."

A short walk in the opposite direction to the one he usually took for the concrete garden, led to a door to a loading bay where a shiny, dark-grey van was waiting. No marks, signs or flashlights, just two rows of black leather seats behind a thick tempered black-out glass dividing the front cabin from the back. No other windows to the outside, just time to get unceremoniously inside, thinking, *if the guy bangs his hand twice on the side to give the go ahead, he's a phoney...*

And it happened! As soon as he was securely fastened to his seat, the guard mumbled, "Bon voyage" in cockney mock-French, shutting the sliding door, before banging on it twice, destination unknown.

Inside, pitch black. Andrew was listening to the engine and gears, trying to make up for the lack of sight, picturing all sorts of possible landscapes in his head. At one point, he was sure they were on the M25 between Potters Bar and Cheshunt... But after what seemed to him a couple of hours, the sequential processes of his brain turned into a doze. Sleeping in the back of a car always gave him dreams. This time, his imagination produced emotions and sensations of fear, horror and distress – a nightmare where he was accused by the police of the murder of Gaia and the kids as a crime of passion. Sentenced to life in prison, his father was going to battle in parliament to reintroduce the death penalty and have him executed.

He was woken by a sharp light entering from the van's side door; he found himself drowsy and covered in sweat. His two escorts were staring at him, behind them, some outstandingly beautiful country landscape, not the concrete walls he had expected. His eyes struggled to cope with the sudden flood of light, as his brain endeavoured to decipher the scene appearing in front of his eyes: *country home, butler-type man, smiley agents. Nothing making sense...*

"Good evening sir, welcome back to Chequers."

Andrew had met the butler a few times before, during his visits to his father's country home, he was Robert's favourite member of staff there. Andrew was in shock. His father had gone so far as having him driven to his country home, meaning that his station in life came with a one-off judiciary pass for his revolutionary son. *I can live with that*, he thought to himself.

"Thank you so kindly, James," he said, jumping out of the van. "Seeing you fills me with absolute joy." He couldn't believe he was a free man walking on the green grass of Buckinghamshire.

"Thanks for the smooth drive guys," turning again towards the agents.

"Have fun lad, your stuff is just here. By the look of it you should be all right," the older agent said, already circling around the van to get back to his seat.

Clearly, they were not too upset about having to release a not-so-dangerous criminal, they held no resentment. Like in the movie *Chinatown*, he was being ushered into impunity. It gave him the feeling of just having been born into light. Looking at the van driving through the front gardens back towards the gates, he thought it was the best sight he'd ever seen.

"Your father is returning from Manchester, he should land in an hour or so."

"Thank you, James."

"We have other guests lodging with us, sir. You will be accommodated in a different room than your usual, the one that was once used by Mary, the younger daughter of Sir Winston Churchill."

"Let's hope she is haunting the place then."

"You are quite right sir, although I gather that it would be a loss if she appeared in her disembodied spirit, sir," James said as he winked.

James' humour and wit worked wonders for Andrew's soul. They chatted as if they were old acquaintances all the way up to Andrew's room. Once inside, Andrew went straight for the minibar, tanking a bottle of beer in a few gulps, followed by a miniature of whisky. He felt much better, he could finally let go a bit. Sitting on the floor, with his back against the antique Victorian bed, he was coming off the largest emotional roller coaster he had ever experienced. The result was that he liked his father a lot and had a newfound respect for him. Half an hour later, he took a shower and tried on some of his dad's clothes that the staff had arranged in the chest of drawers. He looked decent enough, though not the picture of health after the days lying in bed and the few quick drinks he had swallowed.

He had heard a helicopter landing whilst he was still in the shower, meaning his father had arrived. As usual, that wasn't the end of his father's duties, and he wouldn't be seen for a while. Andrew knew he had to wait for contact once work was over.

The butler came to call for supper just after seven o'clock. He was happy to be seeing his father, though he expected to be given a high price to pay for his freedom. He anticipated his father would ask for compensation after having taken the hands of the judicial system off him with a sweep of a magic wand. Andrew almost thought he should consider the scientific curriculum his dad so desperately wanted for him. Most of all, though, he couldn't wait for the second he would taste good food and wine again. The banter with the butler took his mind off the meeting he was about to face. Andrew's relaxed attitude contributed to his astonishment when, entering the dining room, his eyes met the most absurd scene. Robert was sitting at the end of the usual long dining table. On his left flank there were in order Janet Icks, the twins each sitting on top of a sofa cushion each and Sophia. The setup looked surreal even to his movie drenched eyes. He couldn't have expected her to be there and, even so, he wouldn't have imagined it to look so quintessentially intimate, cosy, familiar, like a kind of *My Family* TV show. It was the portrait of the British family he had never had, and it matched perfectly the picture he had carried in his heart all his life, of how he would have liked to be with his mother, father and siblings, sitting around the table for dinner.

He walked slowly, owing to his stupor, advancing at low speed towards the party, struggling to make sense of what he was seeing. They were talking among themselves, taking notice of him only when he was halfway into the room. What also struck him was how beautiful Janet looked, prettier than any of his father's dates, though he hadn't seen many.

"Here comes our movie director..."

"Hi Janet," the closer he got, the more he was shocked to see how much Janet looked like Gaia. A vacuum formed in his throat, forcing his gaze to move on to the boys, who didn't seem to be willing to interact, their eyes stuck on a replay of the *Night Garden* showing on a temporary TV installed at the far end of the table. Sophia instead, raised her eyes from the drawing she was colouring, smiling before whispering, "Mummy's funny friend."

"How are you, Andrew?" Janet asked.

"Alright thanks, amazed to see you here." He was sitting at the table.

"Yes, you look somewhat more bemused than puzzled in fact. Your father has very kindly offered to help us, given the dire circumstances in which we find ourselves."

Robert watched the rapport, hoping that they would naturally make conversation, beyond the difficulty of the situation.

Andrew felt awkward, speaking with Janet in front of his father. She was his late girlfriend's sister and apparently his father's date.

Feeling outdone by his father, Andrew took the only way out that seemed decent to him.

"Hi kids, good to see you again."

Sophia got up from her chair and walked to Andrew, who was now sitting on the right-hand side of his father. When she got close enough, she asked in a soft voice, "Where is your friend?"

Failing to understand, Andrew asked her which friend she meant.

"The sick man…" She was talking about EA1456.

Only then did Andrew recall that, on the way to the lab, Gaia had told the children they were going to help one of his friends, "who's not well and needs a better doctor."

Sophia's question visibly agitated Janet. She worried it could lead to the children asking questions about Gaia. So she got up announcing: "Time for bed I think. Let's go up children. I'll read you a story." The kids had eaten tea already.

"But I want to see the end," whined Matthew.

Determined to break the cause-and-effect process sparked by Sophia's question, she insisted. "Well then, let's watch the end from your tablet in bed."

Janet had to physically lift each of the boys up, as they still had their eyes glued to the screen, but Sophia followed obediently. Andrew got up to help, but Janet was heading towards the door before he could do anything.

"You boys have a chat, I'll be back later." She walked out under their appreciative look.

"Fantastic woman, let's hope she doesn't get crushed by the weight of it all. How are you my boy, happy to be home?"

"Sure, thank you so much for getting me out."

"You owe me a big one. You can thank God for my job, because had I been a movie director, you'd be rotting in there for many more years, before seeing the light of day again."

Andrew nodded, conceding that a father working as a movie director wasn't the coolest thing anymore. Robert understood that his son had changed his point of view and smiled.

"Come here my boy, have a sip of white, it's Italian."

"Thanks, Dad." He moved his glass closer. "So, do you think, I mean, shall I—"

"Go back? Please, no." Robert said raising his eyes to the ceiling, "Unless the lesson has not been clear enough for you? Let's be straight, Andrew," he lowered his voice, "it all became classified ashes, as if by magic." Robert clicked his fingers in mid-air. "Vaporised. No one is going to remember it, as long as you keep your head down, *well* below the parapet, and do as you're told."

Robert sipped some wine, pursing his lips to the vintage glass. "Tomorrow morning, someone's going to see you for a briefing, a sort of induction on how to go about it. It won't be the last, there will be regular refreshes at later stages. *Repetition is the mother of all skills, remember?* You love fiction anyway, you'll take to it like a fish to water. Just for my sake though, remember that our safety depends on how zipped here you stay," he passed his conjoined thumb and forefinger across his lips, "... about the whole affair." He paused. "Nothing's free in life, my son. We both have a price to pay for you chasing skirts and messing with my work... Keep a note of this debt."

Andrew took his slice of humble pie with his sip of wine.

Thankful for his freedom, he was aghast that his father regretted nothing. *He still supported the experiment*, Andrew thought. *All he wanted was to cover his ass, and shag the new bird.*

He also found his father more arrogant than he remembered. "Thank you, Dad," he said coldly, watching his father dishing pasta al pesto onto his plate.

"Now, I'm going to tell you something that will unsettle you. Something I could do nothing about..."

"Couldn't be more upset Dad than I already am."

"Your friend the doctor, Giles... he's gone. Don't ask questions. Stop right there. Just swallow the bitter pill and like me, pray. Pray that five is our lucky number and that we have no more casualties, not one more."

Andrew fought the impulse to throw up. He took the glass of water and drained its contents at the speed of light, unable to rinse away his incredulity, his feeling of loss.

After a good minute of silence, Robert muttered mindlessly whilst chewing, "Eat son, the pesto is made with basil from our gardens."

Andrew struggle to see the point of eating at all; he felt like a dog was gnawing his stomach. His mood was collapsing, the entire happiness of being released and reunited with his father was vanishing.

He couldn't explain how Robert would bother to change TV channels to BBC News. Incredulously, he ended up watching football that followed rugby, that had followed cricket, none of which was in the slightest interesting to either. Still, they watched it, quietly, without talking. Robert eating with a teenager's appetite, Andrew moving pasta bits around the plate, sulking. For him, the reunion wasn't working. It was drifting into a total chaotic awkwardness. The death of an innocent best friend who had offered to help was on a par with watching sports. He was annoyed at his father, who didn't offer any depth for talking things through; no spirit, no interest, while Andrew's world was spinning fast around Giles, Cambridge, the immense gap left by Gaia.

"I'd like to resume studying."

"You mean online, right?"

Andrew was watching Robert dip a piece of baguette in the sauce. "Cambridge would be good," he was careful to avoid any annoyance dripping from his words, to mask the betrayal he felt.

"Seriously? Of all places, you can forget Cambridge for a while. We've been advised on that matter and you have withdrawn from college there. Think of it as a big hole in the ground."

"But—"

"Andrew, leave it, please. This is serious. Your life won't get back as it was for a long time. You're a survivor, please act accordingly. You'll finish your studies elsewhere, things are sorted. In the meantime, study online." Robert wasn't looking at him, busy attacking the cheese board.

Andrew was growing more upset. "That experiment of yours sucked," Andrew said, vexed.

"Oh, but listen to the expert... *Welcome to we're all prime ministers, tonight we're hosting Andrew Hand.*" Robert knew the art of theatrical tones and gestures, "Tell us something about how to run a country?" he asked, leaving his words hanging over a look that meant to abash Andrew.

"No, Dad, please don't get me wrong. I know you're a terrific leader. I just think you've been losing touch with reality in connection with the experiment."

"You, telling me I'm unhinged? After what you've done? Driving a sick patient in the back of your poor auntie's Volvo?"

"How can you compare? I tried to save a life, when you were testing mass genetic manipulation for... for the purification of society."

Robert got the message. "Andrew, for God's sake, what do you know about the issues at stakes? Government isn't like making movies on recycled organic film. You're just like everyone else – want a faster car and a larger house, you want to make a bigger movie. Let me tell you, someone, somewhere, has to get real if you and all the others want to keep creating dreams out of thin air."

Andrew was looking down at his plate again.

"So, tell me, who's lost touch with reality here? Who's real and who's asleep beyond hypocrisy?"

Before they could say a word more, Janet entered the room with a big smile on her face. "Ahh, they were so sweet. Andrew, you know the boys remembered about you?" She was talking in a high pitched tone. She had managed to put the kids to bed and was satisfied with herself. She cherished every little sign of her relationship with them developing.

Both Robert and Andrew replied with contrite smiles. Janet immediately perceived that the conversation had been unpleasant. She continued in their silence, readjusting her tone accordingly. "I hope my pasta's still warm."

Stillness descended over the dining table. Above their quietness, the TV played the catchy BBC News jingle. A new round of news was starting with the main headlines.

"Police confirmed the collision which took place on the M3 near Cobham, Surrey, this morning at 7.10 a.m. resulted in the death of the 38-year-old entrepreneur, Bill Haugan.

"Good evening this is the BBC News at 7.30 p.m."

The screen showed the face of the news anchor, a man in his forties with a large forehead and short white hair. "Our main story tonight: a fatal road accident has claimed the lives of Britain's best-known entrepreneur, Bill Haugan, and his driver. Police and fire crews were called to the scene after a black Aston Martin travelling along the M3 towards London was involved in a collision and came to a stop on the side of the road near Cobham Common in Surrey. Both bodies were cut from the wreckage and pronounced dead at the scene. Police have begun an investigation into the cause of the accident. In a statement, Buckingham Palace said the King and Queen were deeply, "shocked and distressed." Tributes have already been pouring in from around the world, where Mr. Haugan was known for his business and charitable work. Bill Haugan leaves behind a vast empire of companies without an heir.

A shuffled clip of blurred images was playing. Police slowing traffic, a congested motorway, a crane removing the wreckage of the car, a team of fire-fighters walking back to their trucks.

Janet watched with her mouth half-open, unable to complete chewing the first two penne quills she had inserted in her mouth since she had returned to the table. Andrew reacted by raising his eyebrows incredulously, his eyes close to popping out on stalks.

Robert on the other hand, was more composed, calmer, mangling a piece of bread in his hands. Of course, this wasn't news to him, he was making himself ready for the scrutiny that would follow the news report. He anticipated all eyes being quickly on him, and from both sides of the table Janet and Andrew were already staring, waiting for answers.

Making sure he wasn't overheard by serving personnel, he spoke. He was dignified, with the formality of the stateliness he represented for a living.

"Hypocrisy isn't on tonight's menu. Let's be straight about it, the experiment had turned into an epidemic, the outbreak of a contagious disease, spreading rapidly and widely over the lives of everyone involved." He paused. "Now that I have it firmly under control, I request you to stick to my condition: that no information is leaked. No one will ever have to question whether any of us three had a role in it. We had no part in it. We shall protect each other and move on."

Silence wrapped his statement. After a while, Janet asked in an abated tone, "Was the driver... necessary?"

"More necessary than you'd ever think."

3.9 – July 3rd

Nestling between a disused power station and a brown canal, lost in the English nowhere, it was a building that didn't belong to the landscape. On the edge of a small town, that seemed reverentially limited in size and scope, the enormous long blue box looked like a smear of summer sky on the damp industrial landscape. The inside was flooded by sharp white light, with hundreds of workers wearing orange vests, like convicts or their mining ancestors, pushing trolleys around a space the size of 20 football pitches. All eyes were fixed down on handheld screens, dispensing directions, where to walk, what to pick, where to take it.

"And they don't dawdle either. The mobile devices also measure their productivity in real time. They might each walk about 30 miles today." The director of operations and efficiency was gleaming. A white coat against his pale complexion, he faded into the distance except for his large blue eyes covered by electronic glassware. Born computer, he perspired gigabytes. He possessed a desire for replacing every walking human on *his* floor with the robots, which were already moving alongside the automated humans.

"They're used for the easier shaped objects," signalling that he was working on teaching robots to replace men filling shelves, picking products, packing boxes. Later, Robert noticed he broadcasted text messages to workers, instructing them to walk faster and refrain from talking.

"We receive 350 orders per second; three loaded trucks leave the bays every five minutes. And this, it's our state-of-the-art security gate, scanning every employee to guarantee our theft recovery rate at 100 percent," his self-congratulatory smiles failing to impress the Prime Minister.

Robert walked along the first floor balcony suspended over the large hall; on his left, glass-walled, open plan offices were filled with a different kind of humanoid, the type in white overalls consulting A4-sized tablet computers, moving around a seamless desk-free space, where everything was wireless, with barely a place to sit and no personal belongings.

Robert wondered how long it would take for the whole firm to pack up and flee, struck by the temporary nature it had managed to achieve.

His head roving over the report from the Department of Work and Pensions: No general wealth increase registered since opening… Very scarce job security with minimum salary wages not allowing people to afford spending beyond basic necessities… Workers unable to go outside during breaks because of excessive security… Long hours and intense shifts leaving people too tired to socialise after work…

The internet economic renaissance of post-industrial England was in full swing.

"How many people do you currently employ?" his low-toned voice filling the vacuum of noise.

"23,000," replied the director proudly.

"My figures show less than 10,000."

"A share of my number are temps used to stock up for Christmas," still standing proud, walking side-by-side with the Prime Minister.

Like all other puppets here, he must have sharp answer for everything or he loses his job; good luck now that your master has gone.

"Sixty percent temps, in July… Thank you for showing me around, and my deepest condolences for the loss of your inspiring leader."

The efficiency expert twiddled purposelessly for the first time, looking as if the news of Bill's death had just hit him.

Robert was keen to leave him behind. He looked once more around the vast open space scanning to find a known face, his gaze eventually finding a pretty young woman gesturing an invitation to enter the conference room.

Inside, a long oval table was occupied by delegates from his team and company executives. Robert sat in a prominent position, occupying the seat that had many times seen Bill shouting abuse at his executives and board members.

As soon as he sat down, a tall, white-haired man with glasses, older than the rest of the attendees, announced: "Ladies and gentlemen, I declare the meeting open." He looked over his glasses to see if everyone was following. "The agenda you've all been given contains just one single article. The succession of Mr. Bill Haugan's estate, where among the assets there's the 99 percent shares of the holding company here represented by myself and the law firm Benson & Rockwell."

Another pause allowed everyone to flick the page on the tablet in front of them. "With us today, we have the honour to host Robert Hand, Prime Minister of His Majesty's Government of Britain." All eyes landed on Robert, who looked around the table with a single comprehensive nod. "You may like to address this party, sir," said the Chairman before sitting down.

Robert stood up for a speech without notes. "Ladies, gentlemen, it's a great honour to be invited to the board meeting of the most valuable company in our country. Even when the circumstances of my participation are of the saddest nature." He tactically sipped water to let the gravity of the situation veil the meeting.

"Today, we mourn the loss of the finest entrepreneur that Britain has seen in a long time. We grieve the accidental death of a man who has created vast wealth for himself and the rest of the community. He came from the United States to make Britain his home and, by means of settling here, he increased our wealth as a nation, like no other newcomer had before him. May our sorrow be lightened by the continued prosperity of the businesses he founded in our land."

Robert nodded and sat again without delay. He had already started to hate going through the formalities of government, most of all, despising addressing the public for futile reasons, including thanking the ungrateful dead.

It was time for the Chairman to introduce the second guest to the meeting.

"Thank you Prime Minister. Also today, we are pleased to count among our guests Mayor Collard of

Rugeley, in representation of the local community that holds a special part in the success of our company worldwide." All eyes were now on the stout man in a beige suit, purple shirt and pink tie, the specimen of civil service, involved in exercising his public authority to the point of forgetting about his physical appearance. Scruffy, with greasy skin, bad breath, he stood up to address the congregation.

"Ladies and gentlemen, whereas it's with immense sadness that we see the leader of this company disappear, so young, so early, we want to remain positive and remind ourselves that what he did for this place was bloody great. He came to *this little old place* with spirit and ideas," he was talking with passion. "He came from far away, accomplishing more for this village than we have ourselves managed since the closure of the coal pits. We can only hope that whoever runs this place after him will keep building for our future with the same determination and success." He sat down, looking more pleased with himself than mournful.

From over his glasses, the Chairman turned his attention to the people who sat on his left. "We will now read Mr. Bill Haugan's last will and testament."

A young lawyer, belonging to the legal team that occupied a good 40 percent of the attendees, stood up clearing his throat. He wasn't nervous, but looked concerned, perhaps due to the presence of the Prime Minister, adding a fair amount of expectation to his speech.

"I read on behalf of the deceased, Bill Haugan, born in Austin, Texas, on February the 24th 1988."

Robert was scrolling down the pages while the young solicitor read the appointment of trustees and executors. He was looking for the part that interested him "—die unmarried and childless, I disqualify herein the rest of my family, namely my mother and father and all other next of kin from inheriting my estate. I wish for my fortune to be taken over by the State…"

He put the tablet down and started scrolling messages on his phone, waiting for the end of the reading, the part that saved his kingdom from bankruptcy. He was pleased with himself for having negotiated that clause with Bill himself a good three months before. *The State becoming the only successor to his fortune, should anything have happened to himself in connection with the experiment.* Such an unlikely event that Bill had traded without second thoughts against the sole rights to the Killer App.

Once the solicitor had finished perusing the will, the chairman took the floor again. "It is with our great regret that we acknowledge that Mr. Haugan did not leave a testament towards any other beneficiaries than the State, which we as a board do not see as a natural successor in the going concern of the businesses owned by Mr. Haugan. As such—"

Robert, expecting the Chairman's hostility, knowing it would come at some stage, decided to rebuff it from the start.

"Chairman, please. Let me remind you that we've been offered enough material by Mr. Haugan during these years to take over the businesses, if we wanted to."

The Chairman was turning purple. Robert continued, "Years of tax avoidance, tampering with employment and social security laws would entitle us to acquire these businesses by means of expropriation."

None of the numerous lawyers enlisted by the Chairman for the meeting dared to interrupt the Prime Minister.

"But that will not be necessary, as your inspirational leader has expressed his clear wish of seeing the State inherit his property anyway. Now, if you don't mind, I'd like to hear about the contents of the estate."

Robert enjoyed wielding his absolute power, his words commanding the auditing members of his team to report what possessions were about to fall into the government's hands.

"Sir, to our initial survey, Mr. Haugan's estate, if liquidated, would be worth roughly 250 billion pounds, to which we have to add about 700 million pounds in cash and other securities owned in bank's checking and investment accounts. Lastly, his real estate possessions have an estimated worth of 40 million pounds. This includes everything that we have been able to track as of last night at 1.30 a.m., on His Majesty's Revenues and Customs database, and following contacts with the authorities of Jersey, Guernsey, Isle of Man, Bermuda, Cayman Island, Switzerland and the United States."

The Chairman and other members of the board looked distraught. Robert wanted to wrap up the meeting and leave.

"So, I propose that we set a plan for the liquidation, which will be drafted by the Attorney General's Office in due course. Until then, your owner becomes His Majesty's Treasury, represented here by these gentlemen on my left." Robert pointed to three of his team members. "Now, to everyone, I want to say thank you for your good work and kind co-operation." Robert's words sounded like a drill to which the only response was to stand up. The meeting was over. Robert had just overseen the largest shift of private property into public hands of all times.

In his heart he thanked Bill for his foolishness of dying so young, so rich and unprepared – his generous gift would save the country, literally.

He walked out of the board room shaking hands briskly, planning to leave within minutes, to fly to party headquarters for a quick reception. There would be a press conference to prepare, with the help of the spin doctors. He longed to finish early and get home to Janet at a decent time. He couldn't wait to get back to her, he was falling in love.

One of the company directors took him aside. "Good morning sir, my name is Alex Skrine, before you leave, you might want to take a peek at an unexpected piece of property you have just inherited."

"I've already had the tour, thank you. I'm ready to take off."

Lowering his voice, the man pressed on, "Sir, if I may take the liberty to advise you, you really ought to spare the time to visit this most unexpected facility."

"Facility, for what?" There was a lightning flash of anguish in his heart.

"A secret lab, underneath this estate, sir." Robert scowling, assertiveness winning over doubt.

He agreed unwillingly to follow the director, leaving everyone else including the Chairman standing in the lobby.

They walked down the suspended stairs that led to the ground floor, from where they proceeded into corridors leading to the back of the main building. At the doors, they met with one of Robert's escorting agents.

"Good morning, sir."

Robert offered a thin, limited smile without handshake. He was thinking about how late he would be. *Where the hell are they taking me now?*

They boarded a jeep that drove the three of them to the far end of the estate; a good three minutes' drive away.

Squeezed in the corner of the high security fencing, they saw a cottage in a bad state of repair. Roughly 100 years old, dark bricked, dotted with white windowsills and period decorations, it still carried a *Lodge* sign over its entrance door.

Before pushing the door open, one of the men warned Robert, "Sir, what's down there is pretty discomforting."

"Then tell me what it is, or shut up for God's sake!"

Regretting the loss of patience, he conceded, "Tell me what you think of it while we see it, OK?"

The agent nodded. They entered the abandoned building armed with torches. The first thing they saw inside was an illustrated wall hanging for The North Stafford Miners Federation, showing a man with a pickaxe and a woman harvesting wheat. Hidden behind it, a door opened to what looked like a larder, equipped with a stainless steel ladder leading into the ground.

They descended, the director first, Robert in the middle and the agent closing the line. After three sets of steps, they landed in front of a stainless steel door with a keypad on the right-hand side. The host keyed a twelve digit code he had memorised by heart, and opened the door into a well-lit tunnel which had recently been redecorated with new lights, white walls and tiled flooring.

"These used to be the old shafts and tunnels belonging to the mine, sir."

"Don't look a bit old to me."

Viewing the refurbished tunnel, Robert immediately realised that wherever it led, was going to be related to the experiment; it looked too much like the OGL landscape to be anything else.

They followed the underground tunnel till they found another set of stainless steel doors on their left. The man meaningfully looked Robert in the eyes, before briefly pushing it open, his expression saying, "here we go."

Upon pushing the thick door open, the smell kept Robert and the agent at the edge of the room, the latter offering him a piece of cloth to cover his nose. The view wasn't pretty either. The director took charge to explain, as Robert had requested, speaking from under the hand that was covering his nose.

"It's a laboratory for genetic experiments. We count four main areas," he was pointing with the torch. "A prep station there on the recess, with cold storage room for non-threaded bodies there on the left, followed by," Robert's eyes moving slower than his vocal description, "an operating theatre here in the middle, a post-surgery recovery area, there, and a waste area…"

Silence.

Robert was letting the magnitude of madness be absorbed.

"See the two chimpanzees looking at us, there? That tells you the area isn't contaminated," his voice sounding muffled by the handkerchief. At the far end of the room, the two animals were quizzically observing them.

"I was in charge of setting up this place on behalf of Mr. Haugan, but I still don't have any idea of what it could be used for."

I do have a bloody good idea, thought Robert, before asking, "Do you reckon there's any human material here?"

"Something dead is definitely still in the waste area, hence the smell..."

"Yes, it's terrible, let's close it for now." They recoiled into the corridor, shutting the door and resuming more normal breathing. An image crossed Robert's mind, a picture of dead children crushed in a collection bin.

"Have you told anyone else?"

"No sir. But three Russian scientists worked here full time. I haven't seen them for days now."

"And you, have you called anyone?" Robert was addressing the agent.

"I would have called for reinforcements straight away sir, but I thought they would have called you at some point before intervening, so because you were here already I decided to just tell you direct."

Robert remained silent for a moment, inwardly thanking the agent's foresight.

"Well done, good thinking." He was staring at the dark end of the tunnel, shocked at how far Bill had pushed his genetic manipulation ideas.

"Right, we own this place, whatever shit is under here is ours now. Let's keep it tight. Instead of asking your command straight away, please get in contact with Marshall McLeod from the RAF. He'll make sure they come up with something that doesn't arouse any suspicions with the workers, the community or the press." He feared being linked with butchering people for mass genetic exercises. "I want a small team, restricted to specialists. I must know if there is more to this, in any shape or form, before everything else."

"Yes sir."

"Let's go back to the offices, I think my diary is going to suffer a bit…"

Robert felt an immense relief upon reaching the outside of the lodge, where the jeep was parked. He needed the fresh air badly; the view and the smell of the secret lab were so revolting that he had had to suppress the urge to vomit. Worst of all, he was very disappointed to see that his association with Bill had resurfaced with all its danger.

He regretted not having been savvier about him when they first met. But he could not show he was too worried. He thought about whether or not he was going to tell Janet. "How did you decide to disclose this?" he asked the director as they were walking to the jeep.

"I hated this assignment, sir. I thought there was something wrong about it."

Robert nodded at the man. "You've done the right thing. Just don't ever talk to anyone else about it and you'll be fine."

They drove back to the front of the lobby this time. Almost everybody had left, only Robert's helicopter crew members were still there, occupying a seating area in one corner of the foyer. Robert whispered to the agent, "Someone quietly tell the guys we're not taking off just yet." Meanwhile he headed towards the receptionist who had shown him the conference room earlier. She was now standing behind a high desk near the main set of stairs.

"Hello Susanne," he read from her name tag. "I'm Robert, would it be possible to use Mr. Haugan's office, if you don't mind? We have a change of plan and I may stay here longer than I originally envisaged."

Susanne wasn't tall, but had pretty features including short brown hair and full lips.

"Of course sir, let me call the director—"

"No no, please don't bother him, we just need some privacy, thank you."

"Oh, I understand. Just be aware these aren't the headquarters of the company sir, and Mr. Haugan only had a small room here," she said with a pleasant Midlands accent.

"Haven't seen anything small here yet…"

She smiled, revealing her good natured personality. She left the desk and said, "Please, follow me."

After two flights of stairs, a long corridor brought them to a far extremity of the building. She let the Prime Minister and the agent enter a contemporary room, ten meters wide by 20 meters long, featuring floor-to-ceiling glass windows on the far end. *Small room,* Robert thought grinning to the secretary who ushered them in.

"If you need anything, just dial nine from any phone, sir." Once she closed the door, the agent looked around a little bit before sitting on an arm chair around the coffee table, close to the entrance door. Behind him, a bookshelf contained a few pictures, folders and magazines. Robert's footsteps to the large desk arranged at the far end of the room were the only noise in the room. A glass wall, sleek furniture, pictures, objects, all arranged by an interior designer, beauty without personality.

"Ok, call the Marshall, tell him I'm here, and ask him to inform your command."

"Yes sir," he replied, going on his phone at once.

Robert sat on the black leather chair once belonging to Bill, testing the various commands placed under the armrests, *gotta get one of these*. He reclined it and put his feet up on a pedestal looking out of the window and thinking, *soothing views*.

He could hear the voice of the agent reporting in the background. He experienced a disassociation of the senses, where his eyes looked at the moving foliage at the top of trees under a light drizzle, and his ears listened to the phone conversation.

"—I reckon, yes, code 600 should do. Also reporting potentially hazardous biological waste…" It seemed to him that no matter his policies, harmony between nature and mankind was forever lost.

"—Here with us, sir, expecting your call," the agent continued.

Last winter on the Swiss Alps, that was the last short parenthesis of congruity with nature. After that, free fall. Not Janet of course, not Janet.

He felt the urge to speak with her, he needed to feel her close.

The agent was off the phones again, expecting instruction from his command.

He started to slowly travel around the neat and tidy office. The original 1927 picture from the Solvay Conference, a selfie from an astronaut wearing a space uniform sponsored by the BIG. No one was speaking. Robert was still looking outside, absorbed. The agent, perhaps incited by his green investigative itch, started to browse one the folders on the shelf. His attention was caught by a binder marked 'Speeches.'

He discovered it contained chronologically ordered photocopies of all of Robert's public addresses and newspaper cuts, highlighted in fluorescent marker.

"Mr. Haugan was a real fan of yours, sir, he has a complete collection of your public appearances!"

"Beg your pardon?" Robert replied distractedly, without turning to look away from the window, still drawn by the harmony of the landscape outside.

"The spiralling cost of pension, health and social care for the elderly…" the agent read in his county Durham accent, whilst slowly pacing towards Robert.

He then handed the binder to Robert, who skimmed it, quickly realising that Bill had put together a file with his last five years of speeches, key pictures, interviews and public appearances. It was a neat job; a framing job… *A bit of research on the political connection who sponsors…*

"Check around, I want to know if there's anything like it on other people too."

"The next one is on Ms. Janet Icks, sir," said the agent, who had already started to look into the rest of the folders and binders in the bookcase behind the sofa.

"The index reads Scholarship, PhD and labs…"

The End

9 780992 837310